Lost in the Darkness

William Mark

Published by:
Southern Yellow Pine (SYP) Publishing
4351 Natural Bridge Rd.
Tallahassee, FL 32305

www.syppublishing.com

This is a work of fiction. Names, characters, places, and events that occur either are the products of the author's imagination or are used fictitiously. Any resemblance to actual persons, places, or events is purely co-incidental.

The contents and opinions expressed in this book do not necessarily reflect the views and opinions of Southern Yellow Pine Publishing, nor does the mention of brands or trade names constitute endorsement.

ISBN-10: 1940869307
ISBN-13: 978-1-940869-30-8
ISBN-13: 978-1-940869-37-7 ePub

Front Cover Design: Jim Hamer

Printed in the United States of America
First Edition
Feb. 2015

Acknowledgements

Special thanks to Lori, Keith and Christopher.

Dedication

For all three of my bears,
I would go to the ends of the earth.

Chapter 1

The helpless feeling never left. It loomed overhead like a constant darkness that beckoned him from the edge of the abyss. The thought of never seeing his son again weighed heavier on his soul with every day that passed. The thought that his son was taken, angered him to the core.

The city was busy and moving fast around Curtis Walker, but the small, wallet-size photograph held his focus. He slid it back into the crease of the speedometer, temporarily removing him from the world around him and the operation that was under way. The black Crown Vic sat inconspicuously at the end of the quiet row of townhomes. He watched the front door, waiting for his opportunity to move in. The sun had set an hour ago, and the pale, orange glow of the street lights cast shadows of the night. A bitter cold breeze rolled in from the bay, sending a chill throughout his body. He reached for the small, round medallion of St. Anthony hanging from his neck and rubbed it between his thumb and forefinger feeling the small bumps of detail on the charm. It was a calming mechanism when stress was building.

The photograph pulled his gaze yet again. He stared at the toothless grin of the young boy in the little picture with the tattered corners. A pang kicked in his heart, followed by a dreadful sorrow reminding him of his mission. He forced the anger and rage back, allowing himself to focus on the job at hand. It was an important job that he took seriously— despite the costs. He resituated in the seat of the Crown Vic and kept his eyes on the front door of the two-story brownstone.

The row of townhomes in the Russian Hill neighborhood was built in the late fifties but survived the political unrest that plagued the city of San Francisco in the following decades. These neighborhoods had sat patiently, waiting to be revived in the late nineties to outfit more middle class families, gay and straight. The two story brownstone he watched sat on one of the outlying blocks of the neighborhood more famously known for having the "crookedest" street in America, Lombard St. The tourists were far removed from this particular street as it was quiet except for the late evening strollers and dog walkers.

There had been no activity at the brownstone since the woman returned home with the child and turned on the porch lights. The blinds were still shut. There was no need to cover the back. A lone garage house with secrets of its own hid within the secrecy of a high wooden privacy fence. His instincts told him that wasn't an option as an avenue of escape.

"I thought it was summer? Was I wrong? Did I miss something? Does my calendar deceive me?" A whiny voice crackled sarcastically through the ear bud nestled in his ear. The voice was annoying enough but not nearly as annoying as the person to whom it belonged. As usual, he ignored the grumbles of the constant complainer.

The whiny voice went on ignored.

"Seriously, is this opposite world or something? It's late August, and it's freaking cold!" The squeaky voice of Louis Melton was normally ignored by the team, but he did have a point; it was cold.

A moment later, another voice, female, asked, "You never heard the famous quote about San Fran?"

"No."

"Some guy said, 'The coldest winter I ever spent was a summer in San Francisco.'"

The radio transmission held silent for a moment. "That's stupid," Louis added.

Alone in the Crown Vic, Curt Walker sat restless and was subjected to the chatter that came with the boredom of surveillance, but their work was necessary, and he above all others had to be a believer.

"Mark Twain..." Curt added to break the following silence. "Mark Twain was given credit for the saying."

Sitting on a park bench at the other end of the block from where Curt sat in the Crown Vic, Melinda Dalton was battling the summer chill with a Grande-sized latte from Starbucks and pretending to be reading from an iPad as her cover. She nodded upon hearing the famous author was responsible for the witty saying and was equally impressed that Curt not only knew that fact but contributed to the conversation. She shot a glance down the street to the blacked out sedan and smiled; then she looked back over her shoulder to the large conversion van parked down the cross street behind her position.

Melinda glanced back at the target brownstone, but there was nothing new to report, just a slow parade of pedestrians returning home from whatever after work or school activities normal people do. She wondered about how oblivious these people were to the evil that was going on next door. It never ceased to amaze her just how blissful ignorance can be.

Louis Melton popped up from his computer console and walked to the driver's seat of the Mercedes G-45 Sprinter van and cranked up the engine, blasting the heater to combat the cold chills that had seeped inside the mobile hub.

"Coldest winter is a summer…seriously?" He mumbled to himself as he sat back down in front of his work station, rubbing his arms furiously trying to warm up. The back end of the van was outfitted with a high end computer. It was upgraded with a top of the line processor and server connection that allowed Louis to explore any database or search for any information that assisted the team's mission. Louis, the self-proclaimed genius, was quick to brag that there was no firewall he couldn't penetrate, no matter the cyber security installed. He had built the machine by hand and installed its components without direction but managed to get results. Although they were aware of the legal ramifications, they trusted Louis was as good as he boasted and that he made sure he left no trace behind.

Louis settled into his work station and absorbed the data, checked the screen, and prepared to move into the next phase of the operation. He was ready to "do battle" as he called it. He checked the fit of the head strap and boom mic that reached around to the front of his mouth, making sure he was ready. He took a bite of his preferred battle food, Twizzlers, washed down by a large, bladder-busting Mountain Dew fountain drink, and awaited orders.

Curt checked his wrist watch, and the hour was approaching eight o'clock; it was nearly time. He grew irritated at something and checked the screen of his phone, nothing.

"She back yet?" He asked over the radio, clearly annoyed.

"Not yet, maybe there was traffic," answered Louis.

"No, we keep a schedule for this no matter what. I don't care that she pays the bills. There is a set time and place for a reason; it is to ensure the success of the mission, and that is all that matters. We'll go with or without her."

Silence followed the sharp words.

"Relax Curt, the bill payer is here, and yes, there was traffic that couldn't be avoided." A smooth, calm voice with a mature and sexy tone came over the radio. "The new girl is here too. We'll get started in just a minute."

Louis sank slightly in his chair while three women climbed into the back of the van. Two he knew; the third was new. He blushed at the presence of the women and quickly blurted into the boom mic around his head, "Sorry Curtis. They walked in while you were talking."

Curt ignored the apology; it didn't matter.

Alexis Vanderhill took the captain's chair behind the front passenger seat of the van, grabbed a lever under the seat, turned towards the new face, and invited her to take a seat. She looked around the interior skeptically, but in following the spirit of adventure that led her to this point, she climbed in without further hesitation.

Behind the driver's seat was the panel door, and beyond that was a small bench seat along the length of the van wall, cream-colored leather with light gray trim to match the carpeting of the van. Across from the bench and behind the captain's chair was a mini fridge-bar combination that would be expected in any party limousine, not a conversion van on a secret mission, but it appeared to be stocked with Mountain Dew instead of the expected liquor assortment. However, what gave the new girl pause was the elaborate computer station, complete with three monitors, police scanners, a printer, copier, fax, phone, and a white, dry erase board in the very rear of the van. A mousy, early-twenties-something man sat in a small office chair and shyly looked at her through black, thick-rimmed glasses as she climbed in and sat down on the bench seat.

She was a pretty woman with long, blonde hair pulled back tight against her scalp in a neat ponytail. Her high cheek bones and full lips accented her beauty, but she was dressed down in a casual manner with modest make-up. She was physically strong from years of martial arts training and had an athletic build. She was average height and had large breasts she hid in loose-fitting clothes.

A thin, dark-haired woman, noticeably younger than the others, stood behind the new girl waiting for her to get inside the van. After she climbed in, she followed and jumped quietly into the front passenger seat.

"Hey Beth," Louis said, directed at the young dark-haired woman.

"Hey, Louis. You got it warm enough in here?"

"Ha! It's friggin summer, and the wind chill outside is like thirty degrees or something."

Alexis directed Louis' attention back to the new girl, "Louis, this is Rachel Goodwin."

"Hi, I'm Louie, but everyone calls me Louis. You can call me whatever you like." Louis twisted around in his seat and shook Rachel's hand. She had a strong grip, and he figured that she was clearly much stronger than him.

"Okay, nice to meet you Louis."

"And you will soon meet Melinda and Curtis who are out on other posts for this mission. You already met Beth on the drive over."

Rachel looked at the front seat at Beth who had already gotten comfortable with her bare feet propped up on the dash.

"Louis, will you put on the speaker inside the van so we can all talk please. And get Rachel outfitted for an ear bud later tonight, okay?"

"Yes ma'am." Louis pecked at the keyboard and flipped a switch on the panel next to the monitor. The quiet hum from the open radio channel filled the interior of the van.

"Test, test?" Louis said.

"You're good." Melinda's voice boomed loud and clear inside the van. Louis immediately dialed a knob lowering the volume.

"Melinda?" Alexis asked, "I want to introduce you to Rachel, our newest member."

"Hi, Rachel," she answered with genuine courtesy.

"And Curt is the last member of the team who reminded us of the importance of maintaining a schedule."

Curt didn't answer.

"So, let's get Rachel up to speed," Alexis ordered.

Beth Young jumped up from her relaxed position and walked past Alexis and Rachel to grab a folder from a small counter space next to Louis' workstation. She hadn't bothered to put her shoes back on. She handed the packet to Rachel and silently moved back to the front seat. Unsure what she was supposed to do with the folder, Rachel thumbed it open and started reading. On the front page was a picture of a beautiful little girl with blonde locks falling down the sides of a cherub-like face; she couldn't be more than six years old. The name Charlotte was written above the picture. The next few pages appeared to be some type of police report of a missing girl, dated four years ago. She had gone missing from a museum while on a school field trip in nearby San Jose. Rachel looked up at Alexis confused; Louis was looking at her, waiting for a response.

She kept reading the packet. In additional to the police report, there was a series of photographs. The subject of the surveillance photo was clearly unaware the pictures were being taken. The angle suggested the girl was in some kind of clothing store with an older, cold-looking woman, but they were clearly very recent. Rachel studied the surveillance photos and flipped back to the picture labeled Charlotte. She moved back to the photos and back to Charlotte comparing the images. She cracked a smile and looked back at Alexis who was smiling back at her. Beth was twisted around in her seat and watched with anticipation.

"You found her? But how?"

Rachel was astonished at the fact this team she had agreed to help had managed to defy the odds and find a girl missing for the last four years. She held an amazed look as she looked around the van.

"That's what we do, Rachel. And that's what you are going to do— find missing children."

Chapter 2

But how did you find her?" Rachel asked, incredulously. "I mean, I don't get it. The police report says all the leads went cold, and the last update was...." She looked back at the packet of paper to find the correct date. "It was two years ago!"

"We're good at what we do," Louis chimed in arrogantly, looking over at Alexis.

"We are motivated, to say the least. But we do enjoy a high success rate."

"So, okay. What's the secret though? You still haven't answered how."

"Curtis, man. It was all Curtis. It usually is. The guy is gifted when it comes to this."

Rachel looked over at Louis. He sat impressed while speaking of his teammate, and then she looked over at Alexis who held a confirming look on her face. Rachel's question wasn't met, but she grew curious about who Curtis was. Having just started the trial run she agreed to, she expected the answers would come.

Louis explained that the team moved from city to city at random and searched for missing children. Although they were not affiliated with law enforcement, Curt and Melinda were both former cops and sometimes used their sources to facilitate the rescue of children.

"Sounds like a needle in a haystack."

"That's what I say, but it's more like a microscopic needle in a haystack the size of Texas."

"So what do y'all do that cops can't?"

"First of all, we have the time. Second, we've been in the business long enough now that we've gotten good at what we do."

***

Rachel had agreed to meet Alexis in San Francisco on the chance to work for her in the arena of missing children. Alexis had vaguely told her the job would be highly satisfying, and if she wanted to know more, she would have to come see how the team worked first hand. Rachel was skeptical at first but longed for a more worthy cause than her constant stressful and systematically flawed position with the Department of Children and Family Services. She was a case worker, had been for eight years and had seen more kids failed by the red tape of bureaucracy than helped. The victories, it seemed, were fewer and farther apart, and she longed for something more.

She had come across Alexis at a missing children's conference held in Atlanta four months earlier—a conference Rachel attended regularly to honor her sister who went missing from their West Houston home when she was only twelve years old. The memory of her loss still haunted her and provided the motivation necessary to keep making a difference. She recalled Alexis seeking her out amongst the droves of the attendees and proposing to her that if she desired a real chance to help missing children and make a difference, to give her a call. Then Alexis handed her a business card, and Rachel took the card and lost Alexis in the crowd.

After weeks of thinking over the proposal and Googling Alexis Vanderhill, she figured the daughter of a multi-million dollar media mogul and award-winning journalist who featured several exposés on child welfare was worth a chance. Her spirit of adventure led her to pick up the phone and call. Two days later she was meeting Alexis at the airport in San Francisco.

***

The story of Charlotte had started the day before.

"It's getting late, and I'm getting hungry," came the normal and expectant whine of Louis Melton.

"We have been at it for over four hours; it may be time to move on to another location," Melinda added with a tone on secession.

"Curtis? Whaddya say?"

"No, not yet."

The team members collectively shrugged their shoulders at the exhaustive thought of remaining at their posts any longer. But they all remained, each vigilant in their duties for the good of the mission. Louis was behind the monitor screens in the van, Melinda was strolling up and down the long sidewalk of the strip mall, and Curt was posted up in his Crown Vic in the parking lot. Beth intermingled inside several stores, pretending to shop, which was never a bad gig and came natural to the young woman.

The day started to move into the late afternoon. Curt wanted to stay at it for just a moment longer. Questioning the decision, he glanced up and keyed in on a little girl holding her mother's hand through the rear view mirror. They approached the back of his car from the bus stop at the end of the parking lot and walked past the black Crown Vic. The little girl passed by, and Curt locked eyes with her as she walked towards the store. He felt the young girl's heart cry out to him through her stare. She was one of the lost...he could feel it. There was a darkness hidden behind her eyes, a darkness that he had become used to battling. It was easy to recognize something in others that was hidden inside oneself. The familiar feeling in his gut, which he had learned to listen to rather than ignore, returned. He pulled the door handle of the car and slowly got out. He wore a long, tan trench coat, and it fell straight when he stood up. He kept his eyes on the little girl.

"I may have something." The silence over the radio finally broke, and the team noticed the hint of excitement in Curt's voice. "A little brown-haired girl walking into Old Navy with her mother."

Beth piped up, "I'll be there in just a minute. I'm like three stores down."

"I'm piggy-backing on the store's security feed and should have visual...." Louis worked the keyboard like a pianist during a concerto, "Voila. I am GOOD!" The sixteen-screen security camera bank flashed to life on Louis' monitor. He quickly entered a command and focused on the front door, anticipating the dark-haired girl entering the store.

Curt started to move slowly behind the young girl and her mother. As a matter of habit, he felt the Glock .40 holstered on his hip through the trench coat. It was always there just in case he needed it.

Melinda made her way towards the adjacent store to keep eyes on the entrance and exit.

As the team converged, Beth, who could easily pass as a young college co-ed out clothes shopping, beat the young girl and her mother to the store and entered first. Curt brought up the rear but hung back. His appearance, a tan trench coat over a white collared button up shirt and dark khaki pants, didn't necessarily blend him in as a casual shopper.

Beth quickly entered the store and purposely ignored the newly acquired targets. She stood behind the sale rack, off to the side of the entrance for cover. She reached into her purse and slowly pulled out a Nikon camera while she pretended to sift through the clearance rack. The young girl entered the store behind her mother. Beth moved the camera just over the rack of clothes and snapped continuously at the girl. Beth went unnoticed and dropped the camera below rack level and examined her shots. They were clear shots of the girl's face as well as the mother's.

As she zoomed in on the young girl's face, she too saw the gloomy sadness lurking behind her eyes. She could tell something had robbed her of her innocence. It was a look she had become all too familiar with since joining the team. She was amazed at Curt's ability to see inside one's soul, but she wasn't sold that this girl was one of the lost.

"I got 'em," Beth said quietly, trying not to draw attention and stowing the camera back into her purse.

"Good. Let's follow them back to the house when they're done," Curt ordered.

"I got a few stills from the security footage; the resolution is kind of garbage, but I'm running it through the facial recognition software to see if we get a hit."

"Do age regression first." Curt added.

"Dammit!" Louis was angry at himself for not thinking of that first.

"And see if you can change her hair to blonde."

Unbeknownst to each other, all four team members popped their heads up in wonderment over Curt's request about the little girl's hair. They all failed to see the connection but didn't want to question his hunch. He clearly saw something they didn't.

"You got it."

"Blonde hair, Curt?" Beth's curiosity got the better of her.

"Her leg and arm hair is blonde. You can also see her blonde roots deep in the part on her head. It's common for kidnappers to dye the kid's hair, so they are immediately unrecognizable. It makes for an easy get away. That little girl has fair skin, and blonde body hair, she is not a brunette by birth."

Beth pulled out the camera again and verified Curt's observation. He was right—again.

After an hour of shopping in Old Navy and two other clothing stores, the young girl and her mother boarded a bus and headed south. But as the woman stood at the check-out, Louis was ready and set up a tiny hour glass, a "two-minute glass" actually, next to his computer as he waited for the woman to make her purchase. He hoped she used a credit card, and he waited impatiently while he watched on the hijacked security cameras. She pulled out her plastic card and used it to buy the girl's clothes. After the woman used her credit card, she left the store, and Louis set the two-minute glass in action. He vigorously pecked away at his keyboard, hacking into the corporate credit card server and capturing the incoming transaction at the San Francisco outlet store. Once he had the number, he quickly moved into the financial institution that backed the woman's credit card and was able to come up with a name and billing address.

"Ms. Francine Bennett, ladies and gentleman," Louis announced just as the final grains of the two-minute glass fell to the bottom chamber. He followed up with her mailing address, credit report, tax return information, and criminal history. There was nothing significant other than some drunk and disorderly charges from seven years ago.

Louis printed out the found documents, and Beth took the tax return and scanned it over.

"On her tax return, Ms. Bennett claimed a daughter, Charlene. Age eleven."

"That fits." Melinda looked over Beth's shoulder at the tax return.

"Ms. Bennett was never married and worked as a data entry clerk for an HMO according to last year's tax return. She doesn't belong to any groups or charities. She isn't on any social media under that name and seems pretty boring," Louis added.

Curt leaned up against a concrete planter that ran along the sidewalk and watched Francine Bennett moving throughout the mall with Charlene. She was not motherly toward the girl, and she was not warm. He noticed that she addressed the child in a cold manner, and the kid reciprocated. It was not unconditional love. He understood that children

11

get moody, disobedient, and downright annoying at times, but there was always a genuine love that was shared. He didn't see that with Francine and Charlene.

"Louis, pull up past tax returns; how far back was she claiming the kid?"

"Child's play Curtis, child's play!"

"Just do it!"

"Fine." Louis waited for the information to pop onto his screen. "Yep, for the last four years. She didn't claim the kid five years ago. I'll run the social security number to see what pops up."

"Check adoption records from the state."

"Okay, that'll take me a little more time. That stuff is kept in the Fort Knox of cyberspace."

"Whatever…just let me know what you find."

The team followed Francine Bennett and the young Charlene as they took the bus to the Russian Hill neighborhood. Melinda had joined them for the bus ride, and nearing the address Louis found during his search, she remained behind them casually strolling along. Curt watched from his car and Beth from the driver's seat of the Mercedes Sprinter. The mother and daughter ducked into a deli and grabbed dinner to go and soon made it to their two-story brownstone before sunset. The team sat on the residence for the rest of the night until all the lights in the house went out.

It was nearing midnight when Louis was able to confirm Francine Bennett had never adopted a child in the state of California. Beth questioned the scope of his search parameters, but Louis explained that Ms. Bennett, by all accounts, had never left the state of California.

Curt let all the facts they knew to this point soak in. Everything fit. Everything pointed to the possibility that Charlene was one of the lost, but from where was a more important question.

"It's fine. Let's head back to the hotel and pick this up in the morning."

***

The idling engine hum of the Mercedes Sprinter was hushed but sent a soothing vibration resonating throughout the van. Rachel Goodwin sat listening to the background that built up to the operation she had found herself in the middle of. But as she processed the information, she wondered about the legality of their actions.

"So, you just aimlessly hunt for missing children and the basis for selection is the gut feeling of someone?"

At hearing the crude assessment from the new girl, Curt fidgeted in his seat uncomfortably but held his tongue. She was new and just didn't quite understand the complexities of the mission, but if she didn't get with the program, Alexis would give her the boot.

"It sounds a bit simplistic, yes," Alexis chimed in. "But you have to understand, and this is paramount for our existence Rachel, that we live in anonymity and work behind the scenes. It's how we survive in this endeavor. That means we can't go through normal channels asking questions that would draw attention to ourselves."

"Draw attention? You mean from the cops?" Rachel asked.

"Well, yeah!" Louis answered.

"Because you are hacking into corporate and government databases?"

"Hacking is such an ugly word…."

"It's necessary." Curt's voice boomed through the van's speakers causing Rachel to jump. She calmed herself and thought for a minute as Alexis watched her for a reaction.

"So, you picked out the girl; how were you able to figure out she was this Charlotte girl?"

"That's where I come in," said Beth, nodding at the folder in Rachel's lap.

Chapter 3

The pillowy fog rolled in from the south end of the bay and stretched over the water like a fluffy down comforter. The sun began to sneak over the golden hills of the Diablo Mountain Range, bringing a warm light to the coastal city.

Curt was on a post down at the end of the block, same as the day before, after watching Ms. Bennett drag Charlene into the brownstone. He shook off the short night and lack of sleep with a hot cup of coffee. Beth was in a matching jogging outfit and ran a looping track that allowed her to pass by the target apartment. She was already on her second pass, and her heavy breathing was audible through the team's radio system. Melinda remained in the van with Louis watching the front door of the target through a pair of binoculars.

"I've made it into the home's security system network, and in case we miss something, I'll catch it when she sets the alarm."

"If she sets the alarm," Melinda added.

"True."

The team watched for only twenty more minutes. Beth was finishing up her third loop when Francine Bennett's overweight frame stepped out on to the stoop with little Charlene in tow. The girl was dressed in a pretty pink dress, white stockings, a matching coat, and a backpack slung over her right shoulder. They were clearly on their way to school, and for Francine, work at the HMO office that was a few blocks from the school. Curt watched the hefty woman forcefully grab the little girl and pull her along like a dog on a leash. He could feel the bile rising in his throat as he watched in disgust. He knew he was right about her being one of the lost.

As the woman and child made the length of the block, they turned up the street where the Sprinter van was parked and idling. They passed unsuspecting and headed towards the school. The van's heater was keeping Louis Melton and Melinda Dalton warm on the inside. Beth doubled back and watched the pair until they made it to the end of the cross street and far out of sight. She walked back to the van, and the side door slid open. Melinda was poised for her surveillance disguise wearing a dark sweater, dress pants, matching high heels, and carrying a briefcase. To add to the character of a modern businesswoman, she accented the look with rectangular framed glasses and set out to follow the pair. Beth hopped into the van and took Melinda's spot as she fixed herself and set out to follow the targets.

"Are we clear?" Curt could no longer see the woman from his position and anxiously watched the front of the house.

Melinda, walking as stably as she could in the unfamiliar high-heels, looked ahead in the crowd and saw the easily recognizable frame of the bigger woman and the child. She noticed more and more children walking with a parent and figured the school was near.

"Yeah, looks like we are getting close to the school. You should be good to go."

Curt slipped out of the black Crown Vic, checked his hip for the Glock and added an additional check of his trench coat pocket for the tools he would need momentarily. He looked around cautiously and made his way to the back side of the townhomes. He found a narrow alleyway and ducked in unnoticed. The narrow slit between the townhomes intersected another alley that ran behind the length of the townhomes. It bordered all of the small patches of land the homeowners called back yards and was used as a service access for garbage trucks, utility repairmen, and residents who wanted access to their garage.

Curt counted the necessary townhomes from the back to find the target. He waited patiently and asked again if it was clear.

"Yes, the kid is at school, and Bennett's on her way to work." Melinda stood outside the five-story building that housed the HMO and watched Ms. Bennett walk in the front door.

The alley was clear in both directions, and Curt glanced up to the back windows across the passageway that would expose him. He saw that all were either darkened or had the blinds shut. He looked for a back gate to the tall, wooden privacy fence that led to the backside of the brownstone, but when he didn't find one, he gracefully hoisted himself up and over the fence. He dropped down into the small back yard of

Francine Bennett. He sat and waited patiently before approaching the house.

The yard was unkempt and devoid of something he expected to be there, kid toys. There wasn't a swing-set, a ball, hula hoop, bicycle, or anything. There was nothing but a neglected yard with dry, straggly grass. He studied the back door of the brownstone, looking for any additional security measures Louis' research hadn't found. He didn't see anything that caused alarm. Off to his left was a small structure Curt pegged as a garage. He waited for five minutes before moving and made his way to the garage. It was padlocked. He wanted to get into the house first and come back to this if he had time.

The lock on the back door was easy to pick. Curt made sure Louis hacked in and disengaged the alarm before he entered. He didn't want Ms. Bennett to get a phone call at work saying her burglar alarm had been activated and decide to come home.

He slipped in the back door of the house that led to the kitchen. He searched around for anything that could lead them to the real identity of the little girl. She was missing from somewhere; he was sure of it. He just needed proof. Curt made his way to the living room and found it eerie and withdrawn, not comfortable as a home should be. There were no family photos on the wall, and all the mirrors were positioned high on the walls. This was very odd to Curt, and after a moment of thought he realized that the short stature of the child wouldn't allow for her to look in the mirror at that height.

The upstairs was equally abnormal. The house felt distant and cold, not loving and warm. The first bedroom down the hall from the stairwell was clearly an adult's room. It had a large television, laptop, queen-sized bed, and modest furniture, nothing elegant or dainty.

"I got a laptop in the bedroom," Curt updated. He reached in the inner breast pocket of his jacket and removed a small thumb drive. He plugged it in the USB port, and a blue light started to flash on the drive.

"Did you put the thumb drive I gave you in it?"

"Yeah, it's in. The light's flashing."

"Okay, give me a minute." Louis was remotely downloading the contents from the laptop, using a blue-tooth transmitter. He would later sift through the contents, trying to find the secrets she was hiding.

Curt continued his walkthrough and found the little girl's room at the end of the hall. It was not a surprise that the room was as depressing as the rest of the house. He sat down on her perfectly made bed and looked around the room, hoping something would jump out at him. He lay down on the girl's bed, noticing there were no pretty pictures hanging on the wall, no Barbie dolls awaiting a tea party, and no stuffed animals collected on the bed. It was a bleak room. This house reminded him of a very uninteresting museum that no one would ever want to visit.

He looked around the room, hoping to get perspective on how the girl saw the world. He rolled over onto his side and found himself facing a simple wooden desk against the wall, outfitted with a blank note pad, a cup of pencils, and a lamp. There were no pictures pinned to the wall or ribbons to display, nothing. But something drew his attention from this angle. Something was under the desk. He sat upright on the bed, reached under the desk, and pulled a notebook down. It had been taped to the underside of the desk.

This was more like it. The notebook was filled with girlie scribbles and ramblings of a pre-teen girl. She wrote notes to herself about horses, puppies, sharks, Disneyland, and some kids who Curt assumed were her friends at school. This was her one outlet in the otherwise stark prison of a home. He flipped to the first few pages and found that she addressed "Her real mommy and daddy" in the letter. Curt felt adrenaline dump into his veins, hoping the notebook was the proof he was searching for. He quickly continued reading through the pages, hoping to find something tangible to follow up on but found nothing. He scanned the pages for a second time and came to the same conclusion. He closed the book in frustration and let out a defeated sigh. But now the answer was right in front of him. In the bottom corner of the back cover, he noticed the name Charlotte was written.

Curt left the bedroom with a renewed sense of purpose. He'd found a good enough lead with the name Charlotte. It was clearly written with the same girlie handwriting as the rest of the notebook and a glimpse into her world. He quickly retrieved the thumb drive from the laptop and made his way to the back of the house. "I'm coming out, Louis; are you ready?"

Louis snapped to and punched in a quick command to the keyboard in front of him disengaging the alarm again so Curt could slip out the way he came.

"Okay, done. Did you find anything?"

"Yeah, I think so."

Curt shut the back door of the townhouse, leaving it as if he had never been there; he glanced around the backyard and the overlooking neighbors again, seeing if anything had changed. After searching around the eerie house, absent of anything remotely close to what a home should be, he glanced at the garage. He didn't want to leave it unchecked. Maybe it held some secrets worth uncovering.

After a few hard twists and scrub sweeps with the pick, the padlock to the garage went limp in his hand as the clasp opened up. He flipped it off the lock and slid inside the garage and pulled the door shut.

"I'm in the detached garage. Can you guys hear me?"

"Yes, I got you," Louis answered eagerly.

Inside the garage there was a thick layer of dust covering everything. It was a chaotic clutter and collection of useless junk. There were boxes stacked haphazardly with no sense of order, and they appeared unsteady. However, what immediately drew Curt's attention was the vehicle parked amongst the clutter. At first pass, if the bay door was opened from the alleyway, you wouldn't see the car, but from the way Curt entered, he saw it right away. Why would anyone have a car and take the bus? At second glance, he noticed the boxes and clutter were clearly placed around the car in an attempt to conceal it within the garage. Curt thought about this for a moment and decided to investigate further as his instincts were kicking in. He pulled the tarp back to reveal the front left fender of the vehicle; it was a dark blue Ford, possibly a Taurus. He squeezed past another pillar of cardboard boxes, some nearly bursting at the corners, and checked out the rear of the car by lying across the trunk and looking from a nearly inverted angle. He pulled up the tarp so he could read the tag.

"Hey, copy this tag."

"Okay, shoot." Louis was poised, ready to copy down the tag. He had already made it into the California DMV database once he heard Curt mention a garage and had it pulled up on his screen.

Curt read out the tag as best he could in the dim garage light, thick dust, and from an upside-down position.

"Okay, stand by."

He climbed off the trunk and completed his full-circle search of the vehicle. He neared the front passenger fender and lifted the corner of the tarp to take a look. The corner light and grill, along with the tire well, had significant crush damage, but the damage was obviously old, as the creases in the metal had started to rust. Curt kneeled down for a closer look, following his instincts farther down the rabbit hole. He examined the damage and even got on his back to look up underneath of the car. He studied the corner of the undercarriage and saw something that piqued his interest. He reached in his coat pocket for his small flashlight and pulled it out. He needed a better look at what he found. He clicked on the small flashlight and aimed its beam making the object clearer. It was human skin. He looked closer still and saw another small piece, complete with a few hair follicles attached to it. He searched the rest of this corner and saw a powdery red substance in the same area, on the axle, lines, hoses, and the frame itself. Curt backed away from under the car and pulled the tarp back even further, getting an overview of what he found. He pulled away the rest of the tarp to see the passenger side window. It was down, and he stepped over to look in the car. The air inside was stale and dusty, but he could still make out the metallic smell of the aluminum cans and rotting beer remnants in the interior.

Curt flipped the tarp back over and moved the boxes to cover up his swipe marks on the dusty garage floor. He went to the door and carefully opened it up, slipping out, back over the fence, and down the alleyway unnoticed.

"Anything back on the tag?" Curt made his way back to the Crown Vic.

"It's expired by about five years…no liens…no hits in NCIC, and nothing in Carfax."

Curt half-way expected these results from the search. He had pegged the woman for what she truly was as she walked past his car the day before in the mall parking lot, and the lack of information that came back from Louis' search would support that theory.

"Beth? Do your thing with the stuff from the car. Start five years ago and work backwards."

Beth had lost herself in her morning newspaper review of the Chronicle. She snapped to attention at the sound of her name, "Huh? Oh, right, the car. I'm on it."

***

As she sat in the Mercedes Sprinter, Rachel listened to the team's search of Francine Bennett's home. She kept up with the facts as they were relayed to her but still didn't see the hard connection of how they figured out Charlene was the missing Charlotte. She was convinced that they were on to something but couldn't see it herself. Not yet.

"So, how were you able to find out this little girl was the missing girl, Charlotte?"

"Hold on, I'll have to explain later; this is about to go down." Beth gripped the over-sized steering wheel with her small hands, watching Melinda carefully at the front door.

"So now what?"

"Now comes the fun part," Louis added.

Curt grunted at the notion, which was audible through the radio, that the upcoming phase of the operation could be considered fun. Maybe from the front seats of the van it was "fun," but from his point of view, it was anything but "fun." He would agree that it was the pivotal point in their mission. Louis heard the grumble from Curt and sank slightly in his swivel chair.

"This is the reason why we are here, Rachel. At this point, we return the child to her parents where she belongs. That is all that matters," Alexis explained.

"So, what? We just call the cops and tell them what we have figured out, and they come and get her?"

Alexis smiled. Louis turned his attention purposefully towards his screen to avoid answering Rachel, and Beth smirked at the naive statement from the new girl. The radio remained silent to the question as well.

"Okay, so what am I missing?"

"Rachel? I recruited you because I thought you wanted to make a difference."

"I do, but I'm not really understanding what's going on."

20

"Rachel, you worked in the social work field and know how bureaucratic protocol can hinder the progress of justice. Well, let me ask you this—and answer honestly."

"Okay."

"Would you be willing to do the right thing, something you felt deep down in your heart was the right thing to do, no matter what?"

She thought briefly, trying to find the motivation behind the question, "Yes, it's a principle I've lived by."

"What if in doing the right thing you committed some substantial criminal and constitutional law violations for the right reason?"

Rachel was puzzled and looked around the van. She studied Louis, the computers, and thought about the beginning of the story of Charlotte. It clicked. The operation wasn't sanctioned by any government authority. To get the results they desired, at the pace they wanted, they had to skirt some laws to protect the children and get them back to their parents.

"So...you steal them back?"

"Essentially," Alexis agreed. She studied the reaction of her new recruit, hoping she wasn't turned off by the less than legal methods to which she was being exposed, but she felt strongly about the mission of the team and why she founded it—to make a real difference—and she hoped Rachel was willing to get on board.

"So, no wonder I've never seen anything on the news about some vigilante group rescuing a missing child years later!" She stared at the floor of the van lost in thought. She visualized the idea of skirting the system she knew very well in order to do the right thing, as Alexis put it, and making a real difference.

"How many kids have you been able to, you know...save?"

"Over the last five years, since I started this project, we've been able to save nearly 100 children, Charlotte will make number 99."

Rachel was astonished at the number of children the team had been able to save, not only was she impressed at the total number, but how many they'd saved without the first blip on the news media's radar. She found this ironic seeing that Alexis Vanderhill is a notable journalist and the daughter of a media mogul. A sensational story such as this would be a dream story for any journalist. So why the anonymity, she wondered. But then it made sense to her; the illegal methods the team utilized would create more of a problem with the legality of the rescue if they involved the police. But this posed a more perplexing question.

"So, if you don't call the cops and 'steal' the kid back, does that mean the offender gets away with it?"

Curt heard the valid question, and a small crack of a smile broke on his perpetually stoic face. Louis snickered, Alexis smiled, and Beth chuckled from the front seat.

"Not exactly," Beth answered with an enigmatic tone.

Rachel didn't understand what was funny and got a little irritated at being kept in the dark. She searched around the van and among its occupants for an answer but didn't get one.

"It's time; let's move," Curt ordered over the radio.

Alexis saw that Rachel was still in need of an answer and settled her with, "Just wait…you are about to find out."

Beth sprang to life and hopped into the driver's seat of the van. Alexis swung her captain's chair around to face the front and locked it in place. Louis scooted his chair up to his station and pulled a lever in the floor, also locking his chair in place. Rachel felt a twinge of panic wash over her as she watched everyone else within the van prepare for something she was completely unaware of. Alexis glanced over her shoulder, saw the panic, and told her to grab ahold of something. Rachel pushed herself back on the leather bench seat and searched for seat belts but didn't see one available. She braced herself by tensing her arms out to the side for stabilization.

She felt the van jerk into gear, but it didn't move right away. Suddenly, the side door of the van slid open and a thin black woman, late 30s or early 40s, with short hair appeared. She hastily removed a large overcoat and wool blanket from around her body, dropped it on the floor of the van, set down an iPad, and removed a clipboard and briefcase from next to the bench seat. She stood up and took a breath. Alexis smiled at her expectantly. Rachel surmised this must be Melinda, one of the voices over the radio.

"You forgot these Mel," Louis called out to Melinda, extending his arm with a pair of glasses for her to take.

"Oh, thanks." She took the glasses and slid them on her face to resurrect the businesswoman look from earlier.

"Good luck!" Alexis added.

Melinda slid the door shut and took off, walking down the sidewalk of the cross street toward the brownstone. Beth put the van in gear and slowly pulled out onto the street. She stopped at Ms. Bennett's street, made the turn, and parked short. It was in a direct line of sight to the front door.

As the van parked, Rachel took the opportunity to take the front passenger seat of the van to watch the operation unfold. After a moment, Melinda came into view and strolled down the side-walk, clipboard and briefcase in hand, and approached the bottom of the front stairs. She paused, glanced back at the van, and then spoke in a hushed tone.

"Curt, I'm at the front door."

"Okay, I'm in position."

Rachel could hear Louis in the back of the van, typing on his keyboard. Then a strange voice came over a different radio somewhere behind Louis. She looked back at the workstation and saw the green glow of a radio screen next to the panel where she'd seen him hit the switch for the van radio. She listened to the voice speak and quickly recognized that it was a dispatcher coming from a police scanner. She figured it was so they could keep tabs on the police and would be warned if they drew any unwanted attention for this operation.

Rachel felt her heart rate accelerate in anticipation from the building excitement. It was a feeling that had been hard to come by in her world. Melinda knocked on the front door of the brownstone, sending the operation past the point of no return. The porch light flicked on, and Ms. Bennett, dressed in a dingy bathrobe, answered the door.

"Hi, my name is Brenda Martin, and I'm with Windsor Security. We bid for government contracts, and one of your neighbors has applied with us. So, I'm doing a background check to make sure there are no issues or concerns. I do apologize for the late hour, but do you have a moment?"

"Um, sure, but I don't really know any of my neighbors. I really stay to myself." Ms. Bennett was skeptical at the legitimacy of the late caller.

"That's okay. It'll only take a minute."

Curt listened via the ear buds as Melinda worked her magic at the front door. He quickly picked the backdoor lock again and slipped inside careful not to draw any attention. He could hear the muffled voice of Francine Bennett talking with Melinda through the half-opened front door. He moved his thin frame quietly through the kitchen and passed within twenty feet of Ms. Bennett and up the stairs toward Charlotte's room. He calmed his breathing and moved quickly, hearing Melinda struggle to keep the woman's attention.

"Have you known your neighbor to have any late night parties or use any illicit drugs?"

"No, like I said, I don't really know my neighbors, and it's getting late. I need to go."

"Just a few more minutes, ma'am; I promise."

Curt stopped at the girl's door. Once he opened the door, there would be a chain reaction that could not be stopped. But the reason he found himself outside of an eleven year old girl's bedroom was to try and right another wrong in this world.

Charlene Bennett was not asleep as her mother had thought. She had snuck over to her desk and started to write in her secret journal, something that made her feel better inside and kept the loneliness at bay. It kept her connected to the life she once had but for some reason was hard to remember. She had pulled it from the secret hiding place and started to write about a dream she had about her real mother and father. It was about her favorite park that they had taken her to when she was younger. The "shady park," as they affectionately called it because the entire park was covered in shade from large redwoods. It was a favorite memory she visited when not around her new mother. She began to write in the journal and noticed something odd in the back cover. The book didn't close right, like something was stuffed between the pages. She flipped the journal open to the back and there it was, staring back at her. She had never seen it before, but she instantly recognized the smiling faces of her real mother and father, and her smiling too from a seat between them. It was a snapshot taken years ago for the church directory, and somehow it was put inside of her secret journal. She pulled the small photograph from the journal and examined it as if it were a mystical object with great and mysterious powers.

She was so enthralled with the photograph that she failed to notice the strange man standing just behind her watching with soft and sad eyes. He stood still while she carefully studied the picture. He moved just an inch closer and mesmerized himself with the young girl staring at the picture he had placed in her secret journal earlier that morning. The slight movement caught her attention out of her peripheral vision, and she instantly gasped in fright and leapt from her chair, cowering on her bed. Her body began to tremble uncontrollably.

"Charlotte?" Curt stuck his hand out in the friendliest and calming gesture he could manage. "I'm here to help you." His tone was soothing and seemed to ease the frightened girl.

She calmed down and her body stopped trembling. She heard her birth name, and it struck something deep inside. She read the endearing eyes of the strange man in the trench coat and felt he was sincere about helping. She could see the sadness in his eyes too.

"Charlotte, my name is Curt, and I put that picture in there for you to find. Do you know where I got it from?"

She shook her head no.

"Your mother and father gave it to me. I'm here to take you back to them and away from this place."

Charlotte grew quickly confused and hesitant. She withdrew back further on her bed.

"It's true."

"But they're dead. My new mom told me so. She said that bad men came and killed them and they might be after me too, so I had to go with her. She showed me pictures in the newspaper that they're dead. She said I had to change my name for protection."

"No, Charlotte, they aren't dead. There are no bad men that killed them. The woman lied to you. I am here because I want to take you away from here, but we have to go now." Curt tuned into the conversation between Ms. Bennett and Melinda.

"Listen, I've answered your questions lady. I'm sorry; I can't help you any further."

As Ms. Bennett was closing the door, Melinda blurted out, "Listen, I'm willing to pay money for any dirt that can be substantiated. I mean, do you want criminals working on your government contracts? I know I don't."

Ms. Bennett stopped at the mention of money and kept the door cracked so that just her face was visible. Melinda smiled that the stall tactic worked but for how long she didn't know.

Curt stepped toward the girl and extended his hand. She held her arms tightly crossed around her body, still uncertain.

"Listen, we need to go, and we need to go now. I need you to trust me."

"No, my parents are dead! You could be one of the bad men trying to take me away. You need to go!"

Curt couldn't blame the poor girl for not trusting him at first, but he was about to force the issue. He couldn't stand to bear her being in that desolate and loveless house living with a sociopathic woman and away from her loving parents another moment. He stepped closer to the bed and grabbed the girl's arm. She yanked with everything she could and screamed at him to stop.

"No, shhh. Please, Charlotte you have to be quiet."

"No, leave me alone!"

Ms. Bennett heard the scream of Charlene upstairs and looked up towards the second floor, trying to figure out exactly what she heard. She looked back at Melinda with complete suspicion.

"Sounds like someone is up late watching television," Melinda offered. Ms. Bennett wasn't buying it and left the front door headed to the stairs.

Melinda called out after her but failed to hold her attention. "Shit!"

With the ruse no longer in effect, she dropped the briefcase to the ground and pulled out a small eight inch metal cylinder with a rubber grip and followed Ms. Bennett into the house.

"Oh shit!" Louis said from the van. "This is bad."

Rachel spun her head around wondering what she could do to help. Beth dove into her backpack and pulled a notebook out. She flipped frantically through the pages looking for something in her notes, an odd reaction to the situation, Rachel thought.

Curt steadily tried to convince Charlotte Morgan to come with him but wasn't getting anywhere. He heard the failed stall tactic by Melinda at the door and could hear Ms. Bennett calling out for Charlene.

"Call her 'Honey Bear'!" Beth's voice chimed in over the ear bud radio.

Curt paused as he struggled with the child, "Huh?"

"Call her 'Honey Bear,' it's what her parents call her…do it!"

"Honey Bear, your mom and dad called you Honey Bear."

In an instant, Charlotte Morgan stopped fighting the strange man in the trench coat and studied his eyes after he spoke that name.

"What did you say?"

"Honey Bear—that's what your mom and dad called you, isn't it? Is that something a bad man would know? Now, please come with me."

She hadn't heard that name in a long time and knew it only came from one place, home. At the sound of the name, she was instantly reminded of the lazy Saturday mornings she spent in her parent's bed watching cartoons, the late evening strolls around the neighborhood holding hands, and the messy adventures of baking cupcakes for no special reason. Charlotte slowly reached out and took Curt's hand, finally accepting his help. She sprung up, and they quickly made it to the threshold of the bedroom door, but Charlotte yanked free and ran back into the room. Curt immediately thought she duped him, but she reached for something to take with her.

"My journal, please, let me grab it."

Charlotte ran over to her desk, picked up her journal, and ran towards Curt with complete trust. She grabbed him by the hand, and they ran as fast as her small legs would allow her down the stairs.

From the top of the stairs, Curt yelled out to Melinda for her to head toward the van. She had stepped just inside of the door after Ms. Bennett heard the scream and left to investigate. She stood there with an extended ASP baton in her hand. But she had failed to see where Ms. Bennett went once she entered the dark house. Melinda stood in the hallway just inside the door, waiting for Curt to come down with the child. She looked up at the top of the stairs to see Curt with Charlotte. She smiled, for success was theirs and disappeared out the front door obeying his order.

"Come on." Curt squeezed Charlotte's hand giving her the strength to continue with him.

As Curt made it to the bottom of the stairs, a sudden and sharp pain came viciously and unexpectedly to his right leg, causing both of his knees to buckle and fall to the ground. His tight grip of Charlotte's hand pulled her with him, causing her to trip and slide down the hallway next to him. Ms. Bennett stood over him with a wooden baseball bat in her hand and was in the process of another upswing. Curt scurried backwards and shielded the girl from the ensuing blow, but luckily the follow up swing missed leaving Ms. Bennett off balance. Like a magician pulling the missing card from his sleeve, Curt withdrew his

Glock .40 from his hip holster with lightning fast reflexes and aimed it directly at Ms. Bennett's head, stopping her from reloading for another swing.

"Don't even think about it." She froze at the sight of the gun barrel looking dead at her.

"What are doing? You broke into my house, and you're kidnapping my daughter! Child, run; he's one of the bad men coming after you, run!"

"She's not your daughter. Never has been and never will be. She's coming with me." Curt lowered his weapon at the woman's compliance. "Swing on me again, and I'll shoot you in the head!"

Francine Bennett heard the cold and callous demeanor of the man in the trench coat. She believed he was serious and realized this battle was over, and she had lost; so she lowered the bat. The thought of finding another child as she had found Charlene popped into her head.

"What happens now?" She asked pitifully.

"Nothing but to accept the fate you deserve." Curt so badly wanted to shoot the kidnapper because she stood for everything he hated, but he knew it would not solve anything. Her fate was sealed the day he first spotted her at the mall and saw the truth hidden behind the young girl's eyes. This was her creation. Plus, above all else, he knew it would not bring him back.

He looked down and helped Charlotte up from the floor while keeping a close eye on Ms. Bennett. The girl hid behind her savior, hoping her dreams would come true and that she would get to see her real parents and leave behind the hell she was forced into by this woman.

"The police are on their way Ms. Bennett." She snapped back at the sound of her name. She grew paranoid that he knew her name and had figured out her secret and wondered what other secrets these people knew.

"The police are on their way, and this is the deal. You will not tell them about Charlotte, or about us. That will remain our little secret, and you will forget you ever saw us and never bring us up to the authorities."

The woman scoffed, but his confidence caused her concern. "Why should I do that?"

"Because, if you bring it up, you will be exposed as a kidnapper which is a capital felony. That's the gas chamber dumbass."

Francine Bennett didn't understand the deal, it sounded as if it was no harm, no foul to her. She didn't see the catch.

"Okay, so why are the police on their way if I'm to tell them nothing?"

"They will be here…" Curt checked his watch. "…in five minutes to search your garage."

The mention of kidnapping and the gas chamber didn't seem to faze her, the promise of remaining silent about the man in the trench coat did cause some concern, but it was the mention of the police searching her garage that caused her to go into a full blown panic mode.

"B-b-b-but, ww-why would they do that? There's no reason to search my garage; they can't just do that. Not without reason. You put something in there. Didn't you?"

"No we didn't, and rest assured we gave them a good reason to search it." Curt smiled arrogantly. "And you are going to confess to the hit and run murder of Joey Randolph when they get here too!"

"Huh? Who?" She started breathing heavy to the point of hyperventilation. Curt enjoyed seeing the woman squirm. She started pacing back and forth, the bat still draped in her hand and dragging against the laminate flooring.

"You remember him don't ya? The little boy you killed six years ago when you hit him with your car. You were probably too drunk to even notice that you dragged his body for half a mile before leaving him to die."

"But how…." She was dumbfounded at what she heard.

"Because you stole this little girl you piece of trash. Now sit down and wait for the police to get here. If we hear that you failed to confess to the hit and run murder…," Curt paused and made sure she was listening carefully, "…I will come back here, and I will kill you myself."

Ms. Bennett believed the threat as Curt's eyes bore deep into her soul. He had an icy stare when he spoke. She watched helplessly as he left with Charlotte down the stairs and out of her life forever.

"She can't and won't ever hurt you again. I promise." Curt added a smile for her sake. She smiled back, and he noticed the darkness behind her eyes began to fade into a bright sense of hope.

This reminded Curt that there was hope. It existed, and it was real. For another day, for another week, he would be able to hold onto that hope, and he desperately needed to believe there was hope out there, even for him.

Beth pulled the Mercedes Sprinter up in front of the brownstone to receive the girl. Melinda was waiting to take the girl from Curt as they walked down to the sidewalk.

"These are my friends, and they'll take you to your parents. They are waiting to see you."

"You aren't coming?"

"Don't worry. I'll be right behind you."

Melinda greeted Charlotte Morgan with a wide friendly smile and helped her up into the van. Rachel had moved from the passenger seat to the back and helped the little girl climb into the van. Curt looked up and locked eyes with the new girl for the first time. He hoped that she realized what this team and their mission was really about. It was about this moment. She held his stare and instantly felt an odd connection to the man in the trench coat. He nodded to her and shot a glance over to Alexis then turned and walked down the sidewalk toward the Crown Vic. Rachel sat on the rear bench seat and found herself in awe of the little girl next to her and the success of the mission. She was speechless. Once Melinda buttoned up the van, Beth floored the accelerator and headed to the hotel with Charlotte.

The sirens of the approaching police cars grew louder as they approached Francine Bennett's loveless brownstone and her garage that held a terrible secret—a secret that would have gone unchecked had Curt not seen the darkness in a little girl's eyes as she fatefully walked past.

Chapter 4

As the Mercedes Sprinter van pulled up to the front of the towering Grand Hyatt Hotel, Beth turned to look in the back of the van to watch Charlotte as they approached. She wondered if the kid knew what was in store for her. The exterior lights of the hotel reached high up to its roofline, illuminating the giant building, giving it the mystique that it was more than just a hotel; it was an experience. People, tourists, and businessmen and women alike, moved in and around the elegant hotel as the team pulled nonchalantly up to the valet drop off. Beth parked the van short of the valet stand along the half-circle drive-way.

"I'll be right back; stay here." Alexis opened the van door and headed up toward the front of the hotel. This was her hands-on portion of the operation. Rachel studied the faces of the team, searching for a heads up of what was happening next, but as she was learning, this was not a talkative bunch. She focused on keeping Charlotte entertained.

Louis started clicking the keyboards behind Rachel and flipping switches on his machines, slowly powering them down.

With his workstation shut down, Louis slid past Rachel and the girl and stepped out of the van's side door. He stretched his skinny torso and looked around at the passersby. He looked over to the front entrance of the hotel, a huge revolving door large enough for a small group to move through at once, and noticed Alexis making her way out.

Michael and Debbie Morgan were brought to San Francisco on the dime of the Missing Children's Society to participate in the annual dinner the city held to honor and remember the missing children of Northern California, a number too staggering to accept. It was a difficult trip to make to the neighboring city to the north for such a somber reason, but the parents of Charlotte Morgan never gave up hope. They joined advocacy groups in San Jose and the surrounding cities, helped create public awareness of missing children cases, and had even helped in the recovery of three children since Charlotte had gone missing. They agreed it was their duty as parents.

However, there was no dinner and no ceremony to honor missing children. Alexis had paid their way in full under the guise of the awareness banquet and put them up in the expensive hotel all in preparation of reuniting them with Charlotte. Alexis had promised them tickets to the San Francisco Bay Orchestra as thanks for their efforts in the advocacy programs, but like the dinner, there was no concert either.

Once the identity of Charlotte Morgan was made, Alexis had full faith that her team would be able to recover her and bring her safely back to her parents. She was able to track them down quickly in San Jose and, with her influence and money, able to set the subterfuge with good intentions in motion.

Alexis stopped just outside the front door of the hotel and looked toward the van; Louis was now standing outside. She nodded toward the van and saw Beth acknowledge. Alexis had told the couple that she had arranged for their ride to the concert, and she was going to check its status, furthering the ruse. She looked through the front door of the hotel and waved the couple on to join her outside.

As the couple walked outside, in each other's arms and fighting against the brisk summer wind, they stopped next to Alexis and awaited their ride, hoping it would be a fancy limousine. Such luxuries seemed inappropriate for parents of a missing child, but they had decided to allow this in honor of their daughter.

"Michael, Debbie…I have a surprise for you," she said, holding back her excitement that seemed to confuse the forlorn parents. No matter how many times in the past that Alexis had done this, it never stopped causing such an emotional joy inside.

The couple, modest and humble, looked up at Alexis with gratitude.

"Oh, Ms. Vanderhill, you've done enough for us. What more could you possibly do?"

Alexis smiled a knowing smile and could only anticipate the happiness she was about to bring to these fine people. To stop herself from breaking down, she turned back to the van and waved at Beth eagerly.

Debra Morgan had never given up hope that her daughter was alive. She had never given up hope that she would one day return to her, but she questioned God's motives daily as to why He would allow her child to be taken. She prayed each day that God would forgive her for the sin she unknowingly committed causing him to take her precious child. She prayed for forgiveness, not knowing exactly what sin she had committed, but still she prayed. She took this as a sign from God and joined the advocacy group with full force and motivation, knowing if she helped others, she would be rewarded one day. But when the day didn't come, the stress of giving what she didn't have was tremendous and weighed heavily on her relationship with her husband and others. They tried to conceive another child, but they lost two pregnancies to miscarriages. The doctor said that it was nature's way of taking care of things, but she knew it was God's will. She didn't share this with her husband, but she was on the brink of giving up. She felt her small sliver of hope slipping away.

With all Debra had to endure, she saw Alexis Vanderhill standing before her talking of a surprise and looking down the sidewalk to a large black van parked by the sidewalk. Something inside of her stirred. It was hope rising from the depths of her being. Her hold on her husband loosened as she walked toward the van, feeling drawn to it without knowing why. Her husband looked on, trying to assess what was happening but was unable to put it together.

Debra felt herself floating towards the van as her body buzzed with a sense of overwhelming anticipation. She saw a thin dark-haired woman step from the side of the van and stand in front of a nerdy gentleman with a kind face. She stopped as they looked at her in bewilderment. Debra felt stupid, that she had been mistaken. Her hope began to dissipate into nothing.

But there was no mistake. The next set of feet that stepped out of the van belonged to Charlotte, dressed in pink and green pajamas and clutching a worn out notebook. She looked up at the dark-haired woman for direction. She smiled down at her and glanced over at Debra Morgan, not less than fifty feet in front of the van. Charlotte trustingly followed her gaze and locked eyes with her mother…her real mother.

Debra's body went numb; her heart exploded with a euphoric bliss she had been saving specifically for this moment. Her eyes burst with tears, and the stress from four long years of agonizing torture melted away as she finally laid eyes on her child—alive. Her knees buckled, and she fell to the ground, thanking God for finally rewarding her and bringing her beloved Charlotte home.

"Charlotte?" She called out through the sobs as she held her arms open.

Charlotte Morgan had gone through a lot. She had her world thrown into a wild tailspin of confusion that created more questions than answers. She saw the ghostly image of her mother crying on her knees and felt scared, not overjoyed like she had imagined during so many lonely nights in the past four years.

Rachel Goodwin stepped out of the van to watch the reunion and stood next to Beth. She saw the hesitation in the young girl and the confusion set in for the mother.

Charlotte looked up at Rachel with a need of guidance.

Rachel knelt down next to the child, "It's okay, Charlotte." The girl reached around her neck and squeezed, somehow scared to let go of the reality she'd known for the past four years. Rachel knew that children taken at a young age learned to adapt to their surroundings rather quickly and were, in some degree, brainwashed by their captors. Therapy sessions were in the girl's future, but in this moment she wanted to encourage the girl to go to her mother to start the healing process.

"That's your mother, honey, and she misses you so very much. This is where you belong. You can finally go home now."

The hesitation in the child struck a hard shot of fear and anger deep inside Debra's core, but this was her child. She wasn't going to let go without a fight, not when she was so close.

"Charlotte, it's me, Mommy! C'mere Honey Bear!"

Charlotte heard the love and warmth from her mother and let go of Rachel. She let loose a cry of her own and ran straight towards her mother. Charlotte's face was streaming tears of joy as she ran to her mother's open arms. She threw open her little arms and jumped at her mother, hugging her as tight as her small arms could bear.

"Oh, baby, baby, oh Honey Bear, I've missed you so much!" Debra said amidst the barrage of hugs and kisses. "I'm so sorry, baby. I'm so sorry!"

Michael, numb to the scene he just witnessed, snapped to and ran up behind his wife and daughter and hugged them both, failing to hold back a river of tears.

The heart is a strong muscle built to endure many hardships in the physical realm, but watching the reunion brought forth feelings from within that seemed to surpass any physical strain. This was the pinnacle of joy, and the team who made this possible watched for their own benefit and their own gratification, for they knew there would be no press conference, no fanfare, and no acknowledgement. There would be no recognition of the heroism that brought this family back together...so this was it. But it was all they needed to continue in their mission, for this family—and for Charlotte Morgan—they were able to stop the tears of the lost.

Alexis gave the overjoyed family ample time to enjoy the moment all parties had dreamt about since the awful day Charlotte went missing. She explained that the Society dinner and concert were a ruse and that the real reason they were brought to the city was to reunite them with their daughter. They quickly forgave her misrepresentation and begged for repayment, for a favor, anything, for she had given them their life back. Alexis refused any kind of payment and explained that this was her gift to them without consideration, and it was her pleasure. The only thing she asked for in turn was to protect their anonymity. Without hesitation, the Morgan's agreed and thanked her over and over.

"So what do we tell the rest of our family? Our friends? I mean, about how she is suddenly now back home?" Michael asked, worried about how to hold up their end of the bargain.

"That's up to you. You can go on late night talk shows if you want, or you can quietly explain to your family that she just simply returned one day; just keep me and my team out of it...that's all."

"But won't the police come around and start asking questions?"

"Probably, but who's to say Charlotte is too distraught to answer any questions?" Alexis hinted.

Michael Morgan understood what Alexis was asking but didn't understand the reasoning. He simply granted the wish without question, for he was given the best gift of all, his daughter safe and with him and his wife.

Alexis waved the team on, and they piled back into the van and left the area, satisfied at witnessing the beautiful moment of the reunion. She stood outside the hotel and scanned the nearby parking lot. After a minute, she found what she was looking for. Curt was sitting alone in the Crown Vic watching from the corner of the street.

***

Curt Walker sat quietly in his car, focus again held on the smiling brown-haired boy in the tattered picture, waiting to see the reunion he helped bring to fruition. He watched as Alexis pointed the Morgans in the direction of the van and as the mother went to her knees with outstretched hands and the young girl run up for a climactic embrace. He needed to watch the reunion, to feed the small shred of hope he desperately clung to. He didn't bother to wipe away his tears that always followed, so he sat alone and wondered if he'd ever know that same feeling the Morgans felt at holding their child.

After watching the family walk back into the hotel, he saw Alexis Vanderhill stand out front and search for something. He figured she was looking for him. He didn't bother to hide; he wasn't hiding from anything. He just had to do this part alone. She smiled at him in the distance and returned to the hotel. He watched as she pushed through the huge revolving door but saw Charlotte Morgan pop back out and ask Alexis something in a near panic. Her parents were not more than five feet from her as they watched, concerned. Alexis leaned over to listen and nodded at her request. She stood up straight and pointed directly at Curt sitting alone in his car. Charlotte searched with her young eyes, and when she found the dark sedan, she took a few steps toward it and waved. Curt's heart sank a degree at her thoughtfulness, and he cracked a smile.

The girl finished waving and turned back to her proud parents. She was no longer Charlene Bennett. She was Charlotte Morgan.

Chapter 5

Celebration wasn't what the team did after a successful operation. They celebrated quietly in their own way, separate and alone. Curt sat alone at the hotel bar, removed from anyone else, and drank his bourbon quietly. The picture he kept on the dashboard was now tucked safely in the inside breast pocket of his trench coat.

Beth and Melinda were sitting together in the back of the bar waiting for Rachel's decision to choose whether she was going to be a part of the team or not. She had met with Alexis upstairs in her room to finalize the deal. Beth got up and walked up to the bar. She stood next to Curt and ordered another drink.

"You didn't have to pull the gun," she said condescendingly. Beth abhorred any violence and hated that Curt even carried a gun.

Curt, used to the criticism, finished his sip of bourbon and set the glass down while stretching out his leg. He felt a bruise forming where Francine Bennett mistook his kneecap for a baseball.

"She had a baseball bat, and she was going to bash my head in. It was necessary," Curt answered, but he obviously didn't care for her opinion.

"It's dangerous. You could've just snagged her from school."

"Beth…" Curt snapped annoyingly, "…we could've done a lot of things different, but you know what? Taking her from school would've set in panic from anyone if we were seen, just like it would from anywhere else in public." He took the last pull of his drink and set the glass down with authority. "The girl's on her way home safe tonight; that's all that matters isn't it?"

"We could've waited longer. That woman would have left her at some point. I get the feeling you wanted a confrontation with that woman."

Curt stood up and hovered over the smaller Beth Young to make a point. "You're right. I did." Beth backed away but didn't give in. "But make no mistake about it Beth, I was not about to let that girl stay in that house one more second if I could help it. Put yourself in the parents' shoes, and get your head out of your ass!"

The bartender gave Beth her drink, and she walked away without rebuttal. She was a firm believer in a non-violent way to handle conflict and wanted to express her thoughts.

"Yeah, okay. I see your point." She returned back to her table with Melinda, and Curt ordered another.

As Beth got seated, Rachel made her way down to the bar and joined Beth and Melinda in the back. She ordered a club soda with lime from the bar.

"That was some unbelievable stuff earlier. I can't quite wrap my head around it. I was thinking hard about Ms. Vanderhill's offer but after seeing that family together and the immense joy I felt in seeing them hug like that, oh my goodness, it was too much. I told her to sign me up as soon as possible."

"Well, welcome to the team Rachel," Beth said with mediocre enthusiasm.

"Thanks."

"Curt? She said yes," Melinda called out to Curt up at the bar.

He turned around and looked at the new woman, held her stare for a moment, lifted his glass of bourbon in a half-assed salute, and then turned back to the bar.

"Well, okay." She didn't know whether that was customary or an insult but looked back eagerly at the two women with questions she had from the operation.

"So, how did you figure out she was Charlotte Morgan?"

Beth sipped her drink through a long straw; it was some frothy, red, fruit concoction with a pineapple wedge on it. The waitress set Rachel's club soda down and took another order from Melinda.

"Okay, to let you know, we all have different roles on the team, and those roles coincide with our individual talents."

"Like Louis the hacker?"

"Yep, like Louis the hacker."

"So, what's your strong suit?" Rachel asked of Beth.

"Research."

"Okay? Meaning?"

"Like, Louis can access the information, but he can't put it all together. That's where I come in. I took the name Charlotte and searched all missing child reports in Northern California, but I narrowed the search to time frame of when she began showing up on Francine Bennett's tax returns. I took in account her estimated age, and for all his flaws, Curt is usually right, so of those missing girls I limited the list to those who have blonde hair. That narrowed the search significantly, and from there it was just a matter of narrowing down the possibilities."

"How long did that take you?"

She thought honestly for a moment, "About six hours."

"Wow."

"But that's actually pretty fast considering."

"I bet. So why Northern California? Why not the entire U.S.?"

"Huh? Well to be honest with you, she looked like a California girl, especially when you make her a blonde."

Rachel smiled. "And the hit and run murder…that was a bit of good luck?"

"Yeah, I'll say. I'm good at digging up dirt on the kidnappers, but that was one helluva skeleton in her closet."

"So you just dug that up?"

"Yeah, same method. Louis had his work cut out for him because it's hard to get access to unsolved murders. Curt figured it was a hit and run, and I researched the make and model in unsolved hit and run deaths. We figured it happened before the girl was kidnapped, so that narrowed down the timeframe. Then, it was a matter of tracking her whereabouts back that many years and going through the news articles and police reports. We hit pay dirt when I found the headline of a hit and run death of a ten year old boy. It was a neighbor's kid playing one Saturday morning when she came barreling down the street…awful story, awful all around."

"So, now, hopefully, that family will get closure too."

"Yeah, that's the idea."

Rachel sat back in her chair and looked back over her shoulder at Curt who was still alone at the bar.

"But how exactly did you make sure the police would find the car? It's not like we stuck around and opened up the garage for them?"

"No, you're right. We greased the wheels of justice, you could say." Beth took another sip of her sweet drink.

"How so?"

"Well, after we did the morning reconnaissance at the house, I got busy on the computer and found the hit and run report. Knowing we needed to use that to our advantage, we came up with a plan. We needed a way to stay off the police radar but make the search of the garage legit, so it would stick."

Unaware of Fourth Amendment law, Rachel was lost as to how they would overcome that hurdle. "So, how'd you manage that?"

"Acting, really," Melinda offered ambiguously. She threw back the rest of her drink and looked at Rachel. "Basically, I went in the police department as Brenda Martin, neighbor of Francine Bennett, who just happened to have been invited over one day and saw the vehicle in the garage. I asked about the damage, and we spoke about it, and the conversation went toward some type of crash back in the past, and she said something about a little boy getting hurt!"

"So, you lied and set her up?"

"Pretty much. The search had to be valid though to make it work. The police needed a witness to establish probable cause to get in that garage, so we gave them one. Once they got in, it was up to them to find all the necessary evidence to make the charge."

"But what about the police report, the trial? You can't go back as a witness; they'll know you're a fake."

"That's why there won't be a trial. That's why Curt told her that she would confess. That takes the need for a trial right out from under her. It's coerced justice but justice all the same."

Rachel was amazed at the in-depth work the team was capable of on such short notice. She was glad she joined and hoped she was able to keep up and contribute to the mission.

"So, what's your story?" Melinda asked. "Everyone's got one on this team."

"Oh?" she answered evasively.

"Yeah, we all got some unresolved stuff which is what brings us together to carry out this mission."

"What's yours?" Rachel turned it around and back to Melinda.

"Fine, I'll go first. I was a cop in suburban Atlanta, and my family was proud. My sister was proud too, but she was addicted to crack and couldn't stop. She couldn't find a way to leave it behind. That stuff had such a grip on her, she couldn't shake it. She couldn't keep a job, so she walked the streets prostituting herself until one day she overdosed and died. She laid on some dirty floor of an abandoned apartment for three days until someone finally found her."

Melinda relived that moment in her eyes, then added, "It was awful. I get mad at the thought of some asshole John just leaving her there like a piece of trash."

Rachel was taken aback at the bluntness of the woman's story, but her heart went out to her. She could relate in a way. Melinda continued, "So, being a good sister and cop, I tracked down the dealer who gave her the shit and tried to arrest him. I was out of my jurisdiction, but I didn't care. He fought me and pulled a knife, so I shot and killed him."

The air went still in the small hotel lobby while Rachel listened to Melinda tell this part of her past life.

"So, I quit the day after the grand jury cleared me and started in social work, trying to keep kids like my sister off drugs. But you know from being at DCF that it's an uphill battle. I knew we were constantly losing, so one day I ran into this rich white lady who offered me a job. She told me that I could make a real difference. I looked into her, thinking she's either a con-artist or a crazy person and find out she's legit. So, I struck a deal with her. I work for her, and she donates money into the drug rehab place I worked at for better funding, better equipment, and better accommodations for the patients."

"Wow, okay. So the acting? Where does that come from?"

"Five years of working narcotics undercover. I worked one long term case for three years and was someone similar to Ms. Brenda Martin. It was a good cover, so I kept it."

"That makes sense." She took a sip of her club soda and looked at the much younger and less life-experienced Beth Young. "What's your story?"

Beth pulled the rest of the fruity drink through the straw as she poked the alcohol saturated fruit with a tiny yellow parasol. She gulped the last bit and looked at Rachel, starting to feel the buzz.

"Not much to tell. I ran away from my parents' house when I was fourteen...abusive father, alcoholic mother. I ran the streets, stealing anything I could to survive until I tried to steal from some rich white lady...." She mocked Melinda who returned a smile. "And instead of turning me in to the cops, she took me home and treated me like family. She put me through college, so I'm here not out of obligation *per se* but more of a sense of repaying her generosity to those in need. Paying it forward? Kind of."

Rachel nodded seeing her point.

"There are so many kids who leave bad homes like I did. I just want to help those kids who are taken from the good ones."

"So what's up with the computer whiz?" Rachel asked.

"Louis? Ha! That boy ain't right. But he's good. And he ain't shy about his dirt, so just ask him yourself."

Rachel let the backgrounds of the two women sink in and finished up her club soda. She compared their backgrounds to that of her own. She wondered if they knew her story already but was positive they didn't know everything. No one knew, except her. She looked back at the bar and saw Curt was getting up and leaving a tip for the bartender.

"What's his story?" she asked.

Both women looked at Curt with his back turned to them and avoided answering, especially while he was still at the bar. Curt walked past the table of women without saying goodbye and got on the elevator across the marble floor of the hotel lobby.

Beth looked at Melinda expectedly, like she would have to be the one to tell the story.

"I don't want to tell his business, but like us, he's got a rough story too. The difference is he is still dealing with his, whereas we've been able to move on."

Rachel looked over at Beth needing more of an explanation.

"Ehh...I've only been on the team for a year now, so Melinda knows him better than I do. I've had like four or five actual conversations with the man, nothing revealing to say the least."

Melinda finished her drink and offered a tidbit to the curious newcomer. "He was a cop in Tallahassee for like twelve or thirteen years. He was a detective when his son went missing. He's been looking for him ever since."

"How long has he been missing?"

"About three years."

Rachel sat back in her seat wondering about the details of Curt's story and how devastating it must be to live with the pain of having a child missing. She replayed the stories of the two women at the table and figured her own tragedy was what caused Alexis Vanderhill to seek her out. A sense of belonging came over her, which was something she hadn't anticipated.

Chapter 6

A hint of optimism met Rachel Goodwin as she woke up in the extremely comfortable queen-sized bed of the Grand Hyatt hotel. She rolled over and saw the sunlight piercing through the tiny slat in the curtains. She lay on the bed hoping this new chapter in her life would lead to something truly fulfilling. She was losing faith from all the dead ends she managed to find.

She quickly showered, dressed, and packed her belongings. The team was moving on right after breakfast. She took the elevator down to the lobby and found a place to sit in the hotel's restaurant that over looked the atrium. She glanced over the menu and settled for eggs, sausage, and toast with coffee. She unfolded the *Chronicle* and curiously scanned the crime beat for any stories of what happened last night. Her heart skipped a beat as she saw the booking photo of Francine Bennett on the front page of the local crime section. The headline read: "Hit & Run Solved off Tip Seven Years Later." Rachel anxiously scanned the article looking for any hint or mention of the team being involved, but after looking it over carefully, she didn't see anything and relaxed.

"She kept her word...huh!" she said out loud, surprised.

A loud commotion pulled her attention away from the newspaper. It was coming from the front desk area. Curious, she glanced over her shoulder and saw Curt Walker being berated by someone whom Rachel assumed to be the hotel manager, with some kind of security officer. Curt appeared worn down and was taking the verbal assault by the two men. A streak of dried blood from a deep cut had run down his left eye, and his clothes were crinkled and disheveled. She looked around for help, unsure if it was her place to intervene. She stood up from the table looking farther down the hallway for Melinda or Beth, but she figured she may have to step in. She watched Curt try to hold himself up. She noticed his knuckles were also bloody, and his face was ghostly pale and hollow, like he'd been up on an all-night drinking binge. She was embarrassed for him.

Above the protests of the manager and security guard, she heard him calling out, "Mel? Mel?"

As the manager and security officers threatened to call the police, Rachel got up to leave the restaurant when she saw Melinda run over from the elevator and intervene. She took Curt under his arm, held him up straight and addressed the manager. Rachel went back to her seat, unable to look away. Most of the other restaurant goers went back to their breakfasts, but Rachel felt invested in what was going to happen.

The image of that heroic, yet complicated man in the trench coat from the night before was a direct contradiction of what she saw the morning after. She didn't understand what had happened. Rachel remembered hearing that all members of the team had a story...hell her baggage was quite heavy, but how deep was the abyss that Curt was trying to crawl out of, she wondered. Before her was a complete mess of a human being, incapable of even taking care of himself, let alone leading a team of clandestine child rescuers on dangerous missions. She had been content with her decision to join the team; however, seeing this side of Curt gave her second thoughts.

Rachel watched Melinda smooth things over with the manager and the security guard. She figured the envelope that was handed to the man was a bundle of cash to make something go away. Once settled, Melinda walked Curt outside into the bright morning sun and out of Rachel's sight.

Fixated by the dramatic scene at the lobby desk, she failed to notice Alexis Vanderhill approach from behind.

"May I join you?" she asked, startling Rachel.

"Oh my, yes. Please."

"He's flawed, as we all are, but he is necessary to the success of this mission. I hate to see him like that. With all the pain he bears, he uses it to see things no one else sees and gets the results that no one else can...and for that, he is invaluable."

Rachel listened in acceptance. She was learning everything about the team all at once, and with her own background, she didn't feel it necessary to judge anyone. It was just a lot to take in so quickly.

"What happened?"

Alexis thought about the question but answered, "Nothing important to the mission." She bent over and pulled out a letter-sized envelope and slid it across the table to Rachel. "I want you guys to head east and work your way towards Chicago."

"You're not coming?"

"Oh no. I don't work on the team per se. I support the team and work behind the scenes making sure that the mission moves forward, therefore giving you the backing you need to be successful."

"Oh, I thought...." Rachel stopped. She had assumed they all worked together.

"No, this is where we part ways, for now."

Alexis motioned for a waiter who came and took her order for a coffee to go.

"Rachel, do you know why I brought you on to this team?"

"To help..." she looked around for prying ears, "...find missing kids, right? Make a difference by any means?"

"Yes, that's the overview...but the main reason?"

"No, not really."

"Well, Curt is a leader, but he gets in his own way sometimes. He is his own worst enemy. I brought you on because I want you to be the leader that this team needs. I've been looking for someone of your talents to take over and make this good team, great."

Rachel didn't know how to accept the compliment and the responsibility Alexis was giving her.

"It's something I hope to see you grow into. I know jumping in with all of this at one time is asking too much, so let's just ease in to it, okay?"

"Okay, that's sounds doable. Does the rest of the team know about this?"

"No."

Rachel looked dejected. She'd been the new girl a few times with different DCF offices and knew the difficulties some people had with change. She hoped she wasn't going to step on anyone's toes, especially not knowing the pre-existing dynamics of the team, but she trusted Alexis Vanderhill to know what she was doing.

46

"Okay. I guess we'll see what happens on the way to Chicago. Is there anything I need to know about Curt?" She nodded over to where the earlier scene had gone down.

"Not immediately. But in due time, you will. When he's ready."

The waiter came with her coffee and set it down on the table. Alexis pulled out a fifty dollar bill and left it on the table to cover Rachel's and her order, with a considerable tip. Rachel protested, but Alexis smiled as she walked away.

Chapter 7

It was one of his favorite memories of his son.

Josh had just finished his first week in second grade, and as in the two previous years, he got to choose the restaurant for a celebration dinner. He chose his favorite restaurant, a Tallahassee staple on the east side of town off Apalachee Parkway. Barnaby's was labeled as a family tavern with fried chicken, burgers, and their signature pizza on the menu. The dining area remained dimly lit from the stained glass windows, reminiscent of an old English tavern. There were no servers, just a walk up counter that sat in front of three huge brick ovens used for baking the pizzas. A glass partition allowed the patrons to watch the pizza baking process.

But Josh, being the ripe age of seven, wasn't a food connoisseur. Although it was a given, he wanted their signature pizza for dinner. He chose this venue for the small room in the center of the restaurant that housed eight video arcade games, some modern, some retro. While Curt and his wife, Tracy, sat at the table, waiting for their table number to be called, Josh had set his order and bee-lined it to the game room.

"Quarters mom?" Josh begged with his hand held out.

Curt smiled and fished out some change from his pocket before Tracy could. Josh sifted through the pile for the coveted quarters and picked them out with his tiny hands. He watched as Josh concentrated as if the world's fate were in the balance. He gazed at the boy in amazement and felt the warmth within radiate through his body. It was the warmth of pride…the warmth of fatherly love.

"Thanks, Daddy!"

"No problem, buddy!"

Curt smiled as he watched the boy run with complete abandon toward the game room, rip the door open, and disappear inside.

"He's getting so big, isn't he?" Tracy asked rhetorically.

"Yes. Yes, he is."

It was a celebration for the boy, but Curt needed a break from the harsh reality of being a cop. The first week of second grade for Josh coincided with a tough week at work. Curt had just been moved up to the Special Victim's Unit within the Criminal Investigations Division at the Tallahassee Police Department. He transferred from the less glorified unit that investigated property crimes like thefts and burglaries. As a member of the Special Victim's Unit, he worked cases involving crimes that were sexual in nature as well as crimes against children. It took a special kind of person to stomach these investigations; it took an even more extraordinary person to work them.

The first case that dropped onto Curt's desk was a child abuse case. A working mother, careless with whom she left her two kids, was working the night shift at a grocery store and left her loser and aimless boyfriend in charge. Bath time apparently interfered with an important football game he had put money on, and he left the youngest child, not quite two years old, alone in the bathtub. The water that pumped in was straight from the water heater and scalding hot. After the boyfriend set the naked child in the water, he tuned to the more important football game, failing to realize the water was too hot. He ignored the child's screams, for he was too busy screaming at the television, directing his team's quarterback to act accordingly. When the mother returned home, the child still sat helpless in the tub and had sustained second degree burns from the chin down from the blistering hot water. By this time, the skin on the child's legs had blistered up and had begun to slip off. It looked as if the child was wearing loose fitting opaque colored socks. The images seared into Curt's mind as he worked the case.

The child was rushed off to the hospital for treatment, and the boyfriend fled before the patrol officers arrived on scene. Incredulously, the mother attempted to defend the boyfriend's actions and failed to cooperate with the officers, saying the child must have turned the hot water on herself.

Curt did his job and tracked down the boyfriend and appropriately charged him with neglect of the child. During the interview, Curt fought every urge to climb across the table and beat him senseless. His selfish act had left the poor child with blisters and an unhealthy fear of water. The doctors had explained, based on the injuries, the child had stood in the burning hot water for at least twenty five minutes. The vision of the helpless child crying out for her mother while in extreme pain no child should know, fell to the depths of Curt's core and angered him to the point of lashing out at the so-called "man."

As he sat in the interview room, he remembered the video system over his shoulder was aimed at the suspect and figured the beating he deserved would not look good replayed on the evening news. Curt fought the desire to strap the man down to his chair and pour boiling hot water on his scrotum in a sterilization effort, for he did not truly deserve God's gift of a child in his life. But he managed to swallow the anger and play the sympathetic man to the self-centered suspect who tried to excuse his behavior on the over-importance of a football game—a game that was being played hundreds of miles away by men who could care less about his loyalty.

Curt obtained the confession and sent the man off to jail with no fanfare. He felt sorrow for the scarred child left in the wake of his selfishness and noticed a stain was left on his soul from playing into the man's ego instead of the vengeful law man. He went back to work but couldn't shake the feeling of shame and guilt. He left as soon as the paperwork was done and headed straight home.

Upon walking in the door, Josh ran up to him with excitement and gave his father a hug. It was a daily ritual since Josh had learned to walk. Curt knelt down and squeezed him tight vowing he would always love him and protect him and not let some asshole leave him in a tub of scalding, hot water. At that moment, during the embrace of his young son, the stain from earlier was washed away in a tidal wave of love. He instantly felt better and was reminded that the world was not as ugly and that innocence still existed. He was also quickly reminded by his son that it was his choice of restaurant that night for dinner.

"Hey Daddy, they have a new zombie shooting game. Wanna play with me?" Josh had poked his head out of the game room and yelled down the several tables to where his parents sat.

"Sure, buddy." Curt looked at Tracy with a the-boy-needs-his-father look. He explained that he would obviously find no pleasure in a game that required the necessary killing of zombie hoards, for playing the game with him would be more of a duty than anything. She smiled back with a knowing look that her husband would enjoy the arcade game just as much as her son.

"Go!"

"I'll be right back." He kissed his wife on the lips and darted off to the game room.

"Have fun honey!"

The video graphics of the zombie mansion the pair of heroes assaulted was dark and gloomy with enemy zombies and evil monsters popping out at every corner. Curt fought valiantly next to his trusted sidekick with their weapons drawn, a red and blue plastic handgun tethered to the console, and kept firing steadily at the onslaught of the undead. Together, they conquered the first levels of the game until their table number was called over the loud speaker. With the same enthusiasm exhibited when he ran to the game room, Josh dashed out of the small room for the dinner table where a piping-hot pepperoni pizza waited just for him.

That night of celebration, Curt found himself watching his beautiful son in awe. He was a spitting image of himself—dark hair, big brown eyes, and a broad, toothy smile with the cutest dimple in the crease of his left cheek. He wasn't doing anything extraordinary, just being a normal kid that was born out of love, going through life as he knew it. He was unaware of the dark side of reality and the bitter harshness of life. He was still hopeful and constantly optimistic. Curt felt contentment at that moment, despite the ugliness his job brought into his life. He knew he had something truly special and worth fighting for.

As his son picked up his third piece of pepperoni pizza and took another bite, he chewed intently and noticed his father watching him. He swallowed his bite and smiled back at his father, halfway embarrassed at the attention.

"What?" He asked shyly.

"Nothing, buddy. I love you; that's all."

"Daaad!"

Curt smiled at the boy's embarrassment and waved it off as a necessity of fatherhood. He picked up another piece of the pizza and took an over-emphasized bite to make a joke, followed by a comical chomping sound that registered a cute giggle from Josh.

"Nom, nom, nom…." He laughed at his own silliness.

"Curt!" Tracy said, embarrassed herself but overshadowed by the loud giggling of the boy across the booth from Curt.

***

The memories that reminded him of a joyful past had become more and more blurred over the past three years. Pain and helplessness replaced the hope of his past. He forced himself to remember what life felt like then as opposed to the hell it had become. Forcing himself to remember the happiness and purpose his life once held, as opposed to the tragic reality, helped him have a better hold on the hope that one day life would return to normal.

The soothing hum of the Mercedes Sprinter moving at close to 75 mph down the interstate towards Chicago kept Curt in a comatose state as the battle of good memories versus bad waged on in his mind. He slipped in and out of consciousness. He realized he was lying on the floor of the van, tucked away in the back, as the rest of the team ignored him. His pounding headache and throbbing knuckles were obvious signs that it had happened again. A wave of embarrassment washed over him as he fought back the nausea along with the physical pain.

The anguished memories came rushing back, and tears formed in his eyes. He was exhausted. His body was on the brink of shutting down, but he forced himself to continue. He had to keep looking for Josh. He justified the feeling of selfishness in needing time to recuperate by knowing it would be several hours until the team stopped. After fighting away the crushing blow of reality, Curt finally fell back asleep, his eyes filled with tears.

The front passenger seat of the Mercedes Sprinter was very comfortable for Rachel Goodwin. The buttery soft leather seat and armrests held her up, so she could watch the world go by through the large windshield of the van. About an hour outside of San Francisco, she copied Beth's signature position and propped her feet up on the dashboard. She passed the time by reading the full report and background information the team had gathered for the recovery of Charlotte Morgan. The amount of useful information obtained in such a short amount of time was astounding to Rachel. As a DCF case worker and child advocate, it took her years to gather this level of information that the team somehow located in less than a day's time. She wanted to learn more about the people she was teaming up with—trust never coming easy with her—but she stayed silent assuming this was how the group traveled. Especially with one of them passed out drunk in the back.

With the early morning start after the debacle at the hotel, Beth elected to follow the Sprinter in Curt's Crown Victoria as the team made its way toward Chicago. Melinda remained in the back with Curt while Louis drove. Rachel kept tabs on the two in the back and noticed Melinda had dozed off too, leaving her alone with Louis at the helm. However, the normally chatty computer genius remained focused on his driving efforts with little white ear buds playing his music of choice. Rachel ignored the feeling of being out of place and trusted the words of Alexis Vanderhill that this was truly a mission and not a job.

The team stopped at a secluded rest area somewhere in the foothills of the Rocky Mountains to stretch, get some gas, and make a plan for the night. Curt stumbled out of the van, somewhat clear headed, but kept the oversized trench coat on even in the dry heat of the mid-west. He took the keys of the Crown Vic from Beth and agreed to follow the rest of the team towards their destination of the night, somewhere west of Denver, if they couldn't reach Denver by nightfall. Curt didn't bother saying anything about the night before, but Rachel read the embarrassment on his face.

Rachel stood back, letting the team make the decisions as they normally did, getting a feel for the dynamics outside of a dangerous operation like the previous night's. They seemed near flawless during the operation, but she questioned their cohesiveness otherwise.

She found herself watching Curt, during the brief stop. She clearly saw his pain, as he wore it on his sleeve, although he clearly didn't want to talk about it. The rest of the team avoided confronting him and let him deal with his demons in his own way. Curt noticed the attention from the new girl. Before the team filed back into the van, Curt locked eyes with Rachel with an uncertain meaning. As she held his stare, she felt something twinge inside of her heart. Curt broke the connection as he climbed in the Crown Vic ready to follow the Sprinter.

As twilight was upon the team, they were most of the way through the picturesque mountain range that bisected the country. It was getting late and the team was tired of being on the road. They didn't make their planned destination in Denver. They pulled over in the winter haven of Vail, a popular skiing destination during the winter months. In mid-August, the obvious off season of the region, the hotel rates were low, and the population was thin. It was as good as any place to stop for the night.

Melinda took over the driving duties while Rachel moved back to the captain's seat. Beth pulled rank and took back the passenger seat, so she could prop her feet up. Louis was back at his computer station running diagnostics on his machines in the back...or so he said, for Rachel recognized World of Warcraft when she saw it.

Curious, Rachel asked Beth, "I read that whole police report and all the background for the rescue of Charlotte. I didn't see anything about the parents calling her 'honey bear.' That was important; I mean it's what convinced the girl. Where did you come up with that?"

Beth turned around in her seat with mild annoyance at having to explain herself to the new girl.

"It's all in the details. Before Alexis and I picked you up from the airport, we had just met with the Morgan's at the hotel to get them settled in for the fake conference thing. She was holding a picture of Charlotte. It was worn, not like it had been kept in a frame or anything, so it was clearly an important picture to her, something she obviously carried around with her."

Rachel was following, "Okay."

"So, as Alexis talked to them, the mom had the picture out, as a matter of habit I guess, and I saw the back side of it. It had the words 'honey bear' with the year written on it in what I can assume was mom's handwriting. It was the year before she went missing. I made a note of it in case it was helpful, and I was right. That's it."

Beth turned back around in the seat and propped her feet back up on the dash not wanting any kind of attribution or recognition for the work. It was who she was, take it or leave it. Rachel picked up on the hint and let the answer settle. She remained impressed. That was a helluva catch.

The team found a nice Marriott resort in the middle of Vail that sat in the shadow of the mountains. The bare mountain sides were adorned with ski-lifts and were solely operated as people movers for sight-seers this time of year. The mountains looked strangely naked without the customary blanket of snow draped from the top. Instead, the team was greeted with a dismal brown and green grass look which offered a completely different feel to the area.

Melinda parked the Mercedes Sprinter off to the side of the hotel and made all the arrangements inside. Upon her return, she issued out key cards to the team. Curt took his card without saying anything and walked through the front door ahead of everyone. He slung a large duffle bag over his shoulder and walked over to the elevator. Rachel noticed that his knuckles were bandaged up.

"All right, I guess we get another early morning start, and that should put us in Chicago a little after lunchtime tomorrow," Rachel offered to the team.

"Yeah, sounds good," Beth replied dryly.

Rachel wondered if she had already stepped out of bounds but ignored the thought as everyone grabbed their overnight bags and headed inside.

Rachel caught up with Melinda as they walked to their rooms.

"So, does he ever open up at all?" She explained to Melinda that she had witnessed what happened that morning in San Francisco.

"Oh!" She searched for a good answer to the question. "Not really. He's a good man though, just in a lot of pain. I've found it's just best to be there for him when he needs it and not to push."

Rachel listened to the advice and took note. Melinda said good night and disappeared into her hotel room. Rachel found herself worrying about the man she barely knew but felt drawn to, as if she could help in some way. She felt compelled to ease his pain but couldn't explain why.

As Rachel stood at her hotel room door, movement caught her eye to the left. It was Curt, with an empty bucket, in search of ice, still sporting the tan trench coat. He had walked out of the room next to hers. Curt paused noticing Rachel was looking at him and held her stare, again. Unsure how to proceed, he just bowed his head and moved past her in the hallway. Rachel felt stupid for staring at him again, so as he walked past she offered a sincere, "Good night!"

Out of instinct, Curt replied back over his shoulder, "G'night." Rachel smiled, but for what reason she did not know. She slid the card into the door lock, and after hearing the click, she pushed it open and entered the room.

She looked around the hotel room, figuring life on this team and doing this kind of work, she would have to become accustomed to living in and out of hotels. It reminded her about her own dark side. She set her bag down on the bed and kicked off her shoes, trying to get that "at home" feeling. The minibar beckoned from under the television stand/dresser, and she felt the urge to open a bottle of liquor but instead sat down at the edge of the bed and meditated away the urge, repeating her mantra.

She knew the new surroundings would cause her anxiety, but she dealt with the fact she would constantly be on the move as a part of this team. It was a chance to be a part of something special and make a real difference. The mantra calmed her down, but as a matter of habit, she immediately thought of her. She desperately missed her sister, and although it was years ago, it left a scar that would never heal.

Outside of the fourth-story hotel window was the view of a brown and green façade of a beautiful wintery mountain waiting for the winter to bring snow. She figured this room and its view was coveted during the winter season but was nothing special during the summer. Below, she noticed a group of workers knocking off from work and heading out for the night. She moved to the edge of the bed, just an arm's length from the minibar. She opened her luggage and pulled out the framed picture of her sister and herself, a half-posed, half-candid shot of them together at a beach house. She set it up next to the minibar as a reminder. She decided the picture would travel with her everywhere. She remembered the day the picture was taken. It was a day of joy all around, and she prayed that she would know happiness like that again. She felt the emotions welling up inside once more. She wiped a tear away and forced herself to look away from the picture before she was overcome with that emotion. She got up and looked out the window one more time.

Chapter 8

It must have been somewhere in the neighborhood of three in the morning. Rachel had finally managed to doze off, but a distinctive thump brought her back to the conscious world. She tilted her head up to listen for any follow-up noise, but when none came, she nestled back down on the soft hotel pillow.

Thump.

"What the hell?" Rachel asked the empty room.

She sat up in bed, wondering what was making that noise, whether it was some type of disturbance down the hall, a more physical round between two enthusiastic lovebirds, or someone trying to break into a room. She didn't hear any other associated noises but instantly grew frustrated because now she was awake.

She fell back down on the bed and closed her eyes to judge exactly how hard it would be to get back to sleep.

Thump. Thump. Crash!

The sound was more distinctive now. It was coming from the room next to hers...Curt's room, she quickly realized. Rachel jumped out of bed and used the hotel phone to call over to his room. No answer.

"Fine. This is ridiculous."

Rachel opened her door and saw two security officers from the hotel standing outside of Curt's door, waiting for a response from a knock.

One turned to her, "It's okay, ma'am. You can go back to sleep. We'll take care of it."

At that moment, Rachel wasn't as concerned with sleep as much as she was with Curt or what might occur between him and the security officers. A door clicked open from across the hall and Melinda emerged from inside. She shot Rachel a here-we-go-again look and started to address the security officers and smooth things over before it got out of hand.

"Let us handle this please, ma'am," one of them answered.

A moment later, the door to Curt's room broke open, and his face, flushed red and sweaty from some sort of drunken exertion, appeared and answered.

"What?"

"We received several complaints about you disturbing our other guests, sir. Please, we need you to stop or we'll have to ask you to leave the premises."

"Huh?" He answered, half confused, half with contempt.

"Don't huh, me. You are making too much noise, and if you want to play games buddy, I'll kick your ass right out of here!"

The drop in the professional manner by the security officer sent off alarms in Rachel as well as Melinda. They could see Curt beginning to allow anger to break through his drunken state.

Curt's door flung open in a move to clear the area for the impending fight. The security officers braced themselves as one tightened the grip on his Maglight.

"I got this officers; it won't be a problem. He is with me," Melinda said making her way in between the officers and Curt to prevent any type of physical altercation.

"Excuse me ma'am; is he with you?"

"Yes, he's with us, and we'll take responsibility for him. Please, he's just upset and had a few too many. He got passed up on a promotion at work, and they told him while we're out here for some training. Kind of a dick move, right?" Melinda grabbed Curt around the waist; his arm instinctively went around her shoulder, like a crutch.

The officers could see her point and eased in their stance. However, the noise would have to stop, as they explained, or he would have to leave.

Curt looked down at Melinda in bewilderment and at the use of the word "us." He studied her face and looked over at Rachel, standing in her doorway, arms crossed with a worried look on her face. She was wearing a revealing tank top that hugged her curvy body and men's boxers as shorts with the waist line folded over and hugging her hips just below her waistline. He looked her over lustfully with drunken eyes but stopped when a wave of embarrassment came crashing over, and he looked away.

"Poor thing had a lot riding on that promotion, but it won't be a problem anymore sir; I promise, or we'll all check out and forfeit our money…no questions asked."

The security officers agreed and took the deal, knowing management would rather keep the customers happy than unnecessarily involve law enforcement. They left the trouble maker with a stern warning that seemed to be lost on Curt.

Melinda escorted Curt inside of his room, giving Rachel a nod indicating that she could handle the situation from this point, and shut the door behind her. Rachel stood in the hallway with her arms crossed wondering about the true extent of the battle Curt was fighting against his pain—a battle he was clearly losing.

Chapter 9

Morning came like clockwork in the small mountain resort town. Rachel managed a few more hours of sleep, following the episode that ripped her awake in the middle of the night. She thought about Curt and his reckless behavior and wondered if that would cost him in the end. It was clear he was angry and full of rage over his missing son, but there must be a better way to deal with his emotions. She knew first-hand how easy it was to spiral out of control. It was a walk across a tightrope with no net, and losing control could be too costly. She figured if Curt's behavior wasn't kept in check, it would wind up getting someone hurt or worse.

Rachel showered, dressed, and packed her luggage, ready to head on to Chicago. She took the elevator down to the lobby to grab breakfast before the team gathered together to leave. She figured that she would have a little time to herself while Curt recovered from the night before.

As the elevator door opened, she made her way through the lobby to the hotel restaurant. Across the lobby and by the front door, a tall man wearing a tight-fitting white t-shirt, jogging shorts, and running shoes caught her attention. He was panting from a long run, his face beaded with sweat, and his clothes were equally drenched. Rachel noticed the man was athletically fit and had an attractive body, but as she looked closer, she was taken aback. It was Curt.

Rachel didn't notice she had literally stopped mid-stride in the lobby to watch Curt come in the door, cooling down from his run. He pulled the ear buds from his ears and headed to the elevator. He glanced over his shoulder feeling the attention from someone to his right. He locked eyes, again, with Rachel as he passed her.

"Hey!" He said without stopping. He could see the obvious confusion on her face but didn't stop to explain. He was still embarrassed from the night before.

"Hey," she said, almost dumbfounded as she snapped out of her confusion at the sight.

She came to as the elevator doors closed behind Curt. She remembered her original destination and continued to the restaurant, shaking off the confusion of seeing Curt in such an unexpected state. She sat and ordered a coffee while she looked over the menu. She replayed the awkward confrontation in her mind and couldn't stop the smile from appearing on her face. She felt embarrassed by her response to seeing Curt walk through the front door. It was like she had never seen an attractive man before, and she was some awkward teenager. She remembered the inebriated mess he had been only a few hours before, but now he was running like he was training for a marathon. He is a very complex person she figured, and that made her even more curious.

After breakfast, Rachel grabbed a local newspaper and waited in the lobby for everyone to come down and join her so they could leave for Chicago. Beth joined her soon after, and Louis walked in from the parking lot. She finished an article on an upcoming local election where the candidates were debating environmental issues and the legalization of marijuana.

"Hey Curtis. Get a good run in this morning?"

Rachel folded her newspaper down to see a freshly showered and shaved Curt Walker walking toward them at the restaurant. He made coffee in his room and brought it down with him. He was dressed in a white button-up shirt, no tie, dark slacks, and his tan trench coat. He answered Louis and looked over at Rachel.

"Hey?" He said to Rachel as he bent over and searched through her discarded sections of the newspaper.

"Hey."

"I didn't mean to be rude this morning. I had just finished a run and wanted to get showered up so we could all leave on time."

"Oh, that's okay. I was a little shocked, I guess. I mean, I didn't quite recognize you without your trench coat."

Curt stood up straight, looked down at his overcoat, and dropped the newspaper back down without reading it. He threw a quick smile back at her and looked over at Beth and Louis who were watching, interested.

Curt gave a questioning look, and Louis quickly realized what he was waiting for. He had forgotten.

"Sorry…they came in early this morning." He removed a folded piece of paper, what looked like printer paper to Rachel, and handed it to Curt. He unfolded it, eager to read its contents.

"It doesn't look like it's him. One's Hispanic and the other was identified by dental records, obviously not him," Louis added with a sympathetic tone.

Curt read the paper and let out a long breath, like the paper gave him permission to breathe. He was relieved at the information or lack thereof.

Rachel looked puzzled and figured she would be allowed "in" when the time came and thought better of asking about the piece of paper.

"So? We're off to Chicago this morning, right?" Rachel asked, excited to get started in her new job.

"Oh, well…" Louis chimed in, "…we may not be leaving so soon."

"Why not?" Rachel asked.

"Well, I checked on the van this morning, and it didn't want to start, so I disconnected all my equipment, and it started, but barely. I think there is a short somewhere, and it's drawing on the battery. I took it over to a mechanic's shop to have it checked out. I should hear something soon, but we may be grounded for a bit."

"We're not leaving?" Melinda asked, as she walked up and stood next to Curt.

"No, sounds like some electrical issues in the van, so we may need to hang out for a day," answered Curt.

"So, how does that work? I mean, Alexis is expecting us in Chicago; should we call her?"

"No, she doesn't care. It's really a suggestion by her, especially if we find something worthwhile to stay for, but I'll call her and let her know we'll be staying a little longer," Beth answered.

"Oh, well okay. So, what do we do now?"

"I have my laptop, and as long as we don't need any in depth searches into particular databases, I can just hang out here and use the hotel's public Wi-Fi."

Curt looked around. He liked the idea of going out and "fishing" instead of wasting the day waiting around for the van to get fixed.

"We'll need another car," Melinda added. "I don't think the four of us in one car would look that inconspicuous."

Rachel perked up, ready to be part of the team. "I'll go up to the concierge desk and get a rental for the day."

"Alright, you three in the rental, and I'll troll around in the Crown Vic. You can pretend to be on a shopping trip or something."

Beth rolled her eyes and said under her breath, "'Cause that's what we girls live for, shopping," but deep down she was excited for a deserved break.

The group agreed to the plan while they waited on word of the van. Louis got out his laptop and fired it up. Curt studied the hotel lobby and found a secluded spot that was just out of the security camera angles. He didn't want any government agency coming back and finding Louis on his laptop in case he had to hack into some database while using the hotel's Wi-Fi. Louis agreed and moved seats.

The team spent the day looking around the town's malls, libraries, public parks, and other hotspots for child hangouts. School was still in session, and this limited the opportunity to observe kids out in public. The town was pretty quiet in that its off season didn't attract but a quarter of the tourists it would during the winter months.

After finding nothing of interest, the group of three women found themselves in a town center set at the base of a majestic mountain still capped with snow even in the summer months. The center offered specialty clothing stores, restaurants, bars, a few upscale hotels for the more jet-setting snow bunnies, and an open plaza for outdoor concerts and other entertainment. The clothing shops, outside of the tourist trap t-shirts, were showcasing designer, western wear for the ranchers and cowgirls at heart, available with turquoise jewelry and beads to accent the southwestern look fully.

Twisting down the middle of the entertainment center was a rapidly moving river that stretched about twenty feet across through the area. The water was quick this time of year as the snow was melting high on the mountains. The dull roar of the rapids gave the plaza a pleasant background noise which the group was unaccustomed to hearing.

As the three women searched the area for any potential missing kids, they saw advertisements for some type of expo and outdoor sports event coming to the center in the next few days. They discussed possibly staying around the area for the influx of people to come into town, but they passed on the idea when they realized it wasn't necessarily a family type atmosphere for those events.

A pretty, green dress displayed in the window of a clothing boutique caught Beth's eye. The tea length A-line dress was a sexy little number, and she couldn't wait to see how it looked on her. She talked the other two women into joining her for a minute of shopping delight. Her argument was that they all needed a deserved break from the long and arduous time spent on the road and out in the field.

After walking into the boutique and setting off a loud distinguishable ding above the door, Beth went straight for the green dress she saw in the window. Melinda and Rachel perused around the women's sections, looking through the clothing, a more formal and dressier line of clothes neither woman was used to, but they liked what they saw...until they found the price tag.

"Wow...this blouse costs what I made in a week at DCF," Rachel exclaimed.

Melinda smiled at the comment and continued looking through the clothes. She moved on to the designer purses hanging from the wall. Rachel set the expensive shirt down and looked around the boutique to find Beth. She could only imagine how expensive a gorgeous dress like that costs.

From across the store, in the men's section, stood two attractive men looking at dress shirts and jackets from the display table. One glanced up, and Rachel noticed he was fixated on Melinda to her left. She smiled for Melinda's sake but wondered how anyone on this team would have time for a romantic relationship. Clearly, there was no time for dating, as they were on the west coast a day earlier and now smack dab in the middle of the Rocky Mountains. As Rachel thought about it, she preferred it that way.

"Hey, I think he's checking you out!" Rachel warned in a mocked juvenile manner.

"Huh?" Melinda answered.

"That guy over there...blue shirt, dark skin, great smile."

Melinda looked up and returned the gentlemen's look, but indifferent to the attention, she went back to sifting through another rack of clothes.

"Not your type?" Rachel asked.

"Ha! You're more her type than he is," Beth blurted out. She had walked up behind the two women, wearing the glamorous, green dress with her feet bare. She spun around revealing her exposed back, needing the dress to be zipped up in the back.

Rachel looked confused for a second and then realized what Beth meant by her insensitive statement. She looked over at Melinda who kept looking through another rack as she knew Rachel was figuring it out.

Melinda stepped over to Beth and grabbed the zipper, "Yes, I am gay. Is that okay with you?"

"Of course it is. That doesn't bother me at all. I just thought, well…never mind. No, your sexual orientation doesn't bother me at all."

Melinda smiled in acceptance. She turned back to Beth, "You look beautiful dear!"

"Thanks. And no Rachel; we're not a couple. I like boys," Beth said with the same bluntness. Melinda chuckled.

Beth twirled, spinning the silky, knee-length dress around. She stopped in front of a mirror and smoothed it down her stomach and waist. She checked herself out, front and back.

"How much is it?" Rachel asked.

"Oh, four hundred dollars. I may get it; I haven't decided."

"Four hundred!"

"Yeah, sure. Why not?"

"Uh, it's four hundred dollars for starters!"

"Okay, but I have no hobbies. I don't do shoes, and you never know when a dress like this will come in handy. Plus, it makes me feel grown up."

"Okay. It's your money, I guess."

As the three ladies walked outside of the boutique into the cobblestoned walkway of the town center, Curt was posted up against a light pole and a decorative concrete planter. He still sported his tan trench coat. He met their stares with a furrowed brow, questioning with his eyes what they were doing. Rachel felt a slight tinge of guilt as they were caught goofing off and not following the mission. She walked towards him ready to explain, but he lifted a fountain drink and took an exaggerated sip through the straw.

"Find anything good?" He asked.

Beth stepped forward and pulled out the four hundred dollar dress from her bag, proud to show Curt her luxurious find. He liked the dress and explained that he had no luck finding anything around town either. He told the women that he'd found a nice spot in the center for lunch and said he was bringing lunch back to the hotel for Louis. They agreed to continue looking after the local schools let out. If nothing appeared promising, they would call it a day and head out to Chicago later that evening.

Chapter 10

The winding highway that led back to the hotel cut through the valley of the Rocky Mountains. Curt had never been in this part of the country before, and he took in the sights. He liked the picturesque mountains, the small granite, rock-lined streams that ran parallel to the roads, old mining and excavating equipment, and the constant advertisements for ski rentals, mountain gear, and Coors beer.

As Curt neared the service road for the hotel, a radio commercial for an upcoming baseball game between the San Francisco Giants and the nearby Colorado Rockies came over the radio. They were playing an upcoming three game series at Coors Field in Denver. The Giants had been on the east coast and were making the stop in Colorado before returning home. At the mention of the Giants baseball team, Curt's thoughts instantly went to Josh. It was a direct reaction, because of the Giant's all-star catcher, Buster Posey.

Curt remembered the day Posey had played all nine positions in one game while playing for Florida State University. He was there with Josh, watching from the grandstand, as the star catcher completed an interesting, novelty accomplishment in college baseball. It was a warm afternoon in late April in Tallahassee, complete with sunshine, humidity, and solid baseball.

"Daddy, do you think he'll play in the major leagues?" Josh asked of his favorite player, Posey.

"Yeah, buddy. I think he'll be one of the first guys picked in the draft."

"Okay, cool."

Curt sat next to his son in the garnet, plastic grandstand seats in section five. His heavy frame filled out the seat and didn't leave any wiggle room in the average-sized chairs, so he leaned over with an arm around his son so as not to crowd the person to his left. Overhead was a giant propeller fan for cooling spectators in the late spring and early summer heat. Their view was from the first base side and into the visitors' dugout; the Seminoles at home were in the dugout below them. The ever present "green monster" of Dick Howser Stadium, a green colored chain link fence that stretched from the right field foul pole to the alley in right center, loomed over the opposing team's outfielder.

Josh was hugging his customary bucket of popcorn as he and his dad picked away at the snack while watching their favorite team take infield before the start of the game.

"He's going to play at each position during the game, buddy. Isn't that pretty cool?"

"Yeah, wow!" His eight-year-old mind was amazed.

"It takes a special player to do that."

"Well, he's awesome, and he's my favorite player, so he'll be able to do it."

"I think you're right." Curt smiled and looked down at his son, grabbed another handful of popcorn, and saw his son thinking hard about something.

"But…will he still be a catcher, or will he play somewhere else when he plays in the big leagues? He's got to be a catcher. He's too good."

"Oh, I imagine he will play catcher for whatever lucky team gets him."

As Posey moved from catcher to each position around the infield, he managed to wow Josh, and as if scripted, crushed a fastball over the right centerfield fence with the bases loaded for a grand slam. Josh just knew he hit the homerun for him. Curt let him believe that he had.

After the bucket of popcorn seemed to disappear, Josh wanted to walk around the stadium for a little bit. Curt didn't seem to mind as he was content with spending the afternoon away from work with his son. The game was in hand as the Seminoles were already up by several runs. He had always loved the game of baseball and hoped that Josh would develop the same love for the sport, and they would share it together as father and son. So far, Josh was heading in that direction, and that pleased Curt as a father and a baseball fan.

In between the grandstand and the general admission bleacher seats of right field, there was a large, open plaza where pretzel and ice cream venders set up along with the Seminole booster marketing tables. Also, there was normally a table set up for Seminole shirts, hats, posters, stickers, face tattoos, and other memorabilia available for sale. In the back of the plaza, near the entrance were a concession stand and bathrooms.

After grabbing a large souvenir Coke for Josh and him to split, Curt made his way over to the table with the FSU items for sale. Josh had walked over to the right field fence and looked through it to watch the game at field level and possibly snag a foul ball if one were to come his way. Curt looked around at what was displayed and keyed in on a small rubberized wrist band. They were gaining popularity among kids, and Josh had sported a few during recent promotions he was involved with at his school. This particular band was garnet with gold lettering and read, "Unconquered."

The word represented the unconquered spirit of the Seminole nation and the Indian tribe of the same name which the university uses as its beloved mascot. It meant something to Curt, and he liked what it stood for. To him, it meant never to give up and never let anyone stop you from accomplishing your goals. The vision of the awe-inspiring statue on the other side of the football stadium popped in his head. It was of the school's mascot, Chief Osceola on top of his trusted steed, Renegade, reared back on his hind legs with a fiery, feathered spear raised in the air. To a Seminole, it instilled an overwhelming sense of pride and tradition. He bought two of the bands, one for him, one for Josh.

"Daddy, Daddy, Daddy, he's going down to the bull pen."

"Okay buddy, let's go."

Posey was taking the opportunity while the opposition was changing out another pitcher to run down to the bullpen and warm up his arm. It was planned that he would pitch for two outs of the last inning before taking up his last position in the outfield, completing his "around the diamond" feat.

The bullpen was a double-mounded pen directly past the right field bleachers in the shadows of the "green monster." Josh ran ahead of Curt and climbed up the nearly empty bleachers. He stood over the bullpen to watch his favorite player warm up. Curt climbed laboriously up the aluminum bleacher seats behind his excited son and joined him to watch the all-star throw.

"Hey buddy, I got you something."

Josh's head whipped around to see what it was. Curt presented him one of the garnet wrist bands.

"Oh, cool Daddy, thanks."

"Do you see what it says?"

Josh pulled his tiny hand through the band and read it by twisting his wrist around.

"Yeah, Unconquered. Like the Chief Osceola statue?"

"Yeah, buddy, just like it."

"I love it Daddy. It's awesome."

"I got one for me too." Curt flashed the wrist that donned his wrist band. Curt sat down and addressed his son at his level.

"Josh, I want you to keep this with you buddy. Unconquered means never broken, that you never lose sight of who you are, and never let anyone change who you are inside. Do you understand that, buddy?"

Josh studied the wrist band closer, believing that it now held some type of super power and then looked at his father with love in his eyes. He smiled, his cute dimple creasing in the corner of his mouth.

"Yes, Daddy. I understand." He reached over and grabbed Curt's hand and pulled him back over to the edge of the fence to watch Posey finish his warm up session. Curt stood next to him enjoying the moment when Josh looked up at him, "I love you, Dad."

"I love you too, buddy!"

***

The shrill of his cell phone chirped as and vibrated in his pocket. Curt came out of his reverie to realize his cell phone was ringing. He wiped the tears that began to well up in his eyes and fished out the phone from his trench coat breast pocket. It took a moment to get his bearings. He looked around and found himself sitting in the front of the hotel parking lot; the Crown Vic was just idling. He was absentmindedly rubbing the St. Anthony's medallion hanging from his neck, reliving the memory of his son.

He checked the phone. It was Louis. He was waiting for his food. Curt checked the time display in the dash and noticed he had been sitting there for nearly thirty minutes. He extended his right arm and exposed his wrist beyond the coat sleeve to reveal the worn, garnet wrist band, the gold lettering had dulled over time and wear, but the word was still legible. "Unconquered."

Curt wiped the remaining tears away, grabbed the bag of food for Louis, and walked into the hotel.

Chapter 11

A brisk wind rolled over the top of the Rocky Mountains and down into the town cradled in the valley, cooling the late summer evening. The three women decided to explore the rest of the town center when a crowd of teenagers seemed to flood the area after their late lunch. Clearly, school was out for the day. They spread out and focused mainly on the food court and the popular chain stores that anchored the shopping complex. Rachel took up a position overlooking the food court. She felt awkward as she watched a bevy of teenage girls interact with each other. Never a part of the popular girl clique, it was hard for her to decipher exactly what she was watching and the corresponding interaction.

As she watched over the young people in the food court like a protective falcon high on her perch, Rachel watched two girls, in particular, sitting across from each other at a table, disconnected from the larger group. Something about how they sat and talked to each other struck a familiar chord. When the two girls got up from their table, Rachel moved closer and decided to follow them more out of curiosity than suspicion.

The two girls were close in age and size. They talked non-stop as they walked around the entertainment center oblivious to their trailing shadow. They both wore the same hair-style, dark blonde hair pulled back in a ponytail, and they had the same innocent and pretty face. They were sisters Rachel realized. They were the kind of close-knit sisters blessed with being the other's best friend, confidant, debate partner, and backup, all in one faithful and loving person.

Rachel was drawn to the pair of sisters as they found a music store to snoop around in. The smaller of the two then broke away and headed in a different direction. But before doing so, they faced each other and did some kind of hand-slapping ritual and shake with rehearsed lyrics.

Rachel was astounded and watched in amazement as they shared this kind of bond and actually performed their own secret handshake.

Rachel immediately thought of her.

Like the sisters at the town center mall, Rachel and Rhonda had been inseparable. Wherever Rachel went, her little sister, who was only a year and a half younger, would surely follow. They loved the outdoors. Every chance they got to play outside, they took advantage. Whether it was riding their bicycles, playing at the park down the block, or swimming in their aunt's pool across town, they were always outside.

During the middle of spring break when Rachel was fifteen and Rhonda thirteen, the girls had hurried and finished all their chores before their mother got home from work. They were eager to spend their hard earned cash at the convenience store down the road for coveted Jolly Ranchers, a box of grape and watermelon Nerds, a strawberry soda for Rhonda, and a peach soda for Rachel. Gummy Bears were the preferred addition but only if they pooled their leftover change. They barely made it out of the store before ripping into their sugary snacks.

As they pushed their bikes along the sidewalk, feasting on their candy, they immersed themselves in a heated debate on who was the cutest member of New Kids on the Block. Rhonda argued Jordan while Rachel pushed for the more edgy Donnie as her favorite. Both traded off saying their names with the associated last names attached in the fantasy of marrying the band members one day. They giggled together and planned to be married at the same time, and the weddings would precede a concert in their honor.

Neither girl noticed the van from the convenience store following them on the way to the park.

Rachel had blocked out most of the abduction from her memory but remembered that the man was very strong, much too strong for her to fight off and run away. She remembered fighting as hard as she could and screaming as loud as she could until everything went dark. She didn't understand why this had happened and why no one was helping her.

An hour later, their mother ran up and down the neighborhood frantically looking for the girls, but she only found their riderless bikes pushed off into the grass. Just down the street she stopped suddenly, horrified at the emptiness of the scene. Two soda cans were lying on the concrete; their contents had leaked out, staining the dry concrete wet. Half-full candy packages lay discarded on the ground just beyond the soda cans.

The man kept the girls for days in a house somewhere in the greater Houston area, somewhere in the southwest near the Goodwin Home in Missouri City, Texas. Rachel tried to remain strong and fight the man every time he came in the room, but her young muscles were no match for his strength. She was pushed away to the ground as a mere annoyance, while he took Rhonda from the tiny dark room to elsewhere in the house. Rachel knew he was doing bad things to her sister— forbidden things Rhonda shouldn't know about but was forced to endure. She felt powerless as the man took her sister from the room with a glint of evil lust gleaming in his eyes. He would bring her back later, but it happened several times a day. Once returned to their dark prison cell, she wouldn't talk about what happened, only shut down and cry uncontrollably. Rachel would hug her sister tight while she cried herself to sleep, hoping never to let go.

Armed with an idea to stop the violence to her sister, Rachel prepared herself for the next time the man came into the room. Once the heavy stomps on the wood floor neared the tiny, dark room, she hid her sister in the dark corner and stood waiting as the door opened. She could never see his face, the light from the other part of the house flooded the room, casting a dark silhouette on the man. She stood before him, offering herself in place of her fragile, broken little sister. The man contemplated the offer. Rachel, attempting to further entice the man, slid off her shirt, revealing her underdeveloped body, hoping that would steer his attention toward her and not her sister.

She stood there half-naked and exposed for what seemed an eternity, waiting for the man to decide, but suddenly she was pushed aside while he scooped up the younger, defenseless Rhonda and took her from the room. Rachel screamed and pleaded with the man to take her instead. She begged him to take her and leave her sister alone, but her pleas went ignored. She failed.

Rhonda reached out for her sister and their eyes locked as the man carried her out of the tiny, dark room. Rachel tried to convey hope to her sister with a look that everything was going to be alright, but she was met with a defeated and blank stare. She had given up and succumbed to the man and his evil. She mouthed the words, weakly, "It's okay. I love you," as she watched her being taken away. Rachel lunged after the man with every ounce of her being, but he shoved her back in the room and slammed the door. She screamed and pushed against the door, but it was in vain as he locked it, keeping her trapped inside, helpless. She beat and kicked against the door wildly, fueled with rage until she was completely exhausted.

That was the last time she saw her.

The girls had been missing for a total of three days when Rachel was found wandering around a neighborhood in the middle of the night, half naked, dirty, severely dehydrated, and incoherent. She was rushed to the hospital, but because of her delirious state, she was unable to help the police find the house where she and her sister had been held captive. The police covered the area but were unable to retrace the young girl's steps to find any trace of her sister.

While Rachel recovered in the hospital with her mother at her side, the police detectives delivered the awful and heart-breaking news that Rhonda couldn't be located, and the search was being called off. The police searched over three square miles surrounding the spot Rachel had been found wandering, for the better part of two days, but they were unable to find any sign of her sister Rhonda.

The violence inflicted on Rhonda as described by Rachel was unthinkable, and although countless man hours and community support went into the investigation of this heinous act, there was not much to go on. Some leads trickled in, but nothing ever seemed to stick. Rachel tried her best to provide useful details to help the detectives, but her damaged mind became easily stressed. She got confused as she was asked to relive the terrible crime over and over again by the police and psychologists. Every time she tried to picture the man, she could only recall his dark, silhouetted outline standing in the doorway—an image that would haunt her for many years.

Rhonda was never found and was officially presumed dead.

The man responsible for the unforgiveable crime committed against Rhonda and Rachel Goodwin was never found either. He remained a faceless, shadowy monster that loomed in the darkness. This caused Rachel problems after the fact as she felt she was always looking over her shoulder for the man to reappear and drag her back into hell. She started studying martial arts and joined several team sports to get physically strong and take her mind off the tragedy. It helped to focus her pent up anger. But it was only temporary. The anger always lurked in the shadows like a behemoth waiting to be unleashed. Moving through high school, she grew introverted and closed off, afraid to get close to anyone. The relationship with her mother soured as she felt blamed for her sister's disappearance, and her mother never attempted to assuage her guilt. She was too ashamed to explain that she offered herself to the man to help protect her sister, but as her thoughts traveled back to that unbearable time in her life, she questioned why. Why did he choose Rhonda and not her?

Rachel struggled with this question the most and let it eat away and break her self-esteem down to nothing as she moved into adulthood. At the age of sixteen, she started to take up high-risk behavior such as promiscuity and illegal drug use. With her mother still emotionally absent and numb to her fragile emotional state, Rachel used her sexuality to gain attention from whoever was available. This validated her need for acceptance but left her empty and hollow inside. Yet she still craved the attention and was labeled a whore behind her back. She hid the pain through alcohol and drug use and started to engage in more of a physical brand of sex...just to feel something, but it only left her feeling dead inside.

Rachel, at the age of twenty-four, was admitted into the hospital for alcohol poisoning after being left in the back alley of a bar. She was found with her tight-fitting skirt hiked up around her waist, no underwear, and lying in a pool of her own vomit. She couldn't even tell the EMTs what day, month, or even the correct year when she was questioned. She only rambled on about her sister and that she had to find her.

In the hospital, she lay in the bed, thinking about her sister and the pain she would never be able to shake. She overheard one of the nurses, who obviously thought she was out of earshot, say this was the eighth time Rachel had been admitted for some variation of alcohol poisoning. She hadn't realized the number of visits she'd accrued. They snickered at her debilitating weakness and she grew angry and embarrassed. She wanted to lash out and get physical with the bitchy, judgmental women by the nurses' station, but a vision of her sister flashed before her, calming her down. She realized, at that moment, this was her problem and it wasn't going away on its own. She had to deal with it or let it take over. It was no way to honor her sister.

Rachel ripped the IVs out of her arm, got dressed, and walked out of the hospital, never to return as a patient needing to be dried out from alcohol. She quickly found herself turning her life around and enrolled in college classes to finish her degree in social work from Baylor University. She began to take on weight and quit the anorexic behavior she had incorporated for so long to keep the superficial look of being thin and attractive. As the extra weight formed around her mid-section, she found herself content with it, considering how dangerous the alternative had become. She had a few relapses around the anniversary of Rhonda's and her abduction and some shitty days in general, but they waned to nothing as the years went on. Rachel found her niche in helping the less fortunate children. She believed her personal tragedy would allow her to relate better to the children she helped. She took a job with the Department of Children and Family Services out of college and didn't look back, until the day she met Alexis Vanderhill.

Now, she carried with her a framed photograph of her sister from a more joyful and innocent time in their lives, a memorable family trip to the Galveston Beach on the Gulf of Mexico. It reminded her of how low she had once been. Lying in the hospital bed, the vision that flashed before Rachel and pulled her out of the abyss was from that beach vacation with Rhonda.

Rachel's faith in God had disappeared the day she and her sister had their innocence ripped away. Although the path she forged after getting clean was arduous, she found it somewhat fateful that now she was a part of a group that might finally help her find answers about Rhonda.

Chapter 12

After dropping off lunch with Louis at the hotel, Curt headed back out, trying to find another locale suitable for the mission. As the day went on, the sun sat atop the western ridge of the Rockies, leaving long shadows down in the valley town. Curt had to keep moving; he had to keep searching for stolen innocence and remain the beacon of hope he desperately needed, not only for the children he sought but for his own sake.

He moved away from the major streets and avenues of the small town and found his way snaking through back roads and neighborhood streets. Dusk took ahold of the clear mountain sky. A set of lights towered in the distance and caught Curt's attention. As he moved along the road, the lights multiplied into many different, glowing towers, shining brightly in the night. He recognized the sight which bred in him the worst night of his life. A shiver ran through his body from the awful memory, yet he was drawn to the lights like a moth to flame.

Curt made his way through the settling night towards the lights that beckoned. He made his way through the small neighborhood and the sight became clear. He was right. It was a sports complex with a multitude of children, parents, and complex workers moving about and around the cloverleaf of softball fields with a single structure anchoring the center, acting as both a concession stand and field office. His breathing grew rapid beyond his control as the memory came flooding back with the force of a tidal wave. The sight of fathers walking side by side with their sons was the hardest to watch.

Cheers and sideline coaching grew louder as Curt neared the complex. Several miniature football players, clad in oversized pads and legs too short to run that fast, moved around the altered softball fields like a school of fish undulating under the sea. He found a spot to park and just watched.

The picture wedged in the dash pulled his focus like it was calling him by name. He removed the photograph from its place as tears were already falling down both cheeks. He wondered if he would ever run out of tears, but when it came to his son, he would not run out of anything whether it be tears or hope.

***

The vibration of his cell phone buzzed in his pocket. He quietly stepped out of the CID conference room while the others waited patiently. He looked around and fished the phone out of his pocket. The others were waiting for a few more to join the meeting.

"Hey," he answered after reading his wife's name on the caller ID.

"Are you going to be able to make it on time tonight?"

Curt snapped his wrist up flashing his watch. It was nearing 5:30 p.m., "Yeah, we're meeting right now with the command staff and council chair; it shouldn't be too long. I'll run home and grab him, and we'll pick up some food or something on the way."

"Okay, so you know, he won't talk about anything other than watching his daddy play softball tonight!"

"Nice. I hope I don't disappoint."

"Okay, I'll have him ready, but if you run late, I'll just take him with me."

The last anticipated attendee stepped off the elevator with his assistant and Curt's sergeant following. The well-dressed man waved at him as he looked up from his phone call, and Curt waved back. He walked into the conference room and took a seat.

"Okay, I should be there. I gotta go babe…I love you!"

"Love you too."

Curt snapped the phone shut and joined the meeting, hoping to get all the issues ironed out quickly so that he could keep the appointment with his son. Josh loved to be the batboy for his father and his buddies as they played.

The meeting was scheduled amidst the on-going investigation into a serial rapist who was now responsible for six reported sexual batteries, all occurring on the eastside of Tallahassee. Each one was more brutal than the last. The media quickly compared the seriousness of the crimes to the carnage left behind by the renowned serial killer Ted Bundy, who plagued a Florida State University sorority back in the seventies. The unknown suspect was targeting women who were at home alone. He silently stalked them for a bit and then would stealthily break into the house, ambush the women, tie them up, and blindfold them before repeatedly raping them. He left the scene seemingly without a trace, keeping the women's underwear as a trophy of sorts. Curt caught the cases and had been working them non-stop for the last few weeks, trying to stop the sick animal responsible for these atrocious crimes.

The focus of the meeting was to update the higher-ups in command staff and the appointed chairman of the newly formed council on public safety, City Councilman Thomas Pittman. Pittman was selected for this position for his tough-on-crime stance and eagerness to help the police department get the resources they needed along with the city's support. He gained popularity and status in the community by speaking out against the gangs, drug dealers, and thieves of the city. Tallahassee Police Chief Harrison sat next to him at the head of the conference table as Curt walked around the room giving out all the necessary details of the case. He advised them on how they were going to proceed with the investigation.

Pittman was brought in on this case specifically for his willingness to get the resources needed to bring these heinous crimes to a successful resolution. He was also up for re-election the following year, so it wouldn't hurt to help the police bring down a serial rapist.

"In going back and talking with the victims, we were able to determine at least three were members of the same gym, Tallahassee Gym Works on the parkway—something we missed initially. The others were pretty fit and exercised in some way or another outside of the gym. Obviously, this guy has an eye for the athletic type. So based on the normal workout times of the three gym members, we think the suspect is following them home after their work outs, breaking in, tying them up, and raping them after blindfolding them."

Curt signaled his squad-mate, who was sitting in front of a computer in the corner, to activate the projector in the ceiling. After doing so, a wall-sized map of east Tallahassee lit up the screen behind the Chief. The map was marked with six, red pinpoints, one for each of the women's houses and locations of the rapes. He was sticking to a few square miles of territory on the eastside, but unfortunately, the geographic location was home to, or was easily accessed by, nearly a third of Tallahassee's population. The area had been developed rather quickly over the last decade and had grown quite popular.

Curt continued on with the cases providing a brief overview of each attack and any outstanding factors from the case, like if there were witnesses or physical evidence, which were scarce amongst all of the cases. However, once they revisited with each victim and learned of the obvious connection, they were moving fast with follow-up.

"The gym has a good video system, so we're going to explore that first thing tomorrow as well as set up a surveillance operation that is being devised as we speak using the VICE unit. We don't want to move too fast, for our working theory is that the suspect could be an employee of the gym or even a member. So we've requested all member and employee records through the corporate office, which unfortunately is much slower, but we don't want to expose ourselves by going in heavy handed. This guy has proven to be careful. Also, two of the victims said they regularly run or bike up and down Goose Pond Trail, so we're deploying roving units throughout the trail to see if our guy shows up."

Chief Harrison sat back in his chair, pleased with how the investigation was moving forward, but he was eager for it to move forward to a positive outcome and an arrest. He looked over at the councilman, who also had a pleased look.

"So, Chief, what do you need from the council? Name it, and it's yours."

"Well, the overtime budget is getting thin, so honestly, that's what we need to get this resolved. We have the people who are capable; we just need them out there working and getting paid for it."

"Done! Anything else?"

The Chief shot a look at Curt and then over to his sergeant looking for help answering Pittman's question. They responded with blank looks, obviously content with the expanded overtime allowance.

"No, but if something comes up, we'll be sure to contact your office."

"Yes, please do."

Pittman's assistant leaned over and spoke into his ear, causing him to look at his watch and realize something. He addressed the Chief and excused himself from the meeting for another appointment. The meeting adjourned, and while Curt erased his notes on the dry erase board, Pittman approached him.

"Good work detective; are y'all heading out tonight on surveillance? I mean, I have this meeting, but it shouldn't run too late, and I've always wanted to go on a real police stake-out, if that wouldn't be too much trouble."

"Uh, no sir. I actually have plans of my own tonight. I'm taking my son to a softball game. He loves being the batboy. Plus, I haven't been home much lately, as you can tell, so I'm going to take the night off and pick it up in the morning. Hopefully, we'll have the member and employee list by the morning."

"Oh, nice. Good for you. Okay, well let me know about the stake-out. Maybe some other time?"

"Yes, sir."

Curt left the division and made a hasty exit for his unmarked car, a black Ford Crown Victoria. He ran down the stairs and out the back door to the parking lot, wrestling with putting on his trench coat, carrying his case files and his bag of clothes to change into at the ball field. Curt shot a quick call to his wife, giving her an ETA to pick up his son and headed to the game.

***

He looked back in the rear view mirror, waiting for the green arrow light at Easterwood Drive. Josh was sitting in the back of the Crown Vic stuffing his face with Chick-Fil-A nuggets and honey mustard sauce, oblivious to his dad watching. He could watch the boy for hours with all his simple and innocent mannerisms. Curt smiled, watching him figure out the complexities of the proper chicken to dip ratio. He looked over the hills to his left to see the glow of the lights from Tom Brown Park. No matter how many times he'd played over the years, he still had a flutter of butterflies as he made his way to a game.

He pulled the Crown Vic up next to his teammates' cars and helped Josh get out without spilling his drink or food. Curt grabbed his bat bag and change of clothes, and he headed toward the fields. The cloverleaf formation of five softball fields sat in the middle of the athletic complex with a little league field and back to back soccer fields on one side, a larger senior major baseball field and basketball courts bookending the other side. Across the road that wound through the middle of the park was a large, open area used for disc golf and an outdoor concert held every Fourth of July. There were also nature trails, playgrounds, and picnic tables scattered around the 255 acre park on the east side of Tallahassee.

Curt spotted his teammates, off to the side of a field, warming up and running their mouths deep in discussion of nonsense. He'd missed the last few games while working the serial rape case and was glad to be able to make this game along with Josh. Playing the game allowed him to feel somewhat normal and gave him visions of playing alongside of Josh one day.

"Okay, buddy, I need to go to the bathroom and change, okay?"

"All right. Can I go over to the playground?"

"Sure, buddy. I'll just be a minute."

Curt dipped into the bathroom and quickly removed the trench coat, his dress shirt, and pants. He pulled out his game jersey and softball pants, and he slipped them over his hefty 240 pound frame. He noticed in the mirror that he seemed to be filling out his shirt more and more lately. He smirked at the thought, sat down on the bench behind him, and put on his cleats. He packed up his work clothes and shoes in the duffle bag, grabbed it along with his bat bag, and headed out of the bathroom.

He caught the attention of a teammate who waved over at him. Curt sent a head nod back as he shot a look around for Josh. He checked the playground area and saw several kids playing together, but none were Josh. He walked over to the dugout while the rest of his team was getting ready to take the field.

"Hey? You see Josh come over here?"

"Um, no. I haven't."

Curt's face immediately showed concern. He dropped his bags by the dugout and walked back to the playground. An uneasy feeling started to form in his gut. He reminded himself to stay calm and not to freak out. Josh was simply out of sight; he was fine, he told himself.

He walked over, searching the playground and scanning each kid's face for his son, but he wasn't there. He asked the kids if they saw where Josh went, and they were unable to offer any help. He looked around at the nearby dugouts and found a team with a similar color jersey as his team, thinking Josh could've wandered over there by mistake, but he didn't see him there either.

He started asking people he recognized from years of playing softball if they'd seen Josh. The uneasy feeling turned into a panicky sick feeling that was growing exponentially in his stomach, as he was met with no after no.

Curt ran back to the car, hoping to find him there, but he wasn't there either. He ran around the parking lot and started to search the fields again. His team had left the field and started searching for the boy too. A loud PA announcement was made at the concession stand, and all games had come to a halt to search for the boy.

But he was gone.

Patrol officers flooded the area in search of Joshua Walker following a panic stricken 911 phone call from Curt, but all efforts were unsuccessful. One minute he was there with his father; the next he was gone, vanished out of his life. After the initial search ended, Curt sat at the park numb down to his core, blanketed by the overwhelming sense of loss that he was being forced to accept. He needed to leave, he needed to go, and he needed to find his son. But he couldn't. He had no clue where to start looking. He had no leads and no idea why his son was taken, and this alone, paralyzed him to the core. He let out a primal howl that could be heard clear on the other side of the park.

***

The lights of the Vail City Athletic complex were turned off as the last few cars pulled out of the parking lot. Curt remembered the defining and final clicks of the overhead lights being turned off at Tom Brown Park the day Josh went missing. As they went out, he felt something extinguish inside. He snapped to as he realized he was nearly two thousand miles away from home.

He looked down at the picture in the dash.

"I'm sorry, buddy. I haven't given up. I promise I'll never give up." He reached through the steering wheel and removed the picture from the dash. He put it to his lips and kissed the picture, a poor substitute for the real thing, but his only option. He wiped the tears away, started up the Crown Vic, and left the complex.

Curt went back to the hotel to prepare for Chicago in the morning. He ran up to his room and made sure his bags were packed and ready to go. He checked his watch and saw that it was nearing eight o'clock. He realized he hadn't eaten dinner yet, so he walked back down to the hotel's restaurant and sat at the bar.

He ordered a chopped steak and french fries and ate alone. Curt was angry and unable to shake the pain of losing Josh. The thought of him out there in the world without his father's protection was unbearable. He caught the attention of the bartender and ordered a whiskey, which he quickly downed before signaling for another. He felt another rough night brewing.

Chapter 13

He stopped counting after a while, especially when the sting was not as sharp as the first. Curt's painful sorrows were drowning away in a mix of Irish and American whiskies. He had been alternating country of origin just for humor. The purpose was escape. His head was buzzing from the alcohol, and he could feel the rage boiling inside. He hated this part of him and what he'd become and hoped that it would vanish if he was able to find Josh. However, whatever hope he felt was slipping away more and more as time went on.

When he became part of this team, he looked at the parents of these children and compared their devotion to finding their child to his own. He questioned whether or not he was a fool for continuing the search as the odds were clearly stacked so high against him. He once thought the best chance to see Josh again would be at the gates of heaven but thought better of suicide, knowing that if there was a chance he could find his son, albeit miniscule, he was going to take it.

"Ex…excuse me sirrr. Another, pa-leese," Curt slurred his re-order.

"May I join you?" The tender voice of Rachel Goodwin pulled Curt's attention and he turned around on his barstool. He spun slowly, careful not to lose his balance and fall off. He looked at her with skepticism but nodded his head.

"They usually leave me alone when I drink."

"I'm just new and naïve, I guess."

"Hmm."

The bartender slid over another whiskey for Curt and took Rachel's order of a club soda with a lime. Curt heard the order and looked at Rachel, sizing her up and trying to read her thoughts. He leaned away from her taking in a broader look at the new girl. He worked on a thought to himself as he downed the better part of his whiskey in one full gulp. He had figured something out but kept it to himself.

"I just thought we could talk. Something that you clearly don't like to do."

"Talk huh? 'bout what?"

"I don't know. Whatever, I guess."

"Okay, hold that thought then. I have to pee!" Curt put bluntly. He finished the rest of the whiskey and put the empty glass back on the bar with a little authority, causing a loud clank and rattle of the ice within. He turned and made his way to the hotel's bathroom, leaving Rachel alone at the bar with her club soda. She wondered if Curt was even going to return, thinking that this gesture of friendship was a mistake.

To her surprise, Curt made his way back, a degree more sober than when he left.

As Curt saddled up to the bar ready to replace what he just expended. He signaled to the bartender for another drink. The bartender acknowledged the order.

Rachel was about to engage Curt again when a group of four Hispanic men walked past them at the bar. Curt had pegged them earlier as Mexican migrant workers moving through the area before winter. They had taken up a corner booth in the bar when Curt arrived. They were engrossed in a vibrant conversation speaking only Spanish to one another, so Rachel had no clue if they were talking about her, the weather, or the color of the sky.

As they passed by, Curt's head snapped up, recognizing something that was said amongst the group.

"¡Espero que consiga a la Reina de Diamantes esta noche!" One of them said.

Curt's inebriation seemed to vanish instantly as he watched the group of men walk out of the restaurant and into the lobby headed for the parking lot. He strained his ears to pick up what else they were saying.

Clueless and intrigued, Rachel asked, "What? What did I miss?"

Ignoring Rachel, Curt pulled out his cell phone and pushed a button, then placed the phone to his ear. He still kept his stare on the Mexicans.

"Yeah, it's me. Get a tracker out and down to the lobby, now!" Curt's tone was serious and surprisingly sober.

He listened to the other end for a moment and replied, "Doesn't matter which one, just one that we can slap and go."

Curt squeezed the phone shut and looked at Rachel who still had no idea what he was doing.

"You're going to have to explain to me; what's going on? What did that guy say?"

His thoughts were bouncing around his head at warp speed, and the alcohol intake didn't help matters as he sifted through the drunken haze, trying to formulate a plan.

"I'll explain later, can you drive? I've been...."

"Yeah, no problem. But tell me what's going on."

"Human trafficking," Curt said matter-of-factly.

With his answer, Rachel grew even more confused. How did he get human trafficking from a group of migrant workers walking past him in a hotel restaurant?

"I thought we were looking for lost and kidnapped children."

"We are. This is worse. I need you to round up the others and check on the van to see if it's up and running. If you see Louis, tell him I'll be waiting in the parking lot."

"Okay." Rachel stopped trying to figure what was going on and just followed orders. Obviously, Curt was keyed in on something important enough to leave the bar mid-drink.

Louis nearly walked by Curt who had taken up a post by the far end of the front valet drop-off to the hotel. He was watching the parking lot as the group of Mexican workers made their way to their vehicle. Curt just needed to figure out which one.

"Here," Louis said, handing over a small, round disc-like object. It was a simple tracker actually made by Louis. It was a small plastic container that housed a cell phone, equipped with GPS, and affixed to a powerful magnet.

"Did you put the extra battery pack in there this time?"

"Yes." Louis popped open the lid to show Curt the smaller back up battery source for the cell phone.

"Okay, good."

Curt took the tracker and tucked it under his arm like a football and made his way inconspicuously into the parking lot. He managed to out flank the group of men who were heading to the back of the parking lot. Ahead of them Curt saw a dusty, white Ford F-350 with a lot of lawn maintenance tools and equipment in the bed. He hated adhering to a stereotype, but in this case, it seemed to fit. He crept between the other parked cars and remained within the shadows as the group moved slowly and unsuspectingly toward the truck.

The Ford F-350 was definitely their truck, he concluded. Curt was able to read the company logo stamped on the side of the truck which matched the color and logos on the men's shirts.

Louis watched intently as Curt made his way deeper into the parking lot. His gaze switched from Curt to the group of Mexicans and back. Rachel, who had just summoned Melinda and Beth from their rooms, joined him at the front of the hotel. The other two were getting dressed and heading down. They didn't question Rachel when she described Curt's vague, yet tenacious directives.

Curt crawled under a vehicle parked next to the large Ford truck and sat there, holding onto the tracker in his left hand. He felt it pull toward the undercarriage of the car he was under. He fought against the magnetic pull and kept it tucked tight against his body. As he waited for the men to load up into the truck, he suddenly realized his body was now small enough to fit underneath a regular sized sedan.

The loud roar of the F-350's engine was deafening for Curt. He was too close to the exhaust pipe of the large truck as the driver cranked it up. He waited for all four doors to shut and quickly scooted from the neighboring sedan to underneath the truck. Curt reached up blindly into the undercarriage of the truck in search of a concealed hiding spot for the tracker. He couldn't see what he was doing because the street lights didn't reach underneath the truck. He found what he hoped was the ideal place and shoved the tracker up and waited for the magnet to pull it to final rest. The tracker didn't take hold. Curt held it flush against something solid but still it didn't stick. He started to move it around, trying to find something that would grab the magnet. Suddenly, the truck began to roll forward out of its spot. Instinctively, Curt grabbed ahold of something with his free hand and prayed his hand wasn't going to get chopped off in the process. He held on tight as the truck moved out into the driving lane headed toward the highway exit. He hoisted the tracker up to a different spot with his left hand while hanging on with his right. He was being dragged across the parking lot by the work truck.

"C'mon, dammit!" He cursed.

The truck started to pick up speed as it neared the exit. Curt felt the loose gravel scratching his back through his trench coat and white dress shirt. He pulled himself up in a last ditch attempt, knowing this impromptu plan would not last long and would certainly end in painful failure if the truck pulled out onto the highway. With a tight grip from his right hand holding on to the truck, he shoved the tracker up and far to the right until he finally felt the magnetic bite against something metal. The tracker clanked dully against the truck's chassis but was washed out by the loud Mariachi music that was blaring from the cab. He prayed the tracker stayed put long enough to find out where they were going.

The tracker took hold just as the truck pulled to a stop at the main road, waiting to enter traffic. Curt let go and lay still on the road, letting the large work truck lurch forward out into traffic, leaving him in the middle of the entrance/exit way. The loud exhaust of the heavy truck roared out into the highway and dissipated as it left the area, heading west out of town.

Curt lay in place on the cold asphalt for a few moments before moving, realizing how dumb that was. He figured the remaining alcohol in his system was numbing the inevitable pain that would come from being dragged a hundred yards across the parking lot. His body would pay the consequences later. Now, there was work to do.

Rachel and Louis ran over and helped Curt up from the road. They looked him over for any sign of serious injury. He told them he was fine and checked the back of his overcoat. It sustained some rips and tears, but when he noticed they were minor and there was no blood, he felt a sense of relief.

"Dude, that was awesome!" Louis stared at Curt in awe. "We could see you being dragged from across the parking lot!"

"Louis!" Rachel admonished. She turned to Curt with scolding eyes, "Seriously, that was pretty dumb! Now, are you going to let us in on what all that was about?"

"Sure!" Curt said, looking around for the Sprinter van. He started to walk toward it and signaled for the team to follow. "Van's good to go right?"

"Yep, just needed a belt change."

Curt continued, "At the bar, I heard the guy say, '¡Espero que consiga a la Reina de Diamantes esta noche!'"

"Okay, and for those who don't speak Spanish?" Rachel said, looking around at the group.

Beth offered, "Queen of Diamonds? But what the hell does that mean?"

"And how does that relate to human trafficking? They could be on the way to a late night poker game for all we know!" Rachel added.

Beth quickly figured Curt's angle and nodded in acceptance.

"He said, 'I hope I get the Queen of Diamonds tonight,'" Curt translated. Rachel was still lost, as was Louis. "Do they look like the cigar smoking, bourbon drinking, high-stakes poker types?"

"No, but they can just be playing amongst themselves for whatever else they have to gamble."

"True, but why would they say specifically they wanted the 'Queen of Diamonds,' especially when the Ace of Spades rules that game?"

"Okay, I'll bite, but seriously, how are you stretching that phrase into human trafficking?"

Beth answered for the uninformed. "The 'Johns' will sometimes come and meet the pimp outside and pay for a 'card,' not for sex per se. So the John will take the card which allows him entry into the house, and he finds the coinciding card. Behind that card will be a girl waiting to have sex. She collects the card; and at the end of the night, she is paid for every card she collects, usually something in the area of ten or twenty bucks per sex act."

"That's awful!" Melinda offered. She was no stranger to the world of prostitution, being a former undercover cop and sister of a drug addicted prostitute, but what Beth was describing was a different level of inhumane.

"And they usually have around ten to fifteen 'Johns' per night!" Beth added.

Rachel seethed with anger at the thought of defenseless girls being held captive and raped for an insulting pittance. It awoke a hatred deep inside her soul that had been hidden away for a very long time. She grew angry at the images of those poor women forced to endure sex. She wanted in on whatever plan Curt was in the process of hatching. Images from her own haunting past flashed in her mind as a shiver rolled down her body.

"Okay, I've heard about that happening in Mexico, India, and third world countries, but here?" Louis added.

"It happens everywhere. We had a case like that in Tallahassee when I was on patrol," Curt stated. "The girls were basically kidnapped and brought to America on false pretenses, then forced into prostitution to pay a debt."

"How does that even happen?" Rachel asked.

"Get the tracker on-line while we figure out our plan." Curt directed Louis who nodded and fired up his machine in the back of the van.

He addressed Rachel, "It's rather brutal. There is usually some dolled up older woman, drives a fancy car, wears tons of jewelry, and looks like a million bucks. She drives through these small, poor towns in whatever Latin country you can think of and knocks on the door to ask if there are any able bodied females looking for real work in America."

"Okay?"

"So of course she only visits the poor and ignorant people who'll believe her without question and are just desperate enough to buy into what she's selling."

"But she has to lie to them or something. I don't want to believe they'll just agree to be some prostitute in America just to leave some shit-hole country?"

"No, she lures them in with offers of a job in an American restaurant, hotel, or somewhere nice where they can get paid American wages and send home money to help the family. The woman sells them on the fantasy by telling them that is how she became so rich, by following this path to America, and now, she is opening up the door for these poor girls."

"So with no other viable option to get out of the poverty stricken life, they send the unsuspecting girls with the lady?" Rachel surmised.

"Right. But then, that's where it gets messed up," Beth chimed in. "Once the family agrees to send the girl, who is usually between the ages of thirteen and sixteen, they have to come up with a large amount of money to pay the coyote to get them smuggled into the country. It's usually more than the family makes in two years, so they are loaned the money and wind up agreeing to work it off once they land in America."

"But, that's not what actually happens," Melinda figured.

"Nope! Once they are successfully smuggled in, which is usually in the dark trunk of some smelly car and takes days to do, they are shipped off to wherever the network of traffickers needs them. Sometimes the girls have no idea what city or state they're in, but they are now trapped and indebted to the traffickers."

"And, on top of all that, the traffickers usually rape them first, keep them drugged up for weeks at a time, and then tell them if they think about running away, the tyrannical American police will either kill them, arrest them, or send them back to whatever country they're from. That's why they are normally allowed to come and go as they please, because they are more scared of being arrested and sent back to their families with nothing, than fighting against the traffickers. They are totally brainwashed."

"That is truly awful."

"Yes, it is."

"The tracker's on-line Curtis. They are still west of town, heading up north off some road that seems to lead to nowhere," Louis updated.

"If I'm right, they're going to where the girls are being kept. Let's go."

"Hold on, hold on. What's the plan?" Rachel asked.

Curt paused for a moment realizing he was being challenged and let the anger toward the new girl dissipate. However, he understood her reasoning. They did need a plan.

"We go and do some initial surveillance, find out how many girls are being held, how many pimps, guards, fortifications, and then we'll figure how to deal with it once we know all that."

"Okay, so we are just taking a look?"

"Yes, but I could be off and there could be nothing going on with those guys at all."

"Okay, let's go. I'm driving remember?" Rachel stuck her hand out waiting for Curt's keys. He hesitated for a second and then fished them out of his pocket and handed them to Rachel.

Chapter 14

Curt stood outside of the Crown Vic after they pulled over to the side of a two lane mountain road. He peered through a pair of Nikon binoculars across a deep ravine at a nice two-story chalet settled on a picturesque bluff. There was a long, winding dirt road that led away from the house back up toward the mountain road. It was very dark under the night sky offering concealment from the house across the ravine.

The house was well lit from the exterior, which offered good intelligence to Curt as he formulated his plan. The group had followed the tracker data to the mountain house and stopped short to let Curt and Rachel conduct reconnaissance and validate his theory, before moving forward. The van stayed parked down the hill about a half-mile away.

The migrant workers' F-350 was parked in front of the mansion on a large, circular driveway along with three other cars. The driveway encircled an ornate concrete tiered fountain which sat dry. A black Range Rover was combat parked off to the side near a detached garage. This was looking promising, Curt thought. This was clearly not a house befitting the blue-collar workers, especially if they were innocently looking for a game of cards.

This house was for people who had money, based on the feel, its size, location, and spectacular view of the mountainous valley; he could tell it was not for the common working man. If he was right about this house being used for human trafficking, they were well connected and had deep pockets. Two things, Curt figured, that made the traffickers that much more dangerous.

"See anything helpful yet?" Rachel asked, fighting off a chill from the incoming autumn winds.

"Not yet."

Curt had been watching for nearly an hour and didn't really see anything confirming his suspicions. The alcohol in his system had evaporated and left his head throbbing. That and the lack of activity to prove his hunch was making him irritable. He needed something to happen.

Just as his patience was about to be lost, the group of Mexican immigrants exited out of the chalet's massive front door. They were jovial, drunk on spirits, and lustfully satisfied from the sex slaves within who had fulfilled their needs. They lingered in front of the house, talking loudly in Spanish and slapping each other on the backs and shoulders in joking camaraderie. Their voices carried over the ravine and up to where Rachel and Curt were positioned. The men's carefree attitude only made her angrier at the possible horrors that went on inside the house.

A well-dressed man with jet black hair and tanned skinned followed the group out. He stood on the top steps of the chalet's porch and conversed in Spanish with them for a moment. They listened intently, and when he was done talking they quickly piled into the F-350 and left the house, traveling back down the dirt road.

"Is the tracker still working, Louis?" He eyed the truck as it made its way down the long, winding road back toward the main road.

"Yes, Curtis, it's got them leaving the house now."

"Okay, let me know where they stop for the night."

"Will do."

The well-dressed man returned inside, but only for a moment as he exited from a side door that was out of Curt's view, and he climbed into the Range Rover. He looked around, taking in the scenic view like he'd never seen it before. He lit a cigarette, and after the first drag he took out a cell phone and began talking.

"He's got a cell phone. Louis, can we do anything with that?"

"Uhh, I can try...but without knowing the number, it will be very tough."

"Okay."

Curt kept watching. The man moved with confidence and purpose around the house, much like a general as he inspected the barracks.

Over the next twenty minutes, two more men, who accounted for two of the other three cars, exited and left the house. The well-dressed man saw each one out, hugged the last guy like they were close friends, and walked back inside the house. Hosting was clearly one of his duties.

After the last car left the house, the well-dressed man stalked the front yard area, smoking another cigarette. He was on and off his cell phone, talking to someone. As Curt watched carefully from the concealment across the ravine, movement from the front door caught his attention. A demure female, dressed in a silky robe and high heels, stepped to the threshold of the door. She peered outside and spoke out to the man. He quickly barked something back at the girl which Curt couldn't make out, but he figured out he was yelling at her and shooed her back in the house.

"Did you see that?" Rachel asked excitedly.

"Yeah," Curt said, keeping his watch through the binoculars.

"Well, what do you think?"

"I think he could be a controlling asshole yelling at his young girlfriend after hosting a party for friends...."

"What?"

"We don't know enough yet. There is a lot here that suggests human trafficking, but we don't have the smoking gun yet. Let's just wait a bit longer."

"Fine. She's an awfully young girlfriend if you ask me." Rachel walked back to the car in search of a jacket or sweater to combat the cold mountain air.

Thirty more minutes of waiting, and it was nearing midnight. The group was getting tired and wanted to call it a night. Curt was steadily watching the face of the beautiful chalet through the binoculars, fighting off his own exhaustion. He could feel that he was right, but he needed more. He offered to stay while the team went back, but just as they were packing up, Curt's patience paid off.

"I got something." A slight degree of excitement in his voice woke up the team. Rachel perked up from her near slumber in the front seat of the Crown Vic. She jumped out of the car and walked up to Curt.

"What's going on?"

"Look." Curt passed the binos over to Rachel.

Rachel looked through the binoculars and saw a large panel van pulling up the circular driveway to the chalet's front door. The well-dressed host was standing out front, cigarette hanging from the corner of his mouth, and waving the van in. Once the van stopped, he yelled out to someone inside the house.

"I don't understand; it's just a van," she said, pulling away from the binos.

"Just keep watching."

As Rachel looked back, the oversized front door of the chalet pulled open and a large Hispanic man dressed in a button-up dress shirt and slacks stepped out and looked around. He stepped onto the porch with his partner and waved someone on from inside the house.

Rachel's eyes bulged in astonishment at what she saw next. It inspired a mixture of excitement and disgust.

A train of five girls, all dark-headed with Latin features and tan skin, walked slowly out of the chalet toward the van. They were all dressed provocatively in various outfits to incite the fantasies of the men who visited. One was a school girl, the other a nurse, the girl in the robe from earlier was dressed in black, lacy lingerie and high heels. None of the girls looked mature enough to consent to sex, and all had a defeated look of enslavement. The girls walked slowly, huddled up against the cold night air, and climbed into the van like a matter of habit.

"Give me those back for a second." Curt took back the field glasses from a shocked Rachel Goodwin.

Curt took a step closer to the edge of the ravine and stared purposefully through the binoculars. He was focusing on the larger man loading the girls into the van. After the girls were all loaded, he returned to the porch and locked up the house. Curt studied his waistband. The man didn't hide it well. A nickel plated semi-automatic handgun, possibly a 9 millimeter, was stuffed in the back waistline of his pants. He was the muscle, Curt figured.

As the house was secured, the two traffickers gave the van driver instructions and watched the van drive away. As the van made its way up the dusty road back to the mountain highway, the traffickers got in the Range Rover and followed.

"C'mon, we need to follow them," Curt ordered Rachel, pulling her from the ravine ledge back to the Crown Vic.

"Mel, start making your way up the hill toward the house. We need to follow them out. We'll take the Range Rover, you guys take the van."

"Okay, be there in a sec."

Melinda jumped into the driver's seat of the Mercedes Sprinter and put the van in gear. She pulled out on the street and pushed the accelerator to the floor as the van fought against the gravity of the uphill climb. The engine roared in protest as it labored up the mountainside.

Rachel made her way to the driver's seat, but Curt moved her over and took the wheel without debate. Rachel knew it wasn't worth the time to argue and stayed quiet. Plus, it had been almost three hours since they left the hotel.

They sat in the blacked out car waiting for the headlights of the panel van to make the length of the windy road back to the highway. The Range Rover caught up to the van just at the intersection of the highway.

"Okay Mel, they're at the highway. Standby for direction."

"Copy," she replied.

Curt sat up in his seat ready to crank it back to life and begin the chase. Rachel felt her heart pounding in excitement.

The panel van lurched out onto the dark mountain highway, going west away from town, but before Curt could say anything, the Range Rover made a left heading toward town.

Curt was about to crank up the engine but held off as he noticed the Range Rover was slowing down as it neared their position.

"Shit, get down." Curt lunged over Rachel who crouched down into the floorboard of the passenger seat. Curt wrenched his head around and saw the headlights of the Range Rover slowly approach the driver's side of the Crown Vic. He noticed they were slowing down as if they were stopping.

"Fuck...get out! Get out now!" he ordered.

"What? Out?" Her head was down, and she didn't understand what was going on.

Curt reached over Rachel's huddled body and yanked against the passenger door handle; they only had a second to react. The door opened just wide enough to squeeze their bodies through, and Curt, without preparation, shoved Rachel out of the small opening and followed her. He landed on top of her awkwardly just outside of the car. Thankfully, Curt kept the interior lights disengaged during surveillance, a habit he developed through common sense from operations as a cop.

Rachel lay still with Curt's weight uncomfortably on top of her as she realized the cause for panic. The traffickers had pulled up next to the Crown Vic. She was trying to remain perfectly still and calm her breathing. Curt pushed the passenger door shut just as the Range Rover came to a stop next to the car.

Curt slowly moved off of Rachel and toward the back quarter panel of the vehicle, staying low. The tall grass of the ravine's edge moved slightly as they moved around. Curt had his handgun out and ready. Rachel's excitement had turned into frightful panic as she realized the severe danger she was now facing. She questioned the commitment she made with Alexis, as this wasn't in the fine print. She focused on the matter at hand and remained perfectly still, lying as low as she could, praying the tall grass was enough concealment.

The Range Rover stopped just on the other side of the Crown Vic. If one of the men got out to look around the car, a confrontation was guaranteed and would turn deadly. Curt looked around for an avenue of escape, but there were only a few feet of tall reeds and grass followed by an eighty-foot drop into the ravine. Looking through the grass into the ravine was like looking into an endless abyss. Taking this route posed its own dangers, not to mention the traffickers could hear their escape and still give chase. He gripped his Glock tight…ready.

The two men spoke from inside the Range Rover. They spoke too fast for Curt to translate properly but he heard the word for lamp or light. He looked over at Rachel. She was lying as low as she could against the ground, frozen with fear. He felt sorry for putting her in harm's way, but she had to learn this was part of the job. However, he realized that an armed confrontation with the traffickers would mean any chance of getting to those enslaved girls would be gone.

A beam of light broke through the passenger side window and the vehicle's interior. Curt slunk down as he stayed in a very low crouch up against the back quarter panel. They were searching the interior of the car with a flashlight. He was glad they had not remained inside.

After the beam of light searched the inside of the Crown Vic, the Range Rover pulled forward sending a sense of relief through Curt and Rachel. But, before they could relax, the hiss of slowing brakes and the unmistakable sound of a car door opening broke the silent night air. Curt stared at Rachel, telling her with his eyes, to remain calm and not to move. She fought every urge to run away as flashes of being trapped in that small dark room as an abducted child came over her, but she stayed still. She had no other choice but to trust Curt.

Footsteps against the gravel shoulder of the road resonated loudly over the mountain like death stalking a fresh soul. One of the traffickers walked and now stood at the front of the car. Curt, still in his crouch, aimed the Glock just over Rachel's head toward the hood of the car, should the trafficker make the fatal mistake of looking a few inches to his left. After the footsteps, there was a long pause. Curt watched anxiously and waited for the man to simply pop out.

"*Es Frio!*" The man said. It's cold.

Curt quickly understood what he was doing. It was something he did as a young patrol officer when responding to alarm activations or possible crimes in progress. The man felt the hood, checking its warmth, trying to gauge how long it had sat there. Someone doing surveillance in the cold night air would have left the engine running for warmth, a cold hood meant that it was probably abandoned or simply out of gas, and, therefore, not a threat.

The one who remained in the Range Rover yelled out for the man to come on and not worry about the strange car anymore. Curt felt that the suspicion of the man wouldn't be easily satisfied until he searched the area thoroughly, so he held a sharp eye through the sights of his Glock aimed toward the front of the car. Suddenly, the same footsteps on crunched gravel headed back toward the Range Rover no longer carrying the threat of death. Curt ducked low and watched the man's feet walk. He shut the door, put the SUV in gear, and quickly left the area.

Curt waited until the Range Rover was out of sight before standing up. He scanned the area, in case it was a trap, but it was clear. He holstered his gun and ran out into the road to see if he could see where the SUV went. The brake lights blurred off in the distance, and he realized he would never catch up with them, and even if he did, the traffickers might recognize the Crown Vic and instantly be on edge, causing them to do something rash in response. It wasn't worth the risk at this point to jeopardize their only lead for saving the girls. He walked back around to the passenger side.

"Are you okay?"

Rachel slowly sat up in the tall grass, gathering herself. She nodded at Curt but with a look of bitter disgust. Curt was unsure if it was with him, the traffickers, or something completely different. He stepped forward to help her up when Melinda's voice came over the comms.

"Curt, we never got the direction of the van."

"Shit!" He looked far off to the west in a futile attempt to find the panel van, but like the traffickers, it was gone.

Chapter 15

The team huddled in the corner of the hotel lobby, formulating a game plan to go after the traffickers. It was early morning, and there was a line of guests checking out, so they spoke quietly to keep their plan from the ears of any eavesdroppers. Curt stood over the huddled team, leaning up against the wall, sipping a hot cup of coffee, still wearing the tan trench coat. It carried a few more battle wounds from the night before. He had managed to doze off for only a few hours since leaving the house on the bluff, so he needed the caffeine jolt.

Rachel looked up from the group at Curt who held a distant stare. In a moment of levity, she asked, "Isn't it about time for a new coat? That one's seen better days."

Louis, shocked at what Rachel said, shook his head slowly, trying to warn her not to continue. Rachel read the shock and immediately realized she had crossed some unknown boundary and erased her smile. Curt ignored the comment and let Rachel slide.

Beth Young walked up and delivered a bag of various flavored bagels with cream cheese for the team. Her eyes were puffy and protested the early morning start. They grabbed up the breakfast and began throwing out ideas to help the enslaved girls that Curt and Rachel saw the night before.

Rachel started, "We don't know where they are being housed since they were taken away from the chalet last night. Unfortunately, we couldn't get any usable information on the van that took the girls or the SUV with the traffickers because of our close call."

Melinda, Beth, and Louis all instinctively shot glances up at Curt behind them, wondering exactly how close the call was, as they were in the van a quarter mile down the road, listening helplessly.

"So, they are just using the house for the 'business' then?" Beth asked.

"Looked that way. Louis, can you and Beth do what you do on the house, see who owns it, lives there, visits…whatever we can find out to try and identify the traffickers?"

"Sure, no problem. That should be easy," Louis answered.

"What if they don't come back?" Curt posed the question to the group. Rachel thought, dejected for a second; she had not thought about that possibility. Curt continued, "Most traffickers like to stay on the move, attracts less attention from the cops that way."

"Well, we're probably screwed at that point, so let's hope they feel comfortable enough to use the house again."

"We should try to follow them again, to see if we could sneak them out? I'm sure it would be too dangerous if we do it at that house." Beth offered as an alternative.

The group thought about Beth's plan. Curt rebutted, "I would think wherever they're housed would probably be fortified with tall fences and barbed wire as well as guarded with more men. I've seen it before with the migrant farms back in Florida. They do everything to keep the 'workers' from getting out. It'll be easier at the mansion with what we know than what we don't."

"Okay, fine," she relented.

Louis was working furiously on his laptop to find the ownership of the house. The thought of losing the trail of the traffickers and possibly their only chance of rescuing the young girls they enslaved caused the group to fall silent.

"Got it," Louis piped up, breaking the silence. "The house appears to be vacant and was a foreclosure taken back by the bank earlier this year. Used to be owned by a South Florida family who apparently couldn't sell it when the market tanked, and they just let it foreclose."

"What do they do? Can you tell that?" Asked Curt.

"Um, hang on. I'll check the social media sites to see what I can find."

"So, if we want to move sooner than later, we should just set up surveillance on the house and wait and see if they come back?" Rachel offered as a solid option for getting back on track.

"Looks like the guy is a lawyer of some kind, looks like personal injury and…the wife is a dental hygienist. Not very nefarious sounding are they?"

"I was just curious. I saw the big guy use a key. They could have someone working in local real estate who would know the house is vacant. Check which bank owns it; see if we can find a connection that way.

"I'll head down to the bank, Louis. Just give me the address of their biggest branch." Beth assigned herself.

With a few strokes of the keys by Louis Melton's bony fingers, he had an answer, "That's boring; it's the First National Bank of Colorado." He looked up the address, and Beth plugged it into her phone's GPS. She excused herself and headed up to her room to change for whatever part she had in mind.

"Okay, so assuming they go back to the house, it would be later this afternoon, so we can spot check the house in case anyone shows up early, and in the meantime, see what we can get from the bank?" Rachel asked.

The group nodded, except for Curt. It was a good enough plan, for now, he thought. He was just trying to think of anything they might have missed.

They agreed to meet back in the lobby in ten minutes. They would drive the Sprinter to the bank and let Curt spot check the house up on the bluff. As Louis folded his laptop and was stowing away the power cords, Curt stepped up to him. Rachel had only taken a few steps away and heard Curt ask a question.

"Did you check today? Have anything?" Curt was more worried than curious for the answer. Rachel eavesdropped more out of curiosity than anything.

"Oh, no. Sorry. I did check, and there was nothing today. That's good right?" He said, holding a helpful grin.

"Yeah, I guess. Thanks." Curt looked down in relief, but a shroud of sorrow followed. Rachel wasn't sure what they were talking about, but it was clearly important to Curt. He walked by Louis and offered a friendly hand pat to his shoulder. A gesture that was a little out of character from his gruff nature, as Rachel had started to learn.

***

Mrs. Priscilla Harvey walked into the First National Bank of Colorado wearing black high heels, an elegant red and black dress that hugged her tiny curves, dangling gold earrings, and matching bracelets that jingled as she sashayed through the lobby. She walked with an air of distinction and hid her porcelain like face behind an oversized pair of dark sunglasses. She pulled the attention of the two male tellers and even the young female teller as she passed through the cavernous lobby over to the help desk centered in a massive, gray stone and marble accented floor.

She explained that she and her wealthy husband were looking to purchase some rental property to vacation in during the winter months. It was a common enough request, and the customer service clerk motioned for one of three people who were sitting in glass-walled offices in the corner of the massive lobby. The one available was a plump, thirty-something, white guy with glasses and a thick but groomed beard. He buttoned his suit jacket, ran his hand over and smoothed his stylish, dark brown hair on top of his head, and then he walked toward the customer service desk.

"Hi, I'm Jack Cauldress. How can I help you today?" Cauldress accentuated the greeting with a devilish smile.

"Hi, Jack. I'm Priscilla, and I'm interested in finding something to purchase for a vacation rental. I wanted to just hire a real estate agent, but my husband, ever so frugal he is, asked me to check with the banks first to see if there were any quick claims or foreclosures I could look at first."

"Well, that's not uncommon these days, so if you would...." Cauldress motioned for Mrs. Harvey to walk in the direction of his office, "Right this way, ma'am."

Cauldress followed the attractive woman in the snug dress and looked her up and down, imagining her without any clothes on for the brief walk to his office. He saw a fellow co-worker admiring Priscilla in the same manner and shot him a thumbs up as he passed by.

"So, Mrs....?"

"Harvey, Priscilla Harvey."

"Mrs. Harvey, what exactly do you have in mind?"

"Well, I'm not into skiing much, not yet anyway, I prefer the warmer locales, but my girlfriends back in LA just won't shut up about the Vail winter scene, so here I am. I'm a big view person though, so maybe something with a view…and big for entertaining, of course!"

"Ah, we have a lot of those. What's your budget looking like?"

"Well, I may have to work on my husband a little bit, but I'd say no higher than five million."

Cauldress's eyes lit up at the huge amount his newest and certainly attractive customer offered, as he could just taste the commission check on this sale. He calmed himself and continued to seek out all the requirements of his guest because there was no way he was going to let this whale of a client get away.

After an hour and many sexual innuendos, Cauldress had the rich Mrs. Harvey eating out of his hands. She was primed and ready to buy one of the bank's many foreclosures, at above the market price, if Cauldress had anything to do with it. He had seemingly narrowed down her search to three houses in the greater Vail area, all prime for social interaction, entertaining, and of course, close proximity to good skiing mountains no matter the skill level.

"Oh my, it's getting close to lunch, and I'm starving. Is there a place around here for lunch?" Mrs. Harvey asked.

"Yes, matter of fact, there is a local favorite of mine, just around the corner. A little bistro just down the corner serves the best Rueben sandwiches in the state," Cauldress added with a flirting smile.

Mrs. Harvey smiled back with a little extra gleam in her stare that Cauldress was quick to pick up on.

"You know what, Mrs. Harvey?"

"Please, Priscilla."

He smiled again, pleased with his charm, "Priscilla, I am hungry myself; please let me take you to lunch."

"Oh, that would be nice; thank you. We can discuss which house we can look at first?"

"Exactly."

Jack Cauldress made a quick phone call as Priscilla Harvey waited by the door. He hung up, grabbed some breath spray, and squirted a few hits in his mouth. He checked his tie in the wall mirror, straightened his hair once again, and left his office. Out of the sight of Mrs. Harvey, he walked by the envious co-worker and gave him a high five as he passed.

"If all goes well my friend, I'll see you tomorrow!"

Cauldress took Mrs. Harvey by the hand and escorted her gentlemanly out of the bank and down the street to the quaint bistro. She donned her oversized sunglasses to combat the bright midday sun but more so because it completed her fashionable ensemble. He talked her into ordering a Chardonnay, which she initially declined because it was admittedly a weakness of hers, and he sat close to her at the round patio table. After ordering lunch, she took a few sips of the wine and downed the whole glass in one final gulp. Cauldress impatiently ordered the waitress to come back and refill the glass.

"So Mrs. Harvey, how long are you staying in Vail, and when will Mr. Harvey be joining you?"

"Oh, I don't know. I doubt he'll come; he always has to work, so he says. But, whatever, I'm a big girl and can handle this on my own. Why do you ask?"

"Oh, I don't know. I think we can find that house you are looking for today, and I was thinking of celebrating with you tonight!"

"Oh, really?" Mrs. Harvey asked, as she worked on her second glass of wine. She swayed ever so slightly from the effects of her Chardonnay. She offered her lunch date a flirting smile. He held her stare and softly set his hand on top of hers.

"Yes, really. I think we have a special connection; don't you agree?"

Mrs. Harvey slid up her large rimmed sunglasses to the top of her head and looked at the man tenderly with longing eyes. She carefully looked over to her right out into the large intersection that the Bistro's patio overlooked, but not locking onto anything specific. She let her hand be caressed by Jack Cauldress while she visually searched the area for something.

Annoyed at the sudden diversion of attention, he asked, "What's wrong?"

"Nothing." She said, quick and surprisingly sober. She slid the sunglasses back down over her eyes.

He slid his hand off of hers and looked out over the intersection trying to understand what exactly she was searching for. His annoyance continued to grow.

"What are you looking for?"

Mrs. Priscilla Harvey set down the wine glass and fished out a sheathed iPad from under the table. She opened up the soft cover and powered the device on. She remained silent as she followed this up by removing a set of headphones from her purse and plugging them in to the bottom of the iPad.

"Here, put these in." She handed him the headphones.

"Huh? Why?"

"Just do it." Jack Cauldress realized that the suggestible Mrs. Harvey had had a quick and severe personality change before his eyes. He looked at the iPad and the ear buds and let his spirit of adventure give him the assurance to do what the woman asked. He put them in, however confused he was and held on to the possibility of the sale going through as well as the sex, if he played along.

She angled the iPad so he could just see the face of the screen. She turned her head back toward the intersection and said, "Go ahead."

"Who are you talking—"

Jack cut himself off as he looked down at the screen. A pretty, blonde woman with a serious look on her face was now staring back at him on some video chat. He instantly liked where this was leading. He smiled at the image as she realized he was on the other end of the FaceTime call.

"Hello Jack, my name is Rachel, and you are going to help us rescue several girls who are victims of human trafficking and prostitution." The arrogant smile perpetually pasted on his face vanished as he listened. "And before you get up and walk away, just know that if you don't want your dirty little secrets to make their way to the local police, or your boss, I think you should just sit there and hear me out. We are watching you from across the street, so nod that you understand."

Images of many misdeeds came flooding through the thoughts of Jack Cauldress. He was ashamed to admit it was a long list. He didn't like where this was going, but whatever was going on, he had to play it cool. He could probably bluff his way through this charade, knowing his secrets were well guarded. However, the fear of the unknown kept him in his seat. He slowly nodded at the pretty-faced woman on the screen. Then he figured they were going to extort him and wanted money from the bank. I can handle this, he thought.

"Good, now just in case you think I'm bluffing, we found your little collection of 'trophies' at your apartment this morning while you were busy trying to get in the purse and pants of Mrs. Harvey."

"Bullshit!" He shouted out, catching the attention of the other Bistro patrons.

"Oh, don't believe me? Let's see, the video collection of all those ladies you seduced, probably after having lunch right there at that same little Bistro, probably used that lame Rueben line on them too. The hiding place in the closet, under the carpet and sunk in the floor..., sounding familiar?"

The blood started to drain from Jack Cauldress' body. His head stirred dizzily in confusion, and he grew lightheaded.

"Ahh, now you believe me. Ready to listen?"

"Okay." He mustered weakly. Cauldress felt lost and vulnerable now that his secrets were discovered, but as this woman on the tiny screen described the exact hiding place of his precious videos, he was frozen in place. The rest of his blood drained completely from his body.

Unbeknownst to Cauldress and before Priscilla Harvey entered the bank that morning, Louis had quick success hacking into the bank's security camera system. Most major banks were going to a system that fed the footage wirelessly to a server off site, and First National was no exception. An off-site server served to combat intuitive robbers who would destroy the onsite recorders in attempts to destroy evidence. Louis was able to breach the firewall and piggyback the outgoing feeds and watch inside the bank. It only took about thirty minutes of watching the three potential real estate candidates to peg the plumpy, faux debonair Jack Cauldress as the possible bank connection to the traffickers. As he worked the eager Mrs. Harvey, the team was able to search through his bank accounts, criminal history, and credit reports before hacking into his work computer, which was done while he had stepped away briefly to grab items off the printer. He was too busy oozing his charm over his potential client to notice a thumb drive with blue tooth capabilities had been inserted into his computer.

Turns out that Cauldress had several fraud arrests in Texas, Oklahoma, and Nebraska. Most were schemes involving real estate scams where he would sell lots and houses that were in foreclosure, or so he let the clients believe until that initial check was cashed, then he went on the run until he was caught and did five years in a Texas prison. It wasn't hard to find his bank employee records either. They were obviously a complete work of fiction.

He was a prime candidate for the inside man for the traffickers, but the team still hadn't found a connection. Rachel made the decision to pull Curt off of surveillance to check out Cauldress' apartment.

Curt made quick work of the cheap lock and deadbolt on the exterior door of the small apartment Jack Cauldress called home. He looked around and found it a messy tribute to bachelorhood. There were unfinished food cartons left on the kitchen counter and clothes strewn on the furniture and the floor. The place had a dirty odor to it that annoyed Curt. He moved around the apartment, looking for anything to connect this man to the traffickers. He searched through the desk computer in the corner of the living room but found nothing but porn sites, gambling sites, and other random nonsense in his search history. He plugged in the thumb drive and had Louis remotely download the contents of the computer to be dissected later. He moved through a small filing cabinet that was stuffed full of paperwork from his old arrests, probation period, and some fictitious documents he had used along the way. Curt accidentally dropped them into the shredder after realizing they were fakes.

"Oops," he said to the empty apartment.

Curt looked around and wasn't getting the necessary vibe from the apartment but had an uneasy feeling he was missing something. When he moved to the man's bedroom, the picture started getting clearer. The bedroom was well put together and had a warm, inviting look to it, something that would be alluring to any member of the opposite sex. It was cleaner than the rest of the apartment by far. The odor of an intoxicating cologne hung in the air; it was a scent that Curt had once worn at the request of his wife. He looked over the contents of the closet and found designer clothes and shoes. He had high-dollar, name-brand stuff that he shouldn't be able to afford as a bank real estate salesman and a convicted felon. Now, this guy felt more promising as the inside connection. The bathroom had hair products, facial cleansers, moisturizers, and all things a self-absorbed man would keep on hand to promote his sexuality.

Curt had gotten a feel for the apartment and relayed his assessment over the ear buds, "He over-emphasizes his appearance. He is very into how he looks. He's probably over compensating for something. It wouldn't surprise me if he carried Rufinol on his person, just in case the opportunity presented itself."

After sitting on the edge of the bed for a moment, the feeling of missing something still nagged. He gave the room a second and third look before he saw it. There it was, up in the vent. He saw the reflection of glass from behind the air conditioning vent. He found something to stand on to get a closer look and noticed the object was a camera lens reflecting the light. It was angled toward the bed, but where did it lead? He lifted a few folded shirts on the top ledge of the closet to reveal a small recorder hooked up to the covert camera. He popped the drive open to see it was empty. He looked under the other items on the same ledge but didn't find what he was looking for. Curt searched for any false walls or hidden compartments but didn't have any luck.

His detective skills took over, and he placed himself in the shoes of Jack Cauldress. Curt stepped down and slid to the side searching the walls behind every hanging picture or wall art in the tiny apartment. He still didn't find it. He looked under the bed again and only found a cache of sex toys.

"Eww," he said aloud.

"What?" Rachel asked with worry.

"Trust me; you don't want to know."

Something drew Curt back to the closet. It was where Cauldress had chosen to keep his covert equipment, so he obviously felt secure keeping it there. He flung the clothes to the side and checked the interior walls of the closet but didn't see anywhere he kept a safe. He looked down and saw a small string that protruded from the side of the carpet inconspicuously. He reached down and tugged at the string, and it lifted the corner of the carpet. He peeled it back revealing a large safe underneath.

"Jackpot, found it. It was in the closet."

"I'm going through his computer now. He doesn't have any passwords saved or anything that looks like a combo to the safe. Sorry," Louis offered.

"It's a combination lock. But...." Curt worked through a theory of the man he had profiled thus far. When no one was looking, he would take the easy way for sure. He reached down to the safe door and saw that the dial was left on 68. Curt smiled knowing he was right about the man and thinking this was too easy. He moved the dial one tick to 69 and pulled at the lever. It clicked loose and he pulled open the little door to the safe to reveal a collection of at least thirty micro-CDs with women's names on them written in marker, cataloged by date. Without a doubt, it was clearly a trophy case the deviant man had been collecting for a while. Curt grabbed the latest one with the name Ines written on it. It was dated three days ago. He moved over to the computer and put it in the disk drive.

After opening the file, he hit play, and the quiet groans of a man came through the speakers as did the whimper of a woman. As the video focused, Curt saw a frumpy, white male with perfect brown hair underneath a younger, underdeveloped, Hispanic girl dressed as a school girl. Her shirt had been ripped away, but a plaid mini-skirt and knee high socks remained. Curt instantly recognized the girl as the one from the house who stuck her head out during surveillance. She had that same lost and hollow look as Cauldress thrust inside her. As the video panned out, as directed by the frumpy man via a remote control, he got a better look at the room they were in. Next to the bed was a window that had the same scenic view he was looking at before coming to the apartment. It was the house on the bluff.

The lunch hour traffic made for adequate background noise at the bistro patio. Cauldress leaned forward toward the iPad screen as his face turned completely ashen and pallid.

"What do you want?" He was sick to his stomach and on the verge of retching. He had listened painfully to the vivid details this woman and her accomplices had learned about him with excruciating precision. They knew he was allowing the traffickers to use the empty house on the bluff as their brothel for sex slaves in exchange for free sex.

The traffickers extorted him for his help, and if he didn't, all his videos, to include the one of him and his boss's wife, would be turned over to the police. Cauldress, a self-serving narcissist, quickly dismissed the idea of going back to prison. He would rather go on the run from the traffickers than face life behind bars again. He would agree to whatever the woman on the iPad demanded if it meant saving his own ass. Rachel gave him explicit instructions to follow and told him to go back to work as if nothing happened. They would be in contact shortly.

Mrs. Harvey took the iPad and yanked the headphones from Cauldress' ears, causing him to jump in his seat. The smooth operator was now a ball of nerves. She packed up the device in her purse, left the check on the table, and with the same elegance she entered the bank, she sashayed her way across the street and next to a large, black conversion van parked on the side. Cauldress watched helplessly as his surefire whale of a client and sexual conquest walked away, leaving him feeling vulnerable and empty inside.

Rachel sat in the Captain's chair as the door to the Mercedes Sprinter slid open to reveal the put together and lithe bodied Mrs. Harvey. She smiled in excitement at the successful operation, and Mrs. Harvey smiled back.

"Good work!"

"Thanks," Mrs. Harvey said, as she removed her sunglasses and carefully pulled off the long blonde wig. She kicked off the high heels with a sigh of relief and climbed in the van. She sat on the bench seat for a moment, and Louis handed over a pair of rectangular rimmed glasses. She took them and slid them on, for she was back to being Beth Young.

Chapter 16

W hy me?" Louis' shoulders sagged as he whined in protest.

"Because you are the only one they wouldn't suspect. You don't look like a cop and do not pose as much of a threat," Rachel answered bluntly.

Louis Melton is an imposing threat in the virtual world, confident and dangerous, but in the arena of real life, he is shy, meek, and insecure. Nonetheless, he was chosen to enter the den of wolves in an attempt to rescue the sex slaves that were taken from their homes with promises of a new life in America. However, Rachel was lying to Louis about her reasoning, for it was much simpler than she explained. Basically, the team lacked options. It was either Curt or Louis, as the only male options on the team. If they sent a female in, the traffickers would not believe she would be in search of sex at a place like that, or they would be too interested and demand to watch. So hopefully with that logic, a skinny, nerdy, and unimpressive Louis would fly under the suspicious radar of the traffickers.

The team gathered up around the Mercedes Sprinter as they finalized their operation. Jack Cauldress showed up as directed and surprised Curt by not making a run for it. He had been watching him at the bank since lunch and followed him to the hotel after Rachel called him with his instructions.

After Cauldress made some necessary phone calls, he reported that the girls were delivered back to the house on the bluff. Rachel tried to convince the team to seize this opportunity and make a move to rescue the girls.

Beth stood up and addressed the group. "I'm all for getting those girls out of that situation, but it's too dangerous. This isn't what we normally do. I think we should hold back and try to retrieve them some other way."

"We may not get another chance. They could move the girls after tonight, and then we'd have nothing."

"We have trackers; we have the equipment to watch them and wait for them to make a mistake."

Melinda spoke up. "I agree with Beth. I think we should wait."

"Okay, you're right about the equipment. But what happens to those girls in the meantime? You have no idea the hell they're trapped in." Rachel was adamant and stood tall as she made her point.

Beth looked down as she imagined each girl being subjected to the sexual depravities of a paying customer. It was awful, but she still felt strongly about waiting.

"I know, but we're not superheroes or anything. They have guns, plural, guns! We should be patient."

"If we're quick and calculated, I believe we can simply steal them from under their noses." Curt stepped forward to defend Rachel's plan. He stood with his arms crossed and looked set on moving forward.

"I'm in," Louis added.

"Fine!" Beth agreed begrudgingly and turned angrily toward Jack Cauldress. Men like him are the reason brothels like this exist.

Jack Cauldress sat inside the van, contemplating his shallow, fraudulent life. His head lowered. He searched for the answer to how he managed to screw up enough in life to be forced into this situation, but this was just one hurdle added to the long list of things he had to do to get by.

Louis lifted his shirt and situated the small body wire. "So, why do we need the wire again?"

"Because the comms we use don't exactly get all the surrounding noise. This wire will be ideal. Plus, I want something we can deliver to the police afterwards."

"Okay, so what's the plan?"

"Okay, you go up to the house with Jack and get inside with the girls. Once you are alone with them, Mel and—"

"Hey, Rachel!" Curt interrupted abruptly.

She furrowed her brow, irritated, "Yes?"

"C'mere for a second."

She looked at the faces of the others, searching for the error she made. She read nothing in their reaction and walked to the back of the van, clueless.

"What?"

"I don't think we should make it a habit to talk about our operation in front of our sources." Curt pointed back to Cauldress. "We use him for what we need and tell him only what he needs to know. If things go bad in there, we don't need some scumbag snitch to make it worse for us. If he knows our plan from beginning to end, he could use that somehow and double-cross us or something. He's not to be trusted by any means. He's with us because of a specific need and nothing else."

Rachel was new to all of this and hadn't even thought about this possibility. Jack Cauldress was a deviant con-man with an unhealthy sex addiction who drugged women to have sex with them. Curt was right; he couldn't be trusted. She realized that Curt was looking out for her and the team's interest and that he hadn't challenged her in front of the team, making her look weak.

"Okay, you're right. Thanks."

"I'll walk him down the street to make sure he doesn't get an itch to back out, and you can brief the team."

"Okay, good idea."

Rachel walked back over to the van and excused Cauldress from the briefing. He stepped from the vehicle, and Curt took him out of ear shot—probably to threaten his life if he deviated from the plan in any way.

Rachel went on with the plan and explained everyone's role in the operation. As they loaded up in the van, a sick feeling bubbled up in the pit of her stomach, and a small wave of nausea came over her. She cracked the passenger window of the Sprinter letting the fresh, crisp, mountain air wash over her face, settling her nerves. Curt was driving and looked over at Rachel leaning into the incoming cool air. He'd seen it plenty of times before but wasn't worried. It was important that she was nervous; it meant that she cared. She cared for the operation, she cared for the team that was about to carry out the mission, and she was realizing that if something happened, it was going to be because she put them there. It was the burden of being a leader.

"It's okay, that's normal. If you weren't nervous, I'd be worried." Rachel looked over and smiled at Curt. It was comforting that he noticed and knew what she was feeling. It gave her a much needed boost in her confidence.

***

The huge oversized door of the house on the bluff swung open. The large trafficker from the day before stood in the threshold, peering down at the two men on the foot of the stairs. To Louis Melton, he was a giant. The mountainous man caused stress by the mere sight of him. He questioned immediately if he could continue past this point in the operation. Jack Cauldress, the perpetual con-man, whose life was built on surviving stress situations on the fly, stepped up to smooth over the introduction.

"Julio, hey man. I got my buddy Brian here. He's cool. We're here to do a little partying. I called Cortez a little while ago, so he should be expecting us." Jack leaned in as Julio the trafficker eyeballed Louis carefully, "He's got mucho dinero, my friend!" Cauldress added the international hand gesture of money by rubbing together his thumb with his forefinger and middle finger.

Louis reached inside of his jacket pocket and pulled out a thick wad of cash. He peeled off a couple of one hundred dollar bills and waved them around to distract the trafficker from the real reason he was there.

"I'm here to get my fuck on!" Louis said, in the creepiest voice he could muster.

Rachel shook her head as she listened through her ear bud comms. "Don't overdo it Louis!"

The muscular Julio moved aside. He was obviously comfortable with Jack Cauldress and convinced that the newcomer was a bona-fide customer. He let them inside. Louis looked around the foyer, trying to quell the rising stress from within and taking a deep breath as the door was shut behind him. The house was sparse, as far as furniture was concerned; obviously it was not lived in. There was a bar set up in the corner of what Louis assumed was a formal room just inside of the foyer. This was where the deals were made, as Jack had earlier relayed to the team.

The room was large and caused Louis to feel small. The polished ceramic tile floors and blank walls made every small sound echo needlessly throughout the house. The ceilings were high and accented with ornate crown molding, and the room was lit by a brilliant, crystal chandelier hanging in the center of the room. It was empty, but Louis could tell the inside of the house was elegant and belied the horrors that were happening within.

Julio escorted them in and asked for their drink of choice. Jack ordered vodka tonics with a lime for both Louis and himself while they stood waiting. Louis tried to look around for the girls but saw no sign of them. The bedrooms were elsewhere in the house, he figured. Jack handed Louis the drink, and he, maintaining his character, took the drink in one gulp. It burned like liquid fire as it rolled down his throat and into his stomach. It tasted like astringent floor cleaner with a hint of lime. It was awful, and his face couldn't hide this reaction. He coughed unexpectedly, drawing the attention of Julio and Jack Cauldress. Cauldress patted him on the back, trying to maintain the cover.

"You okay, buddy?"

"Yeah, sorry. Went down the wrong pipe. Sorry, this is good shit here," he said as he lifted the small glass.

Julio wasn't amused but didn't think too much of the reaction. He'd seen a lot of weak, incompetent men come here and act bigger than they were, but he didn't care just so long as their money was green. A moment later, his partner joined the small group in the formal room. He was a tense and serious man—olive, tanned skin, expensive designer clothes, and excessively decorated with jewelry. He introduced himself as Cortez. He spoke broken English and held the grip of Louis Melton for a moment longer than customary as they shook hands. He stared at Louis, looking for weakness within the smaller man as his firm grip squeezed his hand. It was weakness in character, not physical strength.

"So, you know Jack? You want to party here with us, huh?" he asked with the enthusiasm of a car salesman.

"Yeah! Of course," Louis smiled devilishly. "We've been buddies for a little while. He told me this was a good place to party, so I brought money to play."

"Okay, take off your shirt," he ordered. The enthusiasm dissipated quickly and turned into suspicion as his salesman smile went flat.

"Huh?" Louis was unable to hide the panic, and his voice cracked.

"If you know Jack, like you say you do, and you are here to party…," Cortez paused for effect. "Then you know he is a lying sack of shit only out for himself, and he cannot be trusted. So, Amigo, take off your shirt." Cortez unbuttoned his jacket to reveal the pearl handle of a pistol in his waistband. Julio moved in close somewhere behind Louis because he could hear him breathing.

Louis immediately keyed into the handle of the gun but heard the voice of Rachel trying to coach him along through the ear bud.

"Stay cool; we we're ready for this. Just stick to the plan." She was blind to the subtle threat Cortez posed by showing the gun.

"Sure, man. No problem." Louis set down his empty glass and began unbuttoning his shirt slowly from the bottom. He moved slowly so that he could pull off the ruse without slipping up. Cortez waited patiently as the new customer revealed a skinny upper body that was as pale as the blank walls of the formal room. Jack Cauldress had backed up away from Louis and instinctively found himself inching towards the door in order to make a quick exit if things went wrong. Louis slowly pulled back the sides of his shirt and cupped the body wire within. He had run the wire carefully up and inside of the stitching of the shirt, so it moved naturally with the material, mainly to counter this inspection. The small, flat transmitter was no bigger than his palm and slid into a small pocket sewn in the inside of his shirt. Louis palmed it as he held up the sides of his open shirt showing off his skinny waistline. He turned around to give the traffickers the full look of no wire and no weapon.

"Empty your pockets, amigo," he ordered.

Louis slowly pulled out the contents of his pockets: keys, wallet, with fake ID in the window flap, some gum, condoms, and his flashy roll of cash. Julio sifted through the items carefully and moved from behind the bar to pat down the rest of his body. Louis held his composure while the large, Hispanic man groped him up and down. Not finding anything on the skinny, pale man, Julio stood up and shook his head to the other trafficker.

Cortez studied the new customer carefully and scrutinized him closely. After a minute of internal judgment, he was satisfied.

"Gracias, amigo." His demeanor was back to the car salesman.

Louis smiled, overly relieved that he passed the test. He quickly buttoned up his shirt and needed another pull of the vodka to calm his nerves. He held out the empty glass wanting more. The big guy moved back behind the bar and filled it up. The alcohol chased a sigh of relief, but this time he welcomed the sting in his throat, needing to dull the anxiety.

"So, what can I do for you two tonight?"

"Well, I was thinking—" Louis started but was quickly cut off.

"We want to play two hands for the poker game tonight, Amigo." Jack held up two fingers to the trafficker with a lustful look on his face.

He looked surprised but ready to fulfill the request if the money was good. "Two hands, eh?"

Louis quickly caught on, "Yes, two hands."

Rachel looked over angrily at Curt who heard the same thing she did through the comms. He wasn't surprised. She disengaged hers and turned to the side in her seat, looking at Curt.

"What the hell? Why the hell didn't he tell us about the little secret code there?"

Curt shook his head. He held a look of indifference, only because it was past the point of doing anything about it. He pulled out his ear bud for a moment and cupped it in his hand.

"I told you. This is why informants can't be trusted. As soon as we can, we leave him there or dump him somewhere, and leak his videos to the cops anyway."

"I'm so mad at that piece of crap!" Curt laughed at Rachel's frustrations as they put their ear buds back in.

Louis Melton, aka Brian, pulled out a thousand dollars cash from his flash roll and handed it over to Julio. He waved it off and nodded for Louis to lay the money on the bar. After doing so, Julio pulled a deck of cards from his pocket and withdrew two cards from the top. He set them face down next to the money. Louis looked over at Cauldress for a little direction as to what he was supposed to do. He nodded towards the cards, indicating he should pick them up. Louis reached up casually to the bar and took the two dealt cards, the queen of spades and the king of diamonds.

Jack followed suit and set his money down, also receiving two cards from Julio. They finished their drinks and were escorted down a long hallway to the back of the house. Jack was directed into one room, and Louis was sent to the neighboring room.

"Wait here," said Julio unceremoniously and shut the bedroom door. Louis stepped up to the door and listened for the footfalls leading away from the room. He turned around and bee-lined it for the bedroom window.

"I'm in the room; I think he's going to go get the girls and bring them to me," Louis relayed over the comms. He looked out of the window and saw the gravel side yard of the bluff just outside. He checked for an alarm in the window and found it in the top corner. He studied it for a minute and then fished out a small, magnetic strip from inside the flash roll and slid it in between the window sensor and the fixed sensor on the window frame. This would fool the window frame sensor in to believing the window was still closed when it was actually open. Louis held his breath and slid open the window to test it. When no alarm blared, he knew he'd succeeded.

"Okay, Mel, you guys are on standby. You're doing good, Louis," Rachel assured.

"Thanks…my hands are sweating up a storm!"

Louis waited impatiently and nervously on the bed. His leg was impulsively tapping on the floor, and he stared blankly into the wall of the bedroom. He wished he was back in the virtual world where he felt in control, but it was too late to back out. A moment later, the door opened and two young, Hispanic girls dressed provocatively, one in a sexy, black cat outfit and the other in leopard-print lingerie, stepped in the room for approval. Both had forced smiles that hid their disgust and abhorrence of the current situation. Louis waved them in eagerly. Julio stood behind them and watched them lasciviously as they walked into the room and over to the bed. Louis held up the two playing cards he was dealt and handed them each a card. They took the cards and looked back at Julio, making the transaction complete. The large trafficker shut the door and Louis heard the click of the lock. He looked over and realized the door knob was reversed and the locking portion was on the outside.

The two girls, like it was a matter of routine, moved over to the skinny man and started to rub and grope his body. Louis, unfamiliar with the touch of a woman, especially two at once, shied away and moved away from their advances.

"Hold on ladies. Hold on!"

They backed up with puzzled looks on their faces. They didn't quite understand the physical rejection or the English he spoke.

"Que?"

He looked back at the door, hoping Julio wasn't listening in and spoke in a quiet tone.

"I'm not here for sex. I'm actually here to rescue you!"

His heroic statement was met with blank and puzzled stares by the two girls.

"Repeat what I say, Louis," Curt said, stepping in. *"Estoy aqui para ayudarte."* I want to help you.

Louis repeated the Spanish to the girls. They looked even more confused. They looked at each other for the answer but came up empty. They had been subjected to some odd and kinky requests, but this was just weird.

"Que?"

Curt relayed more through the ear buds, *"Te ayudarte a escapar."* I want to help you escape.

The girl in the leopard print lingerie stepped up; she was ready to believe what the skinny, pale man was saying but remained cautious as this could be a trap set up by the traffickers.

"Policia?"

"No, we are not the *policia*," Louis answered shaking his head. *"Tengo amigos fuera y le ayudara a escapar, para ser libre!"* I have friends outside and will help you escape, to be free!

"Gratis?" Free?

"Si, gratis!"

The two enslaved girls seemed hesitant to believe this skinny and pale knight in no armor was actually there to rescue them. They had been beaten and brainwashed into believing this was the only life they were allowed to live, but something in the man's sincere face seemed to register within the girls. They spoke to each other about what they should do, and Curt steadily relayed what to say to keep convincing the girls to go with him.

Minutes later, a loud knock came at the bedroom door, startling Louis and the girls. Louis thought fast.

"What dude? I'm about to start the party…go away!" He hoped the big guy respected the customer's wishes and left it at that but didn't hear him walk away. Louis quickly jumped on the bed and started to make groaning sounds. The girls watched and quickly figured out what he was doing to fool the trafficker outside of the door, and they joined him in making sounds of ecstasy. The act rivaled any adult film, if only in sound, and the trafficker soon walked away from the door.

The girls seemed to buy into what the man was saying, and he was able to finalize the escape plan with the help of Curt's translation.

"Mel, you guys are up." Rachel signaled, while she and Curt took their positions.

Julio stood at the bar waiting for the gringo customers to finish up with the whores in the back rooms. He was feeling rather horny and wanted his turn after they were done. He was imagining taking care of the same two girls after the skinny nerd was done. Clearly, he was more of a man than this Brian, although he was impressed at what he heard coming from his room during his last rounds. But they were customers, and the girls were told to act accordingly to the customers, especially the ones with a lot of cash on hand. He took a sip of his tequila when the doorbell rang. They weren't expecting anyone else, but business is business.

As he opened the oversized door, he was surprised to see two well-dressed women standing there. The first, a short-haired, black woman in a dark gray business suit offered a courteous smile to the large man, and the second, a rich-looking, little white woman, with long, blonde hair in a slim-fitting dress, white fur coat, and high heels stood just behind her. They were clearly not customers, so Julio pulled the door shut as he stepped out onto the covered porch to find out what they wanted. He looked around suspiciously since Jack Cauldress assured them that this house was secluded and "off the books." He buttoned up his tight-fitting jacket to keep his gun out of sight.

"Hi, I'm Brenda Martin with Rocky Mountain Realty. I tried to call earlier, but I realized there is no phone here. I have a client with me who is interested in looking at the house. I know the timing is a little late, but may we come in? Take a look around?"

At the sound of the doorbell, Louis and the girls faked their climax and subsequent collapse on the bed. He quickly went to the window and looked outside. A quick beam of light from a flashlight in the bushes hit him in the eyes; it was Rachel. He smiled back at the girls and slowly lifted the window, letting the cold mountain air filter into the room. The nearly naked skin of the girls quickly displayed goose bumps from the influx of cool air.

Rachel ran up to the side of the house and stood under the open window. Her presence solidified the promise of freedom the skinny, pale knight had made. They didn't hesitate to go with the pretty blonde woman who appeared out of nowhere, because they didn't care what was waiting for them outside of that window. Anything was better than the hell within. Rachel helped the girls climb out of the window—still dressed in racy lingerie and high heels—and directed them to the thick bushes off to the side of the gravel yard. Curt had found a quick path down the ravine to a neighboring driveway. It was ideal to make their escape with the girls. Curt stood at the beginning of the trail, at the edge of the bush line, and welcomed the girls who had shucked their restrictive high heels and ran across the gravel yard barefoot.

He waved them over and told them in Spanish to hide behind the bush line; they would wait for the other girls to join them. Leopard print started to argue they shouldn't wait, for the price of being caught was too costly. Curt snapped back at the terrified girl and explained that they weren't leaving without the other girls, end of argument. She didn't like his rude answer, but his degree of confidence and control eased her anxiety, and she fought hard against the urge to take off running down the trail on her own. Never mind she was barely clothed.

Louis explained that Jack had two of the other girls in the bedroom next to his. Rachel moved over to the neighboring window and knocked softly on the glass. It went unanswered for an uncomfortable amount of time. She grew angry and knocked softly again. She waited impatiently and thought about having Curt go in and force the issue, but just then Cauldress' face appeared behind the curtains. Rachel waved frantically telling him that it was time to move.

"Let's go!" She hissed quietly.

Cauldress nodded and finished zipping up his pants. He pulled out the magnetic strip as directed and slid it in between the sensors and opened the window. The two girls he had ordered were huddled in the corner in each other's arms, scared at the knock on the window and the presence of the strange, white woman. They watched in utter confusion; the woman was yelling at the customer they were just having sex with.

Rachel ordered Cauldress out of the way and addressed the girls in her rusty Spanish. She shot daggers at Cauldress, scolding him for taking advantage of the situation. She shoved him out of the way and worked on convincing the two girls to leave with her. They were hesitant at first, but her kind face and the sincerity in her promise quickly earned the girls' trust. What convinced them to leave was the sight of their friends standing off in the bushes next to a tense looking white man in a tan trench coat. The girls climbed out the window and ran over to them. Curt asked how many girls were remaining, and they answered that there was one more, Alma. The girls explained that they were kept in an upstairs bedroom while waiting for the customers.

"We have to go get her. We can't leave her behind," Rachel pleaded with Curt. It was more of a directive than a request made to Curt.

"Okay." He nodded in agreement. He told the girls to stay huddled behind the bushes, and he would be right back. He moved over to the window, but Rachel was already climbing back in.

"Where are you going?"

"I'm going to find her. You stay here with the girls," Rachel ordered. Curt saw the sheer determination in her eyes. He paused for a moment, wondering if her abilities matched that resolve.

"Fine…I'll be out here."

After Rachel climbed through, she stood up next to Jack Cauldress. She was disgusted that he would take advantage of those girls, knowing what the team and she were there to do. She lured him in with a sexy come hither look, and he immediately took the bait.

"We got time—"

Rachel felt the satisfaction of hearing the crunch of his balls as her knee smashed against them. The blow sent the pathetic man to the ground, writhing in pain.

"Find your own way home, asshole!" Rachel shoved with her foot for good measure as she snuck out of the room in search of the last girl.

"Mel, how is it going up there?" Rachel, Louis, and Curt had moved fast, but Melinda and Beth had stalled as long as they could, trying to convince Julio the trafficker that they had an appointment to look at the house that was for sale. He had called Cortez downstairs, which played in their favor, drawing both traffickers together while they were able to sneak the girls out. However, Cortez was getting impatient at the intrusion of the two women, and with his impatience grew suspicion of their behavior.

"Are you sure we can't just come in and look around. We'll only be a moment?" Melinda begged in a last ditch effort to continue the stall. "My client here is in from California and is very motivated to buy. It would really help me out if we could just look around, please?" Melinda offered her best flirtatious look to the head trafficker. He thought briefly and looked at the client, a dolled up West Coast lady he wouldn't mind having alone, but he decided that this didn't feel right.

"No, I am sorry. Please move on; no one let me know about this appointment. I can't let you in. Come back later." He was abrupt and shoved his muscled partner back inside the house and shut the door.

As Brenda Martin and Priscilla Harvey walked back to their car in the front circular driveway, they stopped to enjoy the view. However, it was Melinda, shielded from the front of the house by Beth, who quickly spoke into her ear bud comm that the ruse was over, and the traffickers were back inside the house.

"Okay, I'm upstairs," Rachel answered. She had managed to check most of the upstairs rooms.

"You need to get out of there!" Melinda pleaded. Curt heard the update and stood tense, watching the upstairs of the house for any signs of danger. Louis heard the update too and started to climb out of the window and over to the huddled girls.

Rachel ignored the pleas. She was not leaving the last girl, Alma, alone in the hell that she knew well from personal experience. As she searched the remaining rooms, she heard the two men talking, their voices carrying up to the second-story from the front formal room. She caught some of the Spanish spoken between them and believed they were talking about the strange visitors.

As Rachel came to the final door upstairs, she heard some faint music coming from within. She stepped up to the door, hoping the remaining girl was behind it. With a slow turn of the knob, she pushed it open and saw a young, Hispanic girl, no more than fifteen years old, listening to music on an iPod, unaware of her surprise visitor.

Rachel moved inside the room and pulled the door shut. She side-stepped slowly trying not to startle the young girl. Suddenly, she looked up but wasn't scared or startled.

"Alma?"

The girl pulled off her headphones but stayed seated.

"Si?"

"I'm here to help you, honey," Rachel said with compassion and care. The girl looked at her confused, and Rachel repeated herself in Spanish. She reached out for the girl to take her hand and offered a comforting smile to the frightened young girl. She smiled back, but as she reached out to take Rachel's hand, her face turned to one of shock and horror. She quickly retracted her outstretched hand and cowered back in the chair. Rachel didn't understand and begged her to come with her, saying that she was there to help.

Rachel failed to notice Cortez had entered the room behind her. He was holding a nickel plated and pearl handled pistol to the back of her head. Rachel spun around to see the barrel of the gun staring back at her. She backed up half a step before being backhanded across the jaw. The blow sent her falling hard to the floor and stars popping in her peripheral vision. She held herself up on all fours as she nearly blacked out from the fierce blow, but before she could stand back up and fight, Cortez had jumped on her, hitting her several more times with the butt of the gun. She was able to block most of the blows with her hands but was stunned by the ones he managed to land. He yelled at her in Spanish, cursing her and calling her names, demanding to know what she was doing in their house.

Rachel tried to focus on surviving at this point but felt her world closing in on her. The same terrified feeling came over her as when she was trapped in that nightmarish prison as a little girl. She forced herself to focus and avoid going back into the abyss, for her life now depended on it.

"Help, please help; he's upstairs." Rachel managed to get out over the comms. But she didn't hear any reaction. No one's voice came through, no answer, no reaction. She was alone. She repeated her cries for help as the trafficker turned his physical abuse on the young girl also knocking her to the floor.

"Stop! Please stop!" Rachel begged the man for the young girl's sake.

He stepped back over to Rachel and backhanded her once more across the face. Blood filled up the inside of her mouth from a cut sustained inside of her cheek. She coughed and spat blood onto the floor.

He stopped for a moment and yelled back downstairs to the other man. Rachel could translate something about checking the rooms. Still no reaction over the comms. She reached up to her ear and instead of feeling the small, plastic, ear bud transmitter, she felt nothing but her own ear. It was gone. It must have fallen out when she was violently backhanded by the trafficker. She frantically searched the floor but couldn't find it.

Without provocation, Rachel was yanked up by the hair and dragged out of the bedroom. Panic took over as she clawed the floor and grabbed for anything to fight against Cortez. The trafficker was deceptively strong and kept her off balance and unable to fight back while dragging her down the hallway. She felt helpless, a feeling she hated and had vowed she would never feel again.

Cortez dragged Rachel down the stairs. Her feet stumbled underneath her causing her body to hit each step as she was pulled down the stairs. Julio had kicked in the door to Louis' bedroom and found the room empty and the window open. With his gun drawn, he kicked Jack's bedroom door open and found him huddled in the corner alone still recovering from the shot to his genitals. Julio read a pathetic and pleading look on Jack's face and quickly put his thoughts together. Without hesitation, he aimed his gun at the conman cowering in the corner and shot him once in the head for his treachery and betrayal.

"Where are they?" Cortez slung Rachel onto the floor of the formal room at the base of the stairs. He had just gotten the report from Julio that the girls were gone, and Cauldress was dead.

"Where are they, punta? Tell me, or I kill you now!"

"I don't know what you're talking about," she answered, refusing to be intimidated by the men.

"Bitch!" Cortez lashed out, striking the woman again across the jaw and following up with a kick to the ribs. He ordered Julio to go outside and search for the girls and the woman's accomplices. He reminded Julio that they were half-naked women in the cold Colorado Mountains and they couldn't have gone far. He had to preserve the enterprise at all costs.

Rachel took the brunt of the kick in the ribs and coughed out in pain as she gasped for breath. She pushed herself upright and against the back wall next to the bar. She looked up, bloody lip and face, and told the trafficker who stood over her, "Go fuck yourself."

Cortez grew angry and stepped up and put the barrel of his gun to the forehead of Rachel Goodwin. Her body went numb, and only thoughts of her sister came to her. If she was in fact dead, she was about to meet up with Rhonda in the afterlife. She realized she found comfort in the thought of seeing her sister again, whether in this world or the next. She closed her eyes in anticipation. She was calm and ready.

The gunshot was much quieter than Rachel would have imagined. And there was no pain. She awaited the reaction and the divine white light to appear—there was no light or harp music—just an odd movement that didn't register until she realized she was not shot and wasn't dead.

Her eyes opened, but she didn't want to believe what she saw. Julio, the muscle bound trafficker was falling backwards into the threshold of the oversized door. Cortez was turning around to find the cause of the disturbance behind him. He held his gun pointed in Rachel's direction. As Julio fell, an image appeared from out of the blackness and into the light of the foyer. The image moved swiftly and with purpose through the open door. Curt moved with such fluid speed and aggression, his trench coat billowed in his wake, like a caped superhero taking control. His Glock 22 was aimed steady in his outstretched hand as he closed the gap to the trafficker standing over Rachel. Cortez watched in shock as his man fell to the ground. He swung the steel plated pistol around to take aim at the apparition coming his way, but before he could gather his focus, Curt fired a double tap into his chest, knocking him backward. Blood spattered from his chest and sprayed across Rachel's face where she was still sitting on the ground below him. As a reaction of being shot, Cortez squeezed the trigger, sending an errant round into the wall behind Curt, narrowly missing his head. She watched in morbid excitement as the despicable man fell to the cold tile floor, gasping for his last breath and in search of an answer for what was happening. Lying on his side dying, Rachel crawled over to him and looked into his eyes.

She met his stare with a look of satisfaction. It was satisfaction from not succumbing to the terror he tried to impose, not at his impending death. It was a triumph she failed to achieve as a victim all those years ago, and she felt vindicated, to a degree, while she watched the life fade from his eyes. As Cortez lay lifeless on the floor, Curt stepped over him and kicked the gun from his dead hand. He transferred the gun to his right hand and reached down and pulled Rachel up with his left.

"Are you okay?"

Stunned more than anything, she felt the blood returning to her body and outer extremities, and she told Curt that she was okay. He tugged her toward the door, telling her they had to leave before the authorities arrived. Her senses quickly returned as thoughts of meeting her presumed dead sister dissipated. She stopped suddenly and met Curt with a questioning look.

"Alma? We have to go get her!"

"We already have; let's go."

Rachel was relieved and followed Curt as he grabbed her hand and lead her away from the house on the bluff. They ran down the trail to the neighboring driveway. Rachel ignored the growing pains from her injuries and followed Curt down the steep path. Louis had cranked up the Mercedes Sprinter and gotten all the girls loaded up just as Rachel and Curt made it down the trail. They jumped into the van and slammed the side door shut as Curt yelled at Louis to drive. The Sprinter lurched forward and knocked the newly liberated girls off balance in the back of van. Rachel looked back at the scantily clad women holding each other in their arms, trying to comfort one another in this moment, wondering if they had made things worse by trusting these strangers. Rachel felt relieved that all five girls were accounted for, and they no longer had to endure the hell of enslavement. The injuries she sustained during the beating from Cortez started to take effect, but she realized it was worth it to save these girls from a life of torment and misery. They stared back at the heroic woman and finally started to believe that they were truly safe.

Chapter 17

He held his eyes closed as hot water cascaded down his body, hoping to wash away the guilt of taking a man's life. Curt had been a cop for nearly fifteen years and worked on this clandestine team of do-gooder Crusaders for the last two, but he had never taken a life. He had been saving that honor for the man who took his son. The guilt was from the fact he didn't care about the men whose lives he took. They were despicable men doing evil in this world, and he would get over it as soon as the shower ended. He knew the operation was risky going into it, but they managed to rescue the girls from their bondage. However, things went wrong. That was the nature of the job, and one of the reasons they operated in secret, but after this, he wondered how long it would remain a secret?

Curt remained in the shower, letting the steamy, hot water soak into his body. It had been a long night, and it was after midnight. The team fled from the house on the bluff quickly after the shootout went down. A late night call to the Orion Project representative in Denver was made, and they had agreed to make the drive into the mountains to Vail. It was the best thing for the girls freed from their sex enslavement.

The Orion Project was founded to help the victims of human trafficking survive the aftermath of their enslavement. They are victim advocates who excel in their work with human trafficking victims. They have counselors to help the girls realize they were brainwashed from the beginning, starting with their recruitment. The problem for these girls, specifically, was that there would be no arrest that coincided with the rescue of the five girls, mainly because Cortez and Julio were now dead. This meant they may not qualify for the T Visa that is normally granted to the victims of human trafficking. However, as in most criminal enterprises, Cortez most likely answered to someone above. But that was no longer the team's problem. They had rescued the girls and needed to slip back into anonymity. Following the evidence up the food chain was someone else's job.

Rachel was taken back to the hotel and cleaned up. She sported a few bumps and bruises from the ordeal, maybe a broken rib from the vicious kicks from Cortez, but otherwise, she was fine. She stood proud with her battle scars displayed openly as the representative from the Orion Project showed up a few hours after. The deal, greased with a substantial anonymous donation made to the project, was simply to take the girls back to Denver and stick to the story that they managed to escape on their own after some kind of home invasion robbery that left the two traffickers dead from gunshot wounds. Their story was that they were hiding in the back and didn't see the robbery go down. Therefore, they could only offer evidence in the trafficking case against the enterprise employing Cortez and Julio, not to the shooting that led to the men's deaths. Before handing over the donation, written from the secret account of Alexis Vanderhill, the Orion Project rep agreed to those terms and didn't ask questions, but he knew they were lies given the presence of Rachel's injuries and the huge sum of money. Nonetheless, the rep was more interested in taking down the enterprise than how the girls came to be freed. It was more important that they were free, no matter the reason. Rachel agreed and they parted ways.

Alexis Vanderhill was attending a late night fundraiser in Charlotte when Beth Young called her and advised her of what happened. She listened without reaction as Beth explained that three men were dead, but five innocent girls were rescued from enslavement. Alexis maintained her composure for appearance's sake, and after hanging up quietly, she excused herself and made arrangements to leave for Colorado at once. There was some exposure that needed to be minimized. She listened as Beth explained that Rachel thought of calling the Orion Project to help take the girls. Alexis agreed and directed her to call the specific representative and authorized the use of a "donation" to make things go smoothly. Beth could tell Alexis was not happy since her answers were short and forced to sound cordial.

Louis remained in the Sprinter, listening to the police scanner for updates. A neighbor down the hill on the bluff had heard the report of gunshots echo down the small canyon as he and his wife were sitting on their porch, enjoying a cool night outside. He called in the suspicious incident, and when the first officer got there, he found the carnage within.

Soon after, the detectives were called, along with the crime scene unit. The theory of a home invasion presented itself over the radio, but as the detective responded, he asked if anything looked like it was taken. The officer, after completing a cursory search of the chalet, couldn't answer with certainty and explained that the house was empty for the most part, except for beds set up in most of the bedrooms along with sexual paraphernalia, condoms, alcohol, and some women's personal items. This assessment led to the detectives silence over the radio. Louis kept tuned into the radio channel for any additional information.

The messy crime scene was quickly controlled, and the radio had little voice traffic. This kept Louis in the dark about what they were learning from the crime scene. After the detective arrived on scene, he sent someone to the neighbor's house. They didn't see anyone related to the shooting but stated that they had seen a dark colored sedan leaving the house about a minute after hearing gun shots. They offered that they had seen the same car driving around the area earlier in the day and the day before. Louis figured they had seen Curt conducting surveillance on the house and hoped that was the extent of what they saw.

As the radio traffic slowed, Louis used the time to inventory the equipment. He checked the ear bud comms from everyone and noticed that they were short one. He pulled up a program on his computer that he designed to help manage and keep track of the team's communications. He had wanted to install GPS in the ear buds, but that wasn't quite feasible with their size at this time or within his budget. So, he activated each ear bud, starting with his. It squelched as he turned up the volume, which meant it was in the box where they're kept. He went down the list checking each one, and when he got to Rachel's, there was no squelch, even at max volume. But if it wasn't in the van, where was it? It was on, according to the program, so he should hear Rachel talking or doing whatever if she forgot to take it out. But what he did hear wasn't her talking. It was rather strange. It was muffled voices. Maybe she set it down somewhere at the hotel, and it was picking up some random conversation. He clicked on a few filters in his program, and the voices cleared but not enough to understand what was being said.

One of the voices got louder and louder; then Louis knew exactly where the ear bud was.

"There was a void in the blood spatter against the wall downstairs like someone was against the wall when the smaller guy was shot. The guy in the foyer dropped where he was shot, and so did the one in the bedroom. That fucker was executed in there, so there was at least one other person here during the shooting other than the doer. I'd say a woman based on all these lotions and make up." The raspy voiced man sounded seasoned and confident in his observations.

"So, what do you make of this?" another voice asked.

The voice and movement got much louder and clearer as if they were right on top of the ear bud. Louis stared at his computer console wide-eyed and frozen, unsure of what to do, but he felt compelled to keep listening.

"Hmm, looks like blood. A few things knocked around up here," the raspy voice said, followed by a pause. "Looks like there was a struggle up here. See that scuff mark on the wall by the vanity?"

The other voice agreed with him. Louis listened carefully as the men moved around the room.

"What's that?" again the raspy voice asked pointedly.

"What?"

Louis had a sinking feeling he knew exactly what they were looking at.

"This? What the hell is this?" Louis dialed back the volume as the detective's loud, raspy voice filled the van's interior to a near deafening level.

Louis stared at the console, knowing if he made a loud noise the man could hear him as well. He went stiff with indecision.

The detective blew on the tiny tan plastic thing he held in between gloved fingers, "Hello?"

Louis, his mouth gaped open, slowly extended out his hand careful not to make a noise and clicked the ear bud off. Silence fell inside of the van, but he was still afraid to make a sound. He looked around and stared at the box of the remaining ear buds. If they found out how to activate the small earpiece, they would be able to listen in on their conversations and subsequent operations.

Chapter 18

The mountain air was still which left a calm eerie silence to the cool night. Curt felt as if the heavens were looking down at him, watching in judgment as he packed his luggage in the Mercedes Sprinter. It was late, and most everyone in the mountain hotel was already asleep. Louis relayed what he heard from Rachel's ear bud to Curt and let the information digest for a moment. The home invasion theory provided to the Orion Project rep might hold up based on what Louis heard, but if they figured out where the ear bud came from or where it led to, the team's existence would be in peril. They would have to figure something out soon.

Louis left Curt and went back inside to pack up his luggage. They decided they needed to head out as soon as possible. On his way back in, Beth passed him with an angry scowl on her face and made her way toward the van, suitcase in tow.

"You didn't have to shoot them Curt, god dammit! We're supposed to be protecting life, not taking it."

Curt looked up at the seething woman but realized he lacked the energy to argue with her and then looked back down not saying anything.

"No, don't ignore me. You killed those men in cold blood. I knew we should have just waited and followed the girls out and then grabbed them later. But No! You just had to go in guns a blazin'."

Beth shook her head. "Hell, you practically executed them as if you were judge, jury, and executioner, but you have to pay the consequences. Alexis is on her way, and she is not happy."

"What do you want me to say, Beth?" Curt said wearily, his shoulders were sagging from fatigue.

"I think you wanted to kill those men. There would've been plenty of opportunities to grab those girls without confrontation, but you went in without even considering the alternatives." Beth was steaming. "You are dangerous, Curt. You can't go around killing anyone who crosses your path—it won't bring your son back!"

Curt had enough. He threw down his luggage with authority and snapped to Beth, mere inches from her face.

"Listen, you little shit! In case you didn't notice the beating those assholes gave Rachel, which she got before they dragged her downstairs and held a gun to her fucking head, they were going to KILL her. Not be mean to her and call her names or put her in timeout or whatever else your fucked up little liberal mind thinks was going to happen. They were going to kill her! But, do you know why?"

Beth and Melinda had been separated from Rachel after everything went down and hadn't actually seen her condition as Curt described. She got the run down from Louis which obviously lacked the full picture of the truth. She shook her head at Curt, no.

"Exactly...because true evil exists in this world, and people like those men do not care what's right and wrong. They only do what they want, and at that moment, it was to kill Rachel because she was trying to help those girls escape. So I stopped that from happening. Get off your self-righteous ass, and grow the fuck up!"

"Killing is still wrong Curt; we could've tried to talk with them...tried something before you went in and shot them!"

Curt shook his head in annoyance. It was clear he wasn't going to convince her that he had no choice, no matter how the scenario played out. He needed to get away from her before he did something to cause her harm, so he left and headed for the bar. This way he could only harm himself, and the alcohol wouldn't pass judgment.

Beth let out a groan of frustration at Curt's unwillingness to listen to reason and stormed back into the hotel lobby and up to her room.

Rachel had walked up behind the heated conversation between Beth and Curt and overheard the justification for his actions. From her view point, he was spot on and completely justified, but she could see Beth's point. She was never a proponent of violence, but the thought of those girls trapped in that house and forced to perform sex acts on complete strangers for a meager existence sent a wave of hate through her body and down to her very core. She wanted those men to pay for what they'd done and was glad they were dead. She wanted them to be held accountable for the terror they caused, unlike the man responsible for her abduction who got away with his evil. She turned and watched Curt walk into the hotel and sit at the bar alone, still furious.

"Hey?" She followed him to the bar and spoke softly.

He looked over; the bruises were taking form on her cheek. "Hey."

She slid onto the stool next to Curt and ordered a club soda with a lime. After the bartender set down the drink, he refilled the whiskey for Curt and walked over to the far side of the bar to talk to another hotel employee. She looked around the bar and restaurant area. It was empty except for them and the two employees.

"I wanted to tell you thank you, Curt. Thank you for saving my life." Rachel spoke with a soft genuineness that awoke something inside of Curt, something that had been dormant for a long time.

He exhaled and lowered his head in acceptance. It was nice to hear those words. Until she said them, he hadn't realized how much he needed to hear them. She reached over and put her arm around him, hugging him tight as a purposeful emphasis of her sincere thanks. The warm touch of a woman resonated through his body. It had been too long since the last time he experienced that feeling. He closed his eyes accepting the embrace and the connection to another human being. After which, he opened his eyes and looked over at her. They locked eyes.

"You're welcome," he said softly with his own brand of sincerity. As he held her stare, he was reminded of her beauty.

"In that moment, when you came through the door, when he had me on the floor and a gun to my head…." She looked over at the bartender to make sure he was out of earshot, "I wanted nothing more than for you to kill them. Not just for what they'd done to me but for what they'd done to those girls. I'm glad they are dead. I'm glad you killed them."

Curt leaned upon the bar with his elbows propped up on the counter. He turned and looked over his hunched shoulders at Rachel. He could see she was being honest, but it came with a hidden restraint.

"Tell me about your son," she requested bluntly, taking the opportunity of the moment to get to know the man she felt drawn to. He had just saved her life hours before, and there—now—a bond existed between them. It was a closeness that was foreign but intriguing. She wanted to know more about him.

He drained the last of the whiskey and crunched an ice cube in his teeth as he let the request simmer. He looked over at the pretty woman next to him with a thought behind it.

"You first; tell me why you were an alcoholic?"

Shocked at the accuracy of his assessment, she withdrew from Curt. She immediately questioned whether it was worth having this conversation with Curt in exchange for the knowledge she sought. But she realized they now shared a rare bond in this world, so she let down her guard. She wanted to know, but she also wanted Curt to know about her.

"How did you know that? Louis?"

"No. I don't make a habit of looking everyone up on the internet." Curt turned in his seat and looked straight at Rachel. "You ordered a club soda that first time at the bar, and I noticed you carry just a little bit of extra weight, like the alcohol was a substitute for food, and now with no alcohol, the weight has come back."

Rachel felt exasperated and fought through the embarrassingly insulting words only because they were the truth and a hidden secret he was able to find, but his tone implied he wasn't prejudging anything. He wanted to know, good or bad, and she realized this.

Curt continued, "Maybe you were plagued by an eating disorder? You are very pretty and carry a confident sexuality about you, but it's distant…like you purposefully keep that part of yourself hidden."

"Oh…I do?" Rachel took a sip of the club soda to try and hide her growing discomfort.

"Yeah, it shows with the way you look at me. But also, I can see a lot of self-hatred in your eyes, or at least there was at one point. My guess is whatever it is that drives you was probably something pretty damn terrible, and it led you to alcohol and some questionable sex habits. But that's your past, not who you are now."

Rachel held a look, the look of exasperation. Was she really that easy to read, or was he really that gifted at looking into people's souls? Not even the people she considered close friends knew that much about her.

"Am I close?"

"Uh, yeah. Close enough," she said with a dose of humiliation.

She shook off the initial shock from the direct hit Curt landed and explained he was right. She told him of the evil that had stolen her innocence as well as her sister's. Rachel explained the disgust she held for herself as she fought for the reasoning behind why her abductor preferred Rhonda over her, and how that eventually led to a dangerous life of intoxication and loveless, sexual encounters that were too numerous to remember. Rachel talked a lot about her younger sister, Rhonda, whom she feared was dead. Rachel relived her epiphany in the hospital years later and how she vowed to honor her sister by helping others.

Rachel watched Curt's facial expressions as she described the painful episodes in her life which led most people to judge her as weak or a whore, or both. But he simply listened. He didn't pass judgment as was the usual scenario when she opened up about her dark past. Curt was different; she found it easy to talk about her dark secrets as he himself was unfortunately no stranger to the darkness. He knew that when evil entered our lives, it was hard to adjust and deal with it. Most people would fail to overcome its aftermath. But there are a few who make it, and of those who crawl out of the abyss, a black stain remains forever branded on their souls and is nearly impossible to erase. Curt knew this all too well.

"So you joined DCF? To try and help children who needed it?"

"Yeah, and I loved my job. But as you know, they have a lot of internal problems and no teeth to really make a difference. So when Alexis asked me to join, at first I was skeptical, but after seeing you guys rescue Charlotte, I was a believer."

"Yeah, I can see that."

Curt ordered another drink and a club soda for Rachel. She looked for hints of judgment and repulsion to come as an afterthought but found none. He was right; it defined her motivation, not who she was.

"So?" she said coyly, taking an exaggerated sip of club soda. "You think I'm pretty?"

Curt couldn't help but smile at the question. It was followed by a quick laugh at the way she asked with feigned innocence, and he nearly choked on his drink.

"Yeah, I do." The smile disappeared, and again they held each other's stare. He was no longer looking into her soul. He was looking at her. She was beautiful, and he could see so much strength in her character that was built from such a horrendous tragedy and followed by the reckless period of her life. It gave her balance to move forward and fight true evil as they saw it.

Rachel was first to look away. She set her drink down and turned in her seat to face him directly. Her legs brushed up against his. Both noticed the touch, but neither pulled away.

"So…your turn."

He downed his whiskey as he lowered his own guard to share his pain with Rachel. He crunched on another piece of ice as he thought about where to start. He hadn't told anyone his story in years. He hated reliving it. He knew that the team knew most of the facts of Josh's disappearance as it was well chronicled in the *Tallahassee Democrat*. It made a hit in some national media outlets as well. A cop's son going missing was sensational news, no matter the geographical location.

Curt told Rachel of that awful night at the softball complex when Josh was with him one minute and gone the next. He explained that he had been working a case that required him to stay late and away from his family for the weeks prior, so he was looking forward to the recreational getaway with his son who enjoyed being the batboy. He was deluged with the emotions of that night as they came flooding back, and he relived the total devastation only a parent can experience from the loss of a child. Rachel didn't have any children but remembered the animosity between herself and her mother that was caused by how she dealt with the loss of Rhonda. She could only imagine the complete helplessness a parent would experience in that situation, but for a police officer, that would have amplified the helplessness.

"You were wearing that trench coat that night?" she asked.

"Yeah."

"So that's why you keep it on all the time?"

"Huh? Oh yeah." He looked down at his coat. "I want him to recognize me when I find him."

Rachel nodded her head in agreement with the sweet gesture. For his sake, she hoped that Josh would recognize him no matter what, because even though it had been over twenty years, she knew she would instantly recognize Rhonda, even if it were only for a split second.

"Do you have a picture of him?" she asked tenderly. "I'd like to see it."

Curt swirled the remnants of the amber liquor in his glass as he considered the request. He set down the glass and reached inside his coat to pull out the well-worn picture he kept on the dash of the Crown Vic. He held it up as if to inspect it again and then held it out for Rachel. She carefully took the picture and looked at it. It was folded in half, but the front half was of an adorable brown-headed boy smiling at the camera with a toothy grin and dimples accenting the corners of his face. He was cute, happy, and appeared to be full of life. Her heart sank at the thought that he was gone. She looked over at Curt. He hadn't bothered to watch her reaction to the picture. He had seen it so many times in the faces of all the people he canvassed that night and in the days following Josh's disappearance. He was tired of seeing sympathy, because sympathy wasn't getting him any closer to his son.

Rachel unfolded the picture to reveal the rest of the photograph. It was of Curt and a woman whom she assumed was his wife. Both were equally as happy as Josh in the picture. It was a nice portrait of the Walker family. Rachel regretted her intrusion and noticed that Curt was much heavier and rotund in the picture, at least forty or fifty pounds extra. She folded the picture back and handed it to him just as carefully as she took it and wondered if he lost the weight because of stress or not eating, or perhaps a page from her past, being anorexic.

"You've lost some weight?" she asked probingly.

Curt looked down at his loose fitting clothes and then figured she had looked at the rest of the picture and made the comparison. "Yeah, a little," he said, without explanation.

Rachel suddenly recalled the image of Curt walking through the hotel lobby just two days before with sweat dripping off his very athletic and attractive body. "From running?"

"Yeah, it helps with the stress of everything, but I could care less about the weight; I was running for something else."

"What?"

"Nothing…it's stupid."

"No, c'mon tell me. We're bonding here, in case you didn't notice. It's not stupid. I'm sure."

"Bonding, huh?" Curt smiled.

"Yeah, c'mon." She scooted over to the edge of her stool and shoulder bumped Curt playfully to coax his answer out of him.

"I've imagined finding Josh a thousand different ways, but my fear...," Curt paused, "my greatest fear is that I will find him, but he'll be just out of my reach. I had nightmares after he was taken that I was chasing the man who took him but couldn't catch him. He was always just out of my reach, and I was too tired to go on and was forced to give up. The next morning, I started running. There's no way I'll ever stop chasing after him. I can't."

She was amazed at the dedication Curt put in place for finding his son. She saw the determination in his eyes and believed that he wouldn't stop until he found Josh. She wanted to know.

"Do you talk to your wife much?" She glanced down at the gold ring on his left hand.

He turned on his stool, looking across the bar at the selection of liquors, seemingly avoiding the issue surrounding his relationship with his wife. He stalled for a moment but felt compelled to answer. He looked down at his left hand and thought about his wife, Tracy.

"Every so often she calls, just to check in, but otherwise not much." He explained. "She'll never say it, but I know she blames me for Josh's disappearance. I could see it in her eyes when she arrived at the park that night. It was blame and disgust, like 'how could you let this happen?'"

"Does she know what you're doing, exactly? You know, with the team and everything?"

"Not really. But she knows I had to do something. I couldn't just go back to our life without him, like nothing happened."

"I can imagine that sort of thing takes a toll."

Rachel could see the pain in his eyes as he relived his own hell. But unlike hers, his was on-going, and he lived it with each and every passing day. Her heart ached for him. She reached up and rubbed his back, consoling him. He looked back at her with gratitude in his eyes. He turned back to the whiskey and downed the rest of the alcohol in a big gulp, holding half in his mouth to savor the burn. He could feel the effects taking hold already.

"You know that's not the answer, right?"

He looked back at the empty glass and smirked.

"Yep."

"So why continue?"

"It helps me sleep. It gets me through the times when I feel completely helpless."

"What do you mean?"

"It means, my kid is out there lost with some faceless monster that I hope I have the pleasure of coming across in a dark alley one day, but until I do, I have no idea where to look. What am I supposed to do? Stop looking?"

Rachel shook her head. His tone turned angry. This notion clearly the motivation for all those destructive nights when hotel rooms were left in shambles.

"No. How does a parent ever stop looking? So that's why I joined this…" He searched for the words to define the group but settled sarcastically on, "team."

"What if he's…you know?"

"Dead?"

She nodded, trying to tread lightly.

"Do you think Rhonda is dead?" he asked bluntly.

She was taken aback for a moment at his question, thinking he was mocking her but realized he was trying to make a point. No one had ever asked her that before, and it gave her pause. She thought about it, leaving her own sadness and anger aside.

"Yes, unfortunately I do."

"Is that because you feel that way in your heart?" Curt had twisted around in his seat and faced Rachel, waiting anxiously for an answer.

"Yes, it is." She hated to admit it out loud.

"Well, I feel in my heart that he is still alive, and I have to hold on to that sliver of hope or else I will fall apart and completely let go. I know the only reason I haven't hurled myself off a cliff or jumped in front of a train is that I truly believe he is alive. I have to. I would give anything to see him for just one moment and to know he was alive and safe, and that it was not just some feeling. It's the not knowing if I'll ever get the chance that keeps me in this hell."

"I hope you do find him one day."

He smiled back at her, wishing his instincts were right and Josh was alive. Her support surprisingly meant a lot to him in that moment as he felt the connection grow. He wanted to stay in that moment with Rachel, but the bartender reminded them the bar was closing. He wanted to order another but looked at Rachel instead. She saw the battle waging inside of him and knew the feeling well. She remained silent, knowing he had to make that decision for himself.

"One more?" the bartender asked.

Curt held the stare of Rachel Goodwin, and without facing the bartender, he declined the drink and put down cash to settle the bill. Rachel smiled at the small victory for her new friend. She knew it was a hard choice to make but was glad he did. As Curt stepped away from the bar, she noticed a small medallion hung loosely around his neck. She recognized it immediately.

"St. Anthony, huh?"

Curt, unsure of where the question came from, looked down and saw the pendant exposed on the outside of his white shirt. He normally kept it underneath his clothes, but it had managed to fall out as he moved away from the bar stool.

"Yeah, it's kind of a good luck charm."

Rachel and Curt kept talking as they walked from the bar down the first floor hallway.

"Alexis gave it to me when I first met her at some fundraiser for missing children in Tallahassee."

"That when she recruited you?"

"Yeah, pretty much."

"Well, St. Anthony was the patron saint of lost items, but many think he was the saint of missing children as well. As your medallion symbolizes, he is carrying a small child, who many say is the young Jesus Christ. He faced all life's difficulties and still heard the call to love and forgive. He looked after the needs of others and dealt with crisis, no matter how big or small, and he remained steadfast with the trusting love of God."

Curt had never heard such elegant words used to describe a patron saint, but listening to her, it was clear why Alexis chose it and why she chose to give it to him. He let Rachel's words settle in. Until then, it was just a trinket and a focus for nervous energy.

She added, "Pretty fitting for what we're doing; isn't it?"

Curt nodded. "Catholic school?" he asked, adding a little levity to the moment.

"Yep, six long years, through high school."

Neither of them noticed that they had walked down the first floor corridor and were currently standing outside of Rachel's room. It felt like the awkward ending to a first date, complete with the anxiety that normally accompanies the less than confident.

Silence fell on the couple in the empty hallway, forcing them to address the awkward situation. Curt nervously looked around as his mind was buzzing in thought but remained speechless. Rachel began to twirl her ponytail that was lying in front of her shoulder. Both were clueless as to what to do next.

Curt moved the half step toward Rachel as her back was to the door. She stood still, not shying away from the approach and put her hand softly on his arm in acceptance. She felt her heart beating rapidly as he gazed down into her eyes. She saw the desire in his eyes earlier in the night as they were trading their tragic stories, but she had put it aside because she had ruined so many past relationships by engaging that desire too early. She liked Curtis Walker, but after a near death experience, where she was saved by his last minute heroics, she couldn't help but be drawn to him. She wanted him. She stared up into his eyes, willing him to make the first move.

Curt stood frozen, unsure of himself, but he wasn't ready or willing to walk away. He stepped even closer, pushing his body up against hers. She welcomed his touch as he put his arm around to the small of her back and pulled her against him. She melted in the warm embrace of his strong arms, and she instinctively reached her arms around his neck. She closed her eyes in anticipation of his lips on hers. He closed his eyes too as he met her supple lips with a soft kiss and held it there while their surroundings seemed to disappear. Time stood still as they held each other close, not as teammates, friends, or even lovers, but as two people who, in that moment, needed each other.

She was the first woman he had kissed, other than his wife, in twenty years. She was gentle at first but turned more assertive as her hands started to explore the rest of his body. Curt felt himself being steered to a point of uneasiness but didn't want to stop either. He hadn't seen his wife in over two years and wondered if she had moved on or even found comfort in another man. He had just left her back in Tallahassee in the search for their son and hadn't been back since. He didn't know where that left their marriage or even if there still was a marriage.

Curt held her tight in his arms and kissed her back with fueled passion, needing her warmth in the world of cold darkness. Suddenly, Rachel stopped and pulled away but held his stare with longing eyes, telling him that she wanted to continue. He opened his eyes and looked down at her, half expecting to see Tracy. There was a slight shock as it was Rachel's pretty but bruised face looking back.

She pulled out her hotel room key and slid it in the door reader with urgency. It beeped and flashed a small, green light unlocking the door. She opened it with an inviting smile. She bit the corner of her bottom lip and nodded toward the room. Even amidst the injuries to her face, she was a very sexual woman and incredibly attractive. His heart thumped loudly, nearly jumping through his chest. He imagined what Rachel would feel like as he made love to her, and although he wanted to make that a reality, he stopped at the door and bowed his head.

"I want to…but…."

Like the alcohol he consumed to help him get by in his miserable existence, this wasn't the answer either. He needed more than just sexual gratification to feel whole again. His stain covered too large an area of his soul.

Rachel smiled back at his refusal with only mild disappointment mixed with respect. She exhaled letting out her own sexual energy and leaned back against the door, holding his gaze. She was actually glad he took the moral high road and stopped before they continued in the hotel room. She wished most of the men in her previous life would have been as strong-willed and done the same.

"It's okay. I understand."

"I'll see you in the morning."

"G'night."

"Good night, Rachel."

Curt headed over to his room and disappeared within. Rachel stepped in and leaned against the door as it shut, reflecting on the moment that had passed and just smiled to herself.

Chapter 19

Detective Edgar Rankin walked away from the house on the bluff, ducked under the crime scene tape, and shoved off the attempts from the gathered news reporters who had caught wind of a deadly shootout. "No comment" was his mantra as he ignored the distraction of the inquisitive and found the way to his unmarked car. He took the final drag of a cigarette and finished a thought while he exhaled. He looked back at the scene and tossed the finished cigarette to the ground. He yelled out for his partner, a junior man ten years younger, to hurry up. His heavy and raspy voice echoed off the walls of the bluff.

The morning sun peeked over the eastern ridge of the mountains, sending rays of warmth down into the heart of the small mountain town. Rankin and his partner stopped at a local coffee shop, grabbed a dozen glazed donuts and a gallon of hot coffee for the rest of the squad, and headed back to the police station. It was going to be a long few days, and there was a lot of work to do.

Rankin addressed the squad and wanted to get the rest of them up to speed. He requested that the crime scene tech deliver a CD of pictures from the crime scene to give them the visual tour of what they'd been working. With the help of the junior partner working the computer, he had the gruesome images displayed on a LCD television mounted to the conference room wall.

The senior detective led the squad on the photographic path of the bloody crime scene, frame by frame. He started through the front door, and the dead bodies of two unidentified Hispanic males distinguished to the squad by the "big one" and the "smaller one." The "big one" was lying on his back a few feet inside the doorway with two bullet holes in his chest and a black semi-automatic handgun just out of reach of his hands. The "smaller one" was deeper inside the house in a formal room to the right of the entrance way. He too was lying on his back with gunshot wounds to his chest and a chrome handgun a few feet away on the tile floor. A large pool of blood had collected underneath his body as a result of a bullet severing his aorta, the detective surmised.

"And we don't know who they are?" someone asked.

"No, no IDs and nothing so far when we ran their prints." The junior detective turned in his seat at the computer to address the squad.

The next few images were others of the formal room, and he skipped over a few shots to get to the blood spatter on the far wall closest to the body of the "smaller one." He told the junior detective to enhance the image on the wall. He stepped up to the television screen and pointed out the void of blood on the wall. He concluded the aorta had been severed by the bullet, and he assumed it exited his back which had caused the blood to spray out on the wall. He pointed out the break in the spatter that defined the void. He paused a moment as something churned within. He stepped back and ordered the junior detective to pan the image outward. As he made the view broader, he saw it.

"See that?" he said excitedly. "See it, right there?"

The squad squinted and stared at the picture on the television, waiting for the image to become apparent. Of course, Rankin had been around for a while, and collectively, the rest of his squad had the same experience, so they kept quiet as they were unsure of what they were supposed to be seeing.

"It's a head!" The junior detective spoke up again from the computer.

"Yes, it's a head. There was someone either sitting there or kneeling or doing something at that level when the 'small one' got zipped."

Ahhs followed by questions and speculations filled the room as Rankin's theory was swirling around in his head. He settled the room and got them back on task as the images continued. He resumed the slide show and turned the angle around in the formal room and showed a close-up of the bullet hole in the wall next to the entrance.

"Return fire?" someone asked, clearly reading the angle of the shooter was the direct opposite of this round.

"I think so too. We found five casings in the room, two near the entrance and one close by the 'small guy,'" Rankin answered.

The action of the shooter was pretty much a consensus to this point in the investigation, but Rankin's face held skepticism. He remained silent as he continued the briefing.

Images leading from the formal room flipped by quickly as the view moved down a hallway behind the open stairway and led into a bedroom. It was a tidy room with no discernible disturbance containing a bed and a small night stand. The squad questioned why he slowed down the pictures, but the next image answered their concerns.

"This is Jack Cauldress." Rankin said as the next image clicked over to show a man slumped over on his knees with an apparent gunshot wound to his head. He was half-way dressed, and Rankin added that his wallet and expensive watch were still on him. There were a few sexual paraphernalia items found in a drawer during a search, but nothing else stuck out. Rankin read a few of his team's faces, seeing questions and confusion. He knew the feeling.

Detective Rankin asked the detective to give out the known history and any intelligence on Cauldress. He read of his arrest in Texas for the fraud, suspicion of other frauds in other states, and his job at the bank that tied into real estate.

"We sent some uniforms over to his apartment and found it ransacked."

Surprise and conspiratorial theories spewed forth within the conference room. Rankin explained that nothing from the apartment looked like it was missing. All electronics, valuables, and other high dollar items were left behind, but he mentioned the unlocked and opened floor safe in the closet. They had found it empty and were left with only speculation as to what was inside.

The questions from the squad flooded the room which Rankin quelled quickly. "There's more!" he said, silencing the room.

The presentation of images continued to the bedroom adjacent from where Cauldress was found. It was a mirror image of the first, but no dead body. It too, was neat and tidy. However, the bed was slightly messed up, and the window was left open. Rankin agreed that didn't make sense since the shooter clearly came in through the front door. The visual journey made its way to a back stairwell leading up to the second floor. Upstairs was just as sparse as the rest of the house with a couple of empty bedrooms that the detective flipped past without concern. The view went down to the end of the hallway and into what was assumed to be the master bedroom. Inside were several bags of women's clothes, make-up, jewelry, and personal hygiene products that begged the obvious question, whom does all of this stuff belong to? The detective moved through those images and stopped at a small blood stain on the floor by the bed.

"What was in those bags?" one detective asked.

"Let me guess…more sex toys?" another inquired.

"Yep," Rankin finalized.

"So, the house was a brothel or something?"

"I'm thinking you're probably right," Rankin agreed. "I think there was probably a girl, a prostitute, up here and that she's the void on the wall downstairs. Then the shooter took her with him. Maybe it was about her and not a robbery?"

The squad discussed the ownership of the house and quickly discovered its connection to the First National Bank of Colorado. They weren't surprised to hear that that was where Cauldress worked. Rankin assigned two detectives to follow that angle of the investigation and see what skeletons in Cauldress's closet, literally, had come out and triggered the death of Cauldress and two others.

Rankin allowed the team a quick break as he withheld the last complication from the chaotic crime scene. He shot a knowing glance at his junior partner wondering how it would go over. Once the team settled back in, he grabbed their attention and emphasized the importance of what he was about to say.

"I want to show you guys something odd. I've worked my share of scenes and never found anything like this before, so here goes." He pulled a small, tan, plastic-looking lima bean, packaged in an evidence bag, out of his pocket and tossed it on the center of the table.

"I'm not sure what that is, but we found it upstairs in the bedroom with the bags near the blood stain on the floor."

The squad leaned forward in their chairs to examine the small piece of evidence. One curious member reached over and took the bag for a closer look. He pulled it within inches of his eyes and then passed it along.

"An earpiece," he offered confidently. "It's a small transmitting and receiving earpiece. I saw some Special Forces guys use them on some missions in the Army."

Rankin absorbed the detective's conclusion and agreed as it made the most sense. However, as he digested the information, he wasn't sure how it fit into his theory and realized this created a myriad of questions.

"How can you...?" He stopped for a re-thought. "Can you turn it on? Use it?" Rankin asked.

The detective picked up the evidence bag and manipulated it again in his hands.

"I'm not sure how. It looks like it is intact, but it may be accessed remotely."

"Okay, so how do we go about that?" Rankin added a degree of frustration to his tone at his own technical deficiency.

"I'll get up with the tech guys and see what they can do."

"So what the hell does that mean? What do you think really happened?"

"I'm not sure, but I have a feeling that the earpiece is the key to finding out who was responsible for this."

At the tail end of the briefing, a forensic tech popped her head in the room to provide an initial assessment of what she'd been working on. She explained that she found at least ten sets of fingerprints to sift through.

"Ten?" Rankin's harsh voice unexpectedly hit an octave higher.

"Yeah, there were at least four we found around the bar in the formal room, mainly from the high ball glasses. And up in the master bedroom, there were at least five sets that I could see off the bat—mainly from the vanity and in the bathroom. A few more sets were in the bedrooms downstairs. I'd say ten from the initial look. It'll take me the rest of the day to determine if they're the same or all different. So I'll compare them to the victims first and I'll await suspect names and let you know what I find."

"Fuck...ten? That puts a wrinkle in things," offered the junior detective.

Rankin quickly piped up, "Not really. It makes sense actually. How many bags were upstairs?"

Another member quickly looked over his notes and answered, "Five."

"Okay, so there you go; five girls, five different sets of prints. That leaves the three dead guys, eight, and then two offenders. That's good, but that means we have five witnesses out there and unaccounted for."

Detective Rankin nodded. He saw how daunting a task this case was quickly proving to be. To track down five unknown witnesses, most likely prostitutes unwilling to talk to the police and to identify two gun toting victims who weren't in the system and then to find the suspects—and who the hell left the earpiece behind? It was a list that epitomized the old question in detective work, "Who done it?"

Rankin excused the team as they left for their individual follow-up assignments and sat quietly alone in the conference room. He pulled out a cigarette and put it in his mouth. He stopped himself from lighting it. Smoking inside the building had been banned for years, but he remembered the time when he could. He thought about all the evidence on the scene that seemed to leave more answers than questions. He had to remain confident that the answers would come soon enough.

"Detective?" A kind-faced woman, with the title "administrative assistant" on her desk, poked her head through the doors of the conference room.

"Yes, Karen?"

"There is a man on the phone from Denver; says he's from the Orion Project? And says he has information on the homicide you guys are working."

Orion Project? He asked himself, not finding an answer within. "Okay, get a number, and I'll call him back."

The haggard-faced detective left the investigations division and walked through the lobby of the police station where a small throng of media reporters was awaiting a statement. Rankin ducked them but quickly drew the attention of a young, skinny reporter with thick rimmed glasses claiming to be from the *Rocky Mountain News*. The reporter attempted to gain his attention by putting his hand on the detective's shoulder. He remembered seeing him at the crime scene some ten hours before. Rankin sloughed him off, ignored him, and walked outside, lighting up a cigarette.

He took a long, slow drag as he felt the warm, autumn sun beaming down on his tired body. He let the smoke fill his lungs and exhaled, enjoying the nicotine fix that he'd been craving. He fished out his cell phone and dialed the number for the guy at the Orion Project, hoping he wasn't wasting his time. But he remained positive and hopeful about the potential the phone call had, knowing that informational calls such as these, this early in the game, usually meant they were credible.

"Detective Rankin?" a man's voice asked on the other line.

"Yes. I was told you have information on an investigation I'm working?"

"I believe I have five witnesses to your homicide."

"Okay, I'm listening."

Chapter 20

Louis Melton slipped out of the lobby of the Vail Police Department after removing the tiny listening bug from the lapel of the detective's jacket. With the finesse of a pickpocket, he had snuck the bug on him as he left the crime scene earlier that morning without his noticing. The detective had been too annoyed with the reporter's questions to notice he was placing a microscopic transmitter under the lapel of his jacket.

Louis found a quiet café within range of the bug and listened to the briefing held by the senior detective. He eavesdropped on Rankin's briefing, using headphones and giving the appearance he was listening to music. He learned a lot about the investigation and needed to update the team who had left for Denver earlier that morning. As he jumped into the rental car, he placed a call to Alexis who placed him on speaker phone.

Unlike the dingy, bare-walled conference room of the Vail Police Department, Alexis had reserved a much more comfortable board room on the eighth floor of the Coloradan Hotel in downtown Denver for the team to hold conference.

"Hello, Louis?"

"Yes, I'm here."

"Okay, so what do they know? How bad is it?" Alexis showed her concern as she stood at the head of the table instead of sitting. Instinctively, she bit at her nails, a sure sign she was worried.

Through the speaker phone, Louis's whiny voice filled the small meeting room as he relayed the facts as they were given by Detective Rankin. He made sure he mentioned the call from someone at the Orion Project just before he left the police station. The team took a collective gasp as they heard about the call. They delivered the human trafficking victims to a safe haven as planned, and that's what really mattered. For the team to continue to exist and move forward with the mission, this potentially deadly problem must be resolved. While that notion simmered, Louis continued about the evidence left behind and the numerous fingerprints that were found. When he told the team the detective keyed in on the earpiece Rachel lost during her attack by Cortez, she winced at her potential mistake and how it could cost the team.

Alexis excused herself from the meeting to make a phone call to her contact at the Orion Project. The broken deal made her upset. She hissed through the phone at her contact but learned that the contact's supervisor had gone behind their back after learning about the shooting. They had overheard the interviews of the girls and matched it up with the news coverage on television and put it together. It was out of the contact's control. They argued briefly about the arrangement they had agreed upon, but ultimately, the damage was done. She blamed the breach of contract on the political aspirations of the supervisor who wanted to make a name on the sensationalistic story surrounding the rescue of the girls. However, the contact reassured her that no names of the team would ever be mentioned. Alexis hoped that was true.

"Remind me to cancel that check," Alexis said under her breath as she re-entered the meeting.

"So what do we do now?" Beth asked, looking at Alexis.

"Well, we have to keep monitoring the investigation to see how close they get, but we should probably move on like nothing happened," Alexis offered. She searched the room for any dissidence and read the displeasure of how the operation went down on the faces of Melinda and Beth. She looked at Rachel and excused the rest of the team. She wanted to hear from her first-hand the sequence of events from the rescue in Vail. She would hear from Curt later.

The team left the meeting room to find lunch as Rachel stayed behind. She felt like she was in the principal's office after being caught smoking in the bathroom.

The shrill of Alexis's phone came from within the briefcase at her feet. She reached down and pulled it out. She read the caller ID, and her shoulders sagged as she recognized the number.

"Shit!" She said this before answering the phone with the best and the most courteous voice she could manage. Her tone hid the loathsome feelings she had toward the caller.

Rachel and Curt, who now stood outside the room, were both curious as to who the caller was and what he was calling about. Given the timing of the incident the night before and her adverse reaction, they both knew it wasn't good.

They listened as Alexis seemed to deceive the caller who was asking questions about her visit to Denver and the shooting the night before. Alexis denied the two were related and explained her presence in Denver was to visit a sick friend who had quickly fallen ill and that anything else was merely a coincidence. She managed to sound convincing, but her face held a look of skepticism as to whether or not it was working.

After a few minutes, Alexis hung the phone up and glared over at Rachel and then on to Curt.

"That was Tony Mason wanting to know why I was in Denver." She filed her phone away in frustration and then with complete sarcasm asked, "Can this get any better?"

Curt met her look with equal worry on his face, for he knew the name as well. Rachel looked back and forth between Alexis and Curt, trying to figure out who Mason was and why his calling was a bad thing.

Curt answered as he saw Rachel waiting, "He's a dick reporter from L.A. who has been busting her chops for almost a year now about her possible ties to a secret team of Crusaders who operate outside the law."

"Holy shit, really?"

Alexis continued biting at her nails as she was lost in thought.

Curt continued, "He managed to get one of our re-connects to talk, but they didn't say that much initially. But Alexis' name managed to come up, and he jumped all over that because he knew her through the newspaper circles. Needless to say, we reached out to that family and they managed to get the boy to recant before any real damage was done. He's smelled blood in the water ever since."

"So he could blow everything out of the water for us?"

"Pretty much. And the problem is that's what he wants to do. Totally expose us," Alexis answered. "However good he is, he has nothing concrete on us. For now. But that could change, so let's just move on. Rachel, are you ready?"

"Um, yeah."

With patience afforded to Rachel, Alexis listened as she told her how the operation was put into place on the fly and the reasoning behind such haste. They had moved fast but carefully with each step. Rachel continued explaining about putting Louis Melton undercover posing as a "John" and using Melinda and Beth as a realtor and her client for a distraction while she and Curt snuck the girls out of the house. Rachel emphasized that the only reason she decided to alter the plan and go in the house was because not all girls were accounted for. Rachel backed up her decision for going in and reiterated that she would have done it again given the same circumstance. Rachel cited her experience as a child as motivation and why she wasn't going to leave those girls in the house, no matter the danger. Alexis nodded, agreeing, as she was well aware of her tragic past.

Rachel divulged to Alexis that she thought she was going to die at the hands of the traffickers if not for Curt. She begged Alexis not to impose any kind of punishment on him and said she would accept all responsibility. It was a gesture not out of her character and one of the prime reasons Alexis had recruited Rachel to the team in the first place.

"I'll do whatever I need to do to keep the team going."

"I know, but the violence is what brings the attention, and he knows that."

Rachel thought about the tortured man she had kissed the night before after he had saved her life. He was no longer a complete mystery, and that made her feel closer to him. It was difficult to look at him when they first arrived in Denver with what happened the night before. As she sat down in the meeting room, Curt made it easy for her as he greeted her with a warm smile, as if to say, "Everything will be okay."

"Fine. But it was necessary in this case." Rachel got up and left the meeting room. Curt was waiting just outside, sipping on a hot cup of coffee, and standing anxiously in his trench coat. They locked eyes with the same tension as the night before, but the unanswered question still lingered as to what last night meant.

"Come on in, Curtis," Alexis said. He walked in the room and took a seat next to hers at the head of the table.

"You know this exposes us, and Mason calling me now proves that. It doesn't help that the supervisor at the Orion Project is bringing those girls forward. I was hoping there would've been a comfortable grace period before that actually occurred, but it doesn't matter now. Apparently, he got at least one of them to talk about what really happened last night and is putting them in touch with the detectives in Vail. Let's hope they can't identify you and Rachel by name. I'm not happy about the prints, and it will take some serious hacker magic from Louis to make that go away. Plus, the thing with the earpiece is unsettling."

"I'm not going to make an excuse because there is no need. I did the right thing. Those guys were going to kill her, and I don't have to justify myself to you."

Alexis' head snapped up, and she glared at Curt. She had watched him in self-destructive mode for the last two years and gladly cleaned up his messes without question—mainly because he was truly gifted in their pursuit of finding missing children, but his words dug deep into her heart.

Alexis spoke slowly and softly but purposefully at Curt, trying to remain calm. "No, you don't. And I believe that you had no choice in killing those men. If it had to be Rachel or those men, I'm glad it was Rachel who was spared. But what you fail to realize is that there is a greater good here, and I can't have you jeopardizing that in any way. I will protect it no matter what, and if that means I have to sever ties with you, then so be it."

Curt instantly thought about Josh. He had been on a personal rampage looking in all corners of the country for his lost son with nothing to show for it. The hope of finding Josh one day was the only thing keeping him going, and unfortunately, he felt that hope dwindling fast. He knew the best chance of finding Josh was with the help of the team Alexis had put together, and the possibility of his being excused from that team left him empty. The last ounce of control in his life was about to slip away and be lost in the tumultuous whirlwind that surrounded the deaths of two human traffickers. His body started to go numb.

"Don't take this away from me." He realized just how much he needed the team.

"I'm not, Curtis. I'm protecting you, and I promise it's only temporary. Mason will probably be on the hunt soon, so we need to move."

He ignored the tear, letting it roll down his cheek and fall to the floor. He was frozen in his chair. He had been to countless towns and cities looking for Josh and ended up finding other lost children in his place. He proudly brought them back to their parents' loving arms where they belonged. However, it was not enough to wash the stain from his soul.

"So, now what?"

"You lay low. You can help monitor activities from the van, but I don't want you involved. Where is your gun, the one you used last night?"

"On me. Why?"

"We should secure it someplace safe, don't you think?"

Curt didn't see the point of storing it somewhere. If the Vail Police managed to find him for questioning, he would want the gun with him, for he knew he was justified and wouldn't hide beyond that. He also realized that running from the scene had made him look guilty and thus, was why Alexis wanted to secure the gun.

"I'll take care of it," he said, begrudgingly.

"Thank you Curtis."

***

Louis Melton arrived in Denver shortly after lunchtime and met up with the team, except for Alexis and Curt, at the hotel. After finishing up with their food, they figured the best medicine for the climactic drama hangover from the night before was to move on and continue with the mission. They discussed the next step and how they would head for the lower Midwest, starting with Oklahoma City. They would head out first thing in the morning.

"That's some serious bullshit, that guy at Orion ratting us out like that. I mean, Alexis gave them a huge donation, and this is the kind of thanks she gets. I think that's pretty awful," Beth complained.

Rachel stopped eating her lunch and addressed Beth. "Well, I don't like it either, but when you think about it, the guy is just looking out for the best interests of the girls."

"How you figure that?"

"Well, they need that special kind of visa right?"

"Yeah, the T visa."

"Well, by talking to them and getting the truth, they take the first step toward getting that visa; it assures them the safety they need when you think about it."

Beth did think about it but still didn't like it. Melinda looked over at the young girl and her pouty face.

"She's right Beth; they are only looking out for what's best for those girls. They don't really care about what we are doing. So you can't blame them."

"Whatever."

"Do you guys know who Tony Mason is?" Rachel asked.

Beth snapped her head up at the mention of the name. Louis glared wide-eyed in grave concern as Melinda waited for the follow up to the question before reacting.

"Why?" Beth asked.

"He apparently called Alexis just now. He asked about why she was in Denver and if it was related to the shooting in Vail."

"Shit!" Beth and Louis said in sync with equal amounts of concern.

Melinda chimed in, "He's been chasing us for the better part of the last year. You stay clear of him no matter what, and we'll be fine. Alexis is very good at covering her tracks, so let her handle that guy her way."

Rachel's head popped up over the table as she caught Curt stepping off the elevator. He saw them in the hotel restaurant and diverted toward the group as he suddenly realized something. Rachel saw sadness. There was an even deeper sadness than normal looming over him.

Curt walked straight up to the table and skipped any pleasantries. He glared down at Louis who was chewing a large bite of his cheeseburger with an unsaid expectation. He looked up, puzzled at what the man in the trench coat wanted.

"Anything come in this morning?" He asked with a degree of desperation.

Melinda and Beth excused themselves from the table and Rachel stayed. Her body was just now feeling the full brunt of the eventful night before, and she didn't feel like moving unless it was necessary. Louis figured out what he was referring to and rushed his chewing to answer Curt.

"Yes, a white male, but he was too old by like four years," Louis answered. Curt nodded and the desperation lifted for the moment, and he walked away.

"So, what's that about?" Rachel asked inquisitively.

Louis had already crammed another oversized bite of his burger in his mouth, so she waited impatiently for him to finish.

"Dead kid report," he answered with a mouth full of food and between exaggerated chews. He continued stuffing another french fry in his mouth to join the burger.

"Huh? What's that?"

"Oh, that's just what I call it." Louis wiped his mouth and looked around for prying ears. "Basically, I have been able to spy on the NCIC, AP wire, VICAP, and a few other databases to learn when a dead kid's body is discovered somewhere. You know, like they went missing for so many years and were then found dead somewhere."

"Okay, I see what you mean now. So he's waiting to see if his son shows up on the report, right?"

"I guess so. He asked if I could do it shortly after he joined our little merry band of misfits."

"And you give him the report every morning?"

"Yep. Every morning." Louis took the last of a gigantic bite of his burger, filling out his cheeks like a nerdy human squirrel.

Rachel thought about the torture each morning must bring in anticipation of the dreaded query and whether or not that would be how he learned of his son being found. It was truly awful, but then she thought of her own hellish past and the anguish she dealt with each day.

"Can you add one more to your search?"

Chapter 21

The next few days were spent trolling around Oklahoma's capital city and went by at a tortuously slow speed for Curt as he was confined to the back of the Mercedes Sprinter, figuratively handcuffed. He had managed to stay away from alcohol since that fateful night in Vail when he took the advice of Rachel Goodwin. But the liquid escape beckoned his tormented soul when the night grew quiet, and he realized just how alone he was in the world. His body ached as he concentrated on keeping control and not lashing out and destroying everything within reach.

The team had no luck finding any of the lost. All their potential targets were accounted for legitimately. That's how it would go sometimes, but putting that in perspective, it was a good thing. Morale of the team had taken a hit from how things panned out in Vail. They were trying not to get caught up in the wake of the investigation and focused on moving forward. The team seemed just to exist, not prosper.

During the downtime, Beth researched the traffickers and was able to link Julio and Cortez to a dangerous drug cartel with ties in Juarez, Mexico. She connected phone records from Cortez's phone, which mysteriously disappeared from the crime scene, thanks to a chaotic scene and a borrowed Crime Scene Investigator's jacket. From there, she was able to find connections to other trafficking locations and similar brothels in Florida and Texas. She sent anonymous tips with pertinent details and descriptions in conjunction with phone records to those jurisdictions to make the needed connections in the case. She provided the same information to the Vail police as well, hoping they would focus on the criminal enterprise over the murders. It was a gamble, sending help to the investigators, but ultimately, right is right—a life lesson that Beth was trying to grasp.

Louis routinely checked in on the investigation in Vail to keep tabs and to watch for any exposure of the team. He managed to get into the police records' management database and see that no queries were made of the team members directly, which was a good sign. He was able to set up a flag on all their names and aliases in case they were discovered and cross-referenced in the database. With the help of Beth Young's research, in the form of an anonymous tip, the investigators were able to identify the two dead traffickers as illegal aliens and establish a basis for an investigation into their enterprise. This was corroborated by the link to Jack Cauldress and the sex video he had of one of the girls performing a sex act at the house. That too was sent anonymously to the Vail police. The rescued girls proved to be the most damaging as far as exposure to the team was concerned. However, they only provided descriptions of the skinny John that went by the name "Brian" and the heroic woman, nameless, with the blonde ponytail that fought off the traffickers and aided their escape with the white man in the trench coat. It wasn't much to go on, but Louis could attest to the resolve of a determined detective, Curt being the best example of how something as little as a name could yield huge results.

Remarkably, the story had been quelled in the media after the first sensationalistic shock of the shootout broke. Louis was able to find some emails that were sent back and forth from the detective to his supervisors and someone in the local FBI office as to the extent of the human trafficking network they had uncovered. Thanks to Beth and her research, they quickly put a lid on everything to protect the rest of the investigation into the human trafficking that stretched over three states. This was evident as Tony Mason had yet to produce a follow up article to the shootout and his calls to pester Alexis increased.

The third day of fruitless attempts was winding down. Curt grew more and more anxious at the snail's pace. He wanted to be out there looking and leading the way, hunting for the lost. Out of respect for Alexis, he remained on the sidelines for now. But this day stood out amongst all others and crept by even slower. It was the anniversary of Josh's disappearance, and his thoughts remained solely on his missing son. It was to the point where Curt needed the sting of alcohol to distract him from the reminder.

Images from the night Josh went missing flashed through his mind. He relived the incident once more and felt the full range of emotions all over again. From the joy of having his son hanging out with him for the night to the bitter misery of knowing he may never see him again. He was exhausted. He thought about his wife, Tracy, and the look on her face when she learned of Josh's disappearance. The blame in her eyes had always been too much for him to handle, and it drove a wedge through their once strong, loving relationship.

As dusk approached, the sun hung low hovering over the vast plains of the Midwest, casting beautiful, purple and orange hues on the underbelly of the cloud blankets above. A brisk wind swept through as the team exited the van and walked up to the hotel. Another day had passed without knowing where his son was or what had happened to him. The guilt and anger began to boil inside the bowels of Curtis Walker. There was only one way to silence this pain. He turned around and started walking toward the restaurant across the street that was advertising an extended happy hour until closing.

Rachel saw where Curt was headed and called out for him, wanting to change his mind. He simply turned and looked back at her helplessly.

"You don't have to." She put her best inviting look on her face, hoping maybe they could pick-up where they left off in Vail. She offered another bonding experience over coffee instead of booze, but his look of suffering let her know that was not an option. He continued toward the bar in complete shame, wallowing in self-pity and pain.

"Curtis! Curtis!" Louis' whiny voice called out excitedly from the open door of the van and across the parking lot. He held a sheet of paper in his hand, waving it around purposefully. Curt looked over at him and grew annoyed by the hacker who was delaying his desired drunken stupor.

Louis was genuinely excited, and his demeanor carried the promise of good news. Curt's mood quickly changed as faith managed to find its way back into his heart. He was hesitant to acknowledge its presence because it had been cruel over the last three years, but one look at Louis' face made him hurry back to the van. He strode past Rachel who watched eagerly with anticipation.

"What is it?" he asked.

With a brief impromptu ceremony, Louis slowly handed over the printout to Curt, letting him read the information firsthand. Curt read the page, and Rachel could see energy and determination fill his face. He transformed before her eyes as hope prospered. He was not the same broken man he was just moments ago in search of a bottle. Whatever was on the paper was the cause. Rachel felt his excitement vicariously.

"It's a lead man…it's a lead!" Louis said enthusiastically, as Curt finished reading the page.

Curt looked up at the skinny man and broke a small smile but kept his mind rolling in thought. Not that he was known to be talkative in the first place, but Curt was speechless. Rachel stepped up and looked down at the sheet, trying to read what it said.

She looked down at the page and read the Crime Stoppers' logo across the top. Just underneath the logo was a heading, Missing Persons, and the name on the tip was Joshua Walker, the city—Tallahassee, Florida. It was information on his son. She looked up in joyful anticipation and read the eyes of Curtis Walker, a father in search of his lost son. She looked back down and kept reading.

Under a section designated for a narrative, she read:

Caller stated that after seeing the news about the boy's disappearance on this date, she believes she saw the missing boy at the Governor's Square Mall with an unknown white male yesterday. Caller stated the boy got into a silver Honda Accord with the license plate of SX444. Caller was positive that it was the same boy, only slightly older.

"Curt!" Rachel called out in excitement for her friend and to grab his attention; she hugged him from the side.

"Yeah…um…I have to go. Now."

Curt bolted off running back toward the hotel without saying anything further to either Rachel or Louis. Both knew the importance of the information and thought nothing of the abrupt exit. They looked at each other, hoping that the new information would pan out for Curt's and ultimately Josh's sake.

A moment later, the black Crown Vic sped past the Sprinter with a purpose. Rachel and Louis were still standing there as they watched the car race by. Curt wasn't about to waste any more time.

Chapter 22

Although the gauge of the speedometer held steady at 80 mph, Curt's mind was running at light speed. All the intricacies and details of his son's disappearance moved to the front of his consciousness. He was still able to recall most of them in the first few hours of the long drive home. The only other train of thought that broke through was what he was going to do when he found the man in the Silver Honda. Fantasies of heinous, blood curdling torture came to mind. Being this close seemed to enrage him beyond the point of murder, and he wanted the man who took Josh to suffer, just as he had for the last three years. He realized it didn't take much thought or pre-meditation to shoot Julio and Cortez, as the human traffickers were ready to take Rachel's life. He didn't gain satisfaction from killing those men. It was either Rachel or them, and he had made peace with his decision, but he knew he would find pleasure in taking the life of the man responsible for kidnapping his son.

A horn blared off to Curt's right, pulling him back in from his vengeful reverie. He glanced down at the speedometer and noticed he had pushed the Crown Vic up over 100 mph. He let up off the accelerator and tried to keep himself in check. He drew in a deep breath and blew it out slowly, trying to calm down. He told himself to focus. He looked around at his mirrors, looking for any highway Troopers hunting speeders, but there were none. As he checked the rearview mirror, he locked eyes with himself and saw desperation staring back. Exhaustion too. It had taken a toll on his body and mind over the last three years.

Holding onto hope is the hardest aspect of loss. Hope grips your entire being with a promise of one day being whole, and it won't let go, perpetuating the suffering. It would be so easy just to move on and ignore the possibility that Josh would someday return, but Curt couldn't bear the thought of moving on without his son. He would search to the ends of the earth for one last chance to be with Josh—no matter the cost.

Three years had passed since Josh was taken, and he thanked God for the tenderhearted victim's advocate who remained on the case back in Tallahassee. She had assured him that the local media would do a news story on each anniversary of his disappearance. It paid off today. This Crime Stoppers' tip was the first tangible lead since the incident occurred.

Curt searched through his memory of the case and couldn't recall anything about a silver Honda. He remembered a few vehicle descriptions from the canvass at the softball complex, but nothing was consistent enough to focus on. He tried to ignore the sinking feeling he got after thinking about the tip. He knew when new information like this surfaced, it was likely a misidentification and altogether just a case of misunderstanding. The likelihood of some random person seeing a missing child, fugitive, or other key component of a cold case was extremely rare, and the colder the case was, the higher the odds. He tried to focus on the positive aspects that the lead held and the promise it brought.

The pang in his bladder was growing more annoying as he pushed the Crown Vic straight through the eastern half of Oklahoma then Arkansas, and soon he was about halfway through Mississippi. He was making excellent time, but as a distraught father, he couldn't move fast enough. He had always imagined getting news such as this Crime Stoppers' tip while out on the road with the team and he had known he wouldn't hesitate to drop what he was doing to return to following Josh's trail. But, now, he knew he needed help.

He pulled out his cellular phone and dialed a number without taking his eyes off the road.

"Hello…Curtis?" Louis picked up on the first ring.

"I need you to run that tag and give me everything you can find."

"Um, sure. I already have and sent it to your email. I see you're almost in Alabama. You are flying my man!" Louis sounded impressed and hoped the humor hid the fact that he was tracking Curt's phone.

"I guess I am. You sent it already?"

"Yes. Didn't you get it?"

"I haven't checked. Find anything?"

"Well, yes and no; the tag the tipster gave didn't come back to a silver Honda. It came back to a silver Chevy Tahoe. Kinduv a big difference right?"

"Shit!" Curt felt like he was gut-punched, and the sinking feeling returned exponentially. Louis was right. It was hard to mistake a Honda Accord for a Chevy SUV.

"Yeah, no silver Honda. So I ran all the similar characters in the tag given assuming they missed one or it was lost in translation. So the email is a compilation of all the similar tags that came back to cars that look similar to a silver Honda, all in the Tallahassee area."

"Okay, anything stick out?"

"I haven't had time to vet each one, but nothing seemed to stand out. Do you want me to widen the search? Surrounding counties?"

"Yes, I don't want anything to slip through the cracks."

"Not a problem."

A silence fell on the line. Curt could see Louis sitting in the back of the Mercedes Sprinter, at the helm of his computer station, working feverishly for him and ignoring his duties for the team.

"Thank you, Louis." Curt had a sincere tone in his voice.

Louis rarely heard that from the man in the trench coat and was quickly overcome with pride. He couldn't stifle the grin on his face but realized Curt couldn't actually see him, so he let it go.

"Anytime."

Curt hung up the phone at the same time the engine of the Crown Vic started to sputter. Panic set in as any hurdle could prove too costly in catching up with Josh's abductor, but then he noticed the needle on the fuel gauge was past the "E." He looked up and praised the timing of the upcoming exit with at least three options for gas.

As he pumped the gas, Curt took the break to read Louis' email containing all the license tag possibilities. He had not only provided all the alternatives to the tag and similar matching vehicles but also provided a list of the registered owners to include their photo, criminal history, and a last known address for each person. There were nine total potentials, and Curt liked the odds of one of them being the kidnapper whom the tipster saw with Josh at the mall.

Curt studied the list of nine names and focused on their faces, trying to recall that awful night. He strained his memory and forced their faces into his psyche, but nothing stuck. However, it would stand to reason that the kidnapper would have taken great strides to keep out of sight.

As soon as Curt was back on the road, he noticed that Louis had sent him another email. It also had an attachment and the subject read, "God Speed." He clicked on the attached file and held the tiny screen up so he could still keep his focus on the road ahead. It was another list of the same names but with an addition after one of the entries. It was a narrative cut and pasted into the email. He recognized the format. It was from the record's management system from the Tallahassee Police Department. He used it regularly as a detective. The information was collected from all police contacts and reports. He read the narrative that Louis had added. It was under the name Justin Hooks.

The entry was from an FIR (Field Interview Report) dated a week before the tipster saw Josh getting in the silver Honda at the mall. It read:

While on patrol, I observed a silver 2004 Toyota Camry traveling eastbound on Apalachee Pkwy operating with no brake light on the passenger side. I conducted a traffic stop at the intersection of Blairstone Rd and Apalachee Pkwy for the equipment violation. Hooks was the driver and sole occupant of the vehicle. Hooks appeared nervous, and upon running his driver's license, I learned that he was a registered sexual predator. I conducted a consent search in the interior of his vehicle but did not locate any contraband. However, it should be noted that in the backseat, Hooks had a new Xbox gaming system and new games that targeted young children as well as new clothes for a young male approximately 10-12 years of age.

Hooks stated that he had just purchased the items from the mall and they were for a relative who lives elsewhere in the state.

Hooks allowed a search of his person and nothing was found as well. When asked to search Hooks' trunk, he declined consent, so it was not searched. Photographs were taken of the items which were not confiscated.

I contacted Hooks' probation officer and advised him of the items found in Hooks' possession, and the

*probation officer stated that he would follow up with
Hooks and possibly violate his probation.*

Curt could feel blood boiling in his veins as he read the Field Interview Report on Justin Hooks. He engrossed himself in the report to the point that he ignored the road and didn't notice the Crown Vic suddenly shuddering violently underneath him. He looked back at the road and realized he was driving on the shoulder of the highway at nearly 90 mph. He jerked back the wheel to correct but noticed traffic was at a stop because of some crash up the road. If he continued, he would slam into the back of the car, possibly killing them and himself. He quickly pulled the wheel back to his left staying on the grassy shoulder of the median and applied the brakes to slow down. He dropped his phone and gripped the steering wheel with both hands, holding it steady over the bumpy ground of the median. He passed several other drivers who were clearly frightened by this maniac passing them uncontrollably. As soon as he was able to slow the car, he held the brakes until the car slid to a stop on the wet grass. He ignored the yells and honks of the passing motorists and caught his breath. He fished out the worn photograph of Josh from the interior jacket pocket of his trench coat and placed it back on the dash. He stared at the boy with dimples, combed, dark brown hair, and a wide smile that looked back at him. He smiled back. He had to give all of his attention to getting home safely for Josh's sake. He was too close to allow something so stupid to erase all his efforts and allow his son to remain among the lost.

When traffic cleared up, he pulled back into the traffic lane and held a steady course for home. He allowed his thoughts to move back to Justin Hooks. He'd never heard of him or recognized his face, but the fact that he had items for a young boy no less than a week before the tip came in, infuriated him to the point of madness. He realized, as did Louis, that he drove a silver Toyota which is mistaken quite often with a Honda in the eyes of a witness. He quickly glanced back at the report on his phone and read the address Hooks had provided to the officer during the stop. He recognized the address, and he pictured it in his mind. He knew the neighborhood, and it was within a mile of Tom Brown Park. His breathing grew shallow as his rage boiled within. Curt knew his first stop would be at the front door of Justin Hooks.

170

Chapter 23

As he came into town, it was just after noon. The skies were a dull gray, windy, and wet with intermittent rain softening the ground and casting a somber feel for an early fall day. Curt didn't bother making any stops, visiting any friends, seeing Tracy, or even asking for back-up. He headed straight for Hooks' place. He'd kept his badge for just this purpose. It was the spare key he needed to get into places he couldn't otherwise.

He pulled down the cul-de-sac of duplexes where Hooks' house was located and reconnoitered the area. The duplex sat near the end and backed up to a small patch of woods which was the southern boundary of a nearby neighborhood he used to patrol. Curt found a spot to watch the duplex from behind another parked car. He fought every urge to go storming through the door and beat Hooks to death, but he held back for the small possibility that Josh was held elsewhere. Killing Hooks would then destroy the only link he had to finding his son.

The silver Toyota was not there. Curt spent an hour stirring anxiously in the driver's seat of the Crown Vic. It was too quiet. He had grown accustomed to the unnecessary chatter in his ear from Louis or the amusing ruses that Beth and Melinda put on for the requirements of the operation.

After no activity in the cul-de-sac, Curt slipped out of the Crown Vic and walked down the sidewalk to the end near Hooks' apartment. The yard was manicured with small, trimmed, modest foliage that required minimal upkeep. The duplex was painted tan with brown trim, and a small one car garage sat in front. The oil stains on the driveway told Curt that the car was normally parked outside of the garage. The front door was closed, and after looking around for any onlookers, Curt disappeared to the back of the duplex in search of a concealed place to enter. As he crept by the side of the duplex, he passed by a window. It looked into the kitchenette area, but he couldn't see anything through the tiny slits of the blinds. He continued to the back. His blood was pumping furiously through his veins, and his breathing was fast and forced. He stepped up on the small concrete patio that led to French doors and looked inside. He saw a living area that was sparsely decorated with just a couch, a television set, one book shelf, and a computer desk in the corner. He noticed on the floor there were wires to a gaming console strewn out. There were two controllers. He followed the wires away from the TV and noticed a large, bean bag chair. Curt sidestepped to get a clearer picture of the object to the side of it. His eyes widened in anger as he saw a smaller, bean bag chair, meant for a child, beside it. He was going in.

The lock to the French doors was simple. He pulled out his pick set to open the lock, but Curt couldn't control his breathing as he stood at the back door. The thought of his son being on the other side of the hollow, cored door and thin panes of glass was overwhelming. He had waited so long for this moment, yet he had trouble focusing on the task at hand. He exhaled and looked down at his hands. They were shaking uncontrollably, and the pick set was trembling wildly. Picking a lock, even the simplest of ones, required finesse, and his nerves were too shot to continue.

"Fuck it!" he said out loud. He stuffed the pick set in his trench coat pocket, took a step back, and kicked the French doors open, splintering the wood frame into pieces. Instinctually, he whipped back the side of his trench coat and withdrew the Glock from his hip and stared inside for any unexpected resistance. After hearing and seeing nothing, he moved inside, stepping through the busted door frame into the living room area. He looked and listened. There was nothing beyond his own heartbeat thumping in his chest.

The apartment was plain and ordinary, and like thousands of other ones, nothing stood out immediately. He moved around the small room and down the short hallway that led to a bedroom. He stormed through the closed door and found an empty bedroom. It too was sparsely decorated but tidy and orderly. He sifted through the closet, searched under the bed, and looked in the bathroom. Nothing. No signs of Josh.

He moved on to the second bedroom of the apartment, and his heart nearly stopped at what he found inside. Strewn on the bed and the floor was clothing appropriate for a young boy. None looked familiar, but Curt was sure the kidnapper would have found more clothes. While searching the room, he inhaled deeply through his nose, hoping to catch the familiar scent of his son, trying to find anything to validate the Crime Stoppers' tip—but nothing. He ripped open the closet doors to search inside but only found a few toys and a couple of suitcases. Josh was not here.

The garage! He remembered. Curt nearly walked through the walls to get to the garage and kicked open the door leading to it without checking to see if it was unlocked. The door slammed against the near wall and stood open, revealing a cluttered, filled garage. It was filled with boxes stacked on top of boxes, old furniture turned upside down on top of other pieces of furniture, and a small designated area for the washing machine and dryer. It was jam packed, nearly touching the ceiling with only a tight space to navigate around.

"Josh? Josh?" Curt cried out. No answer. Only silence.

He stepped into the garage and started to check the boxes. Some were labeled kitchen, some labeled office. He read: utensils, sheets, books, plates, clothes, baby clothes. Curt squeezed his narrow frame in the tiny pathway, knocking on the boxes, shaking some and moving them around to gauge if they were full or a façade of some kind. He made his way around back where he had started, without finding any sign of his son. Panic gripped him with a vise-like strength, squeezing his last shred of hope.

"Goddammit, Josh!!!" Tears began to fall from his eyes. He took another look at the massive collection and saw that the boxes formed some kind of wall around the center. He wrenched his neck up and lifted his body up on his tiptoes to get a better look at the middle, but he couldn't see what was behind the mountainous walls. There was only one way to find out.

Curt grabbed the top box on the nearest stack and pulled it down, sending the box and its contents crashing down and scattering on the floor. He knocked more over and climbed up them, ignoring the fragile nature of the contents. He clambered over the stack and pulled at the next box and the next until he pulled himself to the middle of the pile. A large dining room table sat at the epicenter of the cardboard mountain. Curt found himself kneeling on the top. A tiny cavern under the table was perfect for someone to hide, so he sat down and kicked with all his strength at the stacks moving them away from the table top. The faint garage light was blocked by the tall stacks and couldn't penetrate underneath the table into the small cubby. Curt quickly flipped over to his stomach and dove under the table into the blackness.

"Josh?"

Nothing. He reached for his flashlight as he strained his eyes looking into the void. He clicked the flashlight to life and shone the beam into the black. Nothing. Nothing was there. He wondered if he was somehow looking into his own soul.

Curt tore down the entire cardboard mountain in a frantic attempt to find answers but only came up with more questions. After exhausting himself from the fruitless search, he walked back into the second bedroom where he found the boy's clothes. He sank down the side of the bed, crying for his lost son as the last piece of hope faded to nothing. But before the darkness engulfed him completely, he would wait for Hooks to return home in the event Josh was with him.

He pulled out the St. Anthony's charm from under his shirt and began to rub the small medallion as he sat alone. As he stood up, his attention was pulled to the night stand on the other side of the bed. It was a picture of a pretty, brown-haired woman with a small boy standing in front of her. The picture was something he failed to register during his initial search. He moved around the bed to get a better look at the picture just as the vibration of his cell phone buzzed in his pocket. He pulled out the phone as he reached the picture.

"Hello?" Curt answered without looking at the caller ID. He picked up the picture and studied it closely. The boy resembled Josh, but it wasn't him.

"Curt, it's Louis. I take it you are at Hooks' place?"

"Yeah. He's not here!" Curt's voice cracked as he stifled the anguish.

"Well, okay. So you went through the place then?"

"Yeah. What Louis? Spit it out."

"It can't be Hooks."

"What do you mean, can't be?"

"Hooks was living in South Florida at the time of Josh's disappearance. I was able to look at his probation records and his qualifying offense happened down there. He served a prison sentence and didn't move to Tallahassee until six months ago after a judge allowed him to move. He was living in a halfway house in Ft. Lauderdale when Josh went missing."

"But, but…the boy's clothes in the room? The close characters of the tag…it has to be it."

Rachel Goodwin was listening in on the phone call as it was on speaker phone. Louis looked at Rachel for guidance. Both could hear the desperation in Curt's voice. Rachel could see that he was blinded by the loss of his son and failed to see any other alternative. She wanted him to find his son as much as he did, but she had to remain objective in this mission—for his sake. She had learned that from Curt and hated that she needed to point it out when he was feeling so vulnerable.

"Curt, we looked into Hooks a little more. Turns out his younger sister and her son have been staying with him for the past month. She just divorced the boy's father, and they moved up to Tallahassee to stay with him temporarily. Apparently, she is an avid Facebook poster and gave all the juicy details online. The clothes are for her son, not Josh. It must have been her son that the tipster saw, not Josh. I'm sorry."

Curt had missed the signs. His judgment was so clouded by the rage built up inside, that he ignored all the obvious signs that this did not fit. The tag did not match, the car did not match, and now the lead was dead.

Hook had a past that suggested he was capable of kidnapping. That and the presence of the young boy's clothes were what screamed out the loudest to Curt. However, it turned out there was a simple explanation. He just didn't want to see it. Plus, the boxes in the garage belonged to the sister, and he had just destroyed her life's possessions for nothing.

He felt foolish and guilty for breaking into the residence based on pure speculation from Hooks' past indiscretions and by being blinded with the slightest possibility that his son could be there.

The muffled sound of a car door shutting came from just beyond the front window of the living room. Panic struck Curt hard and fast as he hung up on Rachel. He peeked out of the living room to see what made the distinct noise. The shadow of Justin Hooks walking up to the front porch froze Curt in his tracks. He was trapped inside. He reached for his gun but thought better of it knowing this time, he was the intruder. He glanced at the back door and realized he would be seen if he made a run for it since Hooks' keys were already engaging the deadbolt at the front door.

"Shit!" he whispered.

As the front door slowly swung open, Curt stealthily slid behind the door and the near wall concealing himself in the makeshift nook just as Hooks stepped in. At first, he was unaware of the uninvited guest and the damage done inside his home, but a quick gust of an autumn wind carrying the dampness of the all-day rain blew in from the back door. Curt's rampage immediately caught his attention. He glared at the back door seeing it splintered out of the frame and the glass shards scattered on the ground. He stepped in cautiously as his mind was trying to figure out what had happened.

"What the hell?" he asked as he reached back and lightly pulled at the front door without taking his eyes off the back. Curt held perfectly still while standing directly behind Hooks. He stepped further into the apartment and looked down the hallway to see if the intruder was still inside. The front door met the door frame, but luckily it didn't fully engage the lock and shut completely. He willed Hooks to move farther down the hallway and out of sight. Hooks fished out his cell phone and called 911 to report the break in. He carefully inched down the hallway, and when he was just at the corner, Curt pulled the door back open slowly and slipped outside unnoticed. He ran to the Crown Vic down the street where he had parked it and scanned the area for any witnesses.

He waited a moment as Hooks ran back outside looking around. He must have noticed that Curt had left the front door open during his escape and realized the perpetrator had doubled back. He sat hunched low in the driver's seat of the Crown Vic and waited. Leaving right now would bring too much attention. After a few minutes, a marked patrol car rushed by Curt, who was hiding in the seat entirely. The cop got out and met Hooks in the front yard and then followed him around to the back of the apartment. Curt took the opportunity and quickly left the area, hoping he hadn't left anything behind.

Chapter 24

After the near miss at Hooks' apartment, Curt had nowhere else to go. Tallahassee had been the place he called home for the better part of thirty years, and yet, all it did now was remind him of the tremendous loss of his son. The lead was a dead end, and the exhaustion of the road trip from the Midwest caught up to him and weighed heavily on his shoulders. He wandered around his hometown looking at all the expansion and the changes made in the two years he had been gone. New restaurants and businesses had taken root, and the old familiar places had been torn down. The small skyline of the downtown area, accented by the twenty-two-story capitol building, stood the same as he remembered. He noticed the town had grown into a full-fledged city.

Curt roamed around and was somehow drawn to the north side of town. Like an old habit, the Crown Vic made the series of lefts and rights as a matter of routine, just as he did when he left work. His neighborhood looked the same as when he left.

He pulled up along the street in front of his house and parked, looking down the slight hill at the red brick-faced, one-story house with black trim. He noticed the yard was slightly unkempt, a responsibility that was his until he left. He remembered the fall season slowed the growth of the grass but littered the yard with a large blanket of fallen leaves. He noticed the gutters were stuffed full of those fallen leaves and needed to be cleaned, a chore he hated. He turned off the engine of the Crown Vic and stared at the house he used to call home. He compared the warm memories of home to the on-the-go lifestyle he had adopted and realized he missed the stability, but he had no choice in the decision to leave. It was either stay and accept Josh's disappearance or leave and do something about it. It was a tough decision but one he made without hesitation, even at a high cost.

After a while, lost in thought, Curt got out of the car and walked down the driveway. He walked to the side door by the garage and checked the knob. It was locked. He assumed the front and back door would be too. He searched his key chain for the key and noticed it felt odd not using a door pick or subterfuge to gain entry. He'd been gone too long, he thought. He found the key, fed the knob, and opened the door. The garage was very much as he had left it. There were some yard tools stored in the corner, car washing and household tools stored on a shelving system. He noticed a tent on the low shelf and remembered the time he and Josh spent the night in the backyard. Curt didn't sleep at all and ended up taking Josh back inside half-way through the night.

He continued further in and noticed his car was covered with a tarp that held a thick layer of dust. He wondered why she hadn't sold it by now and used the money for necessary bills. Obviously, her car was gone. He checked his watch. It read just after 3 pm, and he figured she was still at work. Curt noticed, stowed in the corner was Josh's bike. It too, was covered with dust. The sight of it being unused brought Curt down deeper in depression at his homecoming.

Curt walked into the laundry room from the garage, and memories of Josh running up to him as he returned home from work came flooding back. He imagined, as he now walked in, that Josh would be sitting there watching television, sitting at the table doing homework, or in his room playing video games. He wished more than anything that was the reality, but pushed the thoughts away, knowing the actuality was too harsh.

The house was silent and still. The collage of family portraits had been taken down from the walls and replaced with some themed wall art that matched the rest of the accents in the living room. It was still a home; it just did not feel like his home. Of course he didn't have much say in it anymore. Curt stood in the stillness of the house, wondering if it would ever welcome him back, and if Josh would ever see the inside again. He ignored the closed door to his and Tracy's bedroom, feeling like he would be invading her privacy if he went inside. He turned and walked down the hallway to see Josh's room.

A crooked sign with a young boy's handwriting that read "Josh's Room" still hung in place. Josh had made it during an art project at school, and Curt hung it that evening. He remembered the pride beaming on Josh's face as he brought it home.

Curt stopped at the closed door. He closed his eyes and bowed his head, preparing himself for the emotional tidal wave that was sure to envelop him. He felt compelled to go in, not because it would be therapeutic but because he needed to renew his sense of connectivity. He'd been staring at a small, wallet-sized photograph for the past two years. He needed to see Josh's room, smell his room, feel his energy, and remember him as a loving son, but there was not even a sliver of a chance that Josh was still in his room. It was more a delusion than a reality.

The doorknob squeaked and the door creaked as Curt opened it. Although it was overcast outside, the light from the mid-afternoon seeped in through the open blinds. There was no delusion…Josh was still gone. The room was as still as the rest of the house and looked as it did the day he went missing. The bed was perfectly made, all the toys and clothes were put away, and all the drawers were shut. The baseball themed room was tidy and cute, and a poster of his favorite baseball player, Buster Posey, hung over his bed. Above his desk was a picture handed down from his father that depicted a memorable moment in his own childhood, the play that sent Sid Bream of the Atlanta Braves sliding across home plate to win the deciding Game 6 in the 1992 National League Championship Series against the Pittsburgh Pirates. A priceless heirloom that carried more worth in sentiments than actual cash value. A small bookcase sat in the corner near the window; the top shelf was lined with his favorite kid detective series, knick-knacks, and other keepsakes from his short life. Curt's eyes welled up, knowing the potential for life the room held and the devastating loss that the absence of that life caused. The emotions flooded as expected, and the failure was more devastating than anything. He was so tired. He was tired of the chase, he was tired of not knowing, and he was tired of the bitter feeling of helplessness. No matter how hard he tried, like the lead in Josh's disappearance that fizzled out earlier, it wasn't meant to be.

The small bed was cool and soft. The rain cloud that hovered above the house cast a shadow upon the room. Curt lay down on the bed and cradled the baseball pillow monogrammed with Josh's name on it. He pulled it close as if it were the only chance he had to hold his son again. Tears steadily leaked from his eyes as he just lay there in silence, thinking about his son.

The exhaustion caught up with Curt as his eyes closed in thought, but no matter how hard he fought against it, he was drawn into unconsciousness, and his world faded to black.

***

At first she hesitated at the presence of the Crown Vic parked out on the street. There hadn't been one parked at the house in two years, but she didn't feel the alarm of an intruder. It felt like a ghost from her past was here to visit. The door to the garage was unlocked, and she slowly stepped inside the house. She moved around, trying to find her unexpected guest, and decided to check her son's room after seeing the door to her room still shut. She pushed open the door to find the guest sleeping soundly in a pitiful display of anguish and tribulation.

Tracy Walker hadn't seen her husband in nearly two years and prayed every night for two things to happen. First was the safe return of her son and the second was for her husband to come home. She understood why he left. She read the determination in his eyes the day he told her he was leaving and knew, no matter what she did or said, he was going to move heaven and earth to find their son. She too held onto the shred of hope that one day her son would be found, but it wasn't Josh's choice to leave. He was taken. Curt made the decision to leave her with the burden of an empty home all on his own without any consideration for her well-being.

She wondered if she would break down and cry the day Curt finally came home or slap him or kiss him passionately as they once did. But now, the day had come that her second prayer was fulfilled. She stood leaning up against the doorway of their son's room, watching the broken man in a worn-out trench coat sleep in their son's bed. She felt sorry for him. She fought the urge to wake him and bombard him with questions about where he'd been, what he'd been doing, and why he was back. She was aware the third anniversary of Josh's disappearance had just passed, so maybe that had something to do with his being there, she thought.

The drizzle outside cleared up, and the blanket of gray clouds broke creating small portals to the blue sky above. A large delivery truck rumbled down the street outside of the house, causing a noise that broke through the silence and released Curt from his slumber. His eyes cracked open, and his vision was blurry from sleep. His eyes were puffy from the tearful homecoming as he looked around, trying to remember where he was. As the confusion to his whereabouts was answered, the vision before him began to gain focus. A figure of a woman, beautiful and warm with long, brown hair falling gently behind her, stood in the threshold of the room with a worrisome look on her face. It was a look he remembered well from when he left some two years earlier.

"Hi," she said, softly.

Curt realized where he was and immediately felt like he was trespassing. He sat up on the bed and wiped his face. He was still so very tired. He looked back at his wife apologetically. He hated that he abandoned her. It was a burden he carried alongside the guilt of losing Josh, but he couldn't just sit by and do nothing. Yet, he knew she still blamed him for Josh's disappearance.

"Hey. I'm sorry I didn't call," he said, straightening the bed the way it was before.

"It's okay. Is everything alright?"

"Yeah, I mean…still nothing. But other than that…." Curt quickly remembered the shooting in Vail and the burglary he committed just hours before. There was too much that wasn't alright, but he didn't want to worry her any further.

"You hungry?" she asked invitingly.

He wasn't. "Sure."

Curt stood up and moved next to Tracy. He felt compelled to walk up and kiss her and then hold her as his wife, but the distance of time between them made the gesture feel inappropriate. He chose to just stand and let her dictate any physical greeting.

"You've lost weight? A lot it looks like," she said surprised, deflecting the awkwardness.

Curt looked down at his body. He knew he'd lost weight but never bothered to keep track of it. It was a by-product of his running and the unhealthy lifestyle of frequent binge drinking and the exhausting life on the road.

"Yeah, well. I've been running a little. I guess I hadn't really noticed."

"Well, in that regard you look great."

Curt's brow furrowed from the hidden meaning in her statement. She read the confusion perfectly.

"You look tired and beat, kind of like those long weeks working those drawn out cases."

"Can't argue there."

"C'mon, dinner will only take a minute."

Curt took a seat at the kitchen table, again feeling it would be inappropriate to follow Tracy into the bedroom while she changed out of her work clothes—something he did as a matter of routine while they talked after their days at work. Instead, he sipped on a glass of water but thirsted for something stronger.

She had made lasagna a few nights before and was reheating enough for both. Curt hadn't had anything home-cooked since he left, and the food smelled decadent to the point it resurrected his hunger. He was looking forward to the meal.

Tracy left the bedroom and walked into the kitchen to finalize the meal preparation. Curt watched her move around nervously, knowing that this entire ordeal was just as hard on her as it was on him. He had pushed away those thoughts while he was on the road, trying not to complicate an already extremely complicated situation, but they were in the forefront now as he sat in the kitchen, waiting for dinner.

He watched her as if for the first time but with a distant sense of intimacy. He noticed that she had put on his favorite black, yoga style pants that hugged her curvy legs and round butt, a figure she'd had since the day they met. The t-shirt was from a little league team Josh played on the year before his disappearance, and it hung loose on her torso. They had made it to the city championship that year, and Tracy was a proud team mom. She had pulled back her brown hair into a cute ponytail that whipped around while navigating the kitchen. She stood barefoot, and he noticed that she maintained at least one personal pleasure in her life, which was getting a pedicure on a regular basis. She was stunningly simple and still very beautiful and wholesome. Just for a glimmer, he was transported back to the years when life was good and he was happy.

Tracy pulled the two plates of lasagna out of the oven and noticed Curt was watching her. She didn't know how to react, so she went on like she had been for the last two years without him, on autopilot. She set the food down and joined him at the table after pouring them both a glass of wine.

"So, why now?" She swirled her glass of wine and looked at him with a heavy dose of contempt.

Curt knew she was upset. Why wouldn't she be? "We got a tip that he was spotted at the mall yesterday. I came home as soon as I could to check it out but...." His face grew long and sad.

"What?"

"It was a bad lead. It led to nothing."

The answer Curt gave settled in Tracy's mind, but she wasn't satisfied. He read something in her face; she wasn't surprised to hear of the lead.

"Did you know about the tip?"

"Yeah, they called me yesterday; told me that they already checked it out and found nothing. Said they think the tipster gave the wrong number or the Crime Stoppers' operator transcribed it wrong or whatever."

"Oh," Curt said, somewhat surprised that the detective from the police department would still check in with her and not him.

"Are you going to stay?" Pain hid behind her eyes. It was as if she knew the answer was going to be no but held onto the small chance that it would be yes.

Curt sank in his seat, knowing his answer wouldn't be welcomed. He couldn't look at her, and although she deserved more, he answered softly, "No. I can't."

She waved off the sting of the answer and took a long drink of her wine washing down a small bite of the lasagna. She set the glass down in disappointment. Disappointment in that she allowed her hopes to be up, not that he was going to leave again.

"I can't do this again. Just leave if you're going to leave."

"But Tracy?" He wanted her to understand why he had to be out there looking for their son.

"But what? It's too hard for me to see you leave again, so just go." Her eyes were welling up with tears.

"I'm sorry. But it's what I have to do."

"Why? He's my son too. Why can't you do it from here? Why do you have to run off with some group of people that don't know him, don't care about him like us? Why can't you stay here with me?" Tears fell down her cheeks as her voice strained with emotion.

Curt didn't have a valid answer. Maybe deep down, past the shred of hope that he was desperately holding onto, Curt knew he'd never find his son again, and being a part of the team and doing what they could to find other missing children was a way of finding his own salvation. It wasn't fair that Tracy had to pay the price for his redemption.

When Curt didn't answer, Tracy wiped her tears away and took a deep calming breath.

"Please go," she said.

Without debate, Curt stood up from the table, grabbed his trench coat from the back of the chair, and walked towards the door. He could feel the hate coming from Tracy as he walked away. He would have to add mending their relationship to his long list of to-dos when he finally brought Josh home, because he didn't have time for this right now. Unfortunately, he realized that the search for his son might take too much time, and he could lose his wife forever.

As he walked out the front door, she stood in the doorway watching him leave. It was too painful for her, but she felt compelled to watch.

He heard her crying as he walked along the sidewalk. He didn't want it to end like this; he needed her to understand. He stopped and turned around, looking up at her on the porch.

"I'm sorry, Tracy." She didn't respond, only continued crying. "I have to find him."

"I know," she managed to get out between sobs.

"I know you blame me for his disappearance, and that's why it has to be me. That's why I have to find him. For you. For us."

Tracy's tears stopped. She didn't understand what he said. She took a half-step forward, trying to figure something out in her head.

"Blame you? What are you talking about?"

"C'mon, you blame me for not watching out for him. It was on my watch that he went missing. It's my fault some asshole took him and is doing God knows what or worse. I don't fault you for blaming me; hell, I blame me!"

"Curtis, why would you ever think that I blamed you?"

He was blindsided by her reaction and searched his memory for the reasoning. She never came out and said it, but it was the look she gave him when she got to the ball field. It was seared into his mind just as it was that night.

"When you got to the ballpark that night, that look you gave me, it was like I was responsible for him disappearing. It was blame. You blamed me."

Tracy stepped from the porch and slowly walked out in the damp night air. A breeze bringing more rain rolled through the front yard and brought a sharp bite of a chill with it. She looked into his eyes and reached out for his hands.

"That wasn't blame, Curtis. I don't blame you. You trusted that our son was safe, as you had on plenty of occasions, and I know you, Curtis Walker. I know you better than yourself. You would never turn your back on that boy, and that look of 'blame' was not that. It was a look of 'horrified astonishment' questioning how someone actually managed to catch you with your guard down."

Curtis Walker had not only been living with the devastation of losing his son to an unknown monster but also enduring the blame from Tracy. But he'd only assumed it was blame because of the look she gave him three years ago, and now she was saying it was something else.

"So…what are you saying? You don't blame me?"

"For him going missing? Oh my God, no! I blame the assholes who took him, Curt. Not you!"

She stood directly in front of her husband. Her petite five-foot-four frame seemed smaller with only her bare feet as Curt looked down at her, seeing her eyes plead for his understanding. He reached down and grabbed her up, hugging her in a moment of clarity. She hugged him back tightly as she sobbed in his arms.

"I'm sorry, baby. I'm so sorry," he said.

He held her body tightly against his in the cold night air. The pitter-pat of rain moved down the street and directly on top of them. The inappropriateness from before was gone in an instant, and Curt reached down to kiss his wife. He held the back of her head with his hand and kissed her passionately with the power of a love long subdued by the tragedy surrounding their missing son. The rain failed to dampen the reunion of Curt and his wife, now that the ugly misunderstanding that had driven a one-sided wedge into their marriage was out of the way.

The light rain turned into heavy raindrops that quickly soaked them. They remained in each other's arms kissing each other, needing to be loved. Curt scooped her up in his arms as he did on their wedding day and carried her inside, still kissing her as she held tightly to his strong shoulders and arms. He kicked the door shut and stopped just outside of the bedroom; the door was still shut. Tracy noticed the pause and looked back at her husband. She realized why he stopped and nodded that it was okay to continue. She kept kissing her husband as he managed to hold her, open the bedroom door, and shut it behind them with the determination of a newlywed.

Chapter 25

The constant hum of the beating rain accompanied Curt and Tracy as they made love throughout the night. They forgot about the looming tragedy that engulfed their everyday lives and temporarily found themselves locked in each other's embrace as man and wife. The sex was unfamiliar at first, but as they relearned each other's habits and preferences, time seemed to melt away.

After several bouts of intense lovemaking, Tracy lay nude and cuddled up in Curt's arms. Upon realizing this, she pulled the sheets up awkwardly to cover herself. She marveled at his weight loss and how the endurance training translated well into the bedroom. Normally, Curt would feel guilty about stopping his search for anything pleasurable, but for some reason, being at his house and with his wife, the guilt was suspended. For this reason, he thought maybe he should return home, but settling back into his life without Josh was unacceptable, and he had to pass on the idea.

"So, they were about to shoot Rachel?" Tracy asked. Curt had told her of the team's latest rescue and the harrowing escape they made from the human traffickers and the surrounding media storm that followed.

"Yeah. I heard the shot come from inside the house and ran around to the front. The first guy opened the door and had a gun in his hand, so I shot him first before going in. When I got inside, the other guy had a gun to her head, so…."

Tracy was able to figure out the rest. She'd been a cop's wife for nearly fifteen years and always wondered what to say if her husband had to shoot someone in the line of duty. She listened to him tell the story matter-of-factly and figured he was fine with the outcome, so she didn't press the issue. She knew what truly haunted him was the disappearance of their son and his unending quest to find him.

Curt told her about the fallout with Alexis Vanderhill following the shooting and how she asked him to take a backseat on the team for the time being. He withheld telling her about the kiss he shared with Rachel Goodwin just outside of her hotel room, for he knew the relationship with Tracy was too fragile for that discussion. He explained to her that the attention from the rival news reporter, Tony Mason, could lead to the possible exposure of the team.

"What would happen if the team did get exposed?"

"I don't know exactly. I'd like to think nothing, but you never know in this day and age. But what we're doing is right; I mean, bottom line, who wouldn't want their child back? I know I'll do whatever it takes to get Josh back. So who cares if we cross a few legal lines to do it? It only hurts the people responsible."

"How illegal?"

"Oh, it's very illegal. Like federal time, illegal. That's why we have to be careful. But I wasn't about to let those assholes hurt Rachel, or me, or anyone. I'd do the same thing if I had it to do over again."

They sat up most of the night talking about the adventures of the team and the lives they had changed over the past two years since leaving home and joining the team. It was still a bitter pill in Tracy's mind, so she was trying to understand why Curt was so compelled to leave her and their home to look for Josh.

"We found this one girl, recently in San Francisco. Her name was Charlotte." Curt smiled at the remembered image of the pretty, blonde girl walking from the Sprinter Van to her parents in such a remarkable reunion.

"Yeah?" Tracy saw the highlight bring a small smile to his face.

"Yeah, and I sat there watching her mother thank God for bringing their daughter back to her."

Tracy fought back a tear at the story and at the jealously she felt for the woman.

"And it feels good being able to bring that kind of joy back into someone's life, but at the same time, I feel a piece of me die each time. The sliver of hope that I have keeps getting smaller and smaller, and soon there won't be any left."

"It's all we can do though. Hold onto the hope that he's brought back to us one day."

"And that's where I get angry."

"Why?"

"Because I'm his father," Curt said, anger adding to his tone. "And I shouldn't have to wait on hope. That's why I'm out there looking. We both know no one else is."

It was true, she thought. She maintained her full time job, but on the weekends and on most nights, she routinely drove by the softball complex during softball games, his favorite restaurants, and the movies, hoping to find him. She even checked the ice cream shop where she took him for a sweet treat when his father worked late, hoping beyond hope that his captor was decent enough to let him indulge in a few of his favorite things and that she'd find him there. But, past that, she knew no one else was looking...besides Curt.

A detective from TPD, an old squad mate of Curt's, checked in on the rarest occasion, like when a possible lead came in, but the detective had a case load to attend to and knew that he couldn't dedicate much time, if any, without something tangible to go on. It wouldn't be fair to all of the other victims who needed his attention.

Tracy sat up in the bed, pulling the sheets up with a skeptical look on her face. She looked over at Curt seriously.

"So...what are you going to do now? I assume your team is still back in Oklahoma?"

"Yeah, I don't know. I guess I'll head back and meet back up with them."

"So there's nothing more to do here? I mean, with that Crime Stoppers' tip?"

"Not really. I mean, the tag didn't come back, and the closest we got to a lead didn't pan out, so yeah, I mean, it's done for now."

Tracy thought for a minute and started to bite her tongue but decided otherwise, and she didn't care if she overstepped some boundary.

"Answer me this—would you have stopped at that when you were working a case?"

"Huh?"

"I was never a cop or a detective, but I know you. I've certainly heard enough of your stories and listened to your cases to know you are one persistent dick!"

Unsure if that was an insult or a compliment, Curt looked at her puzzled. "What do you mean?"

"I mean, I remember when you were able to connect the dots in cases that most just ignored or overlooked. You paid attention to details and you stuck to your guns, no matter what. That was what made you a great detective."

Tracy smiled and then looked down bashfully. "You remember how you got me to start dating you?"

Curt chuckled. "Yeah, I do. I must have asked you out ten times before you said yes."

"It was thirteen times, and I only agreed because you swore to never ask again if I went out with you that one time."

Curt smiled at the memory. He was glad he was persistent even back then.

"So what are you saying?"

"I'm saying that you never used to accept 'no' for an answer. So why are you doing it with this tip? Maybe there's something there. What else have we got to lose?"

She was right; there was nothing else. Curt's mind started to race, much like it did when he focused on a case that stood out. He felt reenergized. He thought about the tip and what was specifically said. He put himself in the call taker's place and imagined answering the phone and taking down the information. It was possible that they got the characters of the tag mixed up or wrote it down wrong. Human error was an unfortunate curse in police work but not completely irreparable. He would start there in the morning.

Chapter 26

The lights were dim in the lobby of the Vail Police Department which added to the dreary weather outside casting a gloomy feel on the world. Tony Mason sat patiently in an uncomfortable plastic chair, waiting to speak to the detective in charge of the shooting at the chalet on the bluff. He sat across from a woman and a small child, also waiting, but for a different reason. She had a nice shiner on her left eye which was swollen shut and a deep shade of purple. A busted lip accented the noticeable injury, and she held a disposition reserved only for the abused. She managed to fight through the physical pain to entertain the unsuspecting child who would grow up in a house of violence. Mason avoided eye contact and hoped that she didn't find out he was a news reporter and demand a story about her marital woes.

A few patrol officers walked through, apparently a sign that it was shift change, and they were hitting the streets. One of the officers stopped to talk to the battered woman and began taking her report. Mason looked for the detective, but he wasn't there. Finally, after another ten minutes, a gruff looking man with an unlit cigarette hanging from his mouth leaned through a glass door looking at Mason.

"You the reporter?" he asked. His voice sounded rough like sandpaper.

"Yeah, are you Detective Rankin?"

"Yeah, can we do this outside so I can smoke?"

"Sure, fine with me."

Rankin led the reporter out of the lobby and into the parking lot. He quickly lit up the cigarette and took a long, lingering pull of the nicotine-filled smoke and let it out in the cold damp air. The exhaled plume hung heavy in the wet air, causing Mason to cough.

"Sorry."

"So, I wanted to know if anything panned out further from the girls in Denver. Did they shed any further light on the situation?"

"Yes, actually they did, but we're a little stuck."

"Okay, maybe I can help?"

"How is that?"

"Tell me what you have so far, and I should be able to fill in some gaps."

"You can go fuck yourself with the 'show me yours, and I'll show you mine' crap; I don't have to tell you shit, and you know it. Tell me how you can help, or I go smoke in the back parking lot where you can't go."

Mason hated when the cops stone-walled him like this, but he was right. It was a symbiotic relationship the media shared with the police, both have different motives, both serving a purpose, but neither wished to share. It was common all over the country, and he was used to the game. It was still worth a try.

"Fine. I've been following a lead on a woman who has been funding the efforts of a team that works outside the law and targets missing children." Mason continued by telling the detective what he knew of the team up to this point.

Rankin had been around. He had seen a lot of things in his long law enforcement career and wasn't surprised by much of anything anymore, but this was a first even for him. His face distorted in confusion as Mason explained how he had interviewed a family in southern California who had their child, missing for almost seven years, suddenly reappear. As Mason followed up on the story, the family let it slip that a group of four people had brought their son back to them, no questions asked. He also explained how he learned that it was Alexis Vanderhill who had set up everything with the family for the kid to be returned.

"But before I could print the story, the family recanted for some reason, and I had to pull the story. I tried to run it anyway, but they had some clout, and it was squashed completely."

"Okay, I fail to see the connection. I'm not dealing with missing children, just a dead con-artist and two dead illegals running a whore house in my city."

"I see your point, but I've been keeping tabs on Vanderhill, and she flew into Denver the morning after the shooting."

"And? Denver is a big city, a lot of people visit. Hell, the Broncos play at home this weekend; maybe she's a fan."

"You're right."

The detective grew impatient and threw down his cigarette and stamped it out on the ground. "I'm done unless you have anything more." When Mason didn't say anything, he turned to walk away.

Mason held his ace as long as he could, but it was clear that the detective didn't want the ally, so he needed to convince him otherwise.

"Was one of the 'suspects' a white male wearing a trench coat?"

The detective stopped abruptly and twisted back around. He studied the reporter with aged skepticism. Mason could tell the assessment of his question was churning in his mind. From his obvious body language, the seasoned detective was ready to listen. Rankin reached for another cigarette and lit it without taking his eyes off Mason.

"Okay, you got my attention."

***

Mason picked up take-out Chinese and brought it back to his hotel room after meeting with Detective Rankin. He opened the small, white, cardboard container and dug into his lo mein as he fired up his laptop to get to work. After providing the descriptions of all the players from the missing California boy to the detective, he opened up more and gave him more intimate details about the shooting. He verified that the girls were illegal immigrants somehow smuggled into the country by a network of human trafficking. He stated that ICE and the FBI were heading up that portion of the investigation while he was just focused on the homicide angle. Mason knew he had multiple stories that would spawn from this and made a note to call the Denver field office of the FBI for comments on the trafficking case.

In turn, Rankin provided a more detailed description of the parties involved in the shoot out to compare to what he already knew. He was aware of the man in the trench coat, and that was on point with what the girls reported. They stayed on par when they described a skinny, nerdy looking, white male. Mason remembered that the missing boy from California was fond of the nerdy guy because they played video games together while they drove him home in some kind of large van, but the girls added a new description to fill the role of heroine for the story. Rankin relayed about how this woman climbed in through the window and bravely fought against the traffickers to help free them. Mason was impressed and wished the story had more legs than it did, but he could feel it coming together. It was still in its infancy, and he hoped to cultivate it into something sensational.

Mason added the description of a mid-thirties, white female, blonde hair pulled into a ponytail and strong cheek bones, average height and average weight to his working file of team participants. He leaned back and stared at the words on the screen, hoping they would soon translate into a story he could print.

He devoured the rest of the lo mein, cracked open the fortune cookie, and tossed out the fortune without reading it. He checked his email and updated his status to the supervising editor. He told him that he would have a piece on human trafficking with some quotes from the FBI field office for the next print. He didn't want to say too much about the lead on the secretive team as he wanted everything in line before he printed that story.

After sending the emails, he did a Google search of Alexis Vanderhill. He routinely checked her name, hoping that some connection to the team or their actions would somehow reveal itself, but nothing had panned out yet. There was just something about her that he couldn't ignore.

There was a new entry under the Google search with a link to an article in the society page in the *San Francisco Chronicle*. He clicked the link and saw that it was dated only about two weeks prior. The article covered a fundraising gala for the Missing Person's Society and Alexis Vanderhill, notable advocate for missing children, was present. Mason read the article, and it was filled with a lot of fluff but made its point with the importance of the awareness. As he scrolled down, he saw there were pictures from the gala, and he clicked on the gallery to see all of the guilty, rich people giving away money in order to feel less ostentatious. He found a picture of Alexis Vanderhill and stared for only a moment.

She's pretty hot, he thought to himself with no one to pass judgment.

He continued through the rest of the pictures and didn't recognize anyone else, but when he came to a second picture of Vanderhill in her splendid silver gown, he nearly choked on the last bite of the fortune cookie. In the picture, standing next to Vanderhill, was a blonde woman who appeared to be in her mid-thirties with her hair tightly pulled back in a ponytail. She was dressed a few degrees on the casual side. Unlike the more formal party goers, she sported a modest, dark gray pantsuit. Mason saw that she had well-defined cheek bones and fit the description of the unknown heroine from the shooting in Vail.

He read the caption under the picture:

Alexis Vanderhill, advocate for missing children stands next to Rachel Goodwin who is attending the fundraiser in honor of her missing sister, Rhonda Goodwin, missing over twenty years.

Mason flipped back to the description Rankin gave him as relayed from the trafficking victims of the heroine and then looked back to study the picture of Rachel Goodwin. He was quickly convinced that he had just identified his first team member.

"Hello, Rachel."

Chapter 27

Despite over a decade of waking up in the same house, Curt sprang up in bed confused and disoriented by his surroundings, a by-product of life on the road accompanied by terror filled nightmares. He fell back to the bed exhausted and closed his eyes in relief, remembering the events of the night before—something that wasn't necessarily a given with his drunken binges. He realized he had gotten a restful night's sleep and wondered if that was his subconscious telling him to stay home.

An unfamiliar sound pulled his eyes fully awake as he sat up in the bed. It was the sound of water running. The shower was going, and a small plume of steam billowed from the crack between the door frame and the bathroom door. Tracy's side of their bed was empty and already folded back neatly as if she had never been there. The only trace that remained behind was her sensual and arousing scent.

Curt dressed as the awkwardness began to return, and the feeling of intrusion grew. The shower turned off, and the door opened to air out the steamy room. Tracy stood there, covered in a towel wrapped tightly around her wet body as her wet hair hung to the side. Even in her natural form, she was still stunning. During his absence, Curt held onto her image in his head, but over the course of two years, that image seemed to fade more and more, except for the look of disappointment he had misinterpreted from the night of Josh's disappearance.

He stood there, half stepped into his pants, staring at her. She smiled.

"Hey," she said. "Good morning."

"Hey, g'mornin." He snapped out of the boyish gawking and finished getting dressed.

Tracy went about her morning routine as if the night before had no impact. She was always the first to say if something bothered her or wasn't right, but Curt noticed that she was now skillful in hiding her true emotions. It was something she had obviously developed to help cope with the stress and the horrific situation she was thrown into, as there was no manual for how to deal with a missing child.

After he finished getting dressed and ready for the day, Curt headed for the door. He hated to have to tell Tracy goodbye again, but he knew he had to continue looking for their son. She was right about his not accepting no for an answer. He was so worn down and exhausted that he couldn't take another lead that fizzled out.

She saw something inside of him that he had long since forgotten. It was her unwavering belief that he would one day find Josh and bring him home, and this gave him the hope he needed to continue.

He avoided looking her in the eyes as she stood in the kitchen making breakfast. He wanted to explain what the night before meant to him and that he loved her so very much, but he was not going to stop looking for their son; he just hoped that she could try and understand.

"I need to get going," he said softly.

She didn't bother turning around. "I know."

He looked over at her but failed to find the words to make things right. He knew nothing he could say would ever make it right.

"Goodbye Tracy," he said. He pushed away from the countertop and headed for the door. She stood still with her head bowed, unable to look at him either. She knew he was going to leave, but it still hurt as much as it did the first time.

He closed the front door tightly behind him and walked along the wet sidewalk and up the driveway to the Crown Vic. As he reached the car door, he felt a presence behind him and turned around to see Tracy standing in the driveway. She was looking at him longingly, expecting more from him and as if she had something to say. He stood frozen not knowing how to react.

"I made you some coffee," she said as she walked up to him. She presented him with an old thermos that he used to use to carry his morning coffee into work. It was a subtle reminder of the life he once had. It read: "Bad Cop No Donut," a sentiment he had taken up in an earlier attempt to lose weight.

"I'll be back as soon as I can." It wasn't necessarily a lie but vague enough to avoid committing to a time frame. He sealed the statement with a smile that carried with it a glimmer of the hope that she had rejuvenated.

"You do that, Curtis," she said as she hugged him tightly around the neck. "Go find him, so you can come home!"

***

The Governor's Square Mall sat in the southeast sector of Tallahassee along the main thoroughfare of Apalachee Parkway, just down from the capitol building. One of the city's best views of the capitol was found by coming westbound on the parkway, looking up to the hilltop that holds the first state capitol. The old three-story statehouse sat in the late evening shadow of the massive building just behind it. The view from the top of the capitol reached out for miles around the Big Bend area.

The mall is a staple for trendy shoppers and teenage wanderers. Built in the late seventies, it still remains the main hub for indoor shopping in Tallahassee and the surrounding areas. Outdated décor and the over use of brass railings and trim don't detract from the draw of the popular stores and boutiques within. Had this been a new town the team had come to visit, this would have been one of the first stops.

Curt found a parking spot close by an entrance he knew was near the mall's office and waited for a call back on his cell phone. It was still early, and the sparse foot traffic consisted of mostly employees and the elderly looking for a dry place to exercise.

The phone chirped in his pocket, and he answered it on the first ring, "Hello?"

"Hey man, that's a no-go. The mainframe won't be hard to crack, but the problem is that they don't even record the incoming calls. Plus, they are routed to the nearest office to the caller, not the incident. So getting a trace is nearly impossible."

"Okay, so nothing?"

"Nah, man. I'm sorry. I was able to take a look around, but it's a jumbled friggin' mess. They designed it that way to keep it anonymous, and they did one helluva job. It's like looking in a really messy room when you know something is in there, but there's so much stuff, you still can't find anything. It's friggin' genius is what it is!"

After leaving the house, Curt's first phone call was to Louis Melton with a request to look into the Crime Stoppers' tip about his son, in the internal sense. He wanted to know if he could backtrack to find the caller and see what other information, if any, was crossed up or changed in translation. Getting more information such as where exactly at the mall the boy was seen, what he was wearing, what the man he was with was wearing, any distinguishable features about the car, and anything else that would be helpful to narrow the search. However, with Louis' valiant attempt to hack the Crime Stoppers' database, he was left with the ashes of shredded data designed to protect the caller's identity. The best he was able to offer was that he located the bank account and access number of the caller, but the tip would have to pan out and be verified by a detective before payment was sent. Curt thought about extending the ruse to that point and making the tip payout but held off for the time being. He didn't want to corrupt a system with such good intentions.

His only move left, albeit a long shot, was the video surveillance at the mall. Curt took a walk around the perimeter of the mall after hanging up with Louis, looking for all of the outward cameras and praying that one of them captured what the tipster reported. After making the rounds, he counted eight cameras that pointed to the parking lot. The problem was that the tip never specified time or place within the massive parking lot, only the day on which the boy was spotted. This was another detail he wished to question the tipster about further, but unfortunately, it left Curt a very wide net to cast which was going to be time consuming.

Before walking into the manager's office, Curt made sure his badge was situated straight on his belt next to his holstered Glock. He hoped the security manager was still friendly to law enforcement that needed to take a look at the camera system.

He badged his way past the secretary of the management office with the confidence that he'd done this before, so it came off as legit. He approached the security office and took a deep breath before entering.

"Hey brother; how are you?"

The young security officer spun in his chair and smiled at the presence of a law enforcement officer. Curt felt his luck turn for the better as he immediately pegged the kid as a wannabe cop. Many of the security officers at the mall went on to join the police force. He knew and had worked with several of them and was in luck, figuring this kid would be more than eager to help out in a real police investigation.

Curt explained that he was following up on a carjacking case and needed to review the footage from the exterior of the mall. The kid was helpful but stingy. He wanted to run the controls of the system and not allow Curt blanket access, so he exercised patience and played into the ruse and explained to the security officer that the target car was a silver Honda Accord with some variation of SX444 as the tag and that it was last seen two days prior roaming the parking lot.

"That's all you have to go on?"

"Yeah, unfortunately."

"Wow, that sucks."

"Tell me about it. Needle in a haystack, my friend."

The kid sent a few commands by clicking the mouse and typing in a password. The screen blinked from real time to the recorded time two days prior in a four by four split screen. There were sixteen screens but only eight were for the exterior. Curt noticed the others were all interior angles that captured both sides of each wing as well as multiple angles surrounding the food court. He sat next to the young security officer and watched the monitor intently as the video played on all sixteen screens. He was straining at each and every screen, hoping to catch a glimpse of his son and not Justin Hooks' nephew.

After an hour went by with nothing, the kid needed a break. Curt hadn't moved and remained glued to the monitor. The kid had grown used to him and allowed him to stay in the room alone while he grabbed a snack and a bathroom break. Curt slid over into the main seat and watched closely. His careful gaze bounced from one screen to the other trying not to miss anything.

"Do you know Whigman?"

Curt was too focused on the monitors; he didn't realize the kid had returned and was standing behind him, let alone hear the question he asked.

"Huh? Who?"

"Whigman? Officer Whigman; he's with y'all right?"

"Oh yeah, he is. I think he's still patrol, right?" Curt vaguely remembered the name and believed that the officer he was asking about once worked as security at the mall before joining TPD.

"Uh…no, I'm pretty sure he's in robbery now. Didn't you say you were in robbery?"

"Oh, right. I'm sorry. I'm kind of glued into this at the moment, sorry." Curt maintained a watchful eye on the screen bank in search of his son, but he could feel the suspicion of the kid grow into concern and hoped he didn't call his bluff. He had to placate him for the moment because there was too much video still to be watched.

"So, you gone through the academy yet?"

"Oh no, but I'm putting in for the next class for sure!" he said excitedly as the conversation became about him.

"Really, well, I know the director over the law enforcement class, so if you want, I can put in a good word." Curt didn't know the director personally per se or even if he was still at the academy, but he knew the kid wouldn't know that.

Instantly, the bored security guard with the probing questions was Curt's best friend. He began asking him questions about getting into the academy, advice on surviving the academy, and helpful tips for successful graduation and possible employment. Curt had pegged him right, and this served to pacify any concerns of his ulterior motives as he filled the kid's head with answers he wanted to hear.

It was well after lunch, which Curt skipped except for a protein bar the kid had on hand, and he had still had no luck going through the footage. There had been a few possibilities of silver Honda Accords, but there wasn't a white male driver or a young boy passenger. There were only a few hours left of operating time left on the video recording, and Curt felt his welcome was getting worn out with the kid and his supervisor who had come to check on him several times. He was able to bullshit them enough with the carjacking ruse, but he felt sooner or later, he was going to get exposed.

The sinking feeling of helplessness returned, and he feared that the lead was truly dead, and he was grasping at straws. He was about to call it, but Tracy's voice sounded off in his head. *Go find him.*

"I'm trying."

"What?" said the security officer.

"Nothing, sorry."

"Listen, my shift is up, and we normally don't have someone come in until later to monitor the cameras. Do you want to come back tomorrow?"

"Um, no. I really need to check this off today if you don't mind."

The kid winced in irritation. He didn't want to piss off the detective who was going to smooth his ticket into the academy, but he was done with the tedious police work, and it had cost him a protein bar. "Okay, how about thirty more minutes?"

"Go back!"

"Huh?"

"Go back to that angle a few minutes; go back NOW!" Curt crossed the room and was nearly pushing past the kid's shoulders, pointing to the one camera angle of the Dillard's wing, upstairs.

After he rewound the tape, he hit play, unsure what an interior angle had to do with a carjacking vehicle, but he obliged.

The tiny screen showed a young boy, maybe ten years old, walking with his back turned to the camera. He was walking next to a man dressed in a dark red shirt and blue jeans, his back also to the camera. As the two walked away from the camera, the boy casually stuck his arm out by his side to run his hand loosely along the handrail balusters as he walked alongside hitting each one. At one point, he stopped to tie his shoe, but before he stood back up, he looked back at the camera and then was hurried along by the man in the red shirt.

Curt's heart nearly burst into pieces at the sight of the boy, for he was overcome with excitement that he had recognized his son, Josh. He ordered the security guard to rewind it again, and as the video played out again before him, Curt reached out and touched the screen as he watched his son look back at the camera as if to say, "Here I am Daddy...please come get me."

Curt burst out in a joyful sob that carried excitement but managed to scare the unaware security guard, confusing him to the point that he just remained silent and let the cop have his weird moment. Curt let out the initial wave of emotion but realized the validation of holding onto hope only got him this far, so now he had to complete the mission.

Go Find Him!

He pushed the kid out of the way and commandeered the video system, back tracking and following Josh throughout the mall. He was only inside for about twenty minutes total and seemed to avoid getting close to the camera angles. The kidnapper clearly didn't realize the camera that first captured them was affixed behind him, and luckily for Curt, he was unable to take an evasive maneuver to avoid its eye.

Finally, as it was apparent the man was leaving with Josh, Curt followed their movements outside into the parking lot. It was painful as he watched and wished he were there to stop the man from taking his son; he wanted Josh safely returned to their home. He wished he could somehow jump into the screen and time warp back to this incident and right the wrong. He kept watching and saw the boy accidentally bump into a short, curly-headed woman just outside one of the anchor stores. She did a double take at him and stood still, contemplating something before continuing inside the mall. After this, the man in the red shirt got into a silver Honda Accord parked near the front of the mall, close to the entrance where Curt had parked the Crown Vic. His nose was only inches away from the screen as he willed the Honda to back up toward the camera angle and expose the correct tag.

"C'mon, c'mon you son of a bitch—do it!"

In slow agonizing movements, the car's brake lights flashed, followed by the white reverse lights. The car backed up slowly and turned toward the camera angle. Curt's eyes were wide with anticipation. He tried to read the tag, but it was blurry and unreadable. The car stopped, then drove forward shrinking smaller on the computer screen as it left the area. No matter how hard he strained his eyes, he couldn't make out the tag.

"No, no, NOOO! Goddammit!" Curt yelled frantically. He grabbed the mouse and rewound the footage several times hoping to read the tag, but it was still too blurry to read. He slammed his fists down on the desk vaulting several pens and paperclips into the air and scattering them across the room. He cussed out of frustration at being so close but still so far away.

"You can enhance it a little bit."

Curt's head whipped around at the small security guard. "Huh?"

"Yeah, just freeze frame the video, and we can enhance it." The kid explained that the video records to a digital server in high definition, but distance blurs out details in the regular mode. Once a specific scene is captured on the monitor, he can zoom in to see close up. Curt released the controls of the system and allowed the kid to take over as he anxiously awaited the results.

He captured the frame of the Honda stopped from backing up and its tag facing the camera, then he pulled it from the bank of screens and expanded it in front of the program. Then he clicked and rolled the mouse forward to zoom in on the Honda's tag.

Curt saw in amazing clarity the tag of his son's abductor and the reason why Louis Melton's searches came up with nothing but Justin Hooks as a possible suspect. The tipster had the tag correct all along, and there was nothing lost in translation, for it was clear as day. The tipster, or call taker, failed to relay one important piece of information though, the tag's state of registration. The common Florida license tag has an orange, appropriate and stately, situated in between the tags characters, but Georgia has a peach, also appropriate. From a distance, they look similar, and the kidnapper's tag was no exception—it was a Georgia tag.

Curt faulted himself for not thinking of that earlier, as Leon County, which encompasses Tallahassee, actually borders Georgia, and it was pretty common for people who live in the nearby Georgia counties to visit and go shopping in Tallahassee.

"Do you want a copy of..." the security asked as he turned around to see Curt had already left the room.

He ran out of the mall and jumped into his Crown Vic rejuvenated in the search for his son and fueled by the realization the tag was from Georgia and not Florida as he and everyone else had assumed. His thoughts were flooded with his next set of moves and how he was going to get his son back, for there was nothing that was going to stand in his way.

"I'm coming Josh. I'm coming."

Chapter 28

With the help of Louis Melton and his "crafty" ways of navigating through the firewalls of government databases, Curt had a name for the man in the red shirt. The tag the tipster provided came back to a man living in Valdosta, Georgia, a city just north of the Florida state line off I-75. Curt wasted no time after learning where the man lived and hit the interstate. It was over an hour's drive, but the anticipation of following the legitimate lead made the trip agonizingly long. It seemed like he couldn't get there fast enough. He pushed the Crown Vic up toward 100 mph but dialed it down, trying to avoid any unnecessary attention from watchful state troopers. He didn't want any record of his being in or heading to Valdosta, knowing what the outcome would be for the man who took his son.

The image of the man in the red shirt was stamped clear in his head after watching the footage from the mall. The man had been careful not to reveal his face to the camera, but after seeing him with Josh, he knew he'd never forget his face. He had soulless eyes that were black as night, his face disgustingly distorted from the evil he'd committed, and he had no regard for what he'd put Curt's family through. He was a monster.

However, when Louis sent a picture of Glenn Gregory to Curt's phone, he looked surprisingly human. He appeared clean cut, average, and as for outward appearances, normal. He did not have the face of a monster, but Curt noticed the picture was several years old. He figured something must have sent Gregory spiraling down to the murky bottom of criminality where he dared to kidnap a child.

Without wasting any time, Curt zeroed in on Gregory's residence, located on the west side of town near the interstate. Curt didn't bother stopping for gas, food, or anything. His body was shaking in anticipation when he realized how close he was to finding Josh. His plan was to grab the boy, no matter the obstacle in his way and get back to Tallahassee as soon as possible. He could care less what kind of chaos he left in his wake.

The GPS zeroed in on Gregory's apartment and told Curt to take a right into a large apartment complex. He sucked in a long breath, held it in his lungs to the point they started to sting, and then blew out the return. This calmed him down to a level of functionality as he looked for the apartment.

Gregory lived in a gated apartment complex that was geared toward the young professional or recently married couples waiting to take the plunge into the housing market. It was a nice, landscaped, and seemingly peaceful place to live, but because of the reason Curt was brought here, he found the place repulsive and had to ignore thoughts of burning it to the ground.

He found it...apartment G49. It was on the bottom floor mid-way into the complex. The silver Honda Accord was not there. Curt did a slow search of the entire parking lot and even in the surrounding business parking lots that neighbored the complex, in case Gregory was trying to hide the car. It was not there either. It was nearing five o'clock, and Curt assumed he was still at work. His next move was simple; he was going inside.

He stowed the Crown Vic in the "future residents" spot up front by the office and casually walked back toward Gregory's apartment. He looked around feigning interest in an apartment. When he saw no one was watching, he slipped behind the G building and up to the back door of Gregory's apartment. He noticed he was remarkably calm as compared to when he was standing behind Justin Hooks' townhome the day before. He made quick work of the lock and slipped inside with little effort.

The apartment smelled like gardenias. It was neat and orderly, not the dungeon of horrors Curt imagined where Josh was being held against his will. He looked around and called out for Josh in a whisper, but there was no answer. He searched around the living room and found what he expected—furniture, a coffee table, a moderate sized television, a desk top in the window, knick-knacks displayed here and there, and pictures of Gregory with friends. Curt picked up one of the pictures on a sofa table near the front door, and it showed Gregory in an arm-in-arm embrace with another man. They were too close to just be friends, and

Curt believed they might be romantically involved with each other. He set the picture down as an uneasy feeling began brewing in the pit of his stomach. He fought off the thought, telling himself he was letting his imagination go wild.

Down the small hallway off of the living room were two opposing doors. He opened the first door to the left, and it appeared to be a master bedroom. The other door somehow beckoned Curt, and he held off looking through the master to check the other door. He opened it slowly, and what was inside hurt him down to his core. At the same time it validated the lead. It was a gut punch worth taking.

A mattress with sheets draped on top, sat lonely and shoved in the corner of the room. In the other corner was a dresser, with a small television on top hooked up to a gaming system. The fading sunlight broke through dusty blinds in the window, giving the room a dismal feel. As he looked around, he noticed clothes and shoes for a young boy were strewn all over the carpet. Curt called out for Josh. Still no answer. He searched the closet and found it empty except for a few more clothes.

The unexpected buzz from his pants pocket caught Curt off guard. He checked the caller ID and saw that it was Rachel Goodwin. He hesitated answering it but decided she might have valuable information.

"Hello?" he answered quietly.

"Have you found the place? Gregory's?"

"Yeah."

"Okay, Louis checked his last tax return. No dependents claimed, but we do have a good employer location. He works for a law firm there in Valdosta, apparently he is some kind of paralegal. The firm handles mostly civil cases and adoption."

"Adoption, huh. Okay, thanks." Curt would definitely be sitting on the firmw waiting to follow Gregory if he failed to show at the apartment.

"What are you going to do?"

"What do you mean? I'm here to find my son."

"You know what I mean!"

He did. She was asking if he was going to kill Gregory. Was she making sure he was going to do it, or was she asking because she was hoping that he would not?

"I don't know right now."

"How 'bout you wait for us to get there? Let us help you, Curt. Let us do what we do best."

Curt thought about it but ignored answering the question as he turned back into the closet to keep searching. He reached in and slid the hanging clothes down the pole as he looked closely at each article.

"Hello?" Rachel asked, waiting for a response.

"I'm here."

"Well?"

"I'm sorry. C'mon if you want to, but to be honest, I don't know what I'll do at this point. I just want one thing in this world more than anything...." Curt pushed a jacket aside in the closet, causing the shoulder to droop off of the hanger. He paused mid-sentence with what he saw.

"I know that's what you want, but you know we work better as a team. Please, let us help you."

Another long pause went by as Rachel waited for an answer. Curt snatched the jacket from the hanger and stepped away from the closet and into the remaining sunlight. Rachel called for him again but only got heavy breathing instead.

Inside the jacket, Curt saw the name Josh, handwritten by a child inside the collar, a directive straight from his mother after losing his favorite one at school. He held it and stared at the name, praying to God that this was real and not a hallucination. He held up the jacket and brought it in as if his son were wearing it and hugged the jacket, taking in its smell. For a second, he caught the scent of his son, and he was transported back to a time before his life was so violently turned upside down.

"He's here, Rach...Josh is here," he said, on the brink of joyful tears.

Rachel Goodwin couldn't hold back the grin that crossed her entire face as she listened to the update.

"He's there now? You have him?"

Curt's mind was a whirlwind of emotions. He clung to the jacket as if it were his lost son. He tossed the rest of the small room looking for any more evidence of his son's existence. The clothes on the floor were recently worn, and this told him that Josh had been in that room within the last day. This coincided with the Crime Stoppers' tip that Josh was seen in Tallahassee a few days before. As he recalled that image from the video, he saw the clothes he was wearing, now laying on the floor.

"Um…no, but…," Curt explained to Rachel what he had found, including the name in the jacket. She pleaded with him to leave the apartment and wait for the team to arrive.

Curt thought about the joy he'd seen on the face of Charlotte Morgan's mother that day in San Francisco, just like all the other times he brought a child back to their parent's arms. He'd wondered when the day would come for him to experience that same level of happiness. That day was today.

"Okay, I'll wait—"

Curt cut his sentence off as the unmistakable sound of a car door slamming shut came from just outside of the window. A shadow of a man moved past the window toward the front door to Gregory's apartment. Curt moved to the window and moved the blinds just enough to see out. He saw the silver Honda facing the apartment and the backside of Glenn Gregory walking toward the community mailboxes. He knew it was him as he recognized the man's walk from the security footage at the Governor's Square Mall. He looked back at the Honda, but there was no Josh. He played back the sounds he had just heard and recalled only one door shutting, not two. Where the hell is Josh?

"Everything okay?" Rachel asked, concerned for the sudden silence.

"Gregory's here. I gotta go."

"But Curt—" He pressed end and stuffed the phone in his jacket pocket. He felt the phone buzz again. He was sure Rachel was calling back, but he ignored it and stepped out into the living room. With Gregory showing up, Curt decided he could no longer wait for the team. Gregory was just outside of the apartment, and there was no sign of Josh. He would just have to get the answers from Gregory.

He leaned up against the wall just behind the front door, waiting for him to come in. He withdrew his Glock and held it down by his side. He heard footsteps just on the other side of the door, the jingle of keys followed by Gregory engaging the lock only an arm's length away. Curt took a deep breath as the door opened and enclosed him against the wall. Gregory's hand blindly reached around to the interior side of the door and shut it as he looked down studying his mail. As the door shut, Curt ran up and kicked Gregory as hard as he could in the back of his left knee. Blindsided, Gregory collapsed to the floor. Curt whipped around from the momentum of the kick and smashed the handle of his Glock on the left cheek of the man, knocking him completely to the floor. Gregory's mail sailed across the tile floor as the crushing blow of the ambush kept him on the ground.

Curt stood over the man and kicked him in the side making him roll over onto his back. Gregory winced from the lingering effect of the kicks from his attacker. Looking up at the stranger, Gregory showed little sign of fear at the man in the trench coat. Curt found this odd. He knelt down next to Gregory who was still dazed from the blow and pointed the Glock at his head.

"Where the hell is my son?"

Gregory let out a defeated groan as he leaned up on his elbows. He remained lying on the floor, looking up at Curt with defiant eyes. He ignored the question as he reached up and touched his cheek, assessing the damage. There was a gash in his face from the butt of Curt's gun that caused blood to seep out and run down his cheek.

Curt grew impatient which quickly turned to anger at the man's defiance. He backhanded the bleeding man on the floor for his dissention. He was inches away from his face; spit sprayed wildly in Gregory's face as Curt yelled, "ANSWER ME, DAMMIT!"

The defiance remained unwavering. "You must be the cop." Gregory held a smug look on his face.

Curt was caught off guard by the man's response and reacted without thought. With lightning speed, Curt stood over Gregory and swung the cold, unforgiving steel of his gun hard across the face of the man with every ounce of strength he could find. Gregory's head whipped back violently, absorbing the blow, and sending him into the realm of the unconscious as his body fell limp on the cold tile.

Chapter 29

Investigative journalism was what Tony Mason lived for. The thrill of chasing the unfiltered truth was what fueled his fire. Finding the little connections that spelled out the story that made it truly newsworthy was a satisfying rush. He assumed the feeling was similar for detectives working a case in search of a suspect. He had found a big investigative nugget when he saw the picture of Rachel Goodwin, and he was finally going to get his story, despite the efforts of Alexis Vanderhill.

He stayed up late the night before after identifying the blonde, ponytailed heroine from the human trafficking case and dove head first into her background. He didn't find much on Rachel, but the caption from the society page in *The Chronicle* gave him a lead to follow…her sister.

Mason Googled Rhonda Goodwin's name and found several articles from the 1993 abduction of her and her older sister, Rachel, from their neighborhood in Texas. He read where Rachel was found a few days later, disoriented and dehydrated, wandering around a nearby town. Rhonda was never found and was presumed dead. The suspect was never found or identified. He did find a couple of arrest reports where Rachel had been locked up for drunk and disorderly charges when she was in her early twenties. It didn't give a lot of background, but the abduction angle gave him a theory of how this clandestine team was formed. He jotted down some notes on his notepad to follow up with later.

Before leaving his hotel room, Mason stared at his cell phone and Detective Rankin's card. He considered whether or not to share his findings regarding Rachel Goodwins possible involvement in the shooting. He had laid all his cards on the table and told the detective of Alexis Vanderhill. If he did his own research like Mason did, he should come up with the same results. So with that, he stowed the business card away and walked down to the lobby. He used the business center in the hotel and pulled up the picture of Rachel Goodwin and Alexis Vanderhill from *The Chronicle's* website and printed out the picture he had found the night before. He pulled out his notepad and located the number Rankin had given him for the Orion Project. He dialed the number and talked to someone after identifying himself as a detective working with Rankin on the shooting. He explained that he wanted to fax a picture and have the girls look at the picture, hoping to identify the woman and whether she was involved in the shootout in Vail or not. The person on the other end agreed, and Mason held on the line while the fax went through.

"I got it."

"Alright good; just call me back at this number after you've shown it to the girls, and try to be quick. We want to roll on this as soon as possible, okay?" Mason said in his best cop voice.

"Sure…will do detective."

"Thanks." Mason made sure they had his number and hung up the phone, awaiting the outcome of his little ruse. He walked out of the business center and into the small cafeteria set with a free breakfast. He wasn't that hungry for food, just hungry for the story. He grabbed a coffee and muffin and sat, impatiently waiting for his phone to ring.

Fifteen minutes later, after Mason emptied the cup of coffee, he got up for a refill. As he pushed down the lever to dispense more coffee, his cell phone chirped. He set the cup down even before the coffee was done pouring out, causing it to spill over the counter, and he pulled out his phone.

"Hello?"

"Uh, detective?"

He had forgotten to answer the phone like a cop. He cursed himself for forgetting.

"Yes, sorry. It's me. What did you find out? What did they say?"

"Not all of them, but most of the girls said the woman on the left, in the pants suit, was the woman from the house that night of the shooting."

"What about the woman on the right? Anything there?"

"No, none of them recognized her."

Mason was dejected at the lack of an ID on Vanderhill but was satisfied at the confirmation on Goodwin.

"Excellent…thank you for your help. Oh, and if you don't mind, shred that picture please; we don't want anyone to get any wrong ideas and impede our investigation."

"Oh, sure. We can do that. Glad to help."

Mason left his coffee cup on the counter and ran up to his room to pack. He was eager to head out and follow his new lead. With affirmation that Rachel Goodwin was one of Vanderhill's team members, he knew he was getting close to figuring out exactly who they all were. He could feel the story growing and nearing the point where it was perfectly ripe to pluck and put into words.

***

Mason spent the day canvassing the area hotels. He drove past the house on the bluff for another look and expanded his search outward, assuming they would have used a hotel that was nearby. He checked at least twenty different hotels and resorts ranging from the fleabag variety to the posh, all with no luck. Either they didn't remember seeing Goodwin, or she was never there. Or, Mason thought, she used an alias, which he had no clue what it could be. If that were the case, his investigative nugget would turn into fool's gold.

The chase that started out with such strong motivation that morning waned into an annoying errand to check off a list. Mason questioned his value as an investigative reporter and pulled into the Vail Marriot Resort to continue the search. He remembered what one of his old editors had told him, "If it were easy, anybody could do it." The mountain lodge style hotel was the perfect destination for a winter vacation he thought, but it looked out of place in the summer.

It was getting late, and he had skipped over lunch. This could be his last stop. His stomach protested the idea as he smelled the food wafting in from the restaurant. There was a small line of guests at the desk, so he walked up to the bar, figuring he could grab a quick bite to satisfy the hunger pangs and wait out the line. The bartender took his order and sent it to the kitchen.

"Something to drink?"

"Just water, thanks."

"Sure thing." The bartender used the station in front of Mason to fill the drink order.

Mason took stock in his progress so far, which wasn't much. Getting Goodwin identified as the woman at the house was a huge piece of the puzzle, which he was still withholding from Rankin, but it was only temporary. He wondered if Vanderhill had some kind of safe house in Vail where they were operating out of since he'd struck out at the hotels. He would head to the property appraiser's office next to see if she had any rental properties in the area. They had to have set up camp somewhere; he just had to find out where.

Although it felt like a cliché, Mason pulled out the picture of Rachel Goodwin from a small folder and laid it on the bar. He slid it to the bartender and asked if he'd seen her.

"Why do you ask?" he questioned, guardedly.

That was the first response he'd gotten other than, "No, nope, no sir, or sorry not here" all day. Mason looked at the bartender trying to read his eyes. He saw recognition. He thought about the question posed by the bartender and figured he had to handle this right and really sell the bullshit he was about to give.

Mason smiled, "Look, I'm a private investigator. The chick's old man hired me to see if she's been stepping out, you know? Got some credit card receipts at the hotel here; just wanted to see if the allegations were true. Can you help me out?"

The bartender relaxed just a bit. Mason figured the man had pegged him for a stalker ex-boyfriend or someone with ill intentions, so he went the PI route in the ruse just in case.

"Well, maybe," the bartender offered cryptically.

As a journalist, he dug deep for the truth behind his stories, and sometimes that meant he had to grease the wheels on occasion. He smiled as he pulled out a twenty dollar bill. The bartender looked indifferent until Mason added a fifty.

"Yeah, she was staying here a few days ago. As far as stepping out, I would say it was safe to assume so. Some guy in a trench coat was up at the bar with her. I saw both of them take off for her room at closing time night before last. Haven't seen 'em since."

Mason slid the money across the bar and thanked the bartender, trying his best to hide his excitement. He excused himself and walked over to the front desk to further his pursuit. A young woman, dark-skinned with a bright, white smile greeted him.

"Hello, I'm from Vanderhill Incorporated. I'm just following up a small internal audit within our company, verifying that the employees weren't fudging their travel expense reports, and I just wanted to make sure they were kosher, that's all."

The woman thought briefly about the request, and since they were past guests, he needed to provide the name and date. She was only allowed to verify the information as correct or not. It was slightly odd that they would send someone in person rather than check via email or over the phone.

"Sure, what's the name? I'll check."

Mason gave Goodwin's name and guessed that her check out date was the day of the shooting. He gave her the date as if it were fact, hoping he didn't over sell it. He waited for the information while he nervously tapped the counter for the results.

"Okay, I got her right here. All paid up." The young woman recalled the dates Goodwin stayed there and added that it was a single occupancy room.

"Okay, great. Thank you."

Mason felt validated but was hoping she would have shared a room with one of the other team members, overall, he was happy with the results. He'd found another link and had a solid base to build his story and bring the vigilante team out into the light. The idea of a book deal suddenly crossed his mind, but he would take one step at a time. He thought about asking the desk clerk about the man in the trench coat, for that's all he knew about him, but he was worried she would see through his ploy and possibly call the authorities.

Mason turned to walk back to the restaurant and pick up his food.

"Sir?" the clerk called out stopping Mason.

"Yes, ma'am?"

"Don't you need to check on the other employees she was with?"

Mason smiled at the shift in luck he was being given but maintained the persona of the travel auditor from Vanderhill Incorporated.

"Of course I do."

Chapter 30

For the last three years, Curt had routinely fantasized about having the opportunity to inflict as much pain as possible on the person responsible for taking his son. However, when he was finally in the middle of that reality, he lacked direction. His initial plan of hostile interrogation hadn't worked. Gregory wasn't talking. He had to move on to plan B.

Curt set the bait and was waiting to spring the trap. He had to proceed with the utmost caution because too much was at stake.

He drove the Crown Vic down the main streets of Valdosta, trying to get a bearing on where he was and familiarizing himself with the area. While circling the area, he checked his rear view mirror for anyone following or driving too closely that could possibly figure him out.

The sun hung low as dusk neared, and the small rush hour created congestion on the main highways making it easy for Curt to blend in. He pulled off into a large shopping complex and found a parking spot furthest away from the store and out of earshot.

He pulled out the cell phone and checked it…no response yet.

"C'mon dammit, write back," he said out loud. He watched closely as a vehicle followed him into the parking lot and drove slowly past him. He remained still in the parked car, hoping he would remain unnoticed by the passerby. As the car moved on, Curt noticed he was holding his breath.

He checked the cell phone again. Nothing.

Thump, thump.

Curt looked back through the rearview mirror but didn't move at the odd sound. He heard a dull, muffled voice straining to say something. The noise annoyed him more than it concerned him, but he scanned the area for anyone close enough to hear. It was clear. He found a small nook created by some hedges and a closed business that offered the much needed privacy, so he backed the Crown Vic into the spot next the tall hedges.

Thump, thump, thump.

Curt ignored the noise and sat waiting.

***

Glenn Gregory slowly regained consciousness while Curt implemented plan A. He struggled against the handcuffs that were cinched tight around his wrists. He looked down and noticed the restraints around his ankles. The shackles kept him strapped into a chair situated in the middle of the kitchen and a prisoner in his own home. He was still dazed from the blow he took to the head and needed a minute to figure out what was going on.

Glenn was a pitiful sight as Curt watched, but he had no compassion for the man. Dried blood streaked down his face where the butt of Curt's gun violently met the boney end of Gregory's left cheek.

Once Gregory became aware of his surroundings, Curt stepped up to him and bent at the waist, meeting him eye to eye. He held his stare, hoping the man could read the unadulterated hate glaring in his eyes. Curt wanted to make it clear to Gregory that nothing was going to stand in the way of his finding his son. Curt's nostrils flared and his jaw clenched as he conveyed non-verbally that he was willing to bury him if necessary.

Gregory looked back into the blackness of his eyes. Fear gripped him like a vise and squeezed to the point he was about lose control of his bowels. His only reaction was to scream.

Curt anticipated the man yelling for help, so after the shriek let loose, he stuffed Gregory's mouth with a folded pair of socks. They were the dirty ones he'd found on the floor in Josh's bedroom. It stifled the noise, and before he could spit out the socks, Curt followed up with a strip of duct tape across his mouth to hold them in place.

Gregory's eyes bulged with fear, and he stopped screaming. A new level of panic set in.

"They can't hear you. No one is coming to help you." Curt's tone was minimal and calm, very matter of fact.

217

The man shook his head back and forth in a futile attempt to loosen the sock and tape gag, but Curt had been unforgiving and merciless as he sealed the tape tightly across Gregory's mouth. His eyes started to roll back in his head as his gag reflex took over. Curt didn't care if the man suffered, but he needed him alive for now. He couldn't afford for him to choke on his own vomit and die before he had the location of his son. He watched for just a moment longer to see if he could manage. When the dry heaving started, Curt knew the play was over and he ripped off the tape and sock gag, letting the man gasp for air.

He coughed and spit while he sucked air back into his lungs.

"Yell again, and I'll put it back on and walk out that door."

Gregory looked back at him and nodded in agreement.

"You know why I am here, so don't bullshit me. You tell me where my son is, and you get to walk out of here. If not, you'll be carried out in a body bag." Curt remained within inches of the kidnapper's face.

Gregory smiled and chucked a defeated laugh. "I don't know."

"You don't know, or you won't tell me?" Curt stood up and stepped back to the counter.

"I don't know…and I won't tell you."

Curt grabbed a kitchen towel from the counter and began to wrap it tightly around his right hand.

"You know, I was hoping you would say that." Curt jumped violently at the man and brought his fist crashing down against the top of his already injured left cheek bone, ripping open the freshly clotted wound. Blood started to ooze past the already dried blood as Gregory nearly fainted again from the powerful blow.

Curt pushed his head back up to face him again. He bent down to look him in the eye and hold his stare. Gregory remained defiant. Without any follow up questions or warning, Curt reared back and punched Gregory square in the nose, knocking his head back and lifting the front two legs of his chair a few inches off the ground. The chair rocked back down as more blood began to drain from his nostrils. Gregory gagged and spit blood as it began to flow down the back of his throat.

"Tell me."

"I can't." Gregory was gargling blood and saliva.

"Tell me! Where is he?"

Gregory closed his eyes, and tears rolled out and down his bloody cheek.

"Tell me, and I'll stop, GOD DAMN you!"

"I don't know. I can't...."

"Fine. I'm not leaving without answers."

Curt stepped back to the counter and pulled out a small plastic bottle of industrial glue. He poured it onto a plate until it was empty. Next, he found where Gregory kept his glassware and took one out of the cabinet. He wrapped the empty glass in another towel and smashed it with a rolling pin. The glass shards crunched against the countertop as Curt smoothed the glass with the rolling pin. After a few extra rolls and crunching the glass into tiny, crushed shards, he opened the towel. He took his right hand, still tightly wrapped with the first towel, dipped it in the glue, knuckles first, and then into the ground up glass. He turned and stared at Gregory while the glue hardened.

"I saw this in a movie once. I'm pretty sure it's going to hurt like hell."

Gregory looked away, whimpering as he bled.

Curt took a deep breath. He managed to find a calm voice to continue questioning Gregory.

"I found his jacket and clothes in your apartment. I have video of you with him at the mall in Tallahassee, and a witness got your tag. I know you have him or you know where he is, so just tell me."

Gregory looked at Curt's right hand and began to panic. He wanted to scream but stopped at the thought of the gag being stuffed back in his mouth. He couldn't take the suffocation again; it was worse than death. He sobbed at what fate had brought him and looked up at the man in the trench coat with a pleading look for sympathy, hoping to find an ounce of mercy.

When it came to who took his son, there would be no mercy. It was clear Gregory wasn't going to answer, so Curt stepped forward and punched Gregory in the same spot on his cheek over and over with precision. He wanted the glass fragments to embed deep into his skin with each strike causing a hellish pain to his face. As he delivered the strikes again and again, Gregory tried to avoid them by wrenching his neck around and moving his head side to side. Curt simply pulled him back into range and let loose another vicious punch.

Curt furiously threw punch after punch, but the man did not reveal where Josh was and absorbed the torture. He could feel the bones on the left side of his face crunch and pulverize further with each blow. Curt started to punch with his uncovered left hand to add to the damage and he quickly grew tired and exhausted.

"JUST TELL ME WHERE HE IS!"

After the onslaught of punches, strikes, and wild haymakers, Curt stepped back, exhausted by the beating he gave Gregory. He hadn't noticed that he sat cuffed to the chair, limp and unconscious with his head bowed down to his chest. He stepped back and looked at himself. He was covered in blood because it had sprayed off his torture victim with each violent blow. The tile floor beneath him looked like it had rained blood, and he noticed his foot prints were in it. He stepped back and leaned against the counter to collect himself. He needed to change tactics. He needed a plan B.

***

While Gregory sat lifeless in the kitchen, Curt moved around the house, looking desperately for any information or lead on Josh's whereabouts. He tore Gregory's room apart, searching for any shred of information, but he didn't find any. He grew angry at the lack of answers. Everything felt clouded and gray, and he couldn't get a clear feel for Gregory or the lead. He searched every crevice and every hiding spot and then entertained thoughts of ripping out the drywall but knew that would cause too much of a disturbance. He couldn't understand why Gregory wasn't talking and for what reason. Clearly, Gregory was the right man. What innocent man would take this much suffering if he wasn't hiding something that was worth it?

Curt yelled out in frustration and collapsed on the couch in the living room.

He caught his breath and sat up on the edge of the couch. He thought to himself, I'm going about this wrong. I'm too close. I need to take a step back.

Curt shut his eyes and tried to focus solely on the case. He had to think like a detective, not a hysterical father. If this were just another case....

"God dammit!" Curt cursed himself at the simplicity of the answer. He stood straight up with a renewed sense of energy and went through Gregory's belongings. He had searched his person and removed his effects before tying him to the chair. Curt grabbed them off the counter and sifted through Gregory's wallet. He found a few business cards that had phone numbers handwritten on the back, but nothing stood out.

His attention turned to Gregory's cell phone. Curt had yet to find a perpetrator who didn't use a cell phone in their criminal endeavors. The more arrogant suspects tended to keep more incriminating evidence that proved damning. Plus, it was the modern day lifeline that people used to stay connected, whether with family, friends, or co-conspirators. It was clear; since Josh wasn't at the apartment, Gregory obviously had help keeping track of the boy. Curt was betting that person would be in Gregory's phone.

Curt clicked on the phone and saw there was a pass code requirement.

"Shit!" If Gregory was willing to take a beating like that and could lead him to Josh, he damn sure wasn't going to tell him the pass code, but this did not deter Curt. He'd seen Louis do this several times when trying to hack into a cell phone. He would say, "Low tech is sometimes the best way to defeat high tech."

Curt never quite understood this saying until now. The pass code required some type of swipe across a four by four pattern of dots. Curt held the phone up to the light in the kitchen and tilted the screen to just the right angle in the light, revealing the oily smudge tracks on the phone. It was in a crisscross and a line up the right side of the pattern. Curt smiled, but in what sequence did the track start and end was the question. If he failed to guess the pass code, he could be locked out and the information lost. If Gregory was the paranoid sort, he would've set up a failsafe to crash the phone after too many failed attempts. He failed at the first try, but after the second try, the screen lit up, and Curt was granted access.

"Low tech." He smiled while looking back at the unconscious Glenn Gregory.

In the phone calls and recent text messages, Curt found a high frequency of calls to a person named "Tobias." He opened the text message thread and found exactly what he was looking for, correspondence back and forth from Gregory and "Tobias" that referenced "the kid."

He found more text messages back on the day that the tipster saw Josh with Gregory in Tallahassee. It read: "I'm headed home; it's your turn. Where do you want to meet up? Dinner?"

"Tobias" replied, "Sure, make it the usual place."

A follow up text from "Tobias."

"You shouldn't have gone there with the kid. Too dangerous, coulda been spotted."

Curt had enough and quit reading. He was convinced already that if Josh wasn't with Gregory, he was with this "Tobias" person. Suddenly, plan B came to light. However, he needed some background. He read some of the other texts to gain an understanding of how they spoke to each other and got an idea of how to get "Tobias" to come to him.

Curt answered the text to "Tobias" to draw him out.

"We need to meet. I have something for the kid."

A few minutes later he got a response, "Fine, give me a li'l bit."

Curt replied, "Just let me know when."

"K."

All kinds of possibilities formulated in his head as to how this ruse would play out, but for now, he had to leave the apartment immediately and somehow take Gregory with him.

***

Dusk brought a curious purple and orange hue to the sky. As he sat in the parking lot waiting, Curt ignored the thumps. He thought about the text messages he had read in Gregory's phone and let the information reverberate back and forth in his mind. They were cryptic in meaning, but he'd been around enough sexual deviants while working in the Special Victim's Unit that he could interpret enough to make sense of the meanings. His son Josh was a possession to the men, not a symbol of affection. The uneasy feeling in his stomach was growing.

His father's curiosity got the better of Curt. He couldn't ignore the feeling any longer. He opened up Gregory's cell phone and searched through the rest of the contents. He came to the photo album and took a deep breath before hitting the image on the screen, opening up the saved pictures. Please don't be there, he said to himself.

There were random pictures of Gregory and several other men at various social gatherings and maybe even some at work but nothing from a hidden dark side. There were some funny pictures Gregory had saved from text messages and emails along with pictures of gourmet dishes of food but nothing deviant. He scrolled up and down and found a few of Josh playing alone in a park. He examined the picture's background for a lead but couldn't help but fixate on the boy's face. The darkness was there—in his eyes, the hollow look of a soul stained by evil.

Curt exited out of the album, but another image caught his attention. It was an icon marked private. The uneasy feeling exploded into a paralyzing fear. He clicked on it, opening up the App. Another pattern pass code requirement but Curt easily defeated it because it was the same as the phone's pass code.

Another deep breath.

He opened up the album, and his worst nightmare became a reality. There were dozens of pictures of Gregory and a man whom he assumed was "Tobias," nude and in various sexual positions with his young son. Drawn to the horrific atrocities that his son was subjected to, bile began to accumulate by the gallon in his stomach. In the past, Curt had the unfortunate duty of working several child pornography cases during his tenure as a Special Victim's detective. Each case and image held its own shock value and abhorrent depravity, but seeing his own son subjected to this was too much.

Curt fell out of the Crown Vic, trying to escape from the nightmare and crawled away from the car. He vomited on the wet ground while on his hands and knees. He retched repeatedly as his body convulsed violently. The shock was too much to bear.

Thump, thump.

All he saw was red—pure, blinding anger and hatred. Curt stood up, snatched the cell phone from the front seat, and stood at the trunk. He popped it open to reveal Glenn Gregory on his side, bound in a sweaty, bloody mess. His hands were still cuffed behind him and a thick strip of duct tape was across his mouth. Curt had left the dirty socks at the apartment in a minor act of mercy, but now he wished he had them after seeing the pictures.

Curt was breathing heavily and was unable to speak. He glared down at Gregory with wide eyes and hate seething from his pores. He wanted to inflict as much pain as he could for what he'd done to Josh. He held up the phone to show Gregory that he had found the disgusting images on his phone.

"You...you...raped him?" Curt's face was fuming with hostility and revenge. He no longer saw Gregory as a man but as a despicable, child-molesting monster.

Gregory read the anger correctly and retracted into the dark, cramped trunk of the Crown Vic, avoiding his impending demise.

"You sick motherfucker! Is that why you took him? To be some kind of sex toy, you piece of shit? What? Did you and this other fuck just pass him around?"

Curt reached in and grabbed Gregory's left ankle and pulled the lower half of his body just outside of the trunk. His feet dangled near the bumper as Curt held him down. He was awkwardly bent over the rim of the trunk, and the handcuffs behind his back made it impossible for Gregory to sit up. Curt searched for something in the trunk while the child molester was whimpering and whining through the duct tape.

Curt withdrew a tire iron from the trunk and raised it high above his head.

"Answer me? Did you just pass him off like some kind of sex toy?"

He didn't need a verbal answer. Curt had been in enough interviews with guilty suspects to see when someone answers with their eyes. Gregory's eyes were saying, yes.

And with that, Curt swung the tire iron down with all his strength, powered by rage, and smashed the narrow metal pipe directly on his genitals. Gregory let out a guttural groan that managed to escape through the tightly sealed duct tape. He howled in agony as his manhood throbbed in impotence. Curt slammed the tire iron down a second time just as hard. Gregory's eyes rolled back in his head as the howl was muffled by the duct tape.

Curt raised the tire iron up again, poised for a follow up blow that would make the impotence permanent. Gregory's eyes bulged at the raised weapon, and he tried to recoil his legs to block another blow. He tried to squirm and kick, but Curt was too strong, and he pinned his upper torso down, keeping him in the position.

Just as Curt was about to send down the follow up strike to his genitalia, Gregory's cell phone bleeped with a reply message from "Tobias." He dropped the tire iron and stepped away to check the phone. He scooped Gregory's legs up and tossed him back inside the trunk but not before giving him a piercing glare that conveyed the message, "I'm not through with you."

Curt slammed the trunk shut and sat back in the driver's seat of the Crown Vic. He gathered control of himself and turned his focus on continuing the plan. He was panting from the exertion. He had worked up a sweat and was getting hot from wearing the trench coat. The text from "Tobias" read, "Ready…where do you want to meet?"

Curt looked up and tried to think back through some of the text messages he read earlier. He needed to pick a place that they both had felt comfortable going to in the past so as not to spook him away. He shot a glance down the busy road and found the answer.

He responded with Taco Bell, a place they apparently had an affinity for or chose to appease their captive, Josh, by taking him there. He didn't know where that came from because Curt didn't remember Josh ever liking Taco Bell.

"k," came a quick response.

Curt cranked up the Crown Vic and drove down the street to the Taco Bell to await "Tobias."

***

It was the beginning of the dinner hour, and there were a fair amount of patrons starting to arrive at the fast food restaurant. Curt watched closely as the people parked and walked up. He kept a watchful eye for anyone who might look like "Tobias." Before he left Gregory's apartment, he snatched the framed picture he saw of Gregory, arm-in-arm with another man, and laid it on the seat next to him for a reference. He assumed that's who it was since it was displayed in the living room as a central, focal point.

He thought back to the day when Josh went missing and the helpless feeling he had in his failure to stop the men from taking his son. He thought about Gregory and this "Tobias" person and how they were not formidable opponents who were ruthless and dangerous as he had imagined. Had Curt had the chance that night at the softball field, he would have easily fought off the men and kept them from taking Josh. They were devious and cunning to have taken him while he changed clothes.

A gold crossover SUV pulled into the parking lot from the highway and found a spot near the front entrance. Curt watched from his position in the back of the parking lot. From that distance, he couldn't tell if it was "Tobias" or not, but it was a white male, same height and weight as him with light brown hair. Curt glanced back down at the picture on the seat and tried to hold a snapshot in his mind. He watched intently as the man stepped out of the small SUV and looked around. He looked irritated and pulled his phone from his pants pocket, checked it briefly, and put it back.

Curt quickly hit the send button making Glenn Gregory's phone call "Tobias," as he continued to watch. The man was still irritated and huffed around the crossover. Curt couldn't see inside the vehicle because of the glare of the low-lying sun, so he kept a watchful eye on the driver. As the phone call connected and started to ring, he saw the man pull out his phone and answer it. He answered the phone just as Curt hit the end button confirming that was "Tobias." Curt stepped out of the Crown Vic and started walking toward the restaurant.

As he walked, he noticed Tobias was getting furious with Gregory who was not answering his call. He started pacing around the SUV trying to call him back. Suddenly, the back door opened up while Tobias wasn't paying attention and two small feet stepped out and away from the vehicle. The door remained open, blocking the view of the small passenger. Curt stepped up onto the sidewalk alongside the restaurant to get a better angle. He tried to see around the SUV door but couldn't without walking through the restaurant.

Tobias addressed the small passenger impatiently and seemed to give in to whatever he was asking. Tobias shut the door and revealed who was with him.

Curt's body went numb at the sight of his son, several yards across a parking lot, alive and healthy. He didn't notice his legs had stopped moving, and he stood smiling at the vision before him, knowing it was not a mirage but a sweet reality. He reached his hand out slowly as if to touch his son.

Tobias saw him first. The man was standing on the sidewalk wearing a trench coat and in some kind of a daze. He'd seen him before and instinctively paused out of paranoia. He shot glances around the parking lot and over his shoulder. Josh sensed the hesitation and looked past Tobias to the cause. He saw the strange man standing on the sidewalk holding his hand out oddly and staring right at him. He looked very familiar. He studied his face for only a moment, and then the trench coat sparked a memory he thought was lost.

"Daddy!" he cried out. "Daddy!" Tobias grabbed the boy as he waited for Curt to react.

The sound of Josh's cries broke Curt from his trance. He stepped forward and indexed his Glock as he watched Tobias hover over Josh. He grabbed him by the arm and dragged him back to the gold SUV. Curt lunged forward but was suddenly blocked by the restaurant door opening up. A party of four adults exited the restaurant and kept Curt from passing. He left his gun in the holster and watched through the glass door. He pushed the unaware bystanders out of his way. He got a few rude comments just as one of the men in the group grabbed hold of Curt's arms.

"Hey, buddy. You need to watch it." The man's grip pulled Curt back.

"No, let me go now!" he hissed back.

He kept his attention on Josh as Tobias pulled him back to the SUV and barely noticed the patron's efforts to pull him back for a confrontation. He yelled something to Curt, trying to show dominance, but he was too focused on Josh to hear. He had to get to him. He was right there! So close and within reach! He stepped forward but was suddenly pulled backwards. Curt quickly whipped around and punched the man who had ahold of him square in the nose, knocking him down from the lightning strike.

"I said let go!" Curt sloughed off the distraction and turned back to see Tobias had shoved Josh in the back seat and started backing up the SUV. He took off at a sprinter's pace for the vehicle and reached the rounded back of the crossover, trying to grab a hold on anything as he accelerated back out toward the exit. There was nothing tangible to grip, and Curt smashed his fist down on the back window, but that had no effect as it pulled away. Curt reached out to jump onto the SUV, but the quick acceleration kept it just out of his reach.

Curt gave chase on foot as Tobias paused at the exit for the traffic on the main highway. Josh's face appeared in the back window of the SUV. He had jumped over the back seat and into the rear compartment and was yelling for his father, beating his small hands on the back window in a futile attempt to get free. Curt caught up to the SUV at the exit, and before Tobias could speed away, he reached out and touched the outside of the glass where Josh held his hand on the inside. They held it there for just a brief, beautiful moment. Tobias cruelly ripped it away as he recklessly pulled out into traffic, causing other cars to swerve out of his way. Curt could hear the boy's voice pleading for his father to do something. He could see the terror on his face. Curt reached for his Glock but let it remain holstered; any shots he made could harm Josh.

As he watched Tobias dive in and out of traffic, escaping with the boy, he thought, *Was this brief moment the last he would be given to see his son one final time?*

"No, NOOOOO!" Curt yelled out at the top of his lungs. He immediately took off running as fast as he could, chasing after the speeding vehicle. There was only slight traffic to help slow him down, but he couldn't give up. He was so close that he could almost touch him. He'd never give up.

He watched the SUV accelerate, moving farther and farther away, as he ran as fast as he could. He disregarded the traffic, forcing cars to go around, honking as they passed completely unaware of the egregious felony that was in progress. Josh's pitiful face looked back at his father in pursuit causing Curt's heart to ache. He fought off the bitter feeling of helplessness that was coming back with every foot Tobias put between him and Curt.

Curt remained in pursuit and ignored the burn of lactic acid building up in his thighs and calves as he pounded the pavement. Fate gave him a favor at the red light ahead catching Tobias at about one hundred and fifty yards ahead. Curt pressed on running through the slowing vehicles trying to catch up.

His lungs started to burn in addition to his legs, but he pushed his body forward, holding the impressive speed and weaving between the stopped traffic. He gained and gained on the SUV and got close enough to see a smile break on Josh's face in reaction to seeing his father chase after him; it was like he knew he was going to be saved. Curt reached out again just as the SUV lurched forward, nearly striking the car in front, and sped off under the fresh green light. Tobias gunned it, switched to the open lane, and pushed the SUV up to sixty miles an hour as Curt looked on helplessly. The smile on Josh's face faded away, and he slipped back into the darkness.

Curt kept running, but the physical limits of his body fought against his will to continue. The SUV created such a distance from Curt that he could no longer see Josh's face or the SUV. He was gone. Again.

Chapter 31

Tobias strained to keep an eye on his rearview mirror, searching for the lunatic in the trench coat. He ignored the cries of the boy and kept the gas pedal to the floor, finalizing the escape. That was close, he thought, too close.

The familiar sight of his condominium complex gave him a reprieve from the chase that nearly cost him everything. He pulled in and quickly parked the car in front of his condo, got the boy out, who was still hysterically crying, and carried him into the apartment.

"Shut up. Now!" he said, with a harsh, hiss-like tone. Josh knew to obey, no matter the circumstances, so he quieted himself on the outside but balled up on the floor crying while Tobias paced around the living room.

"How the hell did he find you?" Tobias asked of himself. He pulled out his cell phone and called Gregory. The phone continued to ring unanswered. Tobias grew angry.

"Where the hell are you, Glenn? Where the hell were you...?" Tobias continued to pace around the living room trying to think and trying to get a grasp of what was happening. He started to wonder if Glenn's little trek back to Tallahassee with the boy had cost them everything. I told him not to go. It was too risky. Then it dawned on him.

"Of course!" he said out loud. The police were able to get something on Gregory, follow him back to Valdosta, and lead them straight to the boy. But they only sent one cop. That didn't make sense.

"Why weren't there more cops?" he asked himself again, confused. The boy's sobbing, however quiet, drew his attention. He looked down at him in thought. Josh was holding his bent legs to his chest and rocking back and forth. Then it hit him. And the answer scared him.

He was too scared at the time to realize what the boy was saying as the man chased after them like a wild maniac. He replayed the memory searching through the hazy panic and remembered that he heard the word "Daddy." It was the boy's father, the cop from Tallahassee.

"Shit!" Tobias paced around the room more frantically. He kept trying Glenn's number and getting no answer. He wasn't sure what to do, but he felt like disappearing. He could pack a few things and be halfway across the country by sunrise tomorrow, but he'd be forced to take the boy. Or…he could dispose of him. Tobias thought about the options, but another idea came to him, an idea that was less complicated than the others. He picked up his cell phone and dialed out.

"I have to call—"

The explosion was so loud and unexpected, Tobias's heart stopped and held its next beat for what seemed like an eternity. The front door to the apartment exploded out of its frame and off the hinges with such force that the entire door slammed to the floor. The wooden frame shattered into pieces and flew through the air like shrapnel. The orange glow of the setting sun followed the man in the trench coat through the door as he stormed in and found Tobias standing, frozen in shock. He was in the middle of the living room, holding his phone with an incredulous look on his face. Curt immediately zeroed in on Tobias and delivered a powerful kick straight to the middle of his chest. The kick sent him flying clear across the room. He landed hard in the corner and knocked his head on an end table rendering him unconscious.

Curt was breathing heavily from the exhaustive chase and couldn't yet speak between breaths. He found the boy curled up on the floor holding his head down, tuning out the world around him, not noticing the arrival of his father. He stepped over to Josh while keeping Tobias in the corner of his eye and knelt down by his side.

He calmed his breathing as fast as he could and as soon as he could speak, he said with a father's warm gentle calmness, "Josh, it's me. It's Daddy."

His small head, with tousled uncombed brown hair that he inherited from his mother, moved slightly inside of his tightly clutched arms at the sound of Curt's voice. He was still sobbing.

"It's me buddy, it's…it's Daddy." Curt gently reached out to touch the boy. His hand rested on the back of his head and neck, and he instinctively ran his fingers through his soft hair, something he did often from before. The connection in just that small touch was so powerful;

Curt had forgotten the immeasurable amount of pain he suffered for the past three years, almost like it had never happened.

Josh looked up at his father with salty tears streaking his cherub-like face as he stopped crying and gave credence to the situation. He reached up and clamped his arms around Curt's neck, squeezing him tight. Curt caught the boy and hugged him in a sweet embrace sheltering him from the rest of the darkness. Curt let loose his own cries. He had finally found his son.

***

After seeing the gold SUV disappear before his eyes with Josh inside, Curt just kept running, determined never to give up and especially not when he was so close. The Crown Vic was too far to go back and get without keeping an eye on the SUV, so he kept running despite the obvious advantage the quick SUV had over Curt's own two feet. He prayed that since Tobias showed up at the Taco Bell rather quickly after sending the text message, he must live relatively close by. For three long years, the search parameters were far too vast to cover. Now, the area was narrowed down to no more than four square miles. Curt wouldn't stop until he turned every inch upside down, but now that he'd seen Tobias' face, he feared that Josh would be killed as a loose end.

As Curt kept running down the highway, he turned down the same neighborhood road the SUV veered onto in the distance. He continued down the road for over a mile, searching for the gold SUV and keeping a pace worthy of top marathon runners. He ignored the pain from the uncomfortable dress shoes he was wearing and pressed forward undeterred. After blindly running nearly two miles from the Taco Bell with sweat pouring down his face and body from running blindly, Curt saw a sign that instantly meant something. As Tobias made his escape, Curt's cop instincts took over, and he scanned the back of the car for identifiable marks along with the tag of the gold SUV. He recalled, as Tobias was pulling away from the Taco Bell, he'd seen a small, green sticker with white lettering in the corner of the rear window. It read: Camellia Gardens. It was a parking decal for the complex. Curt was sure of it; he'd seen many of them while working in Tallahassee with two major universities and nearly 100,000 students living in similar complexes. They were used to identify residents over visitors for compliance of the rules.

When he saw the apartment complex sign with the same lettering, colors, and name, he didn't hesitate searching the area. It was luck that he wasn't going to question. As he slowed his pace, searching the parking lot for the gold SUV, he found it parked in front of an end unit. Curt sped up his pace and charged the door at top speed. He didn't care what opposed him on the other side of the door because he knew the one thing worth fighting for was behind the door, regardless of the danger.

***

The adrenaline pumping excitement of the chase started to wear off, and the stress and fatigue from the exhaustive three-year hunt was now over. Curt reveled in the triumph knowing the odds had been forever stacked against him. He now had his moment…the moments he'd watched nearly a hundred times before and wondered if or when his turn would come. That time was now.

Curt held his son tightly in his arms, vowing never to let him go. Josh pushed back and lifted his head up to say something, but before he spoke, he pulled his right arm from around his father's neck and pulled it in front of him to display his wrist.

"I never forgot Daddy. I never gave up…I stayed Unconquered."

He held his wrist up, proudly displaying the simple gray wristband Curt had gotten him at the baseball game several years before. Unbeknownst to Curt, the little rubber wrist band was his beacon of light in the hellish blizzard of a nightmare Josh had been living. He tried his best to block out the heinous cruelty and focus on the wristband and what his father had explained it meant. Curt looked down at the heart wrenching gesture that defined the boy's innocence and just hugged him even tighter for the special boy he was.

"I know buddy. I know."

Chapter 32

Most of the night was spent watching him sleep. The surreal feeling of seeing their son asleep in his bed gave the parents of Joshua Walker a peace they never thought would return. But now, it was real. To have him under their roof, within their reach, and sheltered by their love—it was real. It was the end of a hellish nightmare.

Curt stood silently in the doorway of Josh's room, watching him sleep, an image he'd dreamt about for the last three years. He looked peaceful and innocent. Josh was still so small even though three years had passed. His captors had inflicted mental and emotional abuse that seemed to stunt his maturation into an adolescent because he didn't look like an eleven year old.

Despite his chronic exhaustion, he remained awake and steadfast by the door. He was afraid that if he closed his eyes, he would wake up in another world where Josh was still missing, and this reality would be gone, or worse, another monster would grab him in the night. It wasn't until Tracy convinced him to trust the reality of his return that he left the bedroom door and made it to bed.

As the bright morning sun shone through the slats in the blinds, Curt came out of the dream world. He shot straight up in the king-sized bed and searched his strange surroundings, trying to remember how he'd gotten there. His mind quickly caught up as he realized he was home. Tracy was gone, her side of the bed perfectly made, so he twisted around to check the clock on the dresser.

It was nearly noon. Curt had slept over twelve hours straight. He lay back down, trying to push off the grogginess. He rubbed his face attempting to wake up as a wave of panic washed over him. *Where's Josh,* he thought. *Was it still true?*

He jumped out of bed wearing only a pair of boxers and walked out of the bedroom, but there were no signs of anyone. The panic grew. He ran down the hall to Josh's bedroom, but he wasn't there either. His bed was made perfectly, like it was the day before, and it had remained the same since his disappearance. Curt started to breathe heavier as the panic started to grip his insides.

The squeak of the heavy door that led into the laundry room from the garage caught his attention, and Curt's first reaction was to become armed, but the sound of Josh's voice followed by the sound of Tracy's calmed him and jolted him back into the coveted reality that he had fought so hard for, it was still true.

The boy and his mother walked in from outside, and Tracy was the first to see him standing confused in the hallway in just his underwear.

"Well, good morning. Uh, you might want to put on a little more than that; there're a lot of reporters out there asking questions, and I don't think you want to go out there dressed like that." She smiled at the thought of Curt dealing with the press in just boxers.

Curt exhaled; Josh was still safe and at home. They had simply walked outside to get the mail. The panic subsided and hopefully, at some point, would stay away on a permanent basis.

After eating breakfast, Curt ignored the press camped out on the street in front of his house, letting their questions go unanswered, and sat quietly on his back deck, drinking coffee from his preferred thermos with the tacky saying "Bad Cop, No Donut." This was a luxury that he had taken for granted before Josh's disappearance, and he wanted to take full advantage now that he had the chance. He looked out to the quiet woods behind his house as the trees swayed gently and the leaves rustled like whispers in the breeze. For once, he did not feel the urge to get up and go searching for his son. A tremendous weight had been lifted from his shoulders, and he would soon know the true meaning of relaxation.

The sun was high in its zenith, and warm rays beamed down through a clearing of tree limbs and onto Curt's face as if aimed by God. He closed his eyes and held his face up toward the sun, feeling its warmth radiate down, giving him the serenity and peace he had exhaustively hunted for since that fateful day. He looked through the living room window where Tracy sat next to Josh, who blankly stared at the television, a sight for which he was forever grateful. He marveled at the accomplishment he had achieved, knowing that all of the exhaustive work, all those hard fought days on the road searching, all the prayers, and even all the distractions were worth this specific outcome. He was content. He closed his eyes again taking in the sun's warmth, and before he knew it, he had fallen back asleep in the deck chair.

***

After crashing through the front door of Tobias Helton, Curt had scooped up his son and carried him away but not before kicking the pedophile kidnapper one more time with authority and handcuffing him to the dining table. Curt stood by while the Valdosta police raced to the scene. He explained who he was and that his son had gone missing three years prior out of Tallahassee. He told the officers about the tip that led him to Valdosta and to the front door of Glenn Gregory, who in turn, led him to Tobias Helton and ultimately to the recovery of his son. The officers worked the call in amazement and disbelief at the sensational story of how the dedicated father tracked down his son's captors.

Curt hesitantly told the cops of the location where his Crown Vic and Glenn Gregory were, but a sergeant who took control of the scene came up to him explaining that they had already found the Crown Vic with Gregory inside. Curt instantly thought he was going to be joining Gregory in jail until the sergeant said they found his stolen car after it was crashed into another car trying to make an escape. Curt looked at the sergeant with a puzzled look, knowing that he had the car's only keys. He was confident Gregory would not have been able to escape his restraints or the trunk and then manage to hotwire the car and drive away.

Before he could ask or set the record straight, the sergeant added, "Yeah, sorry that your car is all messed up; the guy was pretty FUBAR'd too. The crash must have messed him up pretty good, cuts and bruises all over his face, so they took him off to the hospital. If I were you, I wouldn't have left him in the back seat. Hell, I would've stuffed his ass in the trunk."

Curt was stunned into silence. He let the events turn in his favor without dispute. If the truth came out later, he would take responsibility, but for now, he was only focused on getting Josh home.

He had tortured Gregory, plain and simple—however justified in his mind—and left him bound in the trunk of his car. He figured the man would explain the true nature of how he sustained his injuries and at minimum, Curt would face some type of aggravated battery charge. However, the crash gave the story a different angle to explain how Gregory got his injuries.

Curt's phone dinged in his pocket, letting him know a text message was received. He didn't believe it was a random text based on the timing but something to give him an understanding of his situation. He pulled out his phone and opened the message. It was from Rachel Goodwin.

It read: You are welcome.

He looked up from the phone and craned his neck over the sea of blue lights in the condo parking lot that surrounded Helton's apartment. In the distance, he saw Rachel leaning on the side of the Mercedes Sprinter. Louis, Melinda, and Beth were watching through the open side door. She smiled at Curt, and with no particular ceremony or fanfare, she climbed in the van with the rest of the team and shut the door. A moment later the van was gone.

"Expecting someone?" the sergeant asked.

Curt turned his head back to the sergeant, keeping the team's presence hidden from the cops on scene and asked, "Did you get his phone? It has a lot of evidence on it."

"Yeah, my officers already have it impounded. We have this guy, Helton, on the way to the station to talk to the detectives. We're getting a search warrant for his place as well as the other guy's, and we'll get warrants for both of their cars too. Anything you think we missed?"

Curt thought about the execution of a search warrant at Gregory's apartment revealing the real story of what happened to him. He had to remain confident that he had gotten rid of all evidence of the torture before leaving.

"No, sounds like you're good."

"Listen...." The sergeant, a gray-haired man that stood a few inches taller than Curt and with a prominent belly pulled Curt in close. "I wish you would have called us before going all lone-wolf on these guys, but I get it. I'm a father too. So not only would I have gotten those pieces of shit for you, I would'a let you have some time alone, if you know what I mean."

Curt smiled at the comment, beholden to the brotherhood, and thanked the sergeant for the empathy but explained that he just wanted to get the boy home to his mother. He completely understood and directed a nearby officer to give him and the boy a police escort all the way back to Tallahassee since the Crown Vic was totaled. Curt obliged, just so long as his son was with him.

"Helicopter isn't available is it?"

The sergeant howled with laughter and patted his belly in relief. He caught the attention of the crime scene workers who watched in confusion.

"No, son. I'm afraid not. The patrol car is best I can do."

***

The news of Joshua Walker's recovery traveled fast. In a quiet office, the phone was picked up and a number dialed by memory. It rang on the other end twice before it was answered.

"He found the boy. It's all over the news."

"Okay."

"What should we do now?"

"Keep tabs on him like before. We need to know how much he knows, and then we'll deal with it like before."

"Okay. I'll take care of it."

Chapter 33

Tony Mason arrived in Tallahassee with the promise that his story was finally going to make it to print. It was vindicating knowing that he was onto something big when he first learned of the missing boy who mysteriously showed back up in his Southern California home. A person friendly with the boy's family had called, telling him of the return. He did some digging and learned that he had been held in some kind of cult in the hills of Northern California, most likely with the persons responsible for taking him. In doing research into the cult, he found that they were high-tech, powerful people who sometimes taunted the "regulars," as they called the rest of the world. Mason came to the conclusion that whoever found and returned the child to his parents had access to a lot of money, government databases, and must be working unsanctioned. He was instantly intrigued.

Mason searched through the rungs of state law enforcement and some federal branches, hoping to uncover the identity of the entity who did the clandestine work but came up empty. It didn't feel like government work. He assumed that they would most likely focus on something on a more threatening level, such as domestic terrorism. As he went back through his notes, he saw Alexis Vanderhill was involved. He knew her through the journalism world but through reputation only since she operated mainly on the east coast. He noticed that she was there when the boy was brought home…almost like she knew it was going to happen. He figured she was tipped off about the event and got the scoop, but when she never published anything, he grew suspicious of her presence outside of the article and went to interview the boy. That was when he got the full story of the Crusaders who managed to infiltrate the cult and sneak him out of the compound under the veil of night. It was a sensational tale that struck Pulitzer-sized stars in his head, but before he could print it, the boy recanted, and the family had their lawyer threaten to sue if the story was ever printed. Mason didn't have proof, outside of the boy's account, but his gut told him Vanderhill and her substantial influence persuaded the boy to recall this magnificent drama, thus creating the bitter taste in his mouth regarding the rival journalist.

This time he did the legwork beforehand and was ready to spring it on Alexis and her team.

After learning the names of the rest of the team from the desk clerk in Vail, Mason left his hotel for the Denver airport. He was going back home to Los Angeles, and he would write the story on the plane ride. His fingers tingled with excitement.

However, as he waited for the boarding announcement, he tuned into the headline news on the television in the airport's waiting area. One of the lead-in stories was of a Tallahassee cop who tracked down the men responsible for kidnapping his eight-year-old son, three years prior. The footage showed the man at a considerable distance, through a fleet of patrol cars and uniformed officers, kneeling down and hugging his young son. Mason was instantly mesmerized by the story but more for the fact the man was wearing a long, tan trench coat. His heart skipped a beat when the reporter provided the name of Curtis Walker.

It took Mason thirty seconds of deliberation before he got up and exchanged his ticket from LA to Tallahassee, where he was confident he would find the final piece of his story.

Now, Mason joined the crowd of reporters outside of Curtis Walker's home, hoping to get an exclusive interview with the father who took on the investigation of his son's kidnapping all on his own. After growing impatient at the reclusiveness of the family, Mason ignored the respect of the property boundary and walked up to the front door and knocked.

After a second knock and a persistent doorbell ring, the door cracked open. Inside stood the man in the trench coat. Mason identified himself as a reporter from Los Angeles but the door was shut in his face before he could even ask the first question. Curt told him to leave and respect the healing process. He added a threat of prosecution for trespassing if he didn't adhere to the boundary.

Through the closed door, but not loud enough to be heard by the other reporters who watched expecting failure, Mason said matter-of-factly, "I know what happened in Colorado and about the men you killed."

Mason let the statement simmer on the other side of the door as he waited patiently on the outside. The door cracked open, and Curt peered into his eyes, validating the fact that the reporter was at the right place, talking to the right person.

"Do you?" Curt asked skeptically. With everything surrounding the tip and Valdosta, he hadn't thought about the drama that played out at the house in Vail. For the reporter, whose name he knew well, must have flown under the radar of Alexis Vanderhill if he was now at Curt's home asking questions about Colorado.

"Yes. I know it was you and Rachel Goodwin who saved those girls from the traffickers and shot those men. I know about the boy your team rescued from the cult a year and a half ago, and I bet there are many, many more out there. I want to finally bring your story to life. This thing up in Georgia with your son only adds to it. You're a hero. Whaddya say?"

Curt's pulse quickened as he heard Rachel's name spoken out loud by Mason. He was on point with what happened, but the integrity of the team and their anonymity was paramount, especially over glorification of their actions. He could care less about the story surrounding his son. Curt didn't know how to respond to the sudden barrage of information and grew scared at the implications.

"I'm sorry. I can't help you. I don't know what you're talking about," he said. "Please, leave the property."

"Melinda Dalton...."

Curt's head whipped back around and stared at Mason.

"Beth Young...."

"How did you get those names?"

"I guess the new girl wasn't so good at covering her tracks back at the hotel, huh?"

Curt looked down trying to figure out what he meant but quickly realized that Rachel Goodwin had checked everyone in that day and failed to use their alias' instead of their real names. Mason must have swindled a look at the hotel's guest list. His look belied his knowledge of what Mason was saying, but he kept up the silent treatment.

"Sorry, can't help you. You need to leave now."

Mason grew dejected but knew enough of the strong-willed cop to know that he had struck a chord and got him thinking. He wanted to leave him with one final thought.

"I'm printing the story whether you like it or not. I have enough already that Alexis won't be able smooth talk her way out. I'm just offering you a chance to get on the record first. I hope you enjoy the view of reporters out here; it's only going to get worse."

Mason turned and walked down the stairs. The reporters who were watching the interaction chuckled at the rejection, knowing this yahoo from LA wasn't going to get any further than any of them. Mason shot a cocky look back at the crowd, knowing he had the real story.

Curt stood with his back to the door, sick with worry about the exposure of the team and the real ramifications of their methods. So many lives would be turned upside down, the children who had been returned along with their families. People, like Francine Bennett, would be allowed to walk free for their crimes if the truth was known. Not to mention, Federal charges could possibly be filed on the team. So much good work done in a dark world would be ridiculously scrutinized just because one reporter chased a story.

His imagination took off as he thought about the ramifications of exposure and hated the possible outcomes. Curt pulled out his phone and called Alexis.

After a few rings, she answered, "Hey, I'm so happy you finally found Josh. I've been following the story. Are you okay?"

"Yeah, but we have some real problems. Tony Mason knows about Colorado."

Silence fell on the other end.

"How bad?" she asked.

"He seems to know pretty much everything. Knows everyone's name too."

"Shit."

Curt told her everything about the exchange at his front door, including Mason's promise to move forward with the story with or without their cooperation and quoted him back to Alexis, saying that she couldn't smooth this over.

"Okay," she said. "Let me go. I'll handle it. You just stay there with Josh and don't worry about anything."

"All right. Goodbye."

"Goodbye."

It was hard to trust her words that she would take care of everything. It was an extremely tall order from his perspective, but he knew Alexis Vanderhill probably had more at stake than anyone else on the team. He found comfort in her confidence over the phone and hoped it was genuine and not a front used to put him at ease. Curt shook off the exchange with Mason and stopped short of the living room, taking in the scene of his family together again under one roof. He prayed it would stay that way.

Chapter 34

In the days following the recovery of Joshua Walker the story garnered national media attention, headlined with the heroics of a Tallahassee police detective who went on the solitary search for his missing son. It tugged at the hearts of parents across the nation who identified with the actions of the distraught father. Curt declined doing interviews from all who tried and refused to allow anyone to talk to his son. He didn't want any attention or glory. He had the only thing he wanted, his son. The media got agitated at his refusal, but after it was revealed that Josh was subjected to possible molestation from his abductors Glenn Gregory and Tobias Helton, the story took a dark turn, and most reporters understood the father's reluctance.

The Valdosta detectives in charge of the case worked closely with the detectives from Tallahassee. The perpetrators were charged with multiple counts of sexual battery of a minor in Georgia but were charged with the kidnapping in Tallahassee. Surprisingly, both jurisdictions worked hand-in-hand to make the best case possible and send the men to prison. The state where they served their time didn't matter, only that they served a lot of it.

Overwhelming evidence suggested that Josh had been living at both of the apartments belonging to Gregory and Helton. The photographic evidence of sexual activity was undeniable and the biggest piece of proof beyond a reasonable doubt for the prosecution in the sexual battery side of the case. On one hand, Curt was grateful that he found those pictures on Gregory's phone, but he would be forever scarred at the same time. Images like those can't simply be erased, and to a father, they were beyond pure torture. The detectives were able to use the video footage from the Governor's Square Mall against Gregory, which also proved he was familiar enough with Tallahassee to achieve the abduction three years prior.

It proved to be more difficult finding the evidence linking Helton to Tallahassee, until the detectives learned that both men had lived in Tallahassee prior to the abduction and had just relocated to Valdosta several months prior. Gregory had lived in an apartment that was near the softball complex, and it was assumed that he would've been familiar with the park. It was unclear what Helton did for employment, but Gregory was a runner at a local law firm, while he worked toward his paralegal degree from a local trade college.

When detectives searched Gregory's apartment, they found suspicious blood droplets in the kitchen. Samples were examined and collected. After some consideration, it was concluded that Gregory must have cut himself while preparing food before his encounter with Curtis Walker. In a photo album, which Gregory apparently was fond of, as it was displayed on his coffee table, detectives located a picture that appeared several years old; it was of Gregory and a small dog playing in a park. When they were shown the picture, the Tallahassee detectives were able to peg the backdrop as the dog park at Tom Brown Park, and that served as yet another piece for the prosecution.

In Helton's apartment, there were no such damaging photographs, but something else was found that twisted the stomachs of the detectives and made them hate the men even more. There were some toys used as marital aids, which after DNA testing, proved they were used on Josh on at least one occasion.

"I hope these guys burn in hell. Sick fucks...." The Valdosta detective's entire body cringed when he found the evidence in Helton's apartment.

After Gregory was released from surgery to repair several fractures to his orbital and cheek bones, he tried to claim that he was abducted by the boy's father and set-up in the crash. When asked about the abduction, sexual battery, and the evidence on his phone, he remained silent. Based on the case as it stood, it was clear to everyone involved; the outlandish accusations of torture and kidnapping were going to be ignored. The Valdosta authorities balked at his story of the crash being staged. It was obvious he had tried to make an escape using Curt's vehicle. The other driver swore the crazed man ran a stop sign and smashed into her. The police and prosecution never looked twice at Gregory's accusations and focused solely on the case against him instead.

***

Louis Melton was following Curt around Valdosta by watching the triangulation of his phone as Melinda navigated the Mercedes Sprinter through town. Curt had just hung up on Rachel when Gregory came home to his apartment, and the team rushed to try and help. They had just arrived in Tallahassee behind Curt and continued on to Valdosta following the phone call.

As he watched the computer screen, Louis called out the directions and Melinda followed, trying to catch up with Curt. Rachel tried calling back, but he wasn't answering. Just before getting into town, Curt's signal moved from an apartment complex to the area of a large intersection near the Interstate. As they tried to pinpoint his location near a shopping mall, the signal suddenly moved down the street.

Melinda was about to pull back into traffic to follow the signal when Rachel spotted the nose of the Crown Vic in the parking lot of a Taco Bell.

"Hey, there's his car!"

Melinda pulled the van into the parking lot and parked near the Crown Vic. It was unoccupied, and Curt was nowhere to be seen.

As they got out, the sounds of excessive honking from the highway were from confused and irritated motorists blasting their horns at Curt as he chased after Helton and Josh in the gold SUV. However, the team ignored the honks assuming that it was just the mindset of pissed off Valdosta drivers during rush hour.

Louis got out and confirmed it was Curt's Crown Vic and even spotted a phone on the front seat. He knew it wasn't Curt's from the look of it.

"Maybe he got something to eat?" Louis said, staring up at the Taco Bell sign.

"I'll go check inside," said Beth.

Rachel walked around the car looking for anything suspicious and trying his cell phone one more time. Again, no answer. She opened up the car and looked around inside. As she backed out, she noticed a small pile of vomit, which she nearly stepped in, on the ground.

"Eww, gross!"

Just then, she heard an odd thumping sound coming from the trunk. She looked around to see if the noise was coming from somewhere other than the Crown Vic, but it was parked by itself with the nearest car three stalls away. She listened carefully as an uneasy feeling grew in the pit of her stomach.

Thump, thump. She saw the car move slightly from the shifting weight in the trunk.

"Shit…Uh…Louis?"

"Yeah?"

"Open the trunk."

Louis heard the thumps too. He looked at Rachel warily and reached in the car for the trunk release button. Melinda walked over and stood next to Rachel, ready to face whatever or whoever was in the trunk. After looking around for any onlookers, she nodded for him to hit the button.

As the trunk lid opened, a dank foul odor of sweat, urine, and wet metal emanated from within the trunk. The image of Glenn Gregory beaten, bruised, and bound shocked both Rachel and Melinda. Rachel reached down and pulled the tape from his mouth.

"Ahh, thank you. Thank you so much. Please, you have to get me out of here; this madman broke into my house, kidnapped me, and beat me half to death. Please, help me out, please!"

Rachel and Melinda exchanged hesitant looks with each other but didn't make any moves to help Gregory out of the trunk.

"Are you Glenn Gregory?" asked Rachel.

The man's pleading face, seemingly innocent, turned a few shades paler at the sound of his own name. He figured if they knew his name, they were probably helping the man who put him there, and finding him wasn't his good fortune.

Before he decided to answer, Gregory let out a loud scream for help, but Melinda and Rachel both reacted at the same time and shut the trunk, muffling his screams. Louis stood off to the side in amazement as Beth came out of the restaurant, letting the team know Curt wasn't inside. She had heard the murmurs inside the restaurant of some guy in a trench coat chasing a car down the highway just moments ago.

"Sounds like Curt found another suspect," Rachel surmised. Louis took the phone from the front seat and opened it up. He saw the images

Curt had found in a hidden folder and crinkled his face in disgust as he recognized Curt's son in the images. He showed them to Rachel and Melinda who were equally repulsed by the pictures.

Louis took the phone inside the van to download its contents for further dissection. As he hooked it up to his machine, he heard on the police scanner that officers were responding to a kidnapping call where the father of the missing person had one man in custody. The dispatcher added that the boy was also on scene. Louis instantly smiled at the thought of Curt finding his son.

"Hey, he found him. He found Josh! The police are on their way. Looks like they're a few miles down the road."

They all smiled, knowing how much Curt had lost in his search for his son. They hugged and quietly congratulated each other in his absence. But there was a problem still to be dealt with before they could celebrate too much.

"What do we do with this one?" Rachel asked. "Only a matter of time before they come here looking for him."

"What do you mean this one?" Beth perked up. She hadn't seen the battered suspect in the trunk yet. Louis explained, and she took a look for herself. She grew angry at the thought of Curt torturing this man. The impact of the torture didn't lessen when Rachel described the pictures of Josh that were on Gregory's phone.

"We call the police and let them find him like this; that's what we should do. To hell with Curt. If he's going to do stuff like this, then he has to pay the consequences."

"No. I don't think so," Rachel countered. "He's been through enough. I'm not saying what he did was right, but what if that taints the case on his son? Then it will all be for naught, and there will be one more child molester still on the streets. You don't know what's it's like to be pushed to the brink. We're giving him a pass. So let's think."

Beth thought for a moment but remained angry. "So, what do we do? Hell, he's probably coming back to kill him. You want to help him out with that too?"

"No, don't be absurd. We're not going to kill him, but I think I have a way we can keep the case intact and still have the police come get him."

"Are you serious? We're going to help him out after he did something like this? Did you actually look at that guy; he's a bloody mess."

"I'm down with whatever you have in mind, Rachel," Louis said.

"Me too," Melinda joined in. Beth looked at her incredulously. "Sorry, honey. After what he's been through and for what this guy has done to his son…I'm with Rachel."

The vote was settled, and Rachel explained the plan, but they needed to move the Crown Vic before anyone noticed.

"Okay, did he leave the keys for us?"

"No, I checked already," Louis said.

"Hold on." Melinda walked back to the van and got something out of her bag. She returned with a set of keys and gave them to Rachel.

"I made a copy a while back. I needed it a few times when he was on one of his binges, but it's proved its worth at this moment, right?" Rachel smiled.

Melinda assumed the persona of Brenda Martin and was dropped off at the nearest car rental place. She rented a mid-sized SUV and met up with the team a few blocks away in a quiet neighborhood. Rachel, with the help of Louis and Melinda, managed to get the squirming and bloody Gregory out of the trunk and into the driver's seat of the Crown Vic. Next, Rachel jumped in the seat of the rental and backed it up enough of a distance away to make a difference. She tightened her seatbelt and prayed this worked. She stomped the accelerator to the floor and headed straight for the Crown Vic. She braced herself for impact as she pushed the SUV up to nearly forty-five miles an hour and T-boned Curt's car with Gregory in the driver's seat. The crash sent Gregory flying to the other side of the compartment and back to the world of the unconscious. Rachel wondered for a moment if she killed him from the impact, but Melinda checked his pulse and found one. She was almost disappointed that he wasn't dead.

After calling the police and reporting the crash, Melinda removed Gregory's cuffs and replaced them in front of his body. Louis gave Gregory's phone back, and Melinda made sure the phone was left out in the open where the police would easily find it. Louis had taken the liberty of removing the pass code feature and moved the hidden pictures to a more easily accessible location. The police responded quickly, and only Brenda Martin remained on scene with the story of how she simply failed to see the stop sign and accidentally slammed into the Crown Vic. When she went to check on the other driver, she noticed he had been handcuffed and figured he was some escaping felon.

The cops quickly put the pieces together and matched up Gregory to the kidnapping call a few miles away. Rachel's plan had taken root and was working so far. Louis kept listening to the scanner and heard that the illusion of Gregory stealing the car to make an escape was holding up. The hope was that the injuries he sustained would be believed to be caused by the crash and not torture at the hands of Curtis Walker.

After ensuring that Gregory was hauled off by the Valdosta police, the team headed over to the apartment complex where Curt had found Josh. Melinda parked by the entrance where the media had gathered and set up cameras. Rachel got out and saw Curt kneeling next to his son amongst the chaos and the sea of lights. She saw Curt talking to a patrol sergeant with a confused look on his face. Rachel pulled her phone out of her pocket and texted him a simple message. After bearing witness to the humbling scene, the team was ready to call it a night. They agreed to continue with the mission in the morning.

"Can we go back to Taco Bell? I'm hungry!" Louis whined.

Chapter 35

Bitter sweet emotions brought Alexis Vanderhill to the front door of Curtis Walker. She wanted to help his family enjoy their joyous reunion after the hellish nightmare they had been living, which she had seen first-hand, but she had official business as well. Word of the torture he had inflicted on Glenn Gregory reached back to her. This was unacceptable for the team she had worked so hard to create. Emotional reactions like that left ripples on the pond surface that could not be undone. Reactions like that would lead to the team's exposure. Alexis saw herself and the team on the front lines of a battle that was being fought unbeknownst to the other side. The numbers favored the opposition, but a precision strike from within the shadows was what gave them the advantage. Secrecy and anonymity were their biggest weapons in the fight against the darkness. If they were taken away, the battle was lost. Despite Curt being her best asset, she would cut him loose before she ever let that happen.

Alexis awaited the answer to the doorbell while the rest of the team stood behind her. The door opened, and a handsome man in a sharp, navy blue, pinstripe suit stood in the threshold. He shot Alexis a million dollar smile reserved by politicians for their constituents and playboys. She'd been around enough politicians to easily peg Thomas Pittman as one of those politicians.

"Excuse me," Alexis said, as Pittman was on his way out.

"Oh...excuse me." Pittman extended his hand and introduced himself as State Senator Thomas Pittman. Alexis was familiar with the name. He had maintained his "tough on crime" stance and was pushing for harsher gun penalties in the current legislative session. He was good-looking and gaining popularity amongst his peers. Rumor had it that he was aiming for a seat in Washington.

"Nice to meet you, sir. Alexis Vanderhill." The two shook hands, and Curt stepped up from inside the house to greet Alexis and the team.

"Thomas was there for us when Josh went missing. We were working a case, and he was on the city council at the time. Anyway, he has more important things to do than to hang out here."

"Nonsense, Curt. When I heard what happened, I knew I needed to come see you. I'm glad he's back in your arms safely. If you get any flak from these reporter hounds, you let me know."

"Yes, sir. Thanks."

"What line of business are you in, ma'am?" Pittman turned to Alexis as he walked past. He was impressed by the sophistication and demeanor to which she held and never passed up the opportunity to gain more political support.

She met him with a devilish grin, "Reporter hound...but I'm a woman, so that would make me a reporter bitch!"

Pittman managed to hold onto his smile despite having inserted his foot into his mouth. He looked back at Curt, questioning her presence.

"She's fine; she's a friend. Thank you, sir."

"Okay, don't hesitate to call, okay? And wish Josh and Tracy well for me; I'm sorry I missed them."

"Will do."

Pittman left and passed by the rest of the team as they were being invited into the Walker home. Beth Young stood in front of Rachel Goodwin and caught a flirtatious look from the State Senator as he walked by. The attention made her smile, which she held until he walked away. Rachel watched the exchange, and something registered inside of her that felt odd. She ignored it and joined the team inside.

Curt welcomed the team, explaining that Josh and Tracy had run to the grocery store, and they would be back soon. Curt had insisted on going, but Tracy argued and ultimately won. She was determined to impose her motherly love without Curt constantly hovering over the boy. He explained that Josh had been up for most of the night with nightmares and terror sweats. It was something Curt was afraid would happen, given the circumstances.

"Ah, poor thing," Alexis offered.

Rachel ignored her uneasy feeling as she stood in Curt's house. Images of their near indiscretion came to mind. It was obviously not meant to be, so she buried the emotion away and tried to pretend it had never happened.

Tracy soon returned from the store with Josh, and Curt made all the introductions. Rachel felt Tracy stare at her a little longer than the others but passed it off as her inherent paranoia. Louis engaged the boy, and his inner child came out in response to meeting the son of his idol. Josh seemed to respond to Louis who was still young at heart, and he seemed to brighten just a bit. After getting an invite to see his room, Louis stood up next to Curt who watched the boy head off to his room.

"Guess I can stop checking for you now, huh?" Curt smiled widely at the thought of his exhaustive search being over. He no longer had to dread the "dead kid report."

"Yep, I guess so."

Alexis came bearing gifts for Josh, and Tracy invited them all to sit outside on the back deck to enjoy the cool autumn morning. Rachel watched the boy closely and saw that he bore the mark of a damaged spirit. His eyes were still flat and devoid of the life any boy his age should have. Curt hung back in the living room, and Rachel walked up to him.

"Have you thought about therapy?"

"Yeah, I talked to some people over at DCF who I worked with in the past. They referred me to a couple of counselors."

"Good…it's a start." She bowed her head for a moment. "You know he'll never be the same, right?"

"Yeah, I know," Curt said sadly as he bowed his head too.

"I can talk to him, if you want. I mean…as you know, I may be able to relate, ya know?" Curt realized that Rachel and Josh shared a very unfortunate bond. Both were kidnapped at a young age, and although she was never sexually victimized, watching her sister subjected to the same horrors as Josh was just as painful.

Curt knew it was not easy for Rachel to offer such a thing because of how hard it was for her to deal with her own tragic past. He attributed her willingness to help to how close they had grown in the last few weeks. He smiled in acceptance.

"Thank you for that, and thank you for the help in Valdosta. That could've gone in a completely different way if you guys weren't there."

"Like I said in the text, you're welcome!"

They shared another moment, staring in each other's eyes, but the sound of footsteps on the laminate floors caused them to quickly pull away. Alexis asked to speak with Curt privately, and Rachel excused herself.

"What's up?"

"I'm assuming that you are going to remain here with your family?"

"Yes. You knew that when I signed up. I know you probably figured I'd never find him, but yes, I'm staying. Rachel is ready. She has some more learning to do, but she is more than capable."

"Well, she's not you. But yes, I agree that she's capable." Alexis was holding back something else that she wanted to say, and Curt instantly picked up on it.

"Just come out with it."

"Well, what happened in Colorado was unfortunate and honestly, it was just a matter of time before something like that happened. But what happened in Georgia, with the man in your...."

Curt wasn't going to make excuses. He knew he crossed the line, but he willingly stepped over it to find Josh. He would make the same decision if faced with the scenario again. He was grateful for the help altering the story of what happened to Glenn Gregory. However, so long as Josh was safe and brought home, he would accept his fate, whatever it may be.

"Okay...what are you saying, Alexis?"

"I can't have you return to the team. You have proven more than invaluable; don't get me wrong, but this could have exposed us, completely."

Curt recalled the visit from Tony Mason the day before and the fear he instilled because of his pursuit of his missing son. He didn't have an answer for Alexis, but he wasn't going to argue with her decision. It stung, but he was staying home regardless, now that Josh was back home.

"I understand," Curt said solemnly. He hated ending on a bad note, but his role on the team was the result of the worst thing that had ever happened to him, and he was ready to be rid of it all and move on.

"I'm glad and sorry at the same time," she added with a sweet genuineness, leaving the rest of the emotions unspoken.

The team continued to visit a little while longer. It was strange for them to see Curt in such a normal and domesticated mode, and it contrasted with what they'd known of him on the road. In times of crisis, many people adapt to what's necessary and somehow find a way back after the crisis is over. Curt was evidence of that.

As the team left, Curt extended handshakes and hugs. This was goodbye. Even Beth Young put aside her differences and frustrations with Curt Walker and left him with a teary hug. Rachel kept her distance from Curt and offered a platonic handshake that felt more awkward than sincere. Curt watched with Tracy at his side while they loaded up into the Mercedes Sprinter and drove away.

"You didn't tell me how pretty she was," Tracy said with curiosity.

"Alexis? I thought you met her before…when she came three years ago?"

"I'm not talking about her. I'm talking about Rachel."

"Oh, yeah. I guess she is."

Chapter 36

He sprinted down the dark hallway with a sense of urgency and panic. Josh was calling out for him. Another nightmare had ripped him awake. Curt ran to his side taking him in his arms, rocking him back and forth, and stroking the back of his head, calming him as he did when he was a baby.

"Shhh, it's okay, buddy. Daddy's here. It's okay."

Josh held tight to the neck of his father as if his life depended on it. He sobbed hysterically into his chest, frightened out of his mind. Tracy followed Curt to the bedroom and sat next to them on the bed, rubbing Josh's back with tears in her eyes, feeling helpless. Although he was back, the trauma was far from over, and she loathed the men responsible.

Curt avoided talking about the deviant horrors that occurred between Josh and the men who took him. He did nothing wrong, and Curt hoped he would one day understand and accept that. But Rachel was right, he needed therapy. Curt believed he was young enough that the damage could be mitigated, and he could enjoy a normal life. As a cop, he knew the evidence in the case against Gregory and Helton was solid, but that didn't excuse his son from spelling out what happened with enough detail to ensure a successful prosecution.

"Mommy and Daddy are here. You are safe." Curt thought about how unfair it was, being so young and subjected to such cruel events in his life.

"Why did the man take me, Daddy? Why?" Josh cried.

"I don't know son. I just don't know," Curt replied helplessly. He hated the men even more. He wished he had killed them slowly.

"Why did he take me to those men...who...did those things...."

"Who Josh? Who are you talking about?"

"Why Daddy? Why?" Josh's sobs grew louder.

Curt pulled the boy away looking at him face to face, trying to read the meaning in his tear soaked eyes. Confused, he asked again, getting more and more impatient as Josh remained silent.

"What do you mean? Gregory and Helton didn't take you? Did someone else take you? Who was it?"

Josh continued to cry and looked back at Curt blankly with no answers. Curt asked again with more frustration and anger added to his voice. Josh let out a loud sob and went limp in his arms.

"Curtis!" Tracy snapped with concern. "Stop! He's terrified."

He looked back at the boy. His face was full of uncontrollable fear. At the same time, he noticed a wet and warm sensation in his lap where Josh was sitting. He realized Josh had wet himself, and the urine had leaked through his pajamas and onto Curt. He stopped the questioning and handed him over to Tracy who got him cleaned up and eventually put back into bed. Curt felt awful for snapping at his son, but the angry cop and father took over, and he forgot, temporarily, how fragile his son was.

Curt paced the living room unable to sleep. His mind raced after hearing Josh mention that someone else was involved in his abduction. Or, was this simply an aftershock? Was this a response to the traumatizing event from his damaged psyche with no validity? His thoughts swirled around in a maelstrom of information, trying to find the meaning behind Josh's words. He played back the initial information from the investigation three years ago, which wasn't much, and then fast forwarded over all the tips that turned out to be duds, up to the final one that was legit.

Then it dawned on him. It was what Gregory said to him when he first surprised him in his apartment. It had created such anger inside of him; he nearly forgot it was said. While Curt was standing over him he said, "You must be the cop."

It wasn't necessarily what he said that bothered Curt; it was how he said it. It was in that smug tone reserved for the guilty that echoed over and over in his mind. It was as if he was expecting him to show up. To immediately recognize him as "the cop" and not just the boy's father made Curt think there must be a deeper meaning behind his words. At the time, he had been too focused on getting Josh away from those men and home safe to really think about it. He assumed that the man recognized Curt from the press coverage after Josh went missing. They had to know who he was because that would have made it easier to track him to the softball field and strike when they did. Curt recalled the look on Helton's face at the Taco Bell. He instantly recognized him; it would make sense that they would be familiar with Curt so they knew whom to avoid.

Josh's terror filled revelations, if credible, gave Curt a reason to doubt that he had found all of the answers behind his son's abduction. That made Curt want to rethink everything he had learned about the men. If this was new information in any other investigation, Curt would want to go back and re-interview the witness. However, in this case, it was his young and fragile son who was the witness. Going back was not an option. On the other hand, neither was letting this go.

After settling Josh back into bed, Tracy walked out to the living room and found Curt still pacing around the room. He was deep in thought and nervously rubbing a small metal pendant around his neck. She'd never seen him wear the necklace before and figured it was something he picked up on the road.

"He's asleep."

Curt was so buried in his own thoughts that he didn't notice that Tracy had come into the room and sat on the couch. "Huh?"

"Josh, he's asleep," she repeated. He nodded and dove back into his thoughts. "Where are you at right now?" She crossed her legs and folded her arms as she glared at Curt.

"A few things about this are bothering me. About what he said in there."

She had seen this before. Curt had a tendency to dwell on difficult parts of an investigation to the point that sometimes the case consumed him. It was what made him better than other detectives, but it came at a high cost to his sanity and family life. For him, it was hard to compartmentalize the problems and tune them out. He felt compelled to find the answers. They seemed to beckon him, no matter the time.

"What about your son? Can we focus on him first?"

He sighed. She was right; his well-being was paramount at this moment. Anything short of that would have to wait.

"I've tried talking to him, but it's like I don't even know him anymore." Curt sank down into the couch next to Tracy. "He's not the same little boy I took to the softball field. He's distant, like he is still back in Valdosta. I've tried every trick I can think of to get him to open up, but he shuts down every time."

"He's been through a lot. Probably more than we're ever going to know. It's going to take time, Curt."

"That's the thing. I've worked cases like these. I do know. I mean, I don't know how it feels to be in his shoes, but I know what he's gone through. I've seen it in other victims."

Curt quietly cursed his job as a detective. The job came naturally and he was good at it, but what you see can't be unseen. What you learn can't be unlearned. It stays with you, no matter the distraction of booze, women, drugs, or adrenaline. The experiences, good and bad alike, make you a better cop, but they are also a burden you have to bear.

Tracy shook her head, at a loss for words. She put her arm around Curt's shoulders.

He looked over and gave her a hopeful smile. "I'll keep trying. I haven't given up on him yet, no need to fold now, right?"

"Right," she agreed and added her beautiful smile.

Chapter 37

The article was magnificent and, in his opinion, Pulitzer-worthy. Tony Mason made the final corrections and read it one final time. He spelled out the inner workings of the team who worked in secrecy and under the veil of anonymity to find missing children outside of traditional, legal means. He started out with what he knew about the Southern California boy who was saved from the cult but kept it in general terms with no names. He applauded the team for their efforts in the beginning of the article. He carefully chronicled the events surrounding the deadly shootout in Vail which left three men dead. He wrote about the five young women who were illegally smuggled into the country and forced into prostitution and then how they were rescued. Mason criticized the actions of the team as rash and even blood-thirsty, at points acting with no oversight or authority. He painted a picture of the team as paid mercenaries hired by the rich, philanthropist Alexis Vanderhill and her misguided mission to sainthood. He detailed her movements to coincide with these recoveries. She was never on the scene, so as not to get her hands dirty. That was reserved for Curtis Walker. He finalized the article with the motivation of Curtis Walker who was in a desperate search to find his son; he would be willing to kill anyone who got in his way, as he did in Vail. He also speculated that the crash in Valdosta was too convenient and smelled of a cover-up by the team in conjunction with the police.

Mason checked his watch, and it read 11:19 a.m. He was enjoying his stay at the DoubleTree Hotel in downtown Tallahassee, waiting around to see if anything else broke in the Josh Walker case. Everything was done electronically nowadays, and he expected the story to be uploaded to the paper's website by five o'clock on the East Coast. He pictured his editing supervisor, a balding and overweight man, strolling into work on the West Coast with his daily coffee fix from Starbucks and checking all the submitted articles from the night before. Mason saved the article on his laptop and sent it via email, with the subject line reading: Pulitzer?

Tony smiled as he pictured the face of Alexis Vanderhill reading the article and detesting him for finally pushing the story through despite her efforts to kill it. There was nothing she could do about it now; he thought. It was her fault it had come to this adversarial bout of wills; he convinced himself. She was a reporter for Christ's sake. She should completely understand where he was coming from. Hell, he would have co-authored the story with her, but for some reason, she chose to keep it a secret. He was not going to lose any sleep over this by any means.

Mason walked down to the lobby of the hotel and grabbed a local paper. It had full coverage on the Josh Walker case and a lot of follow up on the two men responsible for his abduction. There were some quotes from neighbors of the suspects in the article. "I had no idea. He was a quiet neighbor, never bothered nobody. I saw the boy with him a few times and would've never guessed the truth."

Mason never stopped being amazed at the indifference of people, until it came to their opportunity to speak to the media. Then they sounded off like their opinion really mattered. It was hypocritical, but it made for good news when one of the herd spoke out.

He looked out of the large, sliding door entrance to the hotel. There was a covered drive-thru valet area, and he noticed it was a warm and clear mid-autumn day in Tallahassee. He figured his editor wouldn't get back to him until he had a chance to go over the story a few times and run it through the normal checks. That usually didn't happen until after the second cup of coffee. He checked his watch again. His flight wasn't until later that night, so he decided he would go for a walk.

Outside of the hotel was an elongated park that was bordered by a single-lane road on both sides, one going east, the other west. He noticed the park stretched for several blocks in both directions. It was adorned with paved walkways, cobblestoned in some stretches and bricked in others, with wooden benches along the way. Majestic oak trees were scattered up and down the Chain of Parks offering a canopy of shade for visitors and the casual strollers. Their massive outstretched arms were covered in cloaks of gray Spanish moss, giving them a sense of aged wisdom and distinction.

Mason crossed the street and walked along the path woven between the oak trees. He stopped and wondered about the trees and all that they'd seen and the secrets they kept. Being in a capital city of the Deep South, there was a rich history that included civil turmoil, devastation, adversity, and triumphs. The scars of the city were hidden in the quiet beauty of the giants that loomed downtown.

The California reporter continued walking around the area, taking in the interesting sights of downtown. It seemed extremely small compared to the colossal skyscrapers and the outstretched valleys of Los Angeles, but Mason liked what he saw. He loved LA, but Tallahassee seemed very charming. Maybe he felt that way because it was here where his story finally broke, but nonetheless, he liked the city.

As he walked along the main street that cut through downtown, a hole in the wall sandwich shop caught his eye. The Metro Deli was squeezed between county offices and a local law firm. There was a short awning that stretched over two small tables out front, giving it a big city feel with a bit of quaintness. He stepped in, catching the tail end of the lunch crowd. After studying the menu for a minute, he ordered the Tallahassee sub. *What the hell,* he thought. Essentially, it was a club sandwich with the addition of salami. *When in Rome....*

He sat down at the end of one of the few tables inside the small dining area that was scantily decorated with random pictures and Florida State University paraphernalia. The sandwich was good, and he added a chocolate chip cookie to his order for a pre-celebration. As he finished reading the local paper while waiting on his editor to call him back, he noticed it was nearing eleven o'clock on the West Coast. Mason grew impatient. It shouldn't take this long, he thought.

Finally, his phone rang; he left the tiny restaurant in a rush and headed back toward the hotel.

"Hey, Ed. Jesus, what took you so long?"

"Uh, hey Tony. Sorry about that. I need to talk to you about the article." His editor had always called him "Tone" with his best attempt at an Italian mafia accent. Calling him Tony actually caused him concern.

"Did you like it?"

"Yeah, of course I did. It's good shit, very intriguing...."

"I know it has a lot of bite, but this is just the beginning. If I can track down any more stories like this, I mean, I think they've been at it

262

for a while, and obviously they're good at covering their tracks. The possibilities are endless."

"Yeah, that's good Tony, real good."

There was an awkward pause over the phone. Mason knew something was wrong because his supervisor hated talking on the phone, and yet, he was dragging out the conversation.

"What's the problem now, Ed? For fuck's sake, I've been on this project for over a year."

"I know kid." His heavy breath blew through his end of the phone. "We're not going to run the story."

Mason didn't notice that he had actually stopped walking.

"Come again?"

"Can't print the story, Tony. I'm sorry. It's out of my hands."

"The fuck you can't! Don't do this to me now Ed, come on? What the hell?"

"Came down from the top. I went in fighting. Like you, I smelled a series of articles, and yes, hopefully you could dig up some more stories, but it's a no-go."

Mason begged his editor to reconsider and even asked to speak to the higher-ups. It was all for nothing. The decision was final. He asked if Alexis Vanderhill had anything to do with the decision not to print. He explained she didn't but when Mason demanded a reason, all his editor would say was that it was out of his hands. Mason called him a gutless douche bag and hung up out of frustration. He quickly dialed another reporter to get a real answer.

After a quick ring, the expectant female voice answered.

"Hey Tony, what's up?" She sounded busy.

"Hey, can you tell me why the hell Ed killed my story; it's fucking gold, and I'm getting shit on for no apparent reason!"

"Oh, that was yours?"

"Yeah, what the fuck?"

"I don't know the details but that came in from the top dude. I mean, Ed left out of his office like death had come knocking." This gave Mason confirmation that the decision was made above his supervisor's head. He would have to apologize later, but for now, he had to figure out who axed his article.

"Fuck me. Okay, call me if you hear anything."

Mason made it back to his hotel room to pack his things and get to the airport. He had to hurry up and get home to straighten this mess out. The more he thought about it, the more he knew Alexis Vanderhill had something to do with killing his piece. The article was built on more than just a scared kid from a wealthy family. This time around he made sure what he printed was backed up by provable facts that he had painstakingly checked. He was certain this scoop was beyond the reach of Alexis Vanderhill. He thought about farming the story out to some other paper, but that would probably be a decision with harsh consequences. He vowed to get to the bottom of this catastrophe and get his story printed.

Chapter 38

Within the Unit at the Leon County Jail, there were a few offices for the shift supervisors, a bathroom for jail staff only, and a multi-purpose room that over looked the recreational yard in the center of the jail. At times, one could watch the inmates play basketball, volleyball, or just socialize and soak up the outside air. The Unit sat between the inmate pods on each end of the jail, each floor a cookie cutter of the other. The multi-purpose room was mainly used for interviews with the inmates or meetings with their lawyers. Curt sat impatiently at the table in the multi-purpose room and ignored the sounds of the early morning basketball game outside of his window. He was awaiting the inmate to be brought to the Unit.

Following an awful night, Curt had grabbed his trench coat and flown out the door in search of answers. He needed answers, and he couldn't get them from Josh. He needed them from Gregory. He knew Josh was too fragile, and the statement he made was inconclusive, but his instincts were on overdrive. He knew there was something important that he was missing.

Before entering the jail, he removed his Glock from his holster. It's a secure facility, and not even law enforcement officers were allowed to carry weapons inside. It was actually for their protection since the inmates heavily outnumber the officers inside the jail. Before he stowed the gun away, he stared at it in his hands. *Such a simple and deadly creation*, he thought. The men responsible for taking his son deserved to die, and for a moment, before entering the jail, he asked himself if the answers he sought were more important, enough to allow them to live.

Instead of going through the front of the jail, Curt went through Releasing to avoid the red tape, metal detectors, and cameras. The alternate entrance was on the side of the jail by the sally port where all arrestees are initially brought in and booked. There are holding cells for each gender and transfer cells for those who are housed for longer stays. Releasing was the last stop before leaving the jail.

Curt entered through the small lobby to Releasing and flashed his badge to the deputy working the desk behind the thick, bullet-proof glass. The deputy, accustomed to detectives using this avenue to see inmates, waved him on at the sight of the badge without verification.

"You here to see an inmate?" he said through the small speaker just below the glass.

"Yeah, following up on a case." Curt hoped the vague answer was enough to pacify any curiosity beyond the quick exchange.

"No guns or knives right?"

"Nope!" Curt opened up his trench coat to reveal an empty holster. He patted himself down for added effect. The deputy hit a button on the wall, and soon the steel framed door buzzed and drew open for Curt to pass through. The door rolled slowly shut, and the clank of the internal lock echoed off the concrete walls. Another door opened behind him, allowing access into the jail. He stepped through and walked down the long hallway that led to the housing units and jail pods. As he passed under the watchful eye of the camera system, he subtly reached his arm behind him to the small of his back, adjusting the Glock .40 inside of his waistband. His intentions weren't clear, why he brought the gun, not even to him. But, he wanted it with him anyway as he came seeking answers.

Voices spoke just beyond the multi-purpose door and out in the hallway leading back to the pods. The Unit door opened and a male voice said, "In there."

Curt looked up to see Glenn Gregory make the turn into the room. He walked with a slight limp, and the left side of his face was a brilliant collection of purple and green shades of color, reminiscent of the beating he endured only a few nights before. His eye was still puffy and swollen with a small slit between his eyelids that allowed him to see out, and his face was covered by a patchwork of bandages. He hesitated at the door and looked back at the deputy who escorted him to the Unit. Gregory thought the conspiracy to further torture him for more information would run deep and extend to the jail as well. After seeing the deputy look at him with indifference, he sat down in the room, knowing anything was better than hanging out in the pod with the other inmates. Once they learned he was an accused child molester, the beatings would be more severe than what he had received from an angry father.

Anger settled in Curt's mind as the man sat down across the table. He took a deep breath, feeling the hard edges of the Glock in his waistband push against him, and he focused on why he was there. Answers.

Gregory looked around the small barren room and was drawn to the window that overlooked the rec yard.

"I need answers," Curt said pointedly.

"Why should I tell you anything?" He motioned to his face. The injuries were clear exhibits of his obvious reluctance.

"Because you've done enough to my little boy. He'll be scarred for life, so try and be a decent human being for once. Doesn't that mean anything to you? I want to know why you took him from me!"

Gregory looked away, avoiding eye contact and the consequences of his despicable actions.

"Well, you can't fake another car crash in here. If you beat me, there will be witnesses, so...I think I'll just have my day in court."

Gregory leaned forward to scoot out of his chair. Curt quickly reached up and took a strong grip on his shoulder and shoved him back down in his seat.

"I'm not done! I came to get answers, and I'm not leaving until I do."

"I told you, cop, I'll have my day in court." He leaned back in his chair with the same smugness he had the day Curt waited for him in the apartment.

"I'm not here as a cop. I'm here to get answers. There's no recordings here, no Miranda. I need answers to move on, don't you see?"

"Whatever. You can't trick me like that. This room is probably bugged." Gregory looked up at the ceiling, studying the air vent as if there was a listening device installed prior to his coming to the unit.

"You seemed to know who I was the day we met. How did you know me? I've thought and thought, and I'm positive we've never crossed paths. Is that why you took him, to get at me for some reason?"

Gregory rolled his eyes at Curt's stubbornness and remained silent.

"He said the man took him and brought him to you and Helton. Is that true? Is someone else involved?"

Gregory's face changed slightly, showing a hint of concern and worry. Curt saw it instantly, and it validated what the boy had said.

"There was, wasn't there? Tell me now, dammit! Who the hell else is involved?"

"Hey, I didn't say shit, cop. You won't get me to say anything else, so stop wasting your time."

"No! This is my kid I'm fighting for, so just be a fucking man for once. Tell me what I need to know!"

"I am a man, dammit; fuck you. I'm not telling you anything, so either get on with the beating, or leave me the hell alone!"

Curt held back the overwhelming desire to leap across the table and smash his bruised face against the beveled edge of the table, but the deputy had heard Gregory getting loud and looked through the small window in the door to make sure everything was alright. Curt shot him a look over Gregory's head, indicating things were copacetic.

Curt reminded himself of the loaded Glock in his back waistband but decided against pulling it out for now. Too risky for him to pull a gun on an inmate, no matter how deserving, but more importantly, it wouldn't guarantee him the answers he needed. If he shot him, the answers would die along with Gregory, and he had proven time and again that torturous coercion wouldn't persuade him.

"I told you; I need answers. I need to know why he was taken. Who is this other person?"

"I don't know what you're talking about, so talk to my lawyer. I think I'll start talking to him about harassment charges, maybe even a lawsuit."

His threats were meaningless. Curt had heard this same type of threat from numerous suspects he'd snared in his investigative webs over the years. They didn't faze him; they only confirmed that he was on the right path. It clearly struck a nerve, but the mention of a lawyer sparked a new angle to take.

"Your lawyer, huh?"

"Yeah." Gregory leaned back with a sense of empowerment.

"Who is that, by the way?"

"Donald Carruthers."

The mere mention of the name irritated Curt. He'd arrested plenty of scumbags who were responsible for terrible and heinous acts to women and children, yet Carruthers found a way, on occasion and against Curt only once, to get his clients acquitted from serious charges. During a trial they had together, he questioned Carruthers during a break about his conscience and the ability to sleep at night when defending such depraved individuals. His reply was simply, "If it were you, wouldn't you want me to pull out all the stops and fight like hell?"

It seemed to be different in Curt's eyes. The defense for his actions was that they were necessary, and those of the wicked are inexcusable, but the attorney had a point. If he found himself in trouble and with Tony Mason's article still floating out there, the possibility was high, he would want the best representation he could find. Carruthers was considered one of the best, and it came with a costly bill as well. His shiny Beamer convertible and a beach house on St. George Island were evidence that business was very good.

However, Curt knew Carruthers was defending Gregory and Helton soon after they were formally charged. He figured by his answer that Gregory didn't know the latest update. Curt had used the supervisor's computer to look up a few things on Gregory's case docket while waiting for him to be escorted to the Unit.

"He is, huh?"

"That's what I said." Gregory looked confused by the confidence behind Curt's inference.

"Okay." Curt turned the tables on him and leaned back with his own brand of smugness.

"What?" Curiosity got the better of Gregory.

"Well, if he's your lawyer, then you should know."

"Know what?"

"That he filed a Motion to Sever and a Motion of Conflict."

"Conflict? Sever?"

"Yep."

"C'mon, what are you talking about?"

"It means, he's about to dump your ass. He is severing you and Helton to have you both tried separately, and then the motion of conflict means that he can't be your attorney and Helton's for the same case. I thought you were a paralegal? Shouldn't you know about this kind of stuff?"

Gregory looked on astonished and in stunned disbelief. Curt watched as his mind raced, and he read the fear in his eyes. He knew exactly what Curt was talking about, somewhere deep down. Curt could see Gregory getting angry as he thought about the new information and what it meant for his sake.

"I am. I know what it means, but that doesn't make sense, to sever the case?"

"They do it all the time. It's to make it harder on the state. To make them prove the case on each individual and not the case as a whole. I mean, it was you on the video in Tallahassee. It's your law firm that handles adoptions. I mean, it's not that hard to figure out who the mastermind is in this operation."

Gregory leaned back again, but the smugness was now replaced with deep concern. He folded his arms and immediately started chewing on his fingernails.

"Didn't tell you that, huh?" Curt asked.

"Guess not."

"So, how does a paralegal, who lives in a rented apartment complex, driving a six year old Honda, afford someone like Carruthers in the first place?"

Gregory looked away again. He stared out of the window and into the outside world he no longer knew.

"Helton has less money than you. I checked, but yet—"

"Are you done?" Gregory spat angrily.

"No, because I need answers, and you are too stupid to see that you are getting sold out. You are disposable to whomever you are protecting. They're already cutting ties to you, and your loyalty no longer means shit to them. Don't you see that?"

Gregory thought hard about what Curt was saying. His distrust for the man who fractured multiple bones in his face and nearly castrated him was strong, but he could hear the truth in what he was saying. He silently fought his way through several debates waging in his head as Curt watched patiently.

Gregory needed more proof and remained skeptical. Curt didn't blame him. Curt excused himself and went back to the supervisor's computer, pulling up the court docket for Gregory's case and printing it out. He underlined the two motions that were filed the day before. After he presented Gregory with the proof, he quickly read it and leaned back in the chair for the last time, completely defeated and lost. His thoughts swirled out of control, and he just stared blankly out of the window, wondering if he'd ever see the light of day again as a free man.

"I never met him, never really saw him."

"Who? The man that brought you Josh?"

"Yeah, he knew Toby from somewhere. We met behind some store late at night, and the kid was drugged or something, so I put him in my car while Toby dealt with the guy. Toby didn't tell me his name or anything. I was just excited about having...." Gregory stopped his thought as he noticed Curt was now standing over him.

Curt swallowed his anger and desire to further pummel the man. "So, you never saw him, never spoke to him?"

"No. Never dealt with him again. But Toby knows him somehow."

"How did you know who I was?"

"The guy apparently knew a lot about you; told Toby you were a cop and to steer clear of you and Tallahassee."

"He knew a lot about me?"

"Yeah. Enough about you being a cop. Whoever it was also has a lot of power too, because we had forged adoption papers and other documents later that week."

"Where is that paperwork? I don't think they found that."

"I don't know where Toby put it...his place probably."

Curt hoped the paperwork turned up in the search of Helton's apartment and its existence just hadn't gotten relayed to him. They might not have realized the value of the paperwork and that it could lead them to another conspirator...the one who actually kidnapped Josh.

"Anything else?"

"No."

Gregory was hesitant, but he had given Curt enough to move forward. He needed to track down this paperwork and find out who this third suspect was. But first, he needed to talk to Helton.

Curt looked up the pod where Helton was housed and made a bee-line for that Unit. He asked a deputy to call ahead and have the inmate meet him in the Unit, just like Gregory. As Curt walked across the open center of the jail, he heard a commotion up before him and saw a deputy scurry out of the Unit and down the hallway toward the pod. He was carrying a med-bag.

A sinking feeling in the pit of his stomach crept in as he watched the deputy run with haste. As Curt made it to the other Unit to await Helton, another deputy ran out nearly knocking him over carrying a portable defibrillator. It must be an inmate having a medical issue he thought, and his mind eased. He walked into the unit, but Helton wasn't there. He could have been held up due to the medical issue taking priority. He looked over at the civilian aide sitting inside the control booth in the front of the unit working the electronic door and the radio. She stared back at him with questioning eyes.

"You looking for Helton?" she asked, her voice was muffled by the large metal door and thick safety glass inset.

"Yes."

She looked down, and with no emotion and like it was a matter of habit, she said, "Well, hope you didn't need to talk to him; he just hung himself."

Chapter 39

Helton's side of the pod was cleared out and taped off. Detectives from the Sheriff's Office were already on their way over to work the death investigation. Curt quietly stood by, trying to get as much information as possible without being noticed as an outsider. The timing of this "suicide" was too suspicious. He managed to get a peek into the small pod at the crime scene. He heard Helton hanged himself by leaning forward on his knees and laying his neck across a taut bed sheet tied to the bed post and the bars of the cell door. It was simple yet very effective and ultimately quick. Curt studied the scene for just a moment but didn't see anything out of the ordinary. He was disappointed by the simplistic manner with which Helton took his own life. Curt would have preferred doing it himself or at least to see him dangling lifeless from a noose.

Coward. He wanted to see the man tried for his crime, but he would be amiss if he said he was sad to see him dead. Good riddance.

Curt grew angry at the dead man. Gregory had just given him a direction to follow in finding out who was really behind his son's abduction, but that lead was now dead in a jail cell. He stood outside the pod thinking about his next move. He refused to let this go.

Before leaving the pod, Curt overheard one of the deputies telling his supervisor that he had escorted Helton to the visitor's booth earlier that morning and he seemed fine. Curt thought about the suspicious timing and grew even more wary at the mention of a visitor. There was no way that was a coincidence.

"Okay, pull his phone calls and check the visitor log. The detectives will want to see that," the supervisor ordered.

Good idea, Curt thought as he listened in.

"I checked his account for phone calls, but he hasn't activated it yet, so nothing there. I'll go check his visitors and let you know."

Curt slipped away from the pod and back into the Unit while everyone was busy managing the crime scene. He went back to The Unit computer and pulled up the jail information system, accessing Helton's visitor log. He typed in the command, and the log popped up on the screen.

Curt felt his heart beating faster than normal in his chest. It was possible that the person on the visitor log could be the man who took Josh. He held his breath as he scrolled down. There was only one entry, the mysterious visitor earlier that morning.

In the jail lobby, where the red tape was spun, biographical information from the inmates' visitors was captured along with their addresses and pictures taken at the time of the visits. Curt looked at the photograph of the visitor but grew more confused. He didn't know this person and felt confident that it wasn't someone close to him, as Gregory had led him to believe. This person didn't fit at all.

"Bobby Richards? Who the hell is that?" Curt said out loud.

The name wasn't familiar. Neither was his face. Richards was a black man in his late twenties who wore a look of perpetual contempt. Curt knew the look well. He saw it on the faces of the disenfranchised while working the lower, socio-economic neighborhoods, better known as the "hood" or "ghetto" to its inhabitants. It was no surprise that Richards had a few drug charges, dealing and simple possession in his past. How he fit in with Helton and the kidnapping of his son made absolutely no sense; it only created more questions.

Curt read off Richard's address on the visitor log. He knew exactly where it was. He printed out the log and quickly left the jail. On his way out, he passed the Sheriff's office detectives on their way up to Helton's body. He knew one of the detectives from the academy.

"Hey man, how are you doing?" the detective asked.

"Good, thanks." They quickly shook hands.

"Hey man, sorry to hear about your son, but I'm glad you got him back. I read all about it in the papers. That was some wild ass shit."

"Yeah, thanks. I'm glad too." Curt grew uneasy and tried to pull away without causing a stir. He didn't want any attention about why he was really there; plus he needed to get to Richards, before anyone else did.

"Hey, what are you doing here? Back at work already?"

"Yeah, no rest for the weary. Got to pay the bills, you know." Curt hoped the superficial answer would placate the detective.

He turned to leave, but the detective said, "Okay, well…that's weird."

"What?" Curt said innocently.

"We're on our way to work an inmate death. Actually, one of the guys in your son's case, believe it or not. Apparently, he offed himself in his pod this morning."

"Yeah, I was just up there. I heard. Figured I should leave…it looking bad and all."

"Right. I get it. You didn't kill him, did you?" The detective asked sarcastically.

"No, of course not."

"I know; I'm kidding. I wouldn't blame you though."

"Yeah. Well, I need to head out; good seeing you."

"Yeah, you too. Take care."

***

Bobby Richards lived off one of three streets that made up what was affectionately known as the "horseshoe." The streets made a "U" shape and were historically rampant with illegal narcotic activity, prostitution, gambling, general indecency, and senseless violence. A few respectable houses sat amongst the damned, but the inhabitants were more or less captives in their own homes, surrounded by the violence around them.

Curt pulled up and sat outside of Richard's listed address on the jail visitor log. It was a small, wooden house, a carport on the side, and a small, yet clean yard out front. It wasn't a large house but considered nice given the standards of the poverty-stricken neighborhood. It was a shame that more people in the neighborhood didn't share the same sense of pride.

Curt thought again about how Richards was connected to Helton and the mysterious suspect or even if he was the mysterious suspect, but pieces didn't quite fit. He couldn't place it, no matter what angle he took or how much he thought about it. He knew Richards fit in some way, but how?

Nothing about Richards' personality or presence made sense. First, there was the revelation of the third suspect by Gregory, and then Richards was the only visitor to Helton, mere hours before he took his life. This was not a coincidence. There was a connection, and he just had to find it.

A short black male, head bowed as he listened to his oversized headphones, walked up from behind Curt and up to the house. He eyed Curt as he strolled up to the porch of the house. Curt slowly exited his car, hoping the kid didn't run on him.

"You Bobby Richards?"

The black male lifted his head and looked around before answering. Curt recognized him from the picture taken at the jail; he was still wearing the same black hoodie from the morning.

"Yeah, who you?"

"No one; just need to ask you a question."

"You po-leece?"

"Not really. I mean, yeah, but that's not why I'm here."

"Nah, I ain't doing nothing. Ain't got no warrants. I don't have to talk to you."

Curt walked up to the porch to get close to Richards. He was already growing impatient with his attitude. He'd known too many people like him who just didn't care about anyone outside of their own small worlds, black or white. They wouldn't lift a finger or exert any effort unless it was directly for their own benefit. Curt felt like snatching up the little punk and beating him into submission based on his contempt for authority alone, but he didn't have the time to waste nor was it likely to make a difference.

"What man? Why you getting close?" Richards showed signs of fear of the man in the trench coat.

"You went to the jail this morning and saw this man." Curt pulled out a booking picture of Helton and showed it to Richards. "How do you know him?"

"I don't know that guy," Richards shot back instantly with his same indifferent attitude.

"Excuse me?"

"I said, I don't know that dude; never met him. Couldn't tell you the first thing 'bout him."

Curt's brow furrowed in confusion. He searched around for an explanation. He was missing something.

"Then…why did you visit him at the jail this morning?"

"I didn't."

"The hell you didn't; it's on the log." Curt pulled out the printed out log with Richards's picture on it and shoved it in his face. "You went to see him this morning. Tell me how you know this guy."

"Man, I don't have to talk to you." Richards got up from his small, concrete porch and turned to open up the front door.

"Hey!" Curt shouted.

"Man, fuck off."

Curt stepped up on the porch and pushed the door shut over Richards' shoulder. He hovered over Richards who was several inches shorter. Richards tried to shove the cop away, but Curt grabbed his arm and spun him around, violently slamming him against the door. Curt jacked Richards up and shoved his left forearm into Richards' throat. His eyes widened as he gasped in fear. Richards' feet dangled underneath him, searching for the stable ground.

"I'm not asking anymore, you little fuck! This man took my kid and raped him. You're not who I'm looking for, but I'm trying to find out who helped him, and you're standing in my way!"

Richards struggled but was overpowered by the strong man in the trench coat. He answered with a raspy, choking sound, "Then go ask him yourself."

"I can't. He's dead." Curt emphasized the news of Helton's death by pushing harder against the man's throat.

Richard's attitude changed as he weighed the situation. "He is? Okay, okay. Lemme go."

Curt eased up, letting him down flat on his feet. He eased his forearm off his throat but kept it across his chest as a matter of insurance.

"How do you know Helton?"

"Listen, I don't know that guy. That's the God's honest truth. Some white guy came up to me in the parking lot and gave me two hundred dollars to say I was visiting that guy Helton."

"Why would he have you visit him? Did he give you something to give him or a message of some sort?"

"No, I actually visited my girl. He came in too, but asked for her; then we switched booths. I saw my girl…he saw that guy."

Curt let Richards go and immediately got lost in thought over what he had just heard. Someone was trying to cover his tracks and hiding his connection to Helton. That was the key Curt was looking for, whoever this person was who switched with Richards was the mysterious person or at the very least, directly connected.

"What did he look like?"

"White, fortyish, skinny. I wasn't paying that much attention after he flashed the cash."

"Did he give you a name?"

"Naw, man. I knew enough not to ask."

Curt fished out a hundred bucks from his wallet and handed it to Richards after getting the name of his girlfriend. He left the "horseshoe" and encouraged Richards to keep their interaction to himself, knowing that he would probably be visited by detectives who were following the same lead from the visitor's log. Curt needed to get access to the girlfriend's visitor log before all of the mystery man's loose ends were tied.

Chapter 40

He felt lost without access. The answer was out there and needed to be plucked from cyberspace, but it was just out of Curt's reach. He needed Louis Melton and his computers. Curt knew it was too risky to head back to the jail to get the visitation log of Richards' girlfriend, so he headed to the only other place he could think of, the police station. He parked in the visitor's lot out front and walked in through the lobby like a commoner. He asked the duty officer, a young patrol officer working light-duty, for his old sergeant.

Sgt. Melvin Polk told the duty officer to just give him a visitor badge and buzz him up so that he could make his way through the department. The sergeant assured the rookie that Curt knew the way. Curt felt nostalgic, walking down the hallway past the Watch Commander's office and into the first floor of the crystal palace. It was a name given to the east end expansion of the department due to its overuse of distorted glass tiles that stretched three stories high. He rode the elevator up to the second floor and walked out into the small lobby of the Criminal Investigations Division. An unfamiliar face sat behind the sliding glass window of the administrative aide's desk. He gave a smile and told her that he was there to see Sgt. Polk.

A rotund black man with a graying mustache jutting out under a wide nose pushed through the door. Upon locking eyes with Curt, he gave him a wide and friendly smile then waved him over.

"C'mon in. I can't believe you lost your ID badge. Get in here, son."

"Hey Sarge, how are you?"

"Fine, fine, fine. Let's go to my office. I'm over in homicide now."

"Oh, they let you move on from Special Victims?"

"Yeah, I've been there almost as long as you've been gone. It's been good so far. We're getting a new lieutenant soon; Dylan Akers was here but just got moved away to another position…long story."

"Oh yeah, I remember him. Sharp guy."

As Curt and Sgt. Polk entered his office, Curt took a seat and Polk shut the door, something he used to frown upon. He made it known he liked everything out in the open.

"How've you been, Curt?"

"Good, I mean…horrible for a while as you know, but I found him. So I'm good now, ya know."

"Yeah, that's good. I've followed the story in the news. That's incredible, you finding him on your own like that. But then again, I told everyone around here, if anyone was going to find him, it would be you."

"Thanks."

Sgt. Polk adjusted in his seat and leaned up and on his desk, getting closer to Curt as if to relay top secret information. Curt grew worried and immediately regretted coming to the station.

"I can't help you."

"Huh? What are you talking about?"

"Whatever it is you're working on, and I'm sure it has to do with those men who took your boy, I can't help you! Hell, one of them was found dead in his jail cell this morning."

"Why can't you?" Curt grew angry at the thought of his old sergeant and his own agency not helping him out—unless there was a good reason not to, he thought. A small wave of panic came over him as he wondered what skeleton had been drug out of the closet.

"Curtis," Polk spoke in a soft tone, "I got two detectives flying in from Vail, Colorado tomorrow, and they want to speak to you about something they are working. Something about a triple homicide up there? Happened sometime last week?"

The blood drained from his face, and the air suddenly got much colder in the small office. He felt like running, but there was a reason Sgt. Polk was letting him know this; it was some type of warning.

"Vail, huh?"

"Yeah, and by the look on your face, I take it you know exactly what they're here for."

"But Sarge…."

"Ahh-ahh-ahh, I don't want to know brother. Nope, keep it to yourself. The less I know, the better…you know?"

"Right."

"I know you, son. If you were involved in some shit like that, you had a damn good reason, so I trust that will be evident. But, in the meantime, I can't help you with whatever you're working on, okay?"

"Okay, I understand."

"Now, tell me about Josh. How is he doing?"

Curt tried to shake away the shock of the Vail detectives coming all the way to Florida. How his name came to light concerned him the most. He wondered if Tony Mason had anything to do with it. Either way, it was inevitable that this would happen. He shoved the worry aside and answered Polk's question about his son. He told him about the sleepless nights, post-traumatic stress, and the night terrors but kept the revelation of the third suspect to himself. He was trying to respect the sergeant's wish not to get involved. After talking about the hopeful recovery of Josh, they spoke a little while longer on the progress of Florida State baseball, both were avid fans. Only Curt had fallen off the last three years, for obvious reasons.

"I need to get going. When are the detectives coming in?"

"Not sure, soon though. Maybe tonight, maybe tomorrow. You're not going to do anything stupid are you?"

Curt didn't have a good answer. He wasn't going to lie to him. No matter what the Vail detectives did, he wasn't going to let anything come between him and this third suspect. After that, he didn't care, but he wasn't planning on doing any more running.

"No, sir."

"Good." Polk leaned his hefty body back into his chair, causing it to creak under his shifting weight. He leaned over, opened up a drawer, and pulled out a heavy case file. He slapped it down on the desk and looked directly at Curt.

"What?" Curt didn't understand the meaning of the look. Polk just kept staring back at Curt without explanation.

"I'm going to get some coffee. You can let yourself out with that visitor badge." He purposefully looked down at the file and pushed away from the desk, walked around, and stood behind Curt. "It was good to see you, brother."

Polk placed a gentle hand on his shoulder and left the small office.

Curt leaned forward in his chair and read the name on the file. It read: Joshua Walker. He wasted no time and grabbed the case file, opening it up. Inside were the files from the Valdosta side of the investigation as well as the original missing person's case. He thumbed through the files looking at the property receipts from the search warrant of Helton's apartment. He scanned the list and didn't see where the adoption paperwork was listed or any listed paperwork, for that matter.

"Damn."

He continued to sift through the report. He knew he would have to call the detectives in Valdosta and have them look over their evidence, hoping the paperwork was there, just not labeled. He moved on in the file and came across phone records. A handwritten name of Helton was scribbled on top. Curt quickly pinched out the phone records from the case file and stuffed them in his jacket pocket. This was exactly what he needed. He stood up and quietly slipped out of the office, out of the division, and back out into the visitor's parking lot. He cranked up the car and left the police department unnoticed.

As he passed by the front of the station, he looked longingly at the building. It had been his second home for over twelve years and the source of many great stories, friendships, heartache, and despair. He wondered, based on what Polk just told him of the Vail detectives, if the next time he showed up, he would leave in handcuffs.

Chapter 41

Curt parked in the dusty, gravel lot on the north side of Lake Ella reserved for strollers, picnickers, and duck feeders. Curt couldn't wait any longer to look at the phone logs he had taken out of the case file. He pulled over on the other side of the lake from the police station and began studying the sheets of paper.

The lake was as familiar to him as an old friend he passed by on the way to work every day. The feeling was still there. He used to stroll around the lake with Tracy during their courtship. He had taken Josh on trips to the lake to feed the ducks stale bread and to climb the old oak tree on the south end of the park. It was a necessity of growing up in Tallahassee.

He pushed those memories aside while he searched Helton's phone records for any numbers that stood out. The records went back six months, but he recalled Helton being on the phone as he came crashing through his apartment door to save Josh. In looking back, that phone call must have been significant, given the circumstances. He looked and searched for the corresponding entry. He flipped over the page, found the date, and then scrolled down the list to the corresponding time. It should be the last entry. Helton was arrested moments later after being knocked unconscious.

He found the last entry and read the number. It didn't register like he hoped it would. It was just a random series of ten numbers. The mystery man's identity didn't jump from the pages in a climactic finale. The numbers just stared back. It felt like he'd seen the number before, like knowing the lyrics to a song but not the artist or title. He leaned his head back on the headrest trying to recall where he'd seen it before but couldn't remember. It was an 850 area code which meant it was from Tallahassee. That was promising, but in the age of cell phones and the nearly endless space for contact information, no one bothers to remember a phone number anymore. Curt drew a blank.

He scanned the rest of the records and found the same number popping up on several different occasions. Curt grabbed a notepad and wrote them all out. He had to go old school as he lacked technology access at the moment. He cataloged when the number showed up, the date, duration of the call, and time of call. He noted whether it was Helton calling the number or the number calling Helton. When he was done, he placed the records down and studied the list. There was an obvious pattern. The numbers communicated twice a month, nearly at the same time. On the first of the month, the number called Helton, and around the fifteenth of the month, Helton called the number.

However, there were two anomalies. The first was earlier in the month when Helton called the number, and the date stood out to Curt immediately. It was the anniversary date of Josh's disappearance and coincided with Josh being seen at the mall. Rage slowly began to boil in the pit of his stomach. He remembered reading the text messages on Gregory's phone from Helton admonishing him for taking Josh to Tallahassee saying it was "too risky." It was like Helton was updating the person or possibly giving a warning. The second anomaly was the day Curt found Josh in Helton's apartment.

Curt realized he needed to know who the subscriber to the mystery number was. He pulled out his cell phone and opened the internet application. He punched in the number hoping it would generate a lead. After hitting send, the only hits were information websites that wanted him to pay for access to that number. After years of being a detective and using cell phone numbers as the only lead in some cases, those websites were a joke and never produced any real results. This meant the number belonged exclusively to a cell phone. It was a dead end. He needed access. He needed Louis Melton, but that was no longer an option as Alexis had made that perfectly clear.

The fountain in the middle of Lake Ella sent a stream of water up into the sky nearly sixty feet high which added a simplistic and majestic bliss to the small lake. Curt stared at the fountain while he contemplated his next move. It had always given him a steady calm amid the chaos of detective work. It wasn't working for him in this case which was far too important to fail. In a sense, he felt cornered; there was only one obvious method to find out to whom the number belonged. Call it.

He looked down at his cell phone and weighed the move. He could spook whoever was on the other end if they realized it was Curt calling. Gregory had made it clear that whoever this mystery person was, he knew Curt, and it was understandable that this person would have his number saved in their phone. On the other hand, he would know who the guy was and would be able to move in on him that much quicker.

He dialed the number but didn't hit send. He looked through the windshield, out across the serene lake to the quaint gazebo that sat at the tip of a peninsula added to the park twenty years ago. There was a couple taking engagement pictures, using the picturesque backdrop, and it reminded him of a time in his life when things weren't so complicated. He debated the move and decided he had to know and couldn't wait any longer. He hit the send button.

Shock immediately set in as his heart dropped to the pit of his stomach and rippled all the way up to his head. His heart skipped a beat as he read the name displayed on the phone's tiny screen. It was a named contact…in his phone.

Chapter 42

When building a case, it is essential to answer the basic questions of who, what, when, where, why, and how. In the first five minutes of arriving at any crime scene, the what, when, where, and how are normally answered. On the scene, the where and when are established along with the what, as in, what crime has occurred? While working the scene, looking at the evidence and talking to the witnesses, the how is figured out with close precision. Then all efforts are exhausted trying to figure out the who, as in, whom to arrest and hold responsible for the crime?

But the why will go unanswered most times and is the hardest to answer. Outside of the normal rationale of the armed robber who just wants the money, the murderer who hated his victim or the thief who wanted the financial gain, the why is the most difficult to obtain.

Sitting across the table from a suspect, trying to get him to talk about the what, where, who else, and the how is challenging, even with cooperation, but the why is all too often lost. The why is more likely a guess than something actually figured out. But to a victim, it is the why, he or she wants answered most of all.

As Curt stared down at his phone, the breath left him, and his world went into a tailspin of confusion and anger. The name on his phone read: Thomas Pittman.

Curtis Walker stormed into his house and paced furiously in his living room. The last three years of his life were spent trying to find his son, and at the same time, he was battling to find the why. Why was Josh targeted? Why was he taken instead of another child? As he searched endlessly, he failed to come up with even the tiniest bit of understanding. After a while, he stopped asking because he didn't care why, just so long as Josh was back safely.

After finding Josh in the homes of two homosexual pedophiles, he felt confident that he understood, however revolting, the reason for taking the boy. He was a prize to them. But as Curt found himself running down this latest rabbit hole, he found it led straight to Thomas Pittman. Now his world was turned completely upside down, and the answer to the question of why was more important than ever.

His nervous stomps back and forth drew Tracy from the back of the house.

"What is it; what's wrong?"

He was white hot with confusion and rage. He was speechless. He stared back at Tracy who grew scared with the lost look on her husband's face.

"What is it, Curtis? You're scaring me."

"I...I...I think it was Pittman."

Tracy's brow's furrowed as her face grew furious. She stood erect and folded her arms tightly against her body. She knew exactly what Curt was saying given that he had left early that morning after Josh's outburst during the night.

"Okay, explain."

He explained his day to Tracy. He started with the jail visit and what Gregory said to confirm Josh's statement about a third suspect. He told her about the untimely suicide of Helton and the conversation with Richards about the visitor switch, about getting Helton's phone records from Sgt. Polk, and how Pittman's name came up on the screen when he called the number.

"I came straight home to tell you."

"What should we do? Should we turn him in? You have to do something!"

Curt had thought of several things in response after reading Pittman's name on his phone. Immediately, assassination crossed his mind. He also thought about asking someone he trusted at TPD to follow up, but his detective's mind took over. He asked himself, what proof do you have of Pittman's guilt? Pittman was a former City Councilman and a current State Senator with a lot of political juice and backing. He was the definition of a high profile target and one you don't go after without solid proof. Curt couldn't explain it, but his instincts said Pittman was involved. As Gregory said, it was someone with power and close to him.

Pittman fit both of those requirements at the time of Josh's disappearance.

As far as proof against him, there was nothing but a phone call relationship with Helton. The timing and routine of the calls to Helton were suspicious at best, but any defense attorney would explain that it only proved that they knew each other and nothing else. It was scandalous being connected to two known pedophiles and kidnappers, but having a relationship with them was not illegal. It could derail his political career, but that was not going to get Curt answers. Plus, with Helton now dead, he couldn't testify against Pittman. Also, Gregory said he hadn't actually seen who dropped Josh off that night, so he couldn't testify legitimately against the senator either. There was only one other known witness, Josh.

"No, I don't like it. He's too fragile," Tracy said, after Curt explained he wanted to show Josh a picture of Pittman.

"It's all we've got. If Josh IDs him, then I'll go arrest him right now!"

"NO! He's been through enough. I don't think he's ready, and I don't think he can handle this right now. I don't think he'll ever be ready. And it won't change the fact that he's home safe with us, now."

"So, we just let him get away with it? Until when? Until he does it again? If Josh is the only other person alive that can actually ID him, what do you think he'll do if we don't act first?"

An icy, cold chill crawled down Tracy's spine. She suddenly felt more vulnerable than ever. She hated her choices: making her child relive a hellish nightmare, allowing the man responsible to get away with it—or worse yet, leaving Josh exposed as the next potential murder victim in Pittman's attempt to "tie up loose ends?"

"There's no other way?" she asked.

"I don't see one, no."

She nodded with reluctance as she backed up, allowing Curt to pass by her and go down the hallway. She kept her arms folded tightly, fearing for the worst. Curt took a picture of Pittman and went to show it to Josh in his room. He knew the consequences of pushing a traumatized victim, especially a child, but he felt there was no other option. He paused before going in and stood quietly outside of Josh's door. He debated for any other way and hated what he was about to do.

A moment later, Curt was seething with rage and brushed past Tracy. She heard Josh crying in his room. Her heart immediately sank at the sound of his cries, knowing that he had given the confirmation. Curt went straight for the door without saying anything.

"What are you going to do?" Tracy asked panicked. She had seen this side of him once before. It was the same look he had the day after Josh went missing.

Curt shook his head with no answer.

Tracy stood back, crossed her arms, and looked at Curt expectantly. "When are you coming home?"

"I don't know…later. Go to him; he needs you." Josh's cries were getting louder.

"That's not what I meant. I mean, you've been back for about a week now, but you're not home, Curtis!"

He knew what she meant. He'd been absent for the last three years, and his homecoming hadn't changed anything. He couldn't rest until he had all the answers. He didn't have an answer for Tracy, so he just held an empty stare back at her.

"So, I ask again, what are you going to do?"

He was devastated by what he had just subjected his son to and angry at himself for not protecting him as a father should. But that was about to end. Curt whipped open his trench coat and withdrew his Glock. He pinched back the slide and peeked into the chamber, ensuring there was a round loaded. He hit the magazine release and pulled the mag out, inspected the additional rounds, and slapped it back in the magazine well.

"It's better I don't tell you." Curt walked out of the door before Tracy could respond.

Chapter 43

The drive downtown was a blurred mix of rage and confusion. He barely noticed the red lights and the traffic around him. His thoughts were fixated on Pittman. He was set on killing the man who took Josh.

His rage pushed him through the over-sized door of Pittman's old law firm, which he still used for his Tallahassee headquarters during the legislative session. He yelled at the young woman behind the reception desk, startling her nearly out of her chair.

"Where is he?"

"I need you to calm down, or I'm calling the cops."

"They're already here. Where's Pittman?"

The young woman struggled to understand what the angry man in the trench coat wanted. She had dealt with plenty of disgruntled customers working for a law firm, but she wasn't sure how to handle issues surrounding the senator. She stood up at her desk as she slipped her hand on the panic button under the desk while trying to calm the man as he paced around the small lobby.

"He's not here. Can I help you with something?"

"No, you can't. I need to know where he is."

"Well, I work for the law firm not him, so I'm not sure how to help you."

"If he's not here, find me someone who can help me." Curt stepped up to the top of the desk and loomed over the desk.

The woman picked up the phone and punched some numbers but remained standing, keeping distance between herself and Curt. During the calm, Curt let his eyes wander, and a glossy flyer advertising a fundraiser caught his eye. The guest of honor was Thomas Pittman. He reached over the top of the desk and grabbed the flyer. It was being held that day and within the hour at the University Club at Doak Campbell Stadium.

Curt immediately turned and left the law firm just as two men with shirt and ties came out of a side door behind the receptionist.

"What the hell was that about?" the older of the two asked.

"I don't know. He wanted the Senator but wouldn't say what for."

"Huh. Well, call his assistant, and let him know."

***

Curt sat outside in the parking lot with a blackened heart, contemplating his next move. He'd known Pittman for years from his time as a detective and had considered him a friend. Pittman poured money and resources into finding Josh after his disappearance and had checked in with him almost daily. He was there for him in his family's time of need. He never gave it a second thought when Pittman came to visit just a few days before. Now he realized everything had been for show and to stay close to the investigation. Curt was still fuzzy on the why. Pittman was a State Senator; what reason could he possibly have to take Josh?

The University Club sat on the top floor at the east end of the massive brick behemoth that was Doak Campbell Stadium. Affectionately known as "Doak," the stadium holds 83,000 people to cheer the Seminoles on various Saturdays throughout the fall. The University Club has a bar and dining area that overlooks the field and caters to the more influential boosters. The fundraiser was being held on the fourth floor of the University Club, in a large banquet hall that features a circular window in the far wall, like an oculus that overlooks Tallahassee.

Curt stewed inside of his car, nervously rubbing the small St. Anthony's medallion between his fingers. He was unable to shake the revenge plot that was formulating in his head. Finally, a limousine pulled up to the University Club doors, and out stepped Thomas Pittman, sharply dressed in a shiny, black tuxedo. An equally formally dressed couple followed Pittman out of the limo along with another woman, Pittman's date. She had short, brown hair, a small, fit, and attractive body that was outlined by a silky, green dress. An odd sense of recognition came to Curt as he looked at Pittman's date from afar. She was much too young for him, but she still clung to his arm as they walked up to the entrance.

Curt slid out of his car and made it up to the interior road that encircled the stadium. He paused and watched them walk toward the doors while he stood in the shadows of the Unconquered statue. It depicts Chief Osceola on the back of Renegade rearing high into the sky, holding a flaming spear triumphantly in the air. He watched Pittman with disgust and repulsion. His head was foggy and distant as the hatred drove him to find his revenge. He slowly slid his trench coat to the side and set his hand on the handle of his Glock. The fine line between morality and justice was approaching fast, and once he crossed it, he knew he would never be able to step back. For the past three years, the image of Josh's innocent face fueled Curt's quest to find him, but now, as he stood on an empty shell of desperation, the only image that came to mind was that of Josh cowering in the apartment of Tobias Helton, crying helplessly. This image incited a murderous rage inside him, to the point that there was no other decision to make.

He whipped out the gun in one quick, fluid motion and held it down by his side. He stared across the street at the man responsible for his son's abduction. As the limo slowly pulled away, Curt took a step into the road to get a better shot. Everything was moving in slow motion. His mind wound down, slow enough that he could hear each thump of his heartbeat and the intake of each breath. A calmness engulfed him, giving him a peace he didn't anticipate. The decision was made—Pittman was going to die. As Curt crossed the road, Pittman's date stopped abruptly as they reached the door and looked straight back at Curt, locking eyes with him, as if she knew he was there. The young face staring back at him was Beth Young.

Curt hesitated and snapped out of his vengeful trance as confusion grew to an unexpected level of bewilderment. Just as Pittman felt the tug at his arm, he looked at his date and followed her gaze back toward the parking lot trying to figure out the source of her attention. Curt panicked as the element of surprise was sure to disappear and the opportunity wasted. He had to move, but there was nowhere to hide in an open parking lot.

Before Curt could turn and run, a huge shadow surrounded him as this massive, black flash crossed in front of him, coming between him and Pittman. It knocked him backwards, and he fell to the ground.

292

Curt focused on the giant shadow before him, realizing it was the broad side of the Mercedes Sprinter, mere inches away from where he stood. The huge sliding side door withdrew with purpose, and inside sat Rachel Goodwin staring down at him with disappointment.

"Get in," Rachel said with urgency.

"No, I'm here to take care of something."

"Don't do it. Just get in."

He grew angry at her interference. "What the hell are you doing here? I don't need your help!"

"What are we doing here? Well, we're certainly not here to kill Thomas Pittman in a fit of rage like you are."

Curt was taken aback at her statement. He shamefully hid the Glock that was still in his hand. "Huh?"

"Yeah, we know about Pittman. Now get in."

"Why should I? He has to pay for what he's done. He's gotten away with it for far too long."

"Why should you listen to me? Hmmm. How about the reason why he took your son; would that be worth anything to you?"

Curt's jaw dropped, and his eyes grew wide. "But...but, how?"

"Get in the van, Curtis."

"Goddammit." Curt holstered the gun and looked around for any witnesses.

"Fine," he added.

With no one around, he stepped into the van and took a seat in the back. The door slammed shut, and Melinda Dalton punched the gas, driving the van away in a hurry.

Beth Young quickly focused on the heel of her shoe instead of the commotion out in the street to draw Pittman's attention away to her minor inconvenience. She fixed the phantom issue with the shoe and told her date to proceed with the escort to the fundraiser. He smiled and obliged, leading her through the doors and into the lobby of the University Club.

***

Jeremy Stephens stood at the entrance of the fundraiser, waiting anxiously for his employer, the Senator from Panama City. Stephens had received news from the law firm not more than ten minutes earlier, and he was eager to share the information with the Senator. Pittman followed Priscilla Harvey off the elevator, and they made their way toward the ballroom. Pittman had finished explaining the appeal of his latest bill in Congress when he saw the worried look on Stephens' face.

"Uh, give me a minute dear, would you?"

"Sure. Don't be long."

Pittman smiled, reading the flirtatious smile and its implications on Miss Harvey's face and stepped over to Stephens.

"What?"

"He came to your office looking for you."

The worry immediately transferred over to Pittman's face.

"What did he say?"

"Nothing. He grabbed a flyer for this event and stormed out of there."

"Fuck!" The reaction, although said in a hushed tone, caught the attention of his date who looked over curiously. Pittman turned the façade back on and met her with another smile. She looked away, took out a compact mirror from her clutch, and checked her make-up.

"So, he knows then?" Pittman assessed.

"Yes. Looks that way. What do we do now?"

"What did you find out about that thing in Vail? Did you talk to your guy at the police department yet?"

"Oh, yes. I talked to him this morning. Walker's their suspect. They're flying in to talk with him as we speak. Should I call them? Tell them he's here and to go ahead and make the arrest?"

"Yes, get them here fast. I know him well enough that if he knows I'm here, he'll come straight here, and that could ruin everything."

"I'm on it."

Stephens headed for the elevator as he pulled out his cell phone making a call.

Chapter 44

Alexis Vanderhill watched the drama unfold at the Stadium from the driver's seat of her car. As Curtis Walker hesitantly climbed into the Mercedes Sprinter, she checked herself in the rearview mirror and stepped out of the car. She headed to the same entrance that she had watched Thomas Pittman escort Priscilla Harvey through on their way up to the University Club. She hung back in the lobby, waiting for someone else.

She stood impatiently, checking her watch. Her elegance and beauty were accented by her sparkling, silver dress with a revealing, low cut in the front. The mid-thigh length showed off her stunningly long and lithe legs. She dangled a beautiful diamond necklace around her neck with matching earrings, defining her stylish ambience. She caught the eye of every other partygoer on their way to the elevator as she waited in the lobby and created dissention among the female guests.

After ten minutes of waiting, she grew irritated, knowing it shouldn't have taken this long, not so much for the tardiness or possible absence of her guest but for the fact that it threw a wrench into the plan.

Tony Mason pulled the glass door open and walked into the cavernous lobby. With no sense of urgency, he stuffed both hands in his pockets and leisurely looked around the large room, purposely avoiding eye contact with Alexis. This only angered her more, which he found himself enjoying immensely.

Clutching her small matching purse by her side, she stood angrily with her other arm on her hip as she waited for Mason to stop acting immature.

"Are you done?" she said testily.

He looked past her to see that the lobby led out to the actual football field. The glimpse of green grass and garnet painted letters sent him back to a boyhood fascination, but he'd had his fun and addressed Alexis.

"Ehh. Probably not. I'm not really in the business of catering to Alexis Vanderhill, so...."

"Fair enough, but you'll like what I have to say. I promise."

"Sorry if I don't trust a single word you say. I'm only here because my flight doesn't leave until the morning, and I have nothing else better to do in this humid-filled crap hole. I hate this place. I figured I would at least let you look me in the eye as you try to ruin my career."

Alexis ignored the harsh words from the bitter reporter. He had every right to be mad about how his article was killed, and he would be even more livid if he knew the truth of how his prized expose got scrubbed. That was why she asked him to come to the Stadium, to make amends.

Alexis was overly protective of her team and their mission, just as she was a dogged journalist seeking the truth to report. This was the sole motivation behind killing Mason's feature. The journalist in her hated it, but there was a greater good to protect, and journalistic integrity had to be sacrificed. Nothing within her power was going to jeopardize the mission or the team.

As she remained behind the scenes, she maintained the persona of the team to the families they helped, and until the day before, she had never asked for anything from any of the families. Never asked for any favors and not once for any money, she only asked for their discretion in keeping their secret team, a secret.

After hearing about Mason's visit to Curt's home and the promise to move the story forward, she went into panic mode. Her only move was to re-contact one of the families and ask for help. It was her only option to keep the story out of print.

A few years before, Mason had caught wind of her clandestine team after they rescued a boy from a Northern Californian cult. He'd been missing for seven years, and after an extensive investigation, media campaign, and even private consultants, the team found him and returned him to his family. The kid needed a lot of therapy to reverse the brainwashing from the cult's program, and the team helped him get back on track. Because it was the team who brought him back, the family was most thankful, and they honored her request of anonymity. However, the boy let the word slip out of his rescue and mentioned the team as his heroes. Mason came running for the scoop, but after a quick phone call from Vanderhill to the boy's parents reminding them of their deal, the boy recanted his account to the reporter and ignored further attempts by Mason, much to his disappointment.

What Mason didn't know was that the California boy's father was the head of a major manufacturer of homemade goods in the Southwest United States and they also happened to own one of the biggest advertisement accounts with the LA Times. Unbeknownst to Mason, Vanderhill didn't hesitate to contact the father of the boy and call in a favor. It was dirty pool but necessary to keep the team concealed. It was endearing that the father didn't hesitate or even question the motivation behind her request. He gladly agreed to reach out to the head of the newspaper and have the piece squashed.

"I can never thank you enough Ms. Vanderhill; consider it done," he said.

Now it was time to make nice with Tony Mason.

"So, you gonna piss on me and tell me it's raining?" Mason asked.

"No, I have a story for you."

"I had a story, but you already know that. Oh yeah, you ruined it for me. I don't know how, but I gotta give it to you. I underestimated you, but just so you know, I'm publishing that article…one way or another."

"That's why I called you here. I want to more-or-less trade stories."

"What? Trade? What the hell are you talking about? Why should I even entertain the idea?"

"You're here, aren't you?" Alexis smirked, throwing her perception in Mason's face.

Sheepishly, he conceded to her point and stood listening.

"I'm not going to pretend you're ignorant of what we do, so I'm just going to leave it at that. But there is something going on as we speak, and I think it will be worth your while. Plus, I can't have you sniffing around and getting my team exposed."

The bitterness remained steadfast, and Tony Mason loathed this woman, but he couldn't walk away without listening to her "trade." He admitted that he was intrigued. Alexis Vanderhill had proven herself a worthy adversary, and this made him curious.

He stuffed his hands back into his pockets and looked her in the eyes. He tried to ignore her beauty which he hid behind his hatred for her.

"I'm listening."

"I can't tell you everything...." Mason groaned and spun in his place like a petulant child. He grew annoyed, thinking she was once again playing him for a fool.

"Wait just a minute Tony, and hear me out."

"Fine."

"I can't tell you everything because we are right in the middle of it, but it's big. I need you to keep your nose out of it for now, but once it's done, I will give you exclusive rights to the story, every single detail."

"Okay, so what's the story? I mean, you gotta give me something."

"Well, let's just say there's more than meets the eye to the guest of honor at this fundraiser." Alexis peered behind her toward the elevators. "We expect to have the proof to back that up real soon."

Mason shot a glance over Alexis' shoulder to the marquee sign by the elevators. He read Pittman's name and let it bounce around in his head. He remembered reading the local paper and coming across the name. He remembered Pittman was a State Senator with a tough on crime platform. Was he corrupt? A degenerate? Criminal? He feared for any man who found himself in the crosshairs of Alexis Vanderhill. Mason was now, officially interested, because thanks to Bill Clinton, and many others, America loves a political scandal.

He nodded back at Alexis, understanding the target on which she had set her sights. "Scandal? Like lose his office big or federal prison big?"

"Prison big."

"And I get the exclusive?"

"Yes, sir. In exchange, you drop this crusade you have for me and my team for good and forget about your story, deal?"

"UGH! I knew it. That's a tall order, lady!"

"C'mon Tony, please?"

"This better be big Alexis, or so help me God, I will go through some trash rag like TMZ to get my story out."

"You won't be disappointed." She stuck her hand out for him to shake. Mason hesitated but acquiesced and accepted the deal.

In a flash, Alexis turned and walked to the elevators. Her high heeled steps echoed in the massive lobby, and Mason studied her long and smooth legs as she walked away. He was always so focused on hating her that he never realized just how beautiful she was. As she waited for the ride up to the University Club, she looked back at the LA reporter and noticed that he was staring at her. She smiled at the attention, and he grew embarrassed at having been caught.

***

Mason ambled out of the lobby, wondering whether or not he should uphold his end of the deal. Alexis Vanderhill had royally screwed him several times in his career, so he thought about returning the favor. He stopped at the top of the stairs just outside of the University Club and saw the long shadows of the setting sun stretching far across the vast parking lot.

He looked over and saw a familiar face walking toward him with a purpose. A cigarette was burning in the corner of his mouth.

"Hey, Detective Rankin."

"Reporter," he acknowledged back. Tony was slightly insulted that Rankin didn't remember his name. "What the hell are you doing here?"

"Oh, I thought I'd just visit the school. Good journalism program. What brings you here?"

Rankin paused and looked back at Mason with a look letting him know he wasn't buying that answer for a second.

"Thinking of teaching are you?" Rankin said heavy with sarcasm. He left without waiting for a response, and his junior detective followed and gave the reporter a mocking smile.

***

The elevator dinged and Alexis stepped in, eager to get to the third floor. The doors were caught by an aged hand reaching in from just outside. The doors slid back open, and a haggard, older man stepped inside with her along with a younger man in a crumpled suit. The doors shut, and he punched the already lit three button. Alexis' nostrils were bombarded by the overwhelming stench of cigarette smoke, and she held back a cough.

The men stayed silent, ignoring the elegant woman in the elevator with them. Alexis sized them up and knew they didn't fit in at the hoity-toity fundraiser. They were there for something else altogether.

The younger man adjusted his stance, trying to catch another glance at Alexis. The shine of his badge glared back at her, and she read Vail Police Department engraved on it. She gasped just as the doors opened on the third floor. The older detective turned before he stepped out and looked Alexis over suspiciously; he then continued toward the ballroom without any further thought.

Chapter 45

Curtis Walker stood in the corner of the large banquet room, brooding. He watched Thomas Pittman work the room and jovially converse with the others like he was on top of the world, when in truth, he was a kidnapper. He forced back the swelling anger that wanted to explode into a violent beating of the politician. There was no elegance in that manner of justice but it was guaranteed to make him feel better. After beating Glenn Gregory unconscious, he'd felt a sense of satisfaction, but it was overshadowed at the time by the continued absence of his son.

Curt was on a mission, but now the mission had changed, and one way or another, Pittman was going to pay for what he did.

Curt started to move through the crowd, straight toward Pittman. He stalked him like a lion through tall grass on the Savanna, and the partygoers were his camouflage. As he neared the politician, his full-bellied and hearty laugh resonated outward and was infectious to those around him. It only made Curt nauseous. As he got closer with each step, thoughts of killing Pittman swirled around in his head. The Glock waited patiently on his hip, and at this point, it was just a matter of pulling the trigger.

A tiny voice spoke through the ear bud in Curt's ear.

"Hurry it up. Alexis just sent me a text that the Vail detectives just got off the elevator." There was a tinge of panic in Rachel's voice.

Senator Thomas Pittman was talking to a few fellow legislators and an old colleague who still sat on the City Council. They were rehashing old times and memorable events in past charities. As Pittman downed the rest of his champagne, he felt a presence behind him. The odd look on the Congressman who stood in front of him confirmed this. Pittman turned as he finished the drink to see Curtis Walker standing behind him, a deadpan look on his face.

His stare gave Pittman the uneasy feeling of being exposed, like he could read his innermost thoughts and secrets. Curt's expression was unwavering and caused a stir within the small circle of constituents. Curt was a sight. He was a disheveled mess with an old, worn-out trench coat hanging loose off his body, coupled with distant eyes, and a betrayed look on his face. It gave him the appearance of walking off the street and into the black tie event.

"Curtis! How are you?" Pittman said jovially but secretly met Curt with glaring eyes of contempt.

"I'm fine, Senator. How are you doing?" Curt replied sarcastically.

Pittman handed his empty glass off to someone standing behind him and then excused himself to deal with the man in the trench coat.

With a hidden hiss in his tone, Pittman softly said, "Can we talk over here, please?" Pittman grabbed Curt's arm and pulled him away from the small crowd.

"Sure."

Being a career politician, Pittman quickly explained that the man was a dejected member of his staff who was recently let go and that he needed to deal with something before it got out of hand. He was met with understanding nods.

Once in a private huddle, Pittman said with feigned sincerity, "What are you doing here, Curtis?" There was a slight panic in Pittman's voice, but he was much too cautious to let on that he was concerned. He was holding onto the hope that Curt didn't know just how deep his secret ran.

"Oh, I was just in the neighborhood. Thought I'd stop in and say hi." The sarcasm was still thick and obvious.

"Well, if I'd known that you wanted to come, I would've gotten you and Tracy a ticket."

"Oh, you've done more than enough for my family, Thomas." The deadpan look returned.

Pittman's perpetual smile faded as he realized he had been found out and that Curtis Walker had somehow uncovered the carefully hidden truth. He had ways to deal with this, and he would never let someone like Curtis Walker get over on him. He maintained the façade and made a quick head nod over Curtis' shoulder, as if anticipating this confrontation. Pittman believed in luck but knew he had to make luck work in his favor and sometimes even create his own brand of luck.

Curt turned and saw two men making their way through the crowd. His first thought was that they were goons ready to remove him and "make him disappear." But as the two men got closer, he immediately pegged them as cops, but not local.

"Curtis Walker?" one of the men said in a deep, raspy voice.

"Yes?"

"I'm Detective Edgar Rankin. I'd like to talk to you about an incident that happened a few weeks ago in Vail, Colorado."

Curt didn't react. He slowly looked back at Pittman who had a smug look on his face. He turned and saw a few uniformed officers from TPD standing by the entrances of the ballroom, a contingency plan if he didn't want to go willingly. Finally, he turned back to Rankin and his fellow detective as they were anticipating the worst. Curt noticed Rankin had his hand hiked back and poised to draw his weapon. There was a subtle but palpable tension that came over the room. Pittman and Curt were at the epicenter.

"Sure, I assume we're going back to TPD and not Vail, right?"

"Of course. We've been in contact with your Sergeant Polk. He's expecting us."

Rankin reached up and escorted Curt from the center of the room and through the crowd which drew looks and created murmurs of speculation. Pittman watched as Curt was led away. His smug face appeared strong with his satisfaction and control over the situation. Curt looked back at Pittman with a pathetic look of betrayal and defeat. Pittman only smirked back, knowing his exposure would not come to light, and his dark secret would remain hidden and just that…a dark secret.

"Thanks for the tip, Senator," the junior detective leaned in and said to Pittman.

"No problem detective. I've always been a sounding board for justice, and that includes cops who cross the line. It's sad when that happens, but we're all held accountable for our actions. Do what you must."

"Yes, sir." The junior detective caught up with Rankin to help escort their suspect out of the venue. Pittman smiled arrogantly. A waiter passed by with a tray full of champagne glasses. He reached up and took another while Curt was walked out of the banquet room and toward the elevators.

***

Alexis Vanderhill stood by in the opposite corner and watched helplessly as Curt was escorted away by the Vail detectives. She fought the urge to intervene, but she restrained herself, knowing it would not do any good. As Curt disappeared through the doors of the banquet hall, the hushed murmurs grew into a staccato of loud conversation with a few laughs and high-pitched squeals. These types of events were necessary but were also a huge annoyance as the self-involved people who attended rarely got behind the reason of need. It was used for social interaction and was gaining popularity among the "In Crowd." Sometimes, she was appalled by the misguided elite of society.

"What the hell is going on, Alexis?" Tony Mason decided to catch the elevator after passing Rankin outside. He walked into the banquet room and saw the exchange with Walker and the detectives. He was left wondering if he'd been had since he knew that Curt was a player on her team.

"What do you mean?"

"I mean, I thought this was about Pittman, not Walker. If you lied to me, so help me—"

"Relax Tony. You get ugly when you whine." Alexis turned and looked at Mason and gave him a smile.

Mason saw it and the deviousness that came with it. He caught on quickly and looked back through the crowd at Pittman, who was now the center of attention.

"Plus, who's in control isn't always obvious." Alexis walked away from Mason, leaving him standing alone.

Mason grabbed a flute of champagne from a passing waiter. He tipped it up, emptying it in one gulp. Pondering the events that he had just witnessed, coupled with what he already knew of Alexis Vanderhill, he concluded that he would never want to be on her bad side. "I guess not!"

Chapter 46

The small monitor room on the side of the Criminal Investigations Division was crammed full of onlookers. Most were members of TPD's Command staff along with Sergeant Polk, who all watched the lengthy interview between Curtis Walker and the two detectives from Vail. Each listened intently about the hardship Walker had endured after his son went missing. Most of the department had had no clue of his whereabouts for the past two years. Many had assumed that he had fallen into a life-numbing cocoon of alcoholism and self-blame. So, they were astounded that he had actually been wandering around the country in search of his lost child...literally leaving no stone unturned.

After two and a half hours, Detective Rankin and his partner walked out of the interview room. He had all he needed from the Tallahassee detective and desperately craved a cigarette. Polk explained that the building was smoke-free and escorted them down to the parking garage underneath the Crystal Palace so Rankin could smoke.

"So...what do you think?" Rankin asked of Polk as they waited for the elevator.

"What do you mean?"

"Walker is your guy. Is he being honest?"

Polk didn't want to air any type of laundry to an outsider, but given the circumstances, he wanted to provide honest feedback.

"I think he is. But there's something he's holding back. Putting two-and-two together from your interview, sounds like everything's pretty consistent with what you have on scene, right?"

"Yes, it matches, but he's lying about what led up to the shooting."

"What do you mean? What do you have that says he's lying?"

"The woman...."

Rankin exited the elevator on the bottom floor and quickly lit his cigarette. He took a long drag as if it were air, and he was drowning.

"What woman? The one he rescued from the traffickers?"

"Yes, he didn't acknowledge knowing her. He says he was there following Cauldress who he overheard talking about the prostitutes, and then this woman was just there in a random coincidence. I'm not buying that crap."

"Okay, what you got?"

"Just the evidence on scene. We got her blood, and it's just a matter of time until she turns up. It just doesn't look good for your guy to be holding back." Rankin had sent off the blood from the upstairs bedroom and found it didn't match any of the trafficking victims. According to the lab, it belonged to a female donor. This corroborated the women's story of the heroine helping them escape.

"So, he's truthful with the actual shooting and what happened but not necessarily what led him to be at the house."

"Right?"

"Why would he lie about how he got there but tell the truth about the shooting? I mean, that doesn't really make sense. I get what you're saying though; I'm just not sure what you're looking for. Are you saying Curt and this woman conspired somehow, to kill Cauldress and the traffickers? Did you talk to the girls?"

"Yeah, they said both just showed up, helped them out of the window, and then the shooting happened."

"Kind of backs up their story, huh?"

"Kind of."

"You think they were working together for some unknown reason, but you're still good with how the shooting went down?"

"Yeah, but it still bothers me. Loose ends and all."

"Still sounds like your case is proven," Polk concluded.

"Yeah," Rankin said, followed by a moment in silent thought. "Yeah, looks that way."

"Where are you at with Walker? You gonna charge him?"

"Leaning towards it. I've got a lot of problems with what he's saying. I'm going to run this by my people back in Vail first. Sounds like a righteous shoot despite some of the lies, but I'm stuck on the fact that he hauled ass from Colorado after the shooting. He had time to stage the scene to fit his story of self-defense, because any good cop knows it's better to stick around and at least not say anything rather than running. As you know, running equates to guilt in police work."

"Yeah, that seems to be universal."

"I guess we wait and see," Rankin said, as he tossed down his cigarette and stamped it out with a twist of his foot.

***

Curt sat alone in the interview room while his fate was being settled outside. He gave the detectives everything they needed, short of the real reason for being at the chalet. He owed Alexis Vanderhill that much. He thought about his son at home. He'd been gone all day, chasing the leads about who was behind Josh's kidnapping, and he wanted to get home to see him.

Rankin explained that he was going to contact his agency and give them an update. They would decide whether to arrest Curt later. It was late, and the two Vail detectives left the station in search of food and a hotel while waiting for their superiors to make a decision. Polk agreed to remain behind with their suspect.

"Sergeant Polk, may I have a minute please?" Curt said to the empty room. He knew he was still being watched from the monitor room.

Polk looked around the room to the Command Staff members who looked back expectantly at the sergeant. He had no idea what his detective wanted. He slowly got up and went to the interview room to see what he wanted.

"Hey Curt, what's up?"

"I need to tell you something but not with it rolling." Curt was referring to the video recording equipment in the room.

Sgt. Polk grew leery but could sense the honesty behind the request. He'd known Curtis Walker for a long time, and even though he'd been through some tough times in the last three years, Polk saw the same man he knew. He nodded and requested a minute to shoo away the Command Staff.

"No, I want the Captain and Chief to join us too."

"Okay...." he said skeptically.

A few minutes later, the video recorder was turned off and Curt sat across from Polk, the Captain over investigations, and the Chief.

"What I'm about to tell you cannot leave this room, at least not yet. Can you all agree to that?"

"If you lied to those detectives and want to confess to us, you have no confidentiality here, son!" the Chief said.

"No sir, I didn't lie to them. I gave them everything they need to know. This is about something else. This is about the disappearance of my son and who's responsible."

"Yeah, we know. Those guys from Valdosta."

"No, there's another."

Chapter 47

It all started with a look. Standing outside of the Walker home while a crowd of reporters watched like spectators, Rachel Goodwin noticed the sharply dressed Senator give the younger and more impressionable Beth Young a flirtatious look as he walked by. At least twenty years her senior, it was a lingering look of instant desire, but Rachel read the look as more lascivious and criminal. It stayed with her the whole time she was visiting with Curt, distracting her. It nagged at her. The only time she ignored it was when Tracy Walker walked into the room causing distress, given the moment she had shared with Curt.

After leaving the house, Rachel couldn't let the Senator's look go. She tasked out assignments to the team and asked them to research Pittman, knowing she couldn't go to Curtis with this hunch. She didn't want to be wrong about Pittman and have it cause embarrassment. A false accusation of any kind against a person such as Thomas Pittman could be fatal for the existence of the team.

"Uh, the Senator?" Louis asked skeptically.

"Yeah, something's not right about him."

"Like what?" Beth asked, obviously seeing what she wanted from the charming man.

"I'm not sure. Just take a look and see if anything catches your eye."

Rachel spent most of the day looking at Pittman's profile and trying to learn about him. It was all cookie-cutter stuff that sounded good and nothing that interested her. He was born to and raised in the panhandle of Florida by wealthy parents He went to the University of West Florida for his undergraduate studies and the University of Florida for his master's degree in political science. He moved to Tallahassee and got his law degree from FSU and worked for the State Attorney's Office for several years as a prosecutor before moving into the political arena. He ran for and was elected as a City Councilman at the age of thirty-one and served on the Council for ten years. He was pro tem Mayor for a short term before winning his district for State Senator and moving back home to the panhandle. He still kept an office in Tallahassee to use during session.

She focused on his time in Tallahassee and read more about the oversight committee. Pittman joined the committee a year before Joshua went missing, and he stepped down about six months later to focus on his Senatorial campaign.

Rachel was getting stonewalled by the drab information she found on the internet. It frustrated her because she saw something in Pittman outside of Curt's house. If she failed to validate the feeling, to her that meant she was not capable of leading this team as effectively as Curt. She had seen firsthand his ability to see the darkness within one's soul. She moved through life as guarded as she could, but he managed to read her like an open book on the night of the shooting as they shared their innermost secrets and a kiss. She wanted the same ability, and this was her first test. Not having it was deflating and a waste of time.

"Hey, wanna see something weird?" Louis said, breaking Rachel away from her frustrations.

"Sure."

"I was watching some of the news coverage on Josh's story, and look what I found."

Louis rolled his chair away from his little workstation in the back of the van and twisted the monitor around so that Rachel could see it from the captain's chair. Melinda looked on from the driver's seat.

The footage was from earlier that morning and showed Tracy slowly pulling out of the driveway with Josh in the front seat. The reporters were trying to obtain a sound bite from the mother of the missing child, but she politely smiled and said, "Sorry, no comment." The footage continued and the reporter looked back at the camera and finished the news report. The total clip was about twenty seconds and unsensational to say the least.

"Okay, so? Tracy had no comment. I don't blame her."

"No kidding. That's not it. Did you see past her car?"

"No, play it again."

Louis reloaded the video and hit play. Beth Young stopped what she was doing and watched the computer screen over Rachel's shoulder.

As Tracy's car pulled slowly from the driveway, she addressed the reporters and drove off. As she did, Rachel caught what Louis pegged as "weird." It was a Lincoln Town Car parked off to the side. Sitting behind the wheel was the shadowy figure of a man.

"What time did we get to the house?"

"A little after 10:30 a.m.," Louis answered.

"And this was…."

"Shot at 9:50 a.m., aired at the ten o'clock hour."

"I take it that Curt's neighbor doesn't own a Lincoln?"

"Nope," he answered with a smile, "but you know who was there around ten this morning and drives one?"

"The good Senator," Rachel said.

"Okay, what does that mean?" Beth didn't understand the significance.

"He waited until they left."

"So?"

"Why would you wait until the mother and especially the boy left before visiting? He's a schmoozer and a charmer, why did he wait?"

"That means what exactly? I'm a little lost," Beth questioned.

"Not sure yet, but yes, that is certainly weird."

In the days that followed, Rachel and the team kept digging into the life of Thomas Pittman. They were met with roadblocks along the way, but they were undeterred from continuing. It wasn't until Louis noticed Curt leaving his house early one morning that things started to happen.

"He's headed to the jail."

"The jail?" Rachel asked quizzically.

"Yeah, according to the GPS I put on his car."

"Okay, let's head that way. Do they have their own radio channel at the jail?"

"I'm sure they do. I'll find it on the scanner."

As the team sat in the parking lot of the jail, they listened to the jail radio channel for anything of interest. Rachel perked up when someone asked for inmate Gregory to be taken to the Unit. She had no idea what the "Unit" was, but Gregory, she knew. She hoped Curt wasn't going to do anything foolish while inside the jail. If he did, they might not let him leave.

Louis forced his virtual will on the security measures in the jail's computer system. He started poking around with its features and managed to find the unusual visit by Bobby Richards. After continuing his search, he was able to uncover the mystery man switch rather quickly. Like Curt, they didn't believe Richards was someone who would actually visit a person like Helton. But unlike Curt's limited access, Louis was able to find the girlfriend of Richards and pulled up her visitor log, revealing the mystery man.

"Who the hell is that?" Louis asked.

On the screen was a late twenties, white male with trimmed, low-cut hair, thin-rimmed glasses, and a slight effeminate look. No one on the team had seen him before, and they were at a loss as to who he was.

"Jeremy Stephens," Louis announced, reading from the visitor's log.

"Wait...who?" Rachel asked with urgency.

Louis repeated the name, and Rachel pulled open the laptop Louis loaned her and clicked several times before finding what she was looking for.

"Found him!" Rachel turned the screen around to show the team. They peered at the screen to see the image of a well-dressed man and compared it to the visitor of Bobby Richards' girlfriend. It was the same man, but just as quickly as the comparison was made, the rest of the website that hosted Stephens' picture became known. It was Thomas Pittman's Senatorial page. Rachel found Stephens under the "Meet the Staff" page, and Stephens was listed as a personal assistant.

Just as the team tried to make sense of the latest information, the jail channel came to life, breaking up the silence of the van's interior.

They listened intently to the ensuing confusion and finally heard the name Helton. The radio reported he died by way of hanging himself in his cell. The team sat incredulously thinking about the timing of Helton's death and hoped Curt hadn't become unhinged. When Beth Young spotted Curt walking away from the jail, the team let out a collective sigh of relief. Responsible or not, at least he was leaving on his own accord.

The black Mercedes Sprinter pulled out of the jail parking lot and headed for Pittman's downtown office. Interestingly, it was in the neighborhood just north of Tallahassee Gym Works on the Parkway. Rachel made the connection right away but felt this coincidence was just too good to be true. Obviously, she wanted more. Louis kept tabs on Curt as he watched him move to the Bennett Street address of Bobby Richards. Rachel could only assume Curt had learned of Helton's visitor but not about the switch and was going to question Richards in person.

***

From across the street of Thomas Pittman's office, they could see the black Town car parked around back. There was no doubt that it was the same car from the news footage; the front vanity tag was a dead giveaway. It read "Sen8R."

They sat at his office all morning, watching in silence. They were not really sure how to continue when suddenly Beth Young let out a gasp, setting off alarms inside the van.

"Holy shit!"

"Oh my God; what is it?" Rachel asked.

"I got something, I mean…I think I figured it out.…"

"Okay, let's hear it."

"Doesn't it bother anyone else knowing what case Curt was working on when Josh went missing? As soon as Josh went missing, that case seemed to just disappear with him. At the time, there were at least six rapes that had occurred in the six months preceding the kidnapping, and according to the case files, they were closing in on the suspect."

"So, they're connected? Curt's old case and the kidnapping?"

"Yeah, I don't think it was coincidence."

"So are you saying Pittman is involved in the rapes?" Rachel sounded hopeful.

"Maybe, but listen to this."

Beth Young summarized the rape cases Curt worked prior to the kidnapping. She found another rape that occurred about a month after Josh's disappearance and then noticed they seemed to have stopped altogether. This seemed odd, and she researched any other similar rapes in and around the state. She found five more reported stranger rapes over the following six months that were committed with the same M.O. as the ones in Tallahassee. The women were followed to their homes where the suspect managed to gain entry and then gain control by ambushing them. They were all reported in the Panama City and Panama City Beach area. Beth noted that this was the hometown of Thomas Pittman.

"So…that can't be a coincidence, can it?"

"Uh, no honey; that's damn near probable cause," Melinda added with certainty.

"How do we know it's Pittman and not someone who's working for him? I mean, this Stephens guy is a good candidate, right?"

"Actually…no, I wouldn't think so," Louis chimed in as he was pecking away at his keyboard.

"Why not?"

Louis explained he had found enough information through social media and an unwelcomed glance into his personal emails to indicate he preferred the company of other men, not women.

"I wouldn't think that he fits the profile of a rapist."

"No, I wouldn't think so either," Rachel agreed.

"That fits. I mean, Pittman that is. Politicians often seek office due to a need for power and control. Those are the same traits as a rapist. Is there any evidence from the rapes either here or in Panama City that could be linked to Pittman? Do the police have anything useful?"

"He's good. I mean…real good. He binds the women, assaults them, and keeps them that way even while he cleans up the scene. He leaves them there until they manage to fight through the restraints and free themselves. By then, he's long gone. I've gone over all the forensic reports and there isn't anything there—except for…."

Rachel looked at Beth with a spit-it-out-look.

"I found one more, but it may be a long shot."

Beth explained that in her exhaustive search of the rape cases, she came across a similarly described incident, but the victim was listed as "Jane Doe." The name is reserved for a victim who wants to report the crime but stay anonymous and bypass prosecution. They go through the motions to preserve evidence and testimony, many even withhold the names of the suspect but decline moving the case forward to an arrest and prosecution. It's more about the victim acquiescing to the report and evidence collection, in case she later changes her mind. Many terrified women dread having to relive their encounter and be second-guessed through the court system.

Rachel held a thousand-yard stare as she placed herself in the victim's role, a familiar yet terrorizing place.

"In this case, 'Jane Doe' reported that she saw his face."

"What? That means she can ID him!" Rachel's voice rose with excitement.

"If she remembers, and if she talks to us." Melinda was reminded of the complications in dealing with reticent rape victims.

"The problem is that she's listed as 'Jane Doe,' and there's no way to find her."

"Dammit."

"Hold on. Do you have the report? Let me see it." Melinda's cop skills kicked in. Beth handed her the copy, and Melinda scanned it, searching for something specific. Then, to everyone's surprise, she found what she was looking for.

"There! They put an address for the incident location. That's probably where she lives. He stalked the women and followed them home, right? So this has gotta be her house."

"We need to find her."

***

The Mercedes Sprinter rolled to a stop next to the house of "Jane Doe." It was a long shot but worth trying in order to take down a serial rapist and kidnapper.

The house was modest and on the unkempt side, mostly from neglect, she figured as she walked up to the front door. It was a home built in the late '50s located in the center of town. It had a large front porch and a detached garage in the back. Rachel stepped up the wood, plank stairs and knocked on the door. The house had the feel of old family charm but with an air of sadness.

As the first knock went unanswered, she tried again and noticed the plants off to the side were in desperate need of watering. She shot a glance back to the van and saw the others share a look of disappointment.

Suddenly, the door cracked open, and a demure woman, late thirties, wearing a t-shirt and sweatpants answered. Rachel noticed the woman matched the vague physical description in the report and was hoping she was "Jane Doe."

"Yes?"

"Hi. Um...." Rachel was speechless for a moment as she realized how awkward the reasoning was that brought her to this front porch.

"What do you want?"

"I'm sorry. My name is Rachel Goodwin, and I need your help. You see, my friends and I are trying to stop a man, a very powerful man, from getting away with hurting women as he has for the last several years. I believe we can stop him, but I need your help."

The woman didn't respond. She held Rachel's expectant stare.

"And you're here because? You want some money?"

"Huh? God no! I believe you filed a report about five years ago when you were attacked, here at your home. You were listed as 'Jane Doe.'"

Rachel played her best cards first and waited for the woman to acknowledge that she was "Jane Doe."

"Sorry. I can't help you."

"Okay." Rachel was gut punched and felt the disappointment of everyone, to include Curt's, stacking up against her. "Are you sure?" There was desperation in her voice that was unintended.

"Yes, I'm not that person you're looking for."

The woman closed the door shut. Rachel threw her best card out as a last ditch effort and blurted, "The man also kidnapped a little boy to help cover up his crimes. He won't be stopped unless we do something now!"

Rachel stared at the faded, wood door as it stayed shut. She pleaded through the door for her to find the courage within herself and help. Rachel vowed to walk the path of restoration with her and fight alongside.

"I know what it's like to live in hell every single day. I've been there. I've had to look over my shoulder and wonder if the monster will ever return to finish what he started. The fear is crippling—I know. I have to fight through every day just to survive. I know I can't let him hurt me any longer, and I live my life despite the fear. And if I'm ever given the opportunity, I will not hesitate to bring him to justice for his crimes."

The door remained silent. "Dammit, I'm giving you the chance to fight back, right now! Please, please help!"

She waited for what seemed like an hour and got no response. Defeated, she looked back at the team who watched from the road. As she took a step away, she heard the door crack open. Rachel spun around and saw the woman was crying.

"Can you really help me?"

"Are you 'Jane Doe'?"

With a red nose and teary eyes, the woman nodded her head.

"You're damn right I can."

"Jane Doe" was actually Mirra Teal. She invited Rachel in and explained that she had been scared and living inside of a shell for the past five years. She was afraid to go outside and had even tailored her job so that she could do everything from within the confines of her home. She was a prisoner behind the bars that her rapist had created the night he violated her body, mind, and spirit.

"I don't know if I can do it. Hell, you're the first person outside of my immediate family to come to my door in the past four years. I'm terrified."

"You have every right to be scared. I was a prisoner of sorts for years after my captor released me."

Mirra looked at her, seeking more information. Rachel explained her own nightmare from when she was just a child and the fact that she hadn't seen her sister since. She explained that she too, felt alone and that no one else understood what she had been through. Then, she decided to take it upon herself to make it right and take back control of her life.

"At some point, I knew I had to take a stand, and I know if I ever get a chance to fight back, I will."

"So, they never caught the guy who took you and your sister?"

"No."

Mirra fought an internal battle as she weighed the ramifications of this opportunity. She'd always wondered whether the day would come when she would be given a chance to fight back. She fought hard with her decision. She never told anyone who her attacker was and had only given the police a description. She cringed every time at the sight of Thomas Pittman on the television, making promises to be "tough on crime." She hated him for the hypocritical monster that he was.

"Would I have to appear in court?"

"Maybe, but we can take it one step at a time."

"But I would have to ID him, wouldn't I? Like they do on television…point him out on the stand."

"Yes, if it came to that."

Mirra continued to wage the war inside her head, keeping Rachel on the sidelines.

"What if I had some other piece of evidence?"

"What do you mean?"

Mirra got up from her seat and walked over to a bookshelf in the corner of her living room. It was full of books and old pictures from another generation. She removed two books from the middle shelf and pulled a small, manila envelope from a hidden spot. She turned to look at Rachel while carefully holding it in her hands. She looked down at it, still lost in thought.

After a moment, she took a deep breath and handed it over to Rachel.

"Here. I think you're going to need this."

***

Rachel nearly ran out of Mirra Teal's house and jumped back into the Sprinter. At Rachel's order, Louis got into the Senator's daily schedule and saw that there was a fundraiser at which he was going to be honored that night at the University Club. A Google search of the event told him it was a black tie event that caters to over two hundred guests of the area's politically connected.

"Perfect. Does he have a plus one?"

"Nope."

Rachel looked over at Beth Young with a sly smile, "He does now."

Beth quickly changed into the Priscilla Harvey persona, and after a ten minute phone call, she managed to lure him in with no hesitation. She was now the Senator's date for the fundraiser.

"I get to wear my new dress, yeah!" she said excitedly.

They were heading toward the stadium to set up for the plan when Louis announced that Curt had driven home abnormally fast from the police station, and he speculated as to the reason. They wondered if something happened to Josh. Moments later, Curt left the house and was heading west, toward them, with urgency. Rachel shot a call to Tracy and learned of the identification by Josh and of Curt's unclear intentions to get answers from Pittman. Tracy begged them to help him and to keep him from doing anything drastic.

"I'll try," Rachel said.

As they reached the stadium, they spotted Curt walking near a giant statue of a horse rearing in the air while carrying a man with a feathered spear.

"Over there!"

Curt was holding a gun by his side and staring across the street as Pittman walked up to the University Club. Rachel shouted for Melinda to hurry. She told her to pull the van up next to him before he crossed the small street and intercept him. The van sped up and hit a speed bump nearly causing the van to jump into the air. Melinda held on as she nearly fell out of her seat and stomped on the brakes. She screeched up next to Curt, missing him by mere inches. Rachel flung open the door and spoke to the man in the trench coat.

"Get in!" she ordered.

After a short debate, Curt reluctantly got into the van, and Melinda drove around to the other side of the stadium. Rachel explained what they had learned about the Senator and how they believed he was the rapist responsible for the six reported rapes in Tallahassee and five more in the Panama City area as well as the kidnapping of his son. She detailed the timing of the rapes, and the investigation's momentum timed with his son's disappearance. Rachel spelled out the news articles that Beth found after studying his case files and the existence of the "Jane Doe" case and the new evidence. Curt listened incredulously as he was now provided with the why.

"So, he took Josh to take me off the case. Because I was getting too close?" Curt grew angry. He felt foolish for not seeing the connection, but Pittman proved to be cunning and calculating. It had completely incapacitated him...which was Pittman's intention.

Rachel begged Curt to go along with her plan and expose Pittman for the evil rapist and criminal he was, someone willing to trade the innocence of a child for his own criminal freedom and deviousness.

"All I need is a distraction, and we'll do the rest," Rachel explained.

Curt agreed and as he was being escorted away from the center of the crowd by the Vail detectives. Beth had quickly palmed the stem of

Pittman's champagne flute as he handed it back, while keeping his eyes fixed on Curt. Beth, amongst the confusion, simply handed the glass off to Melinda, dressed in wait-staff garb, who then slid it to Louis, also dressed as wait-staff. Both were already wearing plastic gloves to preserve the integrity of the evidence. Louis placed the glass into a plastic evidence bag and sealed it, keeping the Senator's DNA around the rim of the glass undisturbed until the lab analyst could swab it and compare it to the DNA from Mirra Teal's underwear.

Chapter 48

Rachel saw the first phase of her plan executed seamlessly. She hoped the notion that "the truth will set you free" would prevail in the next phase of her plan. It extended her faith knowing that good things have to happen to good people. This, of course, was aimed at Curt.

After seeing the Vail detectives whisk Curt away from the University Club, she followed them to the police station to bare her soul about that fateful night when the evil men lost their lives. But first, she saw to it that the champagne flute with Pittman's DNA found its way to the private DNA testing lab Alexis had contacted. When the expected outcome was made known, she then provided it to the police on behalf of Mirra Teal.

In the lobby of the Tallahassee Police station, Rachel sat alone. She fought off the unwelcome feeling of helplessness that she correlated with sitting in police stations. After she was found wandering the streets following the escape from her kidnapper, she was subjected to a long and tortuous wait until her mother took her home. It was a feeling she despised.

Up one floor, in the Criminal Investigations Division, Curt invited his sergeant back into the interview room after talking to the Vail detectives. He explained, with vivid detail, the actions he and the team had taken to uncover the truth about Thomas Pittman and why he was responsible for Josh's disappearance. The Chief and Captain left the room to talk over the sensitive information Curt provided. Sgt. Melvin Polk remained and sat back in his chair, astounded by the effort it took for Curt and the team to reach their conclusion. Given the political status of their suspect, Polk was wary about simply using circumstances to prove a case. When Curt explained about the ruse to obtain Pittman's DNA and the existence of DNA linking him to Mirra Teal, he was just about sold.

"Okay, so now what?" Polk leaned his hefty body against the far wall of the interview room, arms crossed.

Curt knew his fate rested on the outcome of the Vail detectives, but he wasn't going to let that stop him from getting justice for his son. He explained that once the DNA comparison was done, someone from the team would send it over, and that's when he offered a solution to catch the Senator in the act and expose him for the monster he truly was.

"He'll argue the validity of the DNA test. It being taken from a third party, non-law enforcement entity doesn't hold up as well as if it were us who collected it."

"Yeah, but that doesn't mean it's not his. Even if he argues that, it's still enough to get a search warrant and compel him to re-do the test anyway."

"That's true," Polk agreed.

"Well, I need to run it up the chain…."

"Keep it as quiet as possible…please Mel?"

"I will, I will. Don't worry. I'll fight for you. I like it, but that's only if the DNA comes back and you're not hauled off to some Colorado prison."

Curt smirked at the notion and cracked a smile. "Fair enough."

***

Unbeknownst to Curt, while he sat in solitude in the interview room, Rachel Goodwin intercepted the Vail detectives and introduced herself as the missing witness. Detective Rankin skeptically studied the pretty, blonde woman and rolled his eyes at her forwardness.

"Of course you are, dear. And why wouldn't my missing witness just randomly show up out of the blue?" Rankin said sarcastically.

He nodded for her to follow him outside so he could smoke while they talked. Rachel explained that she was the missing witness whom Curt had saved from nearly being killed at the hands of the human traffickers. She offered up a full and detailed report of her account so that they would know the truth and, hopefully, would reach the conclusion that it was a justified act.

"Don't you think that is up to a jury, Ms. Goodwin?"

"Not in this case. Others yes, but not this one. Plus, I have some incentive for your consideration."

"Incentive?" he scoffed. "Honey, I'm too old and don't care enough to take a bribe. You gotta do better than that."

"No, detective, not money. Incentive."

Rankin took a step back as a large black van slowly rolled to a stop in the small parking lot at the front of the police department. Rachel took a step back, and with precision timing, the side door rolled open. Rankin thought she was going to make a run for it except that she never took her eyes off the seasoned detective. He remained calm, letting things play out. When the door opened, a nerdy man from inside handed Rachel a small object that she clutched by her side.

"What's that?" the detective's curiosity was peeked. "A video of something? The shooting? Did you get it on video?"

"No, sorry detective. It is a video, just not of the shooting. But it's incentive, nonetheless."

She handed him the video tape. He took it and read the handwritten label on the side. After realizing the implications of what he read, his head shot up, and he stared at the enigmatic woman. She met his stare with the expectancy of his cooperation.

"Where did you get this?"

"Jack Cauldress' closet."

"Holy shit." Rankin clearly recognized the name on the label and that this cassette matched several other sex tapes he found in Cauldress' apartment. Obviously, Rachel and whomever she was working with had made it to the apartment beforehand.

"Well? Is that good enough incentive? I'm pretty sure she was a willing participant and not drugged like most of the other girls. Only my opinion though."

"I could care less, but maybe the Chief will see it your way."

Rachel took that as an agreement that she would provide truthful details in the shooting, and in exchange, they would keep quiet and hand over the only copy of Cauldress having his way with the Vail Police Chief's wife.

Rankin studied the van and the people inside it for a moment while he looked past Rachel. Something clicked inside his mind, and he reached inside his coat pocket and pulled out a small, clear, plastic, evidence bag. Inside the bag was the ear bud comm he had found back in Vail. He'd seen equipment like that before at his own agency—only his technical operation guys had a set-up paid for by taxpayers and not a wealthy philanthropist, so it was more on the economical side.

Rankin wrenched his neck to address the nerdy guy in the van.

"I take it, this is yours?"

Rankin held up the evidence bag for him to see in the street light. Louis' eyes bulged, and he froze with indecision.

"Yes, that is ours. I'll gladly take it back if you're done with it." Rachel stepped into Rankin's field of view.

"Hell, might as well. You people hijacked my case anyway." Rankin tossed it over to Rachel and turned toward his rental car so he could head for the hotel.

"One more thing, detective?"

Rachel explained that she needed one last favor from the Vail detective. Given her recent generosity and discretion, she was confident that Rankin and the Chief would agree to this as well.

She made the request in such a way that it was more or less a directive to the veteran detective. He knew when he was being played, and this was no different. With the leverage this woman was holding over the investigation, he felt powerless to do anything other than comply.

"Anything else?" Rankin was tired and just wanted to go home.

"No, that should be it."

Rachel walked over and got into the large black van. She slid the side door shut and disappeared into the night, leaving the detective to smoke another cigarette. He stared up at the night sky, figuring retirement sounded quite nice at this point.

***

Rachel looked over at Alexis who elegantly occupied the captain's chair in the Sprinter and smiled. It was getting late as they left the Tallahassee Police Department, but there was still more work to be done.

"Your turn," she said to Alexis.

"I think Mr. Mason is going to start to really hate me."

Alexis pulled out her cell phone and after a few rings, Tony Mason answered. She explained that they were in control of the situation, but there was one final request she needed to complete the puzzle, and the story she promised was all but written.

"I can't believe I'm even entertaining this, but fine. What's the angle?"

"C'mon Tony, you're not as cute when you whine!"

Alexis spelled out in detail what she needed of the California reporter and explained that this would be the last hurdle he'd have to jump before the real story was gift wrapped for him. He protested, as expected, but willingly accepted his role. He wondered how the Senator fit in her devious web and tried to foresee the outcome, but the possibilities were endless with Alexis Vanderhill.

"Still not sharing what you have on the Senator?" Mason probed.

"Only after your half of the deal is satisfied…then everything comes out."

"Fine."

Chapter 49

Senator Thomas Pittman awoke with the sun beaming through his skylight and into his bedroom, gently pulling him from a restful slumber. He smiled at the promise of a new day, because he was still in control; he still had his power. The effects from over consumption of the champagne lingered, as well as the disappointment of spending the night alone. He was sure he'd read the flirty signals from Miss Harvey, but somehow, they'd got crossed up. However, the scare from the night before was a close call and sobering enough. He reminded himself to set aside some time to deal with that problem.

He confidently strolled around his sessional townhome in the nude, sipped his coffee, and quickly retrieved the newspaper from his doorstep. This temporary place that was home away from home was conveniently located minutes from the Capital Plaza and close to Midtown, a newer area of Tallahassee that offered locally owned restaurants, bars, and specialty shops. He found himself spending more time there as the legislative session continued. It was prime hunting grounds he discovered.

He sat down on the bar stool, soaking up the sunlight on his naked skin and opened up *The Democrat*. He was shocked at his continued luck and chuckled at the realization that his problem had taken care of itself!

The headline read: Local cop faces murder charges in Colorado. Pittman read the article excitedly and learned that Curtis Walker was responsible for the deaths of at least two men found after a shootout in Vail, Colorado. The article summed up the evidence found on the scene and key witness testimony leading to the identification of Curtis Walker. The piece outlined the theory of the distraught father executing two men in his personal crusade to find his son. The article tied in with his latest heroics of finding his son who had been missing for three years but ended with him possibly facing life in prison for the double murder.

Pittman sat back on the barstool and took a long sip of his coffee. A smile creased his face. He decided that he would call someone in the Colorado State Senate and encourage them to oversee the investigation and admonish the maverick detective's behavior. He hoped it would grease the wheels of justice in his favor. Pittman read the article again and paid closer attention to the part of Walker's missing son. He didn't see anything that hadn't already been covered in the earlier barrage of press coverage. He looked up at the byline and read the name, Tony Mason, Special Reporter to the *Democrat*. He would email Mason and pass on his thanks to him as well.

He flipped open the rest of the paper, searching its columns for something else. After a minute, he found the announcement of his upcoming press conference occurring next week. It was vague, by design, but it hinted at the fact that he was going to announce the kick off to his campaign for a seat in the United States Senate.

Chapter 50

Sgt. Polk waited anxiously in the lobby of the police station for his guest to arrive. He checked his watch nervously and realized it still wasn't quite time. He paced the lobby anyway, annoying the duty officer who sat behind a glass partition.

A week had passed since the news of Curtis Walker's being charged for murder in Colorado came out. The media was gobbling up the story placing TPD as a whole, in an adverse light. As with most police departments their size, it wasn't a new position for the agency to be in the spotlight for something negative, and it always made things tense and awkward for the time following an incident. The public was more skeptical and confrontational when the department had negative exposure, and that made it harder for the police to serve the community properly. It certainly lasted longer than any of the positive recognition they received. It was the true nature of how the world worked.

Sgt. Polk checked his watch again. It was one minute past time, but then he noticed his guest was walking up after exiting a black Lincoln Town car. Senator Thomas Pittman was accompanied by his assistant, Jeremy Stephens, and a few reporters were in tow. No doubt they were tipped off to the reason, most likely by his own office, to maximize the publicity of why he was back at the department.

The reason he was asked to come back was that TPD needed a positive spin on a current development to counter all the recent negativity. In a cold case that had resurfaced, the Senator and former City Councilmen, who once sat on an oversight committee, was asked to help out. The case first became active when he sat on the committee before he was elected to the State Senate. It was decided that Pittman should be invited back to help sell the positive development in the case through the media. He jumped at the chance to continue his "tough on crime" platform and get positive coverage.

As Pittman reached the top step of the police station, he turned to address the reporters.

"As you all know, I have a special place in my heart for Tallahassee. As a former oversight committee member for the Tallahassee Police Department, I've had the privilege of working alongside the detectives as they served and protected this community. Even though one bad apple has been exposed, there are still many hardworking police officers fighting to keep us safe. Now, I have the chance to come back and see the closure of an important case that has remained unsolved until today, thanks to DNA science."

The reporters spoke at once trying to jockey for a follow up question, but the Senator added, "No, sorry, no questions…not until after this case is closed, of course." Pittman smiled his trademark smile, turned, and walked into the police department.

"Thanks for coming Senator; this means a lot to us," Sgt. Polk greeted the handsome politician.

"Sure, anything for you guys. I just need to be somewhere for a press conference I'm holding in about an hour. Hopefully, I can lead with news of an arrest in this case."

"That'd be great."

Stephens took a seat in the lobby and got busy on a tablet he pulled from a briefcase. Polk led Pittman through the lobby, down the hallway, and up to the Criminal Investigation Division. Along the way, he prepped Pittman with the case updates.

"We finally got a hit on that string of rapes that we worked on three years ago. Remember the guy that was targeting the women around Tallahassee Gym Works on the Parkway? It was Walker's case."

Pittman paused at the mention of the case as well as Curtis' name. He smiled back, "Of course, that was right…you know…."

Polk nodded, "Yeah, Josh."

"So I was told you got a suspect?"

"Yeah, he's up in the interview room now. Do you want to watch from the monitor room?"

"Okay, sure. Who is it?" Pittman's curiosity was obvious.

"His name is Brian Clements, long history of voyeurism, exposing himself in public, and burglary. He used to work at that Gym Works during our time frame and lived in the area we thought our suspect might, so he's definitely good for it."

"What about the DNA, my office said you guys got a DNA match?"

"Well, not yet. I mean, it's kind of funny how that worked out."

Polk explained that after three and a half years, an additional victim came forward and disclosed that she held onto a pair of panties she was wearing during her tortuous victimization. She had felt ashamed about the whole experience and withdrew herself from her friends and family. After therapy, she finally came forward with the new evidence. It was after gaining this new piece of evidence, Clements' name came up as a suspect. All that was left was to compare Clements' DNA to the victim's panties.

"So you haven't actually done the testing yet?"

"No, not yet. We're having it delivered to a lab today."

"Sounds good. Good work. I'm glad she finally came around." He hid his concern about the new evidence but outwardly encouraged the Sergeant to press on. He agreed to remain a spectator in the monitor room while they did their jobs, like he had on all the other prior occasions.

Pittman stepped inside the monitor room and instantly stared at the television monitor up on the wall. He wanted to lay his eyes on the suspect. The culprit was not an impressive specimen but gangly and nerdy looking. He wore thick, black rimmed glasses and had greasy black hair. He stood by anxiously to see where this led, but he liked the guy because a predator can always sense another predator.

The interview was underway, and the suspect was steadily talking to the detectives.

"So, you guys drag me down here and accuse me of some serious shit just because I'm a convenient target. I know my history. I know what it says and what you guys think of me, but I can explain all that shit. Misunderstandings is all that was, all a bunch of misunderstandings, and this…this is police harassment!"

"Relax, Brian. You were asked to come here, and you agreed. You know where we stand, and if you have nothing to hide, you have nothing to fear, and should have no reason not to cooperate fully." The detective, out of view of the camera, spoke confidently. Pittman did not recognize his voice.

Pittman watched closely and was standing only a few feet away from the screen. The monitor room door opened, and in walked a younger female detective from the Special Victims Unit. He had seen her talking with Polk before. She was simple and pretty.

"Hi, how are you?" he said, while keeping his eyes on the screen.

"Fine, sir. How are you?"

"Good, good. Are you on this case?" he asked, pointing to the screen.

"Uh, yeah. I mean, we all worked a part of it. I wasn't in the unit when it initially broke, but since we got the new evidence and this guy, we've all been working non-stop."

"I bet, I bet. So the evidence this victim brought in, it was her underwear?"

"Yeah."

"Aren't there some integrity issues with her bringing it in so late in the game?"

"Actually, she mailed them to herself the day after it happened, and it's been sealed since. That was pretty smart in hindsight. I mean, it's not ideal, but with the postmark, it will stand up in court as being untampered. I only wished she had done it earlier. Maybe we would have caught this guy back then."

"Yeah. Possibly."

"Well, I need to get going. FDLE is coming to take the evidence to the lab, so I need to meet the tech in the lobby."

"Okay, don't let me keep you."

"Thanks, nice meeting you."

"You too." Pittman turned back to the television screen as the young detective left, but as soon as the door clicked shut, he poked his head out to see her walking off toward the lobby. Pittman stepped out and looked around. He didn't see anyone paying him any attention, so he quietly followed her out.

She walked down the stairs and out to the front lobby. Pittman hung back in the hallway but was stopped by a uniformed officer of rank that he didn't recognize. The door behind him read "Watch Commander." He explained to the cop that he had stepped out to make a phone call and had gotten turned around. He was shown his way back to the lobby by the unsuspecting cop. Pittman saw the detective meet with the FDLE evidence technician and then step to the elevator to head down to the property and evidence room in the basement. Moments later, the young detective returned with the evidence package in hand. She looked around the lobby for the FDLE tech, unaware that he had stepped outside.

While she stood there, Pittman watched and thought furiously on how to turn this into his advantage. He had to react soon, for his window was rapidly closing. He paused when he saw the young detective answer her cell phone. Her body stiffened, and she immediately spun around and headed back toward Pittman. He turned and ducked down the intersecting hallway and into a small break room to avoid being seen. She sped past the hallway, completely unaware of the Senator, while holding the evidence package in hand.

He followed her back upstairs and into the Criminal Investigations Division. He checked his watch and grew impatient as he had somewhere to be, but this had to be dealt with first. He visually followed her head, just barely showing over the cubicle walls, to her desk in the corner of the Crimes Against Persons section.

"Senator, over here!" Polk shouted over the top of the cubicle farm. Pittman was startled by the Sergeant's voice. His head shot up, and he addressed the Sergeant walking towards him.

"Sorry, I had to step out to make a phone call."

"That's okay. I wondered where you went. We're taking a break right now. This guy's playing hard to get."

"I'm sure you'll break him. Just keep at it."

"Yes, sir. That's the plan."

"Listen, give me a call when you guys are able to make the arrest, and I'll be honored to do the press thing; you know, put a positive note on this down time."

"You don't want to hang out, see how it ends?" Polk sounded disappointed.

"No, I have to hurry up and get down to my press conference. Big day for me. So if you'll excuse me."

"Okay, well...."

"If you need to get back to the case, I understand. I can find my own way out."

"Alright, I'll call you when we're done here."

Pittman shook the man's hand and headed toward the door while placing his cell phone to his ear. There was no phone call. He stood at the door until no one was in sight. He quietly backtracked through the division and over to where he saw the younger detective go with the evidence. This was his only window.

As he crept up quietly to the corner cube, he heard her talking loudly on the phone. Her back was turned, and the evidence was sitting on a chair behind her. With a lightning fast move, Pittman snatched up the small brown evidence package and stuffed it inside of his suit jacket. He walked back to the front of the division and quickly made his way toward the lobby. He barked at Stephens to get up from his seat.

"We need to go, and go now."

He motioned for his assistant to get the car started so that they could make a hasty exit.

"Let's go, Jeremy. We've got to get down to the press conference."

Pittman beat the assistant to the door and opened it up himself. He continued to snap at him to start the car and get moving. Pittman settled in the backseat as his assistant got in and cranked up the car. He kept watch on the front of the police station, expecting the building to suddenly come alive and trap them inside.

"LET'S GO!"

Jeremy jumped in his seat, scared by Pittman's demand. He backed up and sped out of the small, drive-thru parking lot and onto East Seventh Ave. Pittman held his stare on the building as they passed by. Once his assistant made the southbound turn on Monroe Street, he let out a sigh of relief and smiled, thrilled with himself.

Chapter 51

Tony Mason arrived at the press conference early and grabbed a coveted seat in the front row. There were news reporters setting up cameras in the back while the talking heads worked their phones. Butterflies were doing barrel rolls in his stomach. It was an odd sensation in his world of skepticism and harsh realities, but then he knew something the others didn't. He was ready for some form of fireworks when everyone else was prepping for a mundane political announcement piece.

A young female reporter eyed Mason sitting alone, dressed casually in jeans and a Dodger t-shirt and sat next to him. She carried a small cloud of perfume with her and dressed in an off-white blouse and black skirt with heels.

"Hi, I'm Samantha Wallace. I've been covering the political beat for a while now, but I haven't seen you around. You're a reporter, right?"

"Yeah. Tony." They shook hands. "I'm with the LA Times."

Samantha blushed. She was still a small town girl from the panhandle, waiting for her big break. She was thrown back by the unexpected presence of a major West Coast paper.

"Oh, wow! What kind of following does the Senator have in LA?"

"Oh, I don't write the political beat. Not enough blood and guts for me." Mason let the woman hang intentionally as he sat aloof, waiting for her to take the bait.

"What beat are you on?"

"The crime beat."

Reporter Samantha Wallace cocked her eyebrow in confusion. She wasn't getting anywhere with this arrogant jerk from LA, so she wrote him off and checked in with her boss. Mason smiled at himself when he knew she wasn't looking.

***

"Head downtown. There's some big construction going on where they're building a new park, down there where the old Centennial Park was."

"Yes, sir." Jeremy Stephens was wrought with guilt and felt the pendulum swinging back toward his neck. He kept his mouth shut at this point and obeyed what Pittman told him.

Pittman checked his watch. The press conference would start in ten minutes, but he needed to get rid of the evidence. He held up the small manila packaging with the red evidence tape on its edges. It was very non-threatening from the outside, but within, it contained his kryptonite and that could destroy everything.

He tugged at the corner and ripped open the package. He had to see what he had carelessly left behind. Pittman opened it up and peered inside. A small pair of lacy, pink underwear sat stuffed in the bottom crease.

"That's all, huh?" he said to himself.

Pittman looked around and saw they were nearing the park. With all of the construction going on, he could easily dispose of the damning evidence where no one would ever think to look or possibly link it back to him. He looked back down at the underwear. Images from that lustful, power-seeking rampage flooded his mind. He remembered Mirra Teal well. Thoughts of her never went away. She was his first and held a special place in his mind. He felt himself get aroused and flushed in the face, remembering her pathetic pleas for help. He rolled down the window to let the wind cool him down.

Pittman drew a long breath of the outside air and felt refreshed but he was still turned on. He could no longer deny the temptation. He wanted to feel Mirra once again.

He reached in the manila envelope and removed the underwear. They hung loose in his hand as he looked them over. He felt himself breathing heavily, reliving that special night. He rubbed the panties in his hand to get a good feel of the soft fabric. He loved the fact that this garment once touched her most private of areas, and now, he was in possession of it. He put the underwear directly under his nose and inhaled deeply, taking in its scent and the essence of Mirra Teal. Thoughts of keeping it clouded his mind, but it had nearly cost him everything. He had to get rid of them. He would get more, he told himself in consolation.

"It's just ahead, sir," Stephens broke Pittman out of his lascivious reverie.

Pittman looked out of the window and saw a large construction dumpster by a dirt access road. It was already filled to the top with trash and debris which meant it needed to be emptied soon. It was perfect.

"Go over there toward that dumpster in the back."

Stephens maneuvered the Town Car around the park and found an opening where they could access the dumpster. He read the clock in the dash and noticed they had less than three minutes to get to the press conference. He reminded Pittman to keep him on point.

"I know that, dammit. But we have to get rid of this damn thing, or we're both fucked."

"Right."

"Here we are. Want me to do it?" Stephens offered.

"No, I'll do it. Call ahead and let them know we'll be at the press conference in just a bit. Tell them to start the new commercial or something to stall."

Pittman jumped out of the car with the panties and envelope and walked over to the dumpster. He looked around the vast open area that was going to be a large urban park for Tallahasseeans. The coast was clear, and he climbed up on the side of the large metal container and stuffed the evidence inside a dried-out paint bucket. He pushed it farther down in the refuse to hide it even further. He hopped down, wiped his hands, and got back in the Town Car. It was gone. It was over.

***

Mason checked his watch and saw it was nearly the top of the hour. The room was full of media and campaign supporters abuzz with the excitement of Pittman's announcement. The microphones atop the podium were checked one last time for sound, and two large screens on the front wall came to life.

A sinking feeling had started to settle in the pit of his stomach. He felt that he was being played for a fool. He pulled out his phone to call Alexis Vanderhill and declare war with no limits on her and her team.

Before dialing, he stopped as her words from a week ago echoed in his head.

"Who's in control isn't always obvious."

Mason eased back in his front row seat and exercised his lesser virtue of patience. The two screens came to life, and Pittman's new campaign logo appeared. It was sharp and had the expected title of "US Senate" displayed along with his name in red, white, and blue lettering. Some members of his campaign clapped and cheered.

Comments from the crowd began, and Mason looked around watching their reaction. Out of the corner of his eye, a pretty, blonde woman with a ponytail stood in the back. They locked eyes, and Mason made no effort to look away. Rachel Goodwin, he remembered. Her presence was a good thing for this supposed story Alexis promised, but he was getting impatient. He noticed Rachel was standing next to a smaller, brunette woman. She was plain and obviously apprehensive about being in this place. Rachel spoke to her and hugged her from the side. Mason was immediately intrigued and wondered who this woman was.

The lights dimmed, and the crowd was told that the Senator would be arriving momentarily. The dual screens came to life, and Mason turned around in his seat to watch the show.

***

Stephens pulled out of the construction site and paused as he thought about the best way to get back to the press conference. He made a couple of turns to get back to Monroe Street, but the car suddenly stalled, and the engine died. He felt the power steering give out and the brakes stiffen. He stood on the brakes feeling the car roll to a stop.

"What the hell?" Pittman barked.

"I don't know. It just died."

Stephens turned the ignition, and the engine just sputtered and coughed back. He stomped on the gas hoping it would help, but the engine still sputtered.

A tiny ring sounded somewhere in the car that struck both Pittman and Stephens as odd. Pittman ignored it and leaned up between the seats to assist Stephens with the car.

"When'd you get this thing serviced last?"

"Last week, like you told me too. I don't know what's wrong."

"Well, get it working for God's sake." Pittman's tone was full of irritation.

The tiny ring chimed again; this time it was a bit louder.

"And what the hell is that noise?"

"I have no idea."

It sounded again. It was much louder and rang continuously. Pittman leaned back in the seat and zeroed in on the source of the noise. It was coming from the passenger backseat pocket. He reached in and pulled out an iPad. It was ringing. He didn't recognize it as his but opened it up anyway.

Pittman pushed the button bringing the iPad screen to life. The face of Curtis Walker filled the screen and sent shockwaves through the Senator's body.

"Hi there, Thomas." Curt's face was serious.

"Curt? What the hell is this? I thought you were in jail? How'd you get out?"

"I never went."

"I don't understand. What do you want?"

"I want you to confess to the rapes of Mirra Teal and the other eleven women from Tallahassee and Panama City."

"I have no idea what you are talking about."

"You will also confess to the kidnapping of my son, Josh Walker."

Pittman met the request with a conceited laugh full of contempt. "You are insane! I will do no such thing."

"Sure you will. You are guilty of those crimes. If you have any decency, you will confess. There's plenty of evidence against you."

Pittman looked up from the iPad and snapped at Stephens to get the Town Car started and moving. He knew this was a ploy from a desperate man who had no idea that the evidence was now gone.

Confidently, Pittman answered, "No, there's not."

"Okay, I'll admit you were very careful, and the evidence against you is slim, but that's why you're gonna confess."

"Not a chance."

"No?"

"No. Go to hell!" Pittman looked up again, "Jeremy, get us the hell out of here."

"I'm trying."

The car's engine was still stalled, and a series of clicks replaced the sputtering.

A low rumble started to reverberate inside the Town Car, and Pittman felt it vibrating his feet. It caused a mild panic to wash over him. He looked out of the window and didn't see any trucks or cars around, but he instantly realized that the Town Car had come to a stop over a set of railroad tracks. Suddenly, the doors to the Town Car locked on their own. Now, the panic turned into the full blown version.

"What the hell is this, Curt?"

"It's fate Senator, that's what it is. Time to Confess!"

"To what? I've done nothing wrong, and we both know that you can't prove otherwise."

The rumble grew louder. Pittman saw the smoke from the train's exhaust billowing from above the tree line. He tossed the iPad to the side and tugged at the door handle. He pulled at it repeatedly to no avail. He slid across the backseat and tried the other one with the same luck. He slammed his fist against the window in an attempt to break it, but the reinforced safety glass took the beating. Pittman reared back and punched the glass as hard as he could. His knuckles smashed against the solid glass that remained intact. He howled as the sharp pain of defeat resonated through his hand and up his arm.

"Fuck!" He flung his hand wildly, trying to shake off the pain.

Curt's voice yelled out from the iPad screen, "Confess, Senator!"

Pittman grabbed up the iPad and looked at the screen. His face was red hot with fury.

"Listen to me. I'm not confessing to shit because I did nothing worthy of a confession! You can stop your little game here and admit this is some ridiculous ploy."

"No, you listen to me! That train is less than half a mile away, and it will be on top of you in less than two minutes. You don't have much time."

The rumble had grown to a steady rolling of thunder. The train's whistle blared in the short distance, and it was loud and unmistakable.

"You remote accessed the engine and locks didn't you?"

"Something like that."

"You scaring me with the train isn't going to work."

"Tell that to the train."

Pittman looked out of the window. The train was rounding the bend and heading straight for them. The crossing arms started to lower and were accompanied by a dinging sound as the warning lights flashed red.

"Tell him what he wants to know," Stephens begged from the front seat.

"Shut up, Jeremy."

"You should listen to him."

"Curt, stop this now. Turn the car back on, and let's be reasonable about this!"

"You weren't reasonable when you took Josh from me. Why do you deserve anything more?"

Pittman didn't answer. The train was getting closer. Its horn was steadily blaring at the Town Car.

"Curtis, dammit! Do it…turn it back on."

"Not until you confess."

"So you're willing to kill me to get me to confess?"

Curt held a deadpan look giving the Senator his answer.

"Curtis, stop this. You're crazy!"

The train was bearing down at a pace guaranteeing that the smaller Town Car would be smashed into several pieces along with whoever was inside.

"Do you know how long it takes a train to stop?"

"Curtis, I can't!"

"Yes, you can. You did it—NOW ADMIT IT!"

"No…."

The train was less than a hundred yards away. Its horn nearly drowned out the sound of Curt's voice.

"CONFESS YOU MISERABLE SON OF A BITCH!"

Seventy-five yards.

"Fine, fine. I confess. I did it. I did it all!"

Fifty yards.

"Turn the Goddamn car back on, for Christ's sake! You got what you wanted."

"Not even close."

Twenty-five yards.

"CURTIS!" Pittman yelled as the train was nearly on top of them. He read the look on Curt's face. He was seriously considering not releasing the remote hold on the car. Stephens was steadily trying the ignition with no luck. Pittman yelled again, hoping he could be heard over the train's horn, pleading for the Town Car to move.

The engine kicked over, and Stephens stomped on the accelerator. The corner of the freight train's front metal housing nicked the back bumper of the Town Car, knocking it sideways by only a few feet, but it still remained on the road.

"Oh, Jesus!" Pittman said in relief, catching his breath.

Curt watched on the other end of the video chat, contemplating his reasoning for allowing him to live.

Stephens shook off the near death experience and headed for the press conference after asking Pittman what to do. Pittman picked up the iPad and looked at Curt. He wiped his brow with a handkerchief and blotted his face dry before putting it away.

"Good one. I did NOT see that coming."

Curt didn't answer. Pittman thought for a moment and started to laugh.

Curt was immediately annoyed. "What?" he asked.

"You plan to use that in court? That coerced 'confession?'"

"Something like that."

"Well, I got news for you. It was under duress, and I only said whatever it was you wanted to get the car started. It'll never hold up."

"We'll see."

"Not only will it not hold up, anything I say subsequently will be inadmissible as well."

"Like I said, we'll see."

"You arrogant prick! That's why I took Josh in the first place. You were so arrogant, because you just had to have your man, didn't you? I saw you following my trail from such a distance, and I knew you didn't have a real clue. But you persisted because of your arrogance and got too close. But, whatever."

"Arrogance on my part, huh?"

"Yeah, I was enjoying taking my time with Mirra the night before we met for coffee to discuss the oversight committee. How'd'ya like that?"

"I think you're done. You'll never hurt anyone again. Not for the rest of your life."

"On what? That bullshit forced confession? Not a chance."

"No. Not that."

"Then what?"

"You see that little black tube on the ceiling of the Town Car, next to the dome light?"

Pittman searched for what he was talking about and found the small lipstick sized object.

"It's a camera."

"So what?" Pittman's confidence was feigned.

"Nice touch, smelling the panties, you degenerate."

The pit of Senator Thomas Pittman's stomach fell through the floorboard of the Town Car.

"Wh-wh-what are you talking about?"

"Did you think we'd let you just walk out of the police station with our evidence? Our actual real evidence? Now maybe, instead, we'd let you take a pair of panties with a tiny GPS tracker sewn in the elastic band and planted at the station, just for you."

Curt held up the actual package Mirra Teal handed over to Rachel to show the Senator. "This is the real evidence that was compared to your DNA."

"My DNA? You have to have a search warrant or my consent for that. That'll never hold either."

"Yeah, it will. Abandoned property. Got it from your fundraiser. You remember your date right?"

Curt's head moved to the side, and Beth Young appeared. She was dressed much more casually than for the role of Francine Harvey. She waved at Pittman, "Hi" and pulled up a clear plastic evidence bag with his champagne flute inside.

"Wait, you can't do that!"

"Did it and already matched it. Congrats, it's yours."

"Well played, Curtis, well played. But it'll never hold. None of this little charade will hold up in a court of law."

"You may be right."

Pittman smiled, earning a degree of confidence back from Curt's admission.

"I want to show you something first."

"Uh, sir?" Stephens spoke up from the front seat.

"Shut up, Jeremy. What do you want to show me, Curt?"

Curt got up and carried the iPad into a different room from where he was. It was hard to follow as the angle was looking up at Curt's face from waist level.

"Uh, sir?" There was more insistence in Stephen's tone.

"What, dammit! What is it?"

"Look." Stephens was pulling up to where the press conference was being held. A small army of uniformed police officers and FBI agents were standing by awaiting the Senator's arrival.

"Oh shit."

Curt spoke to him through the video chat, "One more thing, Thomas. Have a look; I bet you didn't see this coming either!"

Curt turned the view of his screen outward and panned over a crowd of media and campaign supporters seated in his press conference. He gulped in exasperation but froze at the sight of himself in real time, in the backseat of the Town Car, up on the dual screens. A dumbfounded look unfitting for a distinguished politician remained on his face, until he was removed from the car by uniformed officers and FBI agents.

Pittman was at a loss for words as he was led away in handcuffs with Stephens. Curt stepped outside and made sure Pittman saw him standing there with a look of satisfaction that his brand of justice was served.

***

The crowd who sat waiting for the announcement of Thomas Pittman running for the US Senate got more of a show than they realized. They were in shock from what they just watched on the video screens. Just as the commercial started, it was interrupted, and a live video chat proceeded in its place. It was odd seeing the Senator in the backseat of his Town Car, but the crowd figured it was something new he had come up with for his upcoming campaign.

It wasn't until he began to inappropriately fondle a pair of women's underwear, that the crowd turned silent, realizing it wasn't a joke. A few gasps and choice words followed after watching him smell them. They watched intently as he got rid of the fake evidence and then witnessed his confession made to Curt and the telling conversation that followed.

Pride from his campaign workers dissipated and was replaced by utter abhorrence and loathing. They couldn't believe they had followed a rapist and kidnapper.

Rachel Goodwin turned to Mirra Teal after everything was said and done. She was suddenly standing taller than before. A light from within shone brightly, and she looked at peace. Rachel smiled.

"It was because of your courage that this happened."

Mirra let loose a tear that rolled down her cheek. She nodded acceptingly at Rachel. The scene was empowering on so many different levels. There was a balance that was restored in Mirra's mind. What had incapacitated her for so long was no longer a hindrance in her life. She was set free.

***

Tony Mason was the first to leave the room and he shot a call to Alexis so he could scoop the story. He wanted to get started before the rest of the press could get their legs underneath them and make sense of it all. He walked by Rachel and gave her a smile.

"I know I didn't see that shit coming."

He walked outside and snapped a few pictures of Pittman being hauled away. As the Senator was tucked away in the backseat of an awaiting Crown Vic, he looked over and saw Curtis Walker standing there, watching. Mason's good spirit sobered for a moment, knowing what this meant for the father who had known so much heartache. He raised his phone and snapped a picture of Curt standing proud, draped in a tan trench coat, and looking like an avenging angel watching over his work. It was the perfect picture of justice.

"You can't use that," Curt said, noticing the reporter.

"I'm not. That one is for me."

Chapter 52

With a whirlwind of media attention that stemmed from the sensational arrest of the Senator circling around Curtis Walker, he found refuge by sitting on the floor of his son's bedroom and playing with him. He was desperately trying to reestablish his innocence. In the weeks and months following the arrest of Senator Thomas Pittman, Curt spent most of his time dedicated to the recovery and mental well-being of his son. It was slow going and frustrating at times, but each victory, however minor, was worth the effort. Josh was still having nightmares, and Curt often spent his nights simply holding the boy in his arms, giving him a chance at restful sleep. It was a change from the many restless nights on the road for Curt but an adjustment he welcomed without question.

Curt followed the fallout from the subterfuge that exposed Pittman for the monster he was. The video was played over and over again on the news to the point of nausea. Curt knew the Senator was a craftsman at the law, so he decided instead of attacking him in the courtroom, he would appeal to the higher court of public opinion to try him for his crimes. It worked tremendously well, and he was instantly vilified and disavowed by his political and professional associates. His career was hung by the neck until dead.

The investigation picked up where Curt had left it prior to Josh's disappearance. Curt worked it vicariously through Sergeant Polk. After being confronted with the DNA match from Mirra Teal's underwear, Pittman tried his best to claim it was a consensual encounter and denied anything else ever happened. He fought against the evidence down to the last swab and fingerprint, even after a search of his office in Panama City revealed the same nylon fabric ropes used to bind his victims in both cities. Strands of women's hair were found in the rope fibers that would later be a match for the last Tallahassee victim. But the *coup de gras* was when the investigators found CDs of the victims' taped verbal statements burned onto his hard drive. It was evident that the Senator had worked his way into the investigations of his own criminal acts in order to gain access to their statements.

"So, he wanted to hear first-hand about his power and control through the victim's words?" Curt asked Sgt. Polk after his latest update.

"Looks that way."

"And right under our friggin' noses too. He used his committee seat to spy on his own investigation. Jesus, that's a sick man."

"Yeah, policy changes are sitting on the Chief's desk as we speak. No more civilian oversight committees."

"Good."

The article Tony Mason brought to his editor was the literary equivalent of a stick of dynamite with a lit fuse. He was pleased with the national attention it garnered with lightning speed. It was no surprise given the nature of the corruption, criminality, and especially the subterfuge that was used to bring him to justice. Mason took more credit than he deserved by saying it was he who discovered the link between Pittman and the series of rapes. The only person that could legitimately call him out was Alexis Vanderhill. He counted on her knowing better than to challenge him on this key point and risking exposure to the team. It was a small but pointed victory in his eyes.

The article explained how the one-time City Councilman managed to get inside access to the investigations of the rapes that he had actually committed. Once he learned detectives were closing in on him, he kidnapped the son of the lead detective to derail the investigation. Meanwhile, he continued committing the rapes and moved venues to his hometown, all the while securing an election to the State Senate. It was a Hollywood script that played out in the unsuspecting town of Tallahassee, Florida. Mason kept the term "humid-filled, crap hole" to himself and gave the capital city a more charming demeanor.

The success he found with this story and a pending book deal lessened the sting of Vanderhill killing his earlier story about her and her team, but he still held a grudge. Using the old adage of, "*If you can't beat 'em, join 'em,*" Mason agreed to terms with Vanderhill but with the understanding that he had the exclusive on any of their future ventures.

"That will be fine just so long as I okay the story."

"Alexis, I think this is the beginning of a beautiful friendship."

Alexis rolled her eyes.

Mason added, "We'll always have Vail."

"Are you done?"

"Here's looking at you...."

Alexis groaned at his adolescent attempt at humor and walked away. Mason smiled and finished quoting his favorite movie. "...Kid!" He shouted, knowing she could still hear him, "...of all the stories, in all the towns, in all the world, you had to walk into mine!"

Chapter 53

Three months had passed since the team had managed to bring down the Florida State Senator and his personal assistant, Jeremy Stephens. Stephens was definitely the weak link, and he quickly made a deal with the prosecution. He agreed to testify against the Senator about his knowledge of the rapes and the kidnapping for a reduced sentence. Stephens was the one who actually set up the delivery of Joshua Walker to Tobias Helton on the night of his disappearance. Stephens had known Helton socially and had actually introduced Helton to Gregory with whom he had also taken pre-law classes at FSU. Stephens and Helton had severed their relationship, in light of the kidnapping, so it wouldn't be traced back to the Senator.

Detectives from the Leon County Sheriff's Office found a note Helton had written before committing suicide. He admitted to having done "terrible acts" but did not specify the atrocities he was responsible for perpetrating. He cited the reason for ending his life was not being able to face his inevitable prison sentence and the violence that was sure to greet him at the gate. *Helton was a coward to the end*, Curt thought. He was willing to inflict violence on a weaker person to satisfy his lustful desires, but when the tables turned, he chose to take the path of the gutless.

As for Gregory, he was sentenced to a term of life in the Florida State Prison but only after the death penalty was taken off the table by the prosecution. Curt wasn't happy with the sentence, knowing that nothing short of death was acceptable. However, when Gregory took a plea deal, it meant Josh was spared the trauma of testifying which would reopen his devastating wound. This kept Josh from reliving the nightmares all over again in open court. That made it satisfactory to Curt.

Curtis Walker eased himself back into life as a detective at the Tallahassee Police Department, although he found himself missing the work he did while on Alexis' team. He often thought of them and wondered what they were doing...where they were...whom they were helping. Visions of Louis sitting inches away from a computer screen, Melinda and Beth utilizing their impromptu acting abilities, and especially of Rachel, all ran through his mind. He'd known her the least but missed her the most. She understood him; and as he looked back on the help she gave him in his moment of need, he was the one who was now indebted.

Therapy was going slowly with Josh, and some days, he reverted backwards into a downward spiral of anger and misunderstanding. He would physically lash out toward Curt and Tracy, fighting to understand why this awful thing happened to him. Curt hated to see his child like this but knew of no other way to help him. This led to arguments with Tracy that weren't productive, and her frustrations with his two-year absence finally surfaced after everything calmed down. He tried his best to repair the damage that this nightmare had placed on his family, but it seemed to run even deeper than he thought. It left him wanting to feel that sense of purpose he had while working on the team. It was something he wasn't ready to give up.

***

The Sprinter van was parked in the shadows of the street lights just outside the trailer park. A $90,000 van would be too conspicuous if set up within, Rachel mentioned. After leaving Tallahassee, the team started to work westbound and was currently in a suburb on the east side of Houston, Texas.

Louis Melton worked the computers while Rachel set up inside the park to watch the target trailer. Beth and Melinda were getting acquainted with a nice, elderly neighbor to combat the cold. While hunting earlier that day, Rachel spotted two disheveled children, clearly siblings, following an overly controlling man who constantly snapped at them. Although appalling on some level, there was nothing overly suspicious about this behavior. However, Rachel grew leery of the man and wanted to look into him further. During reconnaissance, she locked eyes with him and could see he was paranoid and hiding something. After running his face through facial recognition software, they learned that he was wanted in Florida for parental abduction and attempted murder. He had lost his two children in a bitter divorce a year prior. Before it was finalized, he ran off with the two children after beating his mother-in-law half to death while she was watching them during the divorce proceedings.

"I'm set up, and I just saw the kids' lights go out," Rachel noted.

"Okay, we're on our second round of hot tea with Granny Stanton over here," Beth said.

"Alright, the plan is simple. Have the old lady call and get him over there to fix something, whatever, and then stall him while I get the kids out."

"Copy that."

As Rachel waited for notification that the phone call was made, the familiar voice of Curtis Walker came over the ear bud comms, "What do you need me to do?"

Rachel instinctively grinned from ear to ear at the sound of his voice but shook it off to continue the illusion of professionalism.

"Couldn't stay away, could you?" she asked with a hint of flirtatiousness.

"No, I guess not."

Without further hesitation, Rachel ordered, "Good, well, come meet up with me, and you can help me take the kids out. I'll brief you in person."

"Alright, I'll be right there."

About the Author

William Mark grew up and currently lives in Tallahassee, Florida with his family. He attended the Tallahassee Community College where he graduated with an AA degree and the Florida State University where he graduated with a BS degree in Criminology and a minor in Psychology.

After college he attended the Pat Thomas Law Enforcement Academy in Midway, Florida. William has fourteen years of police experience, including assignments in Homicide and working as a member of the departments Tactical Apprehension and Control (TAC) team.

William and his family, a wife and three beautiful children, are active members in their church, avid Florida State Seminole fans, and enthusiastic travelers. William's first book is From Behind the Blue Line.